The Four Deadly Seasons

David Hewson

Copyright © 2025 David Hewson

The right of David Hewson to be identified as the Author of the Work has been asserted by him in accordance with the Copyright, Designs and Patents Act 1988.

First published in 2025 by Bloodhound Books.

Apart from any use permitted under UK copyright law, this publication may only be reproduced, stored, or transmitted, in any form, or by any means, with prior permission in writing of the publisher or, in the case of reprographic production, in accordance with the terms of licences issued by the Copyright Licensing Agency.
All characters in this publication are fictitious and any resemblance to real persons, living or dead, is purely coincidental.

www.bloodhoundbooks.com

Print ISBN: 978-1917705394

The animal nature, which chemists call the animal kingdom, acquires by instinct the three means necessary to perpetuate itself. These are three fundamental needs. It must feed itself, and to ensure that this is not merely a need, it experiences the sensation known as appetite, and derives pleasure from satisfying it. Secondly, it must preserve its own species through reproduction, and certainly it would not fulfil this duty, whatever Saint Augustine may say, if it did not derive pleasure from it. Thirdly, it has an irresistible propensity to destroy its enemy; and nothing is more soundly reasoned, for in its duty to preserve itself, it must hate anything that operates towards, or desires its own destruction.

— *The Memoirs of Giacomo Casanova*, translated by Gregory Dowling, to whom I'm indebted as usual for his essential insights into local Venetian matters.

Prelude: The Devil's Tritone

'Is that a gun? Seriously. The mild and scholarly Arnold Clover, with a firearm? Goodness me. What is the world coming to?'

The weapon – a Beretta 92, or so I gathered from the internet – did feel strange in my right hand. Heavy, clammy too. Sweat I imagine, though it was Capodanno, New Year's Eve, a bright, chilly afternoon. Just after two thirty and by the icy waters of the Adriatic the temperature was close to zero, sharpened by a biting offshore breeze. The harsh winter light was softening already, dusk – *crepuscolo,* a lovely word in Italian – looking to drift down from a limpid blue sky as if it were a wispy cloud of smoke.

On the city side of the littoral barges would be in place for the night's fireworks in the Bacino San Marco, restaurants preparing spectacular banquets, all the best tables long reserved for those who could afford the prices. Lobster, scallops and champagne for the wealthy, lentils and earthy *cotechino* for the rest. Prosecco and spritz flowing everywhere while La Fenice would open its doors to the customary orchestral broadcast around the world.

Not that it would be the only music that night. Another,

newer entrant was about to enter the concert lists, the Teatro Maddalena, a place that had occupied me for much of that year across the seasons. A long-hidden architectural gem that would finally open its doors to the public after a saga as strange and mysterious as it was, on occasion, bloody.

I was supposed to be there. Afterwards, while everyone else stayed to enjoy drinks and *cicchetti* before moving on to the lagoon and the fiery show that would turn the velvet sky into a spectacle of noise and flame, I'd slink away, find a quiet place somewhere, watch the show from a distance. New Year's Eve the year before had been a solemn and solitary event for me. A time for remembering what had been lost, to reflect on the frailty, the brevity of life. An attempt to dim that still-flickering flame for my late wife Eleanor who'd died suddenly just before we were due to move to our little apartment in San Pantalon, on the edge of Dorsoduro.

Events, they say, 'conspire', which is plain ridiculous. Only people are capable of that. The unexpected does happen though, and not just to poor Eleanor.

Besides, all this musing was quite hypothetical at that moment. I'd yet to discover whether I'd live to see another day at all.

Though I was starting to feel my feet as a foreigner in Venice, this deserted spot was new to me, home to a bohemian beach bar shuttered for winter. In Rome they have a saying... *non basta una vita.* One lifetime isn't enough. Make that several for the city in the lagoon.

The establishment was mostly driftwood, tables, veranda, sunshades for the summer, even the cabin at the back that must have served as bar and kitchen. Gritty sand and dead marram grass from the dunes were strewn everywhere. Dry thistle heads rolled across the pebble shore caught on the stiff marine breeze. The sea was still and sleepy, devoid of the blue shade of summer. Only the distant outline of a tanker broke the pallid straight ruler of the horizon. Along the finger of rock that formed a narrow promontory into the water there was a *capanno da pesca,* a fisherman's hut on stilts, dangling a square balance net on cables, ready to be lowered if a passing shoal should risk scavenging by the shore.

Not that anyone looked ready to work it now. The two of us were quite alone on the beach beyond Alberoni, the hamlet at the foot of the Lido, one side looking back to the city, the other to the desolate Adriatic. Lazy waves, a feeble tide barely a foot high, murmured ahead of us, accompanied by the sharp cries of gulls and the rattle of the dead limbs and cables of the *capanno.* The place had the crisp smell of winter by the ocean, sand, salt spray and seaweed, rotting away, marooned on lines of washed-up pebbles. Wood smoke too from the logs burning in a brazier by the bench seats where we sat facing one another.

'The gun?' I said eventually and placed the thing on the table. 'It seemed... sensible somehow. After all it came with this when you broke into my flat.'

I placed the scrap of paper between us. Torn from a musical manuscript, two notes separated by a rest, all handwritten in blue ink. A simple message beneath:

It's time for the final act in this long performance,
Arnold Clover. Macondo, 1430. Don't be late.

I had to look it up. Macondo was the name of the shuttered beach bar, a bus journey down the Lido to the terminus where the service stopped and waited for the ferry across the brief stretch of water to Pellestrina. Then a lengthy stroll on a wooden boardwalk past what looked like a shuttered fish processing factory until I emerged by the sea.

No matter how long I live in Venice, the place will always offer up some surprise out of nowhere. Here I was, just a few kilometres as the crow flies from the bustle of San Marco and the happy expectant crowds about to embark on their New Year's Eve revelries, in a place so solitary and deserted I might have been Robinson Crusoe washed ashore on an empty windswept strand, no idea where I was, no map, no clue which way to turn.

Except, of course, I wasn't alone. My Friday was there already, seated at a bleached driftwood table at the front, hands warming over the fresh brazier. Prepared for what was to come. Food too, a wicker picnic basket, leather handles and the label of one of the city's pricier delicatessens, inside packs of cold meat and cheese, bread, *baccalà*, a bottle of Ribolla Gialla and some San Pellegrino.

'Let me see how much you've learned.' A gloved hand passed over a glass of wine then pointed at the two semibreves, one on the staff, the second below. 'What, exactly, is this?'

It had been such a strange year, one that had engaged me in matters of great art, great risk, of life and death. Of music too. I'd always regarded myself as an ignoramus in that regard, corralled once more by my friend Luca Volpetti into something I barely understood, struggling with terms I'd never heard – 'ritornello' and 'ripieno', 'appoggiatura' and 'acciaccatura'.

'C and F-sharp with a semiquaver rest between them.' I did my best to sing it, and the result was awful, which was not simply my dreadful voice.

'Not bad. What do you make of it?'

'The *diabolus in musica*. The Devil's Tritone, of course. Why are we wasting our time with this? You didn't drag me all the way out here for–'

'It's an interval. Which is precisely why you're here. Drink your wine. Grab some food.'

'I am neither thirsty nor hungry. Except for answers.'

A laugh, and it seemed warm and genuine which I hadn't expected. 'Join the club. Intervals. Our lives are composed of them, don't you realise? What would music be if they were absent? Nothing but notes, cacophony, no spaces, no distinction from one to the next. Silence speaks more than sound sometimes.'

A gloved finger tapped on the table, like that of a teacher making a point. 'It's the interval and the emptiness that complete the tale. That fire our imagination and challenge us to comprehend the gap between before and after, one note, one idea and the next. Take the cuckoo.'

I'd no idea what to expect but it wasn't this. 'You're being exceptionally cryptic.'

'No. You're being rather slow. But then you have been all year long, haven't you? Charmingly so I must say but all the same. Cuck-oo...'

Sung out loud. With far more precision than I could ever manage. 'That's how you think it goes. A minor third. But were you to listen to the bird a little later you'd find she changes her tune. First to a major third. Cuck-oo. Then, finally to a fourth...'

'Very good.'

'It's more than good. It's at the heart of everything. A natural progression, in our case from the dissonance of your ugly yet intriguing Devil's Tritone to the fulfilment of a perfect, sonorous response. Unfinished to complete. Promise to delivery. Challenge to success.' A pause then, 'Life to death. The cuckoo begins in a minor key as she seeks out the nests of the birds whose fledglings she wishes to murder and displace with her own. Then, once the egg of the bloodthirsty intruder is in place, she watches, shifts her song slyly from minor to major as the deadly subterfuge begins to work. Finally, when her offspring has disposed of the genuine fledglings in the brood, taken their place, their food, the love of their idiot, unseeing parents and is about to fly and spread the cuckoo race, only then, satisfied, does she express her vocal joy with a perfect fourth. This is her philosophy, cast in blood, in her genes. Life to death for her victims, birth to freedom for her own, with not so much as a scrap of effort on her part after that fateful egg is laid. What more can any creature ask?'

The glove came off, a pen came out. A careful, knowing hand scrawled on the scrap of manuscript I'd brought, changing the F-sharp down a semitone to F-natural.

'Cuck-OO.'

Blue ink.

'But we're not there yet, are we?' I said. 'I'm still stuck in the Devil's Tritone. Not perfection, but cacophony. Or silence. Either way I remain in ignorance. For how much longer?'

A smile, closed eyes and I was beginning to feel yet more uneasy. 'You know why it's called that, surely?'

So much reading, so much research since Luca Volpetti introduced me to a curious collection of musicians, con artists, thieves and liars eight months before.

'I read it was because the early church thought it so ugly, so wrong they believed it to be the music of Satan. And banned it from church.'

'My, my, Arnold. Do I really need to tell a man like you not to believe everything you've read? That's a fairy story. Anyway, we're more sophisticated than that now. Can you name a piece of music that uses it?'

I was sick of being treated like a child, of being asked to play this game.

'Hendrix. "Purple Haze". The opening.' With as little skill as I felt obliged to muster, I grunted the opening notes, that harsh, rough augmented fourth and then the fuzzy riff. 'I must say I feel philosophy and murder make poor bedfellows.'

A pause. A strange look. Half anger, half puzzlement.

'Oh, please. Don't disappoint me now. This is the end of our journey. We must resolve the awkward dissonance. Turn your Devil's Tritone around. Change it to the interval of peace, of silence, of resolution.' A pause and then, 'A suitable conclusion for one who can never quite push the thought of death from his mind. You crave to be close to that, don't you? I've seen it in your face all year long. Why else bring that gun along with you?'

I pushed the blasted weapon across the dusty table, thinking back to how this strange tale began, wondering, too, how the day might end.

There were no easy answers. 'You may find this somewhat hard to believe. But after this distinctly bizarre year I am no stranger to firearms. Furthermore, I rather thought this thing belongs to you.'

Part One

La primavera, Spring

Chapter One

Allegro

'Quick, Arnold! Quick! We mustn't be late!'

April was never the cruellest month, not in Venice anyway. Already, the bare branches of wisteria were coming to life, pushing out plumes of purple blossoms so fragrant they made me sneeze. The natives had begun to cast off their heavy winter clothes, with great caution naturally. One can never be too careful. Venetians seemed inclined to the same view of my old Yorkshire mother... ne'er cast a clout till May be out. The chaos of Easter – too many people in the tourist places, scarcely a soul beyond them – was over. Life had subsided into a brief lull before the next, inevitable wave arrived at Piazzale Roma. A time to pause, to relax, to enjoy.

Or so I'd hoped. Luca Volpetti, as ever, had other ideas.

'Think of the opportunity!' he cried, rocking back and forth on the rolling vaporetto. 'The challenge! The secrets to be revealed!' Gusto was never lacking in my friend. Nor did he seem to feel embarrassment. Nothing would induce me to appear in public wearing the clothes he'd chosen for our journey across the Giudecca Canal that afternoon: mustard trousers, green wax hunting jacket matched with a jaunty Austrian alpine cap complete with feather, a nod to the mysterious Viennese moneybags we were due to meet.

The Number Two boat had scarcely docked at Zitelle, the final jetty on Giudecca, before he leapt off, eager as a puppy, a state which, for him, was quite natural.

I helped an elderly lady with her shopping trolley then meandered along behind, comfy in my jeans and windcheater, feeling, once again, a hint of trepidation. Luca's schemes always started off straightforward but rarely ended that way.

'Ah.' He stopped and checked his watch by a restaurant where a few hardy foreign diners were finishing their tiramisu. The day had the gentle brightness of spring, neither cold nor warm, with no sign of rain. 'We're a touch premature. I've met him once only, but I gather Marcus has a Teutonic fondness for punctuality. Being early is as bad as being late.'

Marcus. The first time I'd heard a name. Over an extended and rather liquid lunch Luca had been unusually cryptic about the task ahead of us. Only to say that it would be highly rewarding, both intellectually and when it came to money too. That latter point had certainly sparked my interest. Life had become more expensive of late what with soaring prices and utility bills, even for a widower living a relatively frugal life on his own. My two pensions – state and civil service from all those years working for the National Archives in Kew – no longer went as far as they used to. Life wasn't hard, just a touch constrained.

Luca knew this and had been gently pushing the odd writing and translation work my way. Then there were the occasional derisory fees I received when called into the San Zaccaria Carabinieri Station by our mutual friend Valentina Fabbri, capitano there, a charming, sly Venetian woman whose company I always appreciated though not without reservations. I felt at home in the city, but I was always aware I lived there as an outsider, accepted but with limits.

Still, for those who knew, there was much to enjoy in Venice even when you were close to broke. Here was one, the view from this vantage point by the vaporetto stop. The rest of the island of Guidecca ran in a straight line to right and left, territory largely foreign to me apart from its two splendid churches on the canal, Zitelle and Redentore. Further to my right stood the marble white Palladian edifice of San Giorgio Maggiore on its tiny island. Across the Bacino San Marco there was that familiar aspect from a million postcards, the needle point of the Punta della Dogana marking the beginning of the Grand Canal, the constant flow of boats and vaporetti edging across the blue water in all directions, the Doge's Palace, the edge of the Piazza San Marco and the basilica behind.

The day was quite still, the tang of brine in the air softer now winter had given way to spring. In London, where I'd lived and worked most of my life, the seasons were marked by little more than temperature and weather, hot or cold, wet or dry. In Venice the changes were both more subtle and more obvious, shifts in light, changes in local habits, periodic unusual holidays and saints' days, parades, regattas, and musical interludes. Food too. Gone were the heavy winter dishes of squash and Treviso radicchio, replaced by fresh delicacies emerging from the fields of Sant'Erasmo: tiny purple artichokes – *castraure*– sweet and crunchy, the first buds of the year; peas and early sprigs of green asparagus; once, when Luca and I struck lucky and we were asked to a trial menu tasting at the restaurant run by Valentina Fabbri's husband, a delicate green risotto made with *bruscandoli,* the tender young shoots of hops newly burst from the soil.

I could have taken a bench seat there and spent an hour or two just looking, dreaming, snoozing after a lazy lunch paid for by Luca as part of his attempt to soften me up for the caper to come. The Archivio di Stato, the city archives which employed him and, on occasion, me, had an outpost here, an industrial-looking warehouse along the waterfront. I'd assumed that was where we were headed.

But no. We turned away from the canal promenade and I followed him into a narrow, gloomy alley then headed into the slender belt of Giudecca's interior, a part of Venice I simply couldn't picture. There were what looked like factory buildings, mostly derelict, modest apartment blocks – low-cost public housing, he said, and a couple of boatyards, not that I saw a sign of them. Only cobbles, elderly people snoozing on chairs in the fading afternoon sun, and the odd dozy cat.

Luca's phone rang. He glanced at a message and harrumphed. 'It seems Marcus has an urgent call. There's an hour to waste.'

'Sounds an elusive fellow.'

Luca scowled at that. 'As I said, I've only met him the once. He seemed... nice enough. Or we wouldn't be here. You do remember what I said back in January, at Epiphany?'

A few cryptic words as we watched a small flotilla of elderly men dressed as witches scull their rowing boats towards a giant sock dangling from the Rialto bridge. The Grand Canal every January the sixth.

'Vaguely. That was months ago, and I seem to recall I was rather tired at the time. Do excuse me if I don't hang on your every word.'

'Vienna! The Red Priest! Revelations!'

'Rings a bell.'

As did the fact he'd caught the train to Austria through the mountains a few weeks back and told me at great length afterwards how beautiful the journey was through a snowy winter landscape.

'A little enthusiasm wouldn't go amiss.'

'I'm English, Luca. I dispense my enthusiasm sparingly since it comes in finite quantities.'

'Vivaldi!'

'The Red Priest. Quite,' I said, and as if on cue I began to hear the strains of a small orchestra playing something I knew all too well, the music that, for much of the world, seemed to sum up Venice entirely. 'I'm a jazz man. As I've explained before. I know nothing at all about anything classical.'

He gave me a wink. 'Stick with it. You're onto what the English call "a bloody good thing". I trust you've a plentiful store of that finite enthusiasm of yours.'

There was a green door in the brick wall ahead, a large, modern sign there saying, 'Private. Keep Out' in English and Italian. The music was coming from there. Luca strode ahead, pushed it open and summoned me through.

I'd no idea what to expect. And if I had, it wouldn't have been this. Behind stood a narrow canal, a wooden bridge over it, brand new by the looks of it, the timber yet to be treated. Across the water lay a garden, or park might be more accurate. It must have run to a good couple of acres, a place, it occurred to me, that would once have been magnificent. There were bowers with trellis arches, a folly with a fountain designed to resemble an ancient Roman nymphaeum. A few statues here and there, mostly broken, all of them classical. The beds were strewn with weeds or bare altogether as if newly dug for planting. The one cared for part of the estate lay in the distance, by the wall that must have bordered the lagoon. There, a lone gardener, a hefty and rather thuggish looking man, laboured with a shovel over a vegetable bed filled with nodding artichokes.

'What on earth is this place?'

'Lately the Palazzo Colonna-Ottoboni. Before that, the former Convent of Maddalena delle Zitelle. A lost wonder few have seen in decades,' Luca said, walking on. He turned and rubbed his fingers together. 'There wasn't the money. Till now. Thank Marcus for that. Now. Let's see if we can find the boss.'

'You mean Marcus?'

He turned shifty quite suddenly. 'All in good time...'

It was pointless pressing for more information. Luca only doled that out when he was so minded. And besides, I'd found myself in a hidden paradise, tucked away among the blocks of apartments and old industrial buildings of Giudecca. It was time, I felt, to observe and enjoy.

Ahead lay two very different buildings, divided by flower beds rampant with weeds and the ruins of a decrepit fountain with a spouting goddess mostly in pieces at the centre. The one to the left seemed to be a large circular church with a domed roof, much like a cut-down version of the Pantheon in Rome, except this one had a Palladian entrance, doors open, the sound of strings and the familiar strains of Vivaldi streaming out into the afternoon. In front a large sign reading 'Teatro Maddalena'.

On the other side was a mansion, a palazzo even. Four storeys high, white Istrian limestone I suspected, Venetian Gothic with the customary tracery windows and loggias on each level. At the summit, half-hidden by scaffolding and builders' boards, was what looked like a roof garden with palm trees and four large purple parasols along the edge.

We stopped by the open doors of the auditorium and listened. The music came to a halt. Luca put a finger to his lips and ushered me into the shadows inside. It was a rehearsal. I knew enough about music to understand that. A small string orchestra was listening to an elderly man talking, inaudibly to me, his voice was so low and clearly foreign. A striking fellow, even seen from the side: pushing eighty perhaps, with a full head of silver hair slicked back in streaks, a craggy face, and a beak-like nose. Hunched over, hands buried beneath his armpits, he reminded me of an American bald eagle, magnificent to look at, a little formidable too. And Samuel Beckett in his later years. Which, given the strange tale that was about to consume me, was, perhaps, more apt.

He finished his little lecture, the musicians heaved a communal sigh and started to get to their feet. I wasn't much of a one for concert-going – the ticket prices were steep in lots of places for one thing. But I was accustomed to seeing smartly dressed players got up to the nines. There was none of that. Scruffy jumpers, threadbare waistcoats, not a dress among the women, only jeans. They made up half the ensemble and seemed mostly young. The men were older, less chatty too.

The Palazzo Colonna-Ottoboni meant nothing to me. But my Italian was good enough to understand the origins of the place – Maddalena delle Zitelle. For most visitors, 'Zitelle' is simply the name of the vaporetto stop on Giudecca, and the church, perhaps by Palladio, perhaps not, nearby. As so often happens in Venice, the truth is rather more complex. 'Zitella' is a word you rarely hear in Italy these days, and then in an insulting fashion, meaning something like 'ugly spinster'. Centuries back, it was the opposite, a term used for young, attractive girls, virgins, often, in the eyes of the church, in danger of falling into prostitution.

The church, which is really called Santa Maria della Presentazione, was part of a complex that gave unmarried young women an escape from poverty by offering accommodation, food and instruction which either led them to marriage, by a dowry paid for by the institution to attract a suitable husband, or the wimple of a nun. In the meantime, they were set to work, making lace for one thing. Someone who had the contract for this place pocketed a fortune selling Louis XIV, the Sun King of France, the ornate lace collar he wore at his coronation, one that took two years to complete. But that, as they say, is another story. Venice has so many, and at times they run into one another with ease.

There, you see the obsessive habits of the archivist in retirement. Forever looking for links, testing them, then peering through the mists of time to see where the connections, if any, might lead. I've been doing that most of my adult life and it's a habit that's impossible to break.

I scanned the musicians packing away their instruments and scores and groaned at the sight of a familiar face. Rupert Hazard – a man more aptly named it would be hard to find – had spotted me already and was waving wildly across the room, cello bow in one hand, the other making the unmistakable gesture of necking a drink.

'You seem to have a friend here already,' Luca noted.

'No. A near neighbour of mine. Once. Always pestering me to go drinking with him. He used to have an apartment along the street. Then before I knew it, he was gone. Some trouble with the landlord maybe. Haven't seen him since.'

'Lucky!' Hazard yelled.

'Lucky?' Luca wondered.

'Don't ask...'

One more tip of the imaginary glass and then he bustled up in front of me, beaming, ruddy cheeked, walrus moustache going grey, full head of hair an artificial tone of boot polish brown, rotund and grinning, a burly man, a rugby player once I seemed to recall.

'Lovely to see you again, old boy. Tinctures round the corner? They're on the house. Palazzo Buckshee this place! My, have we fallen on our feet.'

I smiled. Briefly. Then said, 'We?'

Luca put a hand on my arm. 'Talk to your friend. Just for a few minutes. Then – I know how difficult you find it – but please, for once, try and mingle. I have business...'

Without another word he was gone.

'If music be the food of love...' There was a makeshift bar in a small pavilion next to what I assumed to be the concert hall under construction. Rupert Hazard made for it like a shot, waving his spritz around so wildly the drink spilled everywhere, winning us a caustic glance from the woman behind the counter. '...then I'm bloody starving.'

Not that he was alone. Most of the small orchestra was availing itself of free drink and *cicchetti*, quite expensive looking too. I rather regretted having eaten lunch.

'Can you believe it, Lucky? A man like me, abandoned?'

An odd comment. I'd never seen him with a woman. With anyone. He struck me as a lonely soul.

'It's a pleasure to see you again too.'

'Don't be like that. I had a temporary glitch in my cash flow. The landlord was not in the least understanding. Greedy old bastard couldn't wait to kick me out and turn the place into a sodding Airbnb. Now I'm across the water in a studio in Mestre, god help me. We're not all as lucky as you... Lucky.'

'As you doubtless appreciate, I so wish you wouldn't call me that.'

He gulped down the rest of his spritz then, without a word, placed the glass on the bar to be refilled. As it was, in a silent instant by the glowering barista. 'Clover. Lucky. Makes sense to me. Can you believe it? You never met my Vanessa. She was supposed to come out and join me. Turns out the cow's left me for some jumped-up bassoonist with the London Philharmonic. Not even a good one.' He jabbed his fist into the bowl of crisps then stuffed some into his mouth. Bits flying everywhere he added, 'Never trusted woodwinds. Something about them. Apart from a lovely thing called Gertie back in Berlin. She was a cracker.'

'I have to say you don't look starving. Any more than your fellow players.'

He wasn't listening to a word. 'Well, that stupid bassoonist can put up with her temper and her tantrums. I'm done with the woman. Fifteen years of marriage. And what do I have to show for it?'

I checked my watch and looked round for Luca. Nowhere to be seen.

'No, Arnold,' he said, suddenly serious. 'None of us is starving here. And if you're coming on board, you won't be either. It's curious really. Quite extraordinary.'

'What is?'

'The money. They're chucking it around like they're made of the stuff. Which I assume they are.' He nodded at the church now turning into an auditorium. 'That place. It won't be done till winter. Millions going on it. And the palazzo which is going to be some kind of pad for Marcus and his missus and a posh hotel, pricier even than the Cipriani round the corner I'm told. Then there's bringing in an old warhorse like Kravchuck to tell us how to do it. He may have his limitations these days, but he won't come cheap. If the old chap makes it to the opening night which won't be till November. If... Still, they're paying us hand-somely for rehearsals twice a week even though we're six months off a performance. Want to test the acoustics and

Kravchuck's staying power or something. Can't wait to piss it all away it seems to me, not that I'm reluctant to help.'

Clearly, I looked baffled.

'Kravchuck. Andriy Kravchuck,' he explained. 'A genius once. You should hear some of his recordings.' He grimaced. 'Though no longer...'

'He's the conductor?'

Hazard sighed. 'God, this is hard. We don't need a conductor for The Seasons. We follow the soloist. It used to be Kravchuck, the man's famous for it and quite the scholar too. One of the best in his field. Then...'

That grimace again.

'Then what?'

'Don't you read the papers?'

'Not if I can help it. I fled to Venice to try to escape all that. Too damned depressing.'

'He's Ukrainian. From Kyiv. Poor chap was performing in Crimea the first time Putin's monsters invaded years back. You remember that, surely?'

So many wars of late, so many tragedies. 'Of course.'

'He never talks about it. From what people gather Andriy was kidnapped by some Russian soldiers drunk and high on getting the free run of the place. Being a sound Ukrainian of a patriotic frame of mind he gave them a piece of his mind.' A deep breath. 'They broke his precious Guarneri into pieces in front of his face then chopped off three fingers from his left hand. Threw him bleeding on a bus to Kyiv with them in his pocket.' He held up his left hand and wriggled his fingers. 'No more fiddle playing without these. He's seventy-one, believe it or not. Looks a lot older after an ordeal like that, poor sod.'

'The fellow seemed quite... in control to me.'

Rupert Hazard chuckled at that and tapped the side of his head. 'Oh, he may be frail in body but there's nothing wrong up here. Also, he's got his pretty protégé – I'm assuming that's the right word. At his age. Musicians... you never know.'

'Sorry?'

'His creation. The fellow's been coaching her ever since he lost his fingers. Ellen Kim. Half-American, half-Korean. Quite the looker and damn good with the fiddle too. Only to be expected given who's teaching her.' He squinted at me. 'She wasn't there, was she? You'd have noticed. Pretty little thing comes and goes, floats in and out when she feels like it. Got the impression dear Marcus has his eye on her. Wouldn't want to be around his missus if that came to anything.'

'Too much information,' I said.

'The music or Marcus Haas? Do you have any inkling what I'm on about?'

'Not the faintest.'

'Then how the hell are you going to write this book of theirs? About Vivaldi?'

It took a second or two before I could blurt out... 'What?'

'Ugh.' He waved a dismissive hand in my direction then checked his watch. 'Never mind. No time for idle talk. Appointment in town. Let's pop out for a drink one night. I'm moving to a student flat in Santa Marta. Noisy but cheap.' He waved at someone in the midst of the next gaggle of players. 'Reggie? Come and meet Arnold Clover. An old friend of mine.'

A sturdy woman pushed her way through the mob of players gathered round the bar, smiling as she turned up holding what looked like a Negroni in a half pint beer glass.

'No, Rupert,' she said in a loud, south London tone. 'That's final.'

'I haven't asked for anything.'

'Yet. The answer's no regardless. If he's a friend of yours he must be a reprobate. It's either drink, money, food or company you're after and I'm not in the mood for any of it.'

He put a hand to my shoulder. 'Arnold Clover, Reggie Davies. Her bark is worse than her bite. Nor does Arnold here have a reprobate cell in his body, I promise. He's the latest recruit to the Teatro Maddalena though he appears to know not a single thing about classical music or Vivaldi, it seems to me. Which is odd since a little bird told me he's going to write the seminal biography that brings old Antonio back to life and unveils a good few secrets. Given no one knows much about the old bugger, quite the task. Amuse him, please. I must head for the briny…'

~

'An old friend of Rupert's, eh?' Reggie Davies led me to a bench seat in the anaemic sun by a bower of bay and yew bushes and a lemon tree dropping fragrant old fruit.

'I wouldn't put it quite that way,' I admitted. 'He used to live a few doors down from me. Then he vanished. I couldn't stop the chap banging on my door to be honest. He was quite insistent at times.'

'Odd man, Rupert Hazard. Did you notice his voice?'

'Not really…'

'His speech is firm but furtive and extraordinarily monotone. Key of E-flat. Almost always.' My head was starting to spin as I realised she was quite right. Hazard did speak in an odd way. She harrumphed. 'E-flat minor. Not a key for a level-headed man to embrace. I mean, if the chap were stuck on C-sharp one might, just, forgive him but–'

'Perhaps he doesn't realise.'

I got a hard stare.

'He's a musician, isn't he? Or claims to be.'

She was a striking woman. About fifty I'd guess, with a bohemian appearance so casual and seemingly uncared for it could only have come from much forethought and little in the way of expense. A spiky head of hair dyed a luminescent scarlet bright enough I could imagine it shone in the dark. A round face as expressive as that of an actor. It seemed in constant motion, turning from smile to frown, smirk to dead-eyed stare in a matter of seconds, never once subsiding into idle blankness, torpor or dismay.

She reminded me of an athlete, strong arms, a muscular neck, broad shoulders, the right somewhat lower, the result of a lifetime of bowing I fancied based on no evidence whatsoever. This physicality all became a part of her identity too, since, in performance, she told me, she preferred when allowed what looked like a black, male dinner outfit. And for rehearsals... holed jeans and a worn plaid red and green lumberjack shirt.

Her voice had a huskiness to it from what I suspected was years of cigarettes and booze. It rose a couple of decibels and tones when, after she told me she played first violin, I said I looked forward to hearing her solo.

'Christ almighty... are you having a laugh?'

Ah, I remembered. 'Sorry. Rupert said something about there being a young protégé...'

That brought out a smile. 'Yes! Ellen! She's our soloist which – don't tell anyone – is the only really hard bit in the whole thing. First and second don't involve the fast runs or double stops and you hardly go beyond third position. I mean... it's not exactly Paganini.' All I could do was blink. 'Never mind. Kravchuck's girl can play the lot, as well as he could in his prime, just about. A finer teacher you couldn't ask for. I sat behind him at the Proms back when he had his fingers. Exquisite. Those Russian bastards should be shot.'

'And doubtless for much else besides,' I added.

'Naturally.' She sounded a mite testy. 'Much else. Not that I couldn't play solo if required but Ellen is undoubtedly rather easier on the eye. When the girl shows up that is. Touch of the prima donna there. We're put through the wringer by Andriy every working minute and get hell if we're a second late. Ellen would never screw up the fiddle, but timekeeping is something she might address.'

'I still don't really understand how all this works...'

'It's not a proposition from Wittgenstein as they say. The first and second violins are part of the team. The backing if you like. The soloist is... the soloist. They're different jobs. It's like in cricket. Bowlers, batsmen, wicket keepers, fielders. All essential to the work as a team. Do you know nothing about music?'

'As much as I understand about cricket. Have you been in Venice long?'

'Never been anywhere long. I am what they now call a digital nomad. Though I prefer the term itinerant jack of all trades.'

Not that I asked for it, but she then recounted her life after graduating from the Royal College of Music, all the years she'd spent on the road, a journeyman violinist mainly, appreciated by orchestras across Europe, the US, Australia and Asia, never quite hitting the heights. And finally, Venice and the Teatro Maddalena which would occupy her for another year under contract. After which...

A middling career was better than none, I ventured, the way of the profession for so many in her line of work. I'd known a good few people at Cambridge who'd hoped for careers as professional musicians. Many seemed quite brilliant to my untrained ears. Yet most abandoned the field after a few years. A lack of money, of recognition, occasionally, as they came to accept it, of sufficient talent too, since there was always someone a little better and perhaps more socially connected... all these factors seemed to come into play.

She waved that away. 'Balderdash. Mostly, in my case, it's

down to sheer boredom. I can't do the same thing over and over, no matter how much people want it. No matter how much some fool sponsor is willing to pay. A year here will be a record and frankly I'm not sure I'll make that. I don't like being ordered about, you see.'

'Who does?'

The look I got seemed to say... *Well you, for one thing. Else why are you here?*

'Do you have any idea what I did the moment I flew the nest from the Academy and Marylebone Road?'

'Set out on a steady and well-organised path of career advancement by sending your CV to the very best orchestras you could find?'

Her grey eyes narrowed. 'There's more to you than meets the eye, isn't there?'

'Sorry?'

'Once free of the shackles of academia I temped in a literary agency. Then worked at a publishers manning the photocopier mostly, briefly toying with a career in the book world since there was precious little in the way of work for a musician. That soon became tiresome, so I dyed my hair, got a couple of tattoos and moved to Barcelona. Shacked up with an anarcho-punk outfit there, most of whom couldn't play a note. We did a few gigs as a collective. Anal Seepage, we called ourselves. My idea. They were Catalan. No idea what it meant. All very Nigel Kennedy I suppose. Please tell me you've heard of Nigel Kennedy...'

'Didn't he play Jimi Hendrix?'

She scowled. 'Among other things. He also popularised *The Four Seasons* for an audience who'd never ventured near classical music before. My excuse – for Barcelona and Anal Seepage – is I was young. You?'

Had to think about that. 'Straight after a 2:1 at Cambridge I went on holiday to Mablethorpe with my fiancée. A caravan site. Golden Sands I think they called it. All we could afford. Then we got married. We were soon both in the civil service.'

Reggie Davies didn't look remotely surprised. 'Each to their own. Doubt I'd prosper in anything with the word "civil" in the title.' She narrowed her sharp eyes. 'And you're about to produce a book about Antonio Vivaldi?'

'Rupert would have it so.'

'Have you written a book before?'

'Lots of reports. A few cultural pamphlets here in Venice for the museums and galleries.'

'That's a no, then?' She patted my knee. 'Well at least you'll have a good and sympathetic editor.'

'I will?'

'Yes. A digital nomad. Jack-of-all-trades as I said. Freelance editing's what I do on the trot between gigs. Marcus found out and put it to me along with a reasonably generous fee, for publishing that is. He knows the price of everything that man.' Another pat. 'Don't look so scared. It's not so hard. Stories need three things. A world to enclose them. Characters to populate that world. And events that bring the narrative to life.' She nodded back towards the city. 'You'll get your world easily enough. You're living in it. The rest will come. But you'll need to get your skates on if you're to deliver to the deadline.'

'There's a deadline?'

'The end of January at the latest. Remember that. In my book, authors who miss deadlines would be well advised to focus on that word "dead".'

I could think of nothing to say. Happily, Luca Volpetti was walking back from the palazzo with an elegant blonde woman in the kind of sheer pink silk trouser suit I associated with glamorous stars at the annual film festival.

'Ah,' Reggie said, spotting the pair. 'The Lady Haas. Have you ever seen Verdi's *Macbeth*?'

'There's a musical as well?'

That prompted a theatrical palm of her forehead. 'Good god. What have I let myself in for? Generally, we call them "operas". But I think you're a mischievous man, Arnold Clover, much as you might wish to hide it. I leave you to the charms of Mia. Mrs Marcus. Croatian before you ask, from Dubrovnik. Our real taskmaster round here. Do you know this is my third week *in situ* and I've only seen her mysterious husband once? That time he said he had an acclaimed professional historian lined up to write a book that needed editing.' A quick grin and she raised what little was left of her half pint of Negroni. 'Welcome to show business. Cheers, chuck. His money's real enough anyway.'

'The statue!' Mia Haas clapped her hands as a young woman in a barista's outfit turned up with glasses of fizz and some snacks. 'The statue! *The Penitent Maddalena.* Donatello's darling. She's here, Luca... Do you like my Franciacorta? I know we should drink Prosecco but honestly, it's a special occasion.'

We'd retired to what appeared destined to be the shady theatre foyer, away from the dwindling crowd of musicians. Another young woman turned up with a tray and offered round a plate of tiny pancakes with odd black splodges on them.

'The blinis are from our own kitchen. The caviar is Iranian if you were wondering. Not Russian. Not these days. I wouldn't want to offend poor Andriy. He's always convinced there's a Kremlin poisoner around the corner.' She shook her carefully coiffured shiny blonde head. 'As if...'

Three workmen had unloaded a large wooden box from a boat by the bridge and were lugging it across the grass. From the look on Luca's face, I got the impression he was more than a little exasperated.

'Arnold needs to discuss the commission,' he insisted. 'It's important he agrees. Time is not on our... your side. There's much to do.' He pulled an envelope out of the pocket of his green hunting jacket. 'You need his signature now, work to commence immediately.'

I did my best to smile then said, 'May I point out I haven't agreed to a single thing?'

She wasn't listening to a word. Another striking woman but, quite unlike Reggie Davies. Mia Haas had golden hair and the long, flawless neck, the languidly alluring face of Titian's *Venus of Urbino*, a voice only slightly marked by an indistinct accent and the stance, the stalking feline gait, of a catwalk model. Money too, lots of it, stated very clearly in her clothes and jewellery, heavy bracelets on both wrists, a necklace of pearls, earrings that matched. I felt as if I was in the presence of minor royalty from an obscure foreign dynasty and wondered whether she might expect me to bow.

'I don't write books either,' I explained. 'Or particularly want to.'

Luca mouthed... ssshhhh. Which was unnecessary. Mia Haas still wasn't listening but remained in raptures at the delivery of another ornament for her theatre. We watched as a life-size copy of Donatello's famous Maddalena from Florence was unboxed in front of us and set upon a plinth by a half-built cabin with a box office sign just out of its plastic wrappers. I'd seen the original some years before with Eleanor and this was as good a copy as one might imagine, the oak aged, traces of gilding still visible in places. A haunted, haunting skeletal figure naked beneath rags, hands in prayer, gaunt and tortured face lost in the tragedy of her redeemer's brutal end. I could hardly bear to look at it back then in the warm and well-lit surroundings of the

Duomo museum. Even with the connection in name to this musical venue being created in a hidden corner of Venice, it seemed bizarre to choose such a grim vision to welcome paying customers.

I had to turn away and try to admire what was being made of the palazzo across the way and the rambling gardens that ran onto the furthest wall by the water. An old-fashioned hothouse stood there, ornate windows green with algae, and a spiked decorative roof.

The curious history of the estate only came to me later. To begin with it was much simpler, accommodation for the young women, the Zitelle, taken into the care of the institution which sought to protect them. This part of the complex was then sold to a noble family, the Colonna-Ottoboni, as a private residence, much altered and improved by the money they spent on it. The palazzo they created was surely noble, perhaps inspired by the Ca' d'Oro on the Grand Canal. Even covered in scaffolding and timber, workmen painting and chipping away at its ornate exterior, I could imagine the spot as yet one more fancy boutique hotel in a city that so often seemed to want to suck in more tourists than it could possibly handle. Not that overcrowding was likely to be a problem in this isolated spot.

'Do you not find my Maddalena fetching, Arnold?' Mia asked, clearly noting my reaction.

'I find her memorable. As I did in Florence. A very good copy. As disturbing as the original.'

'It should be. Seeing what she cost.'

'Mia...' Luca waved his envelope.

'Of course. The matter must be dealt with.' In an instant she turned serious and businesslike and the image I felt she first wished to project – that of an elegant but rather empty-headed woman of substance – vanished. 'The arrangement is this...'

I listened in astonishment, soon certain this was Luca

Volpetti's doing, another of his efforts to ease my financial short-comings. No short-term translations or appointments to accompany visiting dignitaries around the Archivio di Stato. Instead, I was to devote the rest of the year to writing a book that would mark the reopening of the Teatro Maddalena as a concert hall with a neighbouring hotel, all a tribute to the works and memory of Antonio Lucio Vivaldi. The most illustrious composer in the world to some, a genius whose *The Four Seasons* was a modern icon for many who knew little or nothing about classical music. A master of his craft who, Luca revealed, twice conducted his own work in the Teatro Maddalena where we stood when, three centuries ago under the Colonna-Ottoboni, the former private chapel of the Zitelle was briefly a concert hall.

'Well?' asked Mia as Luca flourished the contract and a pen. 'What do you think?'

'Is the contract with you? Or with your husband?'

Her smile was fixed and unconvincing. 'With both of us. Or rather our companies. Marcus had hoped to meet you, but he's indisposed just now. He's not been himself of late.'

Luca looked puzzled by that. 'He seemed fine when we spoke last week.'

The smile hardened. 'That was last week.'

'All the same,' I said, 'I think you've got the wrong man...'

Luca was grimacing unseen by her and rubbing his fingers together... money.

'Why do you say that, Arnold Clover?' she wondered.

'Because I've never written a book in my life. I know nothing about classical music. Nothing about Vivaldi.'

'But you're an archivist, aren't you? Someone who finds things out. Sorts and sifts. Places them in a logical order. What is a book, a biography, but that?'

'Archivist or writer, one still requires sources.'

'And if,' she went on, 'I were to say you'd be the first man in three centuries to lay your eyes on a unique and newly discovered treasure trove of original material. Vivaldi's journals, his letters...' She hesitated for effect. 'His autograph scores...'

'His what?'

'The original music for *The Four Seasons*. In the composer's own flowing hand. Thought utterly lost, along with his private papers.'

I felt desperately out of my depth. 'You mean that's not what people play today?'

'Arnold, Arnold,' said Luca. 'I can explain all this in detail later. The Seasons as we know it is performed from copies published in Amsterdam. We've ninety per cent of Vivaldi's other autograph scores in Turin at the National Library. But not the work he's most famous for. Vanished, everyone thought. What you hear now in...' He grimaced. '...every pizza parlour you enter is like a Shakespeare play. A version copied from the original. We listen to it second-hand.'

'The original's different?'

They glanced at one another.

'We've yet to receive the material,' Mia Haas said. 'That's down to Marcus. We honestly don't know. All the same—'

'It strikes me you need an expert.'

'Stop this!' Luca looked quite cross. 'There will be experts. This material, when we have hold of it, will be made available to all the academics who need it. But first Mia and Marcus require a quick, readable, accessible piece of non-fiction for a general readership. Like an extended pamphlet for one of the museum exhibitions you've worked on.' He paused then added, 'With a little of the colour of actual fiction, of course. I'm sure you're up to that.'

'Oomph,' Mia went on, with a wag of her finger. 'That's what we seek. A tale to whet the public's appetite. With a touch of sensation, which I am promised.'

'Sensation...?' I murmured.

'Art and beauty and perhaps even a touch of the erotic,' she said to my surprise. 'What more can one ask? His relationship with the singer Anna Girò. Listen to me. I worked in public relations before I married Marcus. I promise I'll make this a sensation. Your name shall be on the front. Eight per cent of all sales net will go to you as royalties, once the advance is earned out, of course.'

I sighed. 'Let me think about it.'

She smiled, a winning one I imagine you'd call it. 'You are tempted then?'

'There's no time to waste.' Luca waved the pen at me. 'You need to start work now. Mia wishes to soft launch the venue in October. Then go fully public in the spring with the first open concert and the hotel. The Seasons, naturally, played by the small and authentic orchestra you see here under the guidance of Andriy Kravchuck. The book must be ready by then.'

For a second she seemed downcast, regretful. 'If only poor Andriy could play too but at least he can make sure our small orchestra delivers the goods. December is more likely for the soft launch of the concert hall by the way. Perhaps for New Year's Eve. Capodanno. Let's not try to fool our friend, Luca. He's an archivist. Trained to spot frauds surely.'

'Still...'

She took out a notebook and found the right page. 'The sums are settled already. Your initial advance will be paid monthly in six instalments each of €3,000. Starting today if you sign now. Then a further €18,000 on delivery. And a final €18,000 on publication. We will meet all reasonable expenses, of course, including any travel that's necessary and expert opinions. That's €54,000 in all, plus generous royalties. For six to eight month's work. A reasonable offer I believe.'

I was dumbfounded. This one commission would solve all

my short-term financial problems and stave off any future ones for a good while.

'It seems an awful lot...'

'Luca assures me you're a highly qualified expert who's worked on such things as the royal papers back in London.'

'That's true but–'

'If it would make things easier, I could pay you less...'

Luca growled as he glared at me.

'I wasn't suggesting that but...'

Andriy Kravchuck saved me further embarrassment. He was out of his chair, staring at the gaggle of musicians, roaring with fury.

It was, I assumed, in his native tongue, so I couldn't make out a word, but it was clear the old man was not happy at all.

'Excuse me,' she said and placed a gentle hand on my arm. 'I must deal with this. When I return, please tell me you've signed the contract. I asked Luca for your bank details since he has them from your work with the Archivio. I can have the money with you this afternoon.'

Kravchuck, realising no one could understand him, had switched to heavily accented English and was berating the players of his little group for being late back from their break and drinking alcohol. Rupert Hazard looked admonished, which was perhaps an act. Reggie Davies merely smiled. The rest just shuffled to their seats and picked up their instruments. I thought to count them, since this was not what I thought of as an orchestra. Six violins, what I took to be a viola, Hazard on cello and a rather nervous looking woman behind a modern-looking harpsichord. Space at the front for the missing soloist, I guessed. With a little help I felt I could get the hang of all this.

It took a few words from Mia Haas to calm Kravchuck. That and the arrival of a slim and beautiful woman in a red silk dress covered in ornate dragons, Ellen Kim, the half-Korean soloist I imagined given the smile she got out of the old man and the brief bow.

She took prime position at the front. The strings started to warm up. The maestro closed his eyes, listened to a few bars, then waved his hands and told them to give up for the day.

'Your inattention has been noted and now I am no longer in the mood,' he declared in an accent so thick I struggled to make out the words, though his face conveyed the message just as well.

Luca dragged me away as the musicians began to file out, Ellen Kim too after a brief word with her mentor.

'I simply cannot believe you're hesitating,' he grumbled when we were well past that disturbing statue of the Maddalena.

'It's just—'

'I've been working on this for months. You need the money. It's obvious. Valentina and I are agreed...'

That puzzled me. 'Valentina? What on earth has this to do with the Carabinieri?'

'She's trying to help.'

'I'm sure she is. What's in it for her?'

'That's not fair.'

'Why's a Carabinieri capitano interested in this place?'

'She isn't. She's interested in you. Concerned about you. Because she's your friend. As am I. Two of the only friends you have in Venice as far as we can see. Close enough to know you're struggling with money and too proud to admit it. Close enough to observe you need to find a project, a problem. A bone to chew on. You're not a slothful man by nature, Arnold. Yet how do you spend your days?'

I beamed. 'In blissful idleness. Dreaming. Reading. Loafing. It's a talent. I'm working on it and there's no better place on the planet to do that than here.'

'It's not you.'

'I said... I'm working on it.'

He waved the pen at me again. 'Think of the money.'

'I am...'

'Think of the challenge.'

'That too. I know nothing about music, Luca!'

'Which is precisely what they require! Someone who can make all this accessible to the public. Not a scholar who'll write a book so highbrow only his or her fellow academics can understand it. Those will come. But first... you once told me ignorance was a blessing. It meant you came to problems with no preconceptions. An open mind.'

'A blank mind in this instance. Can I count on your help?'

He wriggled and it was obvious this was a question he didn't want. 'As much as I can. The Archivio has precious little on Vivaldi.'

'You're joking.'

'He was a churchman. Not all those records came our way. This new material Marcus seems to have located sounds far more promising.'

To break the awkward moment, he took a sip of his fizz, and a sample of the caviar the woman had left us. Then he wrinkled his nose. 'Not used to this stuff. Tastes a bit fishy.'

'Not the only thing, is it?'

'What?'

I nodded at the buildings. 'Fishy. All this. The millions they must be spending. Where does it come from?'

'Finance, I gather.'

'Which means what?'

'Ask Marcus when you talk. I did and it was gobbledegook

about bitcoin and derivatives and stuff that's well beyond me. Who cares? I despair of you sometimes. Imagine you were a shopkeeper and someone walks in and wishes to buy the most expensive object you own. Would you ask him where he got his money?'

The players were dispersing, some to the bridge and the vaporetto stop I imagine. A few hanging round the grounds, muttering among themselves. The small orchestra of the Teatro Maddalena was doubtless well paid. But that does not necessarily make for happiness.

'I'm not a shopkeeper.'

'No, you're a highly intelligent Englishman allowing your talents to go to waste through nothing more than idleness and boredom. One last time...' The pen again. 'Even if the money offends you...'

That made me laugh.

'Even,' he added, 'if the fact this comes as a gift from me with Valentina's blessing pricks your obvious English pride...'

'I am grateful, Luca. Honestly.'

'Then for pity's sake... sign. Marcus promised me you'd get your hands on material no one has seen for centuries. Touch the same paper Vivaldi did with his quill and intellect. How can a man like you turn that down?'

I grabbed the pen and the contract then signed without reading a single word. What was the point? Luca was right. I had been lazy of late. I craved some kind of intellectual adventure as much as I needed the money. And I'd enjoyed talking to Reggie Davies too. The idea she'd be the editor, a source of advice and encouragement when I needed it, was intriguing.

'Hope I don't regret that...'

'The English,' he murmured. 'Do you not have a saying about looking a ghost horse in the mouth?'

'Gift horse,' I corrected him.

'Ah. I suppose that makes a little more sense.'

Although I was soon to learn a ghost horse would have been equally appropriate.

~

Mia Haas returned, a fresh glass in her hand alongside another round of caviar blinis.

'Well?'

Luca held up the contract and pointed to my signature.

She waved it away. 'I've put the money in Arnold's account already. Done.'

I'd heard my phone buzz a few minutes before, too busy to wonder what it might be. Sure enough, when I looked there was a payment of €3,000 in the account, from a company in Bucharest with the odd name Wurdulac.

'You'll get the same each month,' she added. 'The companies may change. Marcus runs a complex financial ship.' She smiled broadly for the first time, and of course it was a showbiz smile, perfect teeth, very white. 'Don't ask me how or why. I leave all that to him.'

I asked the obvious questions... when I was I to start? And how? Where was this new material and how would I be allowed to examine it? An office in the palazzo it seemed, one on the top floor near the Haas's private quarters. All prepared with a computer and internet access.

'May I see it?'

'No need now,' she insisted. 'The first thing we must arrange is for you to sit down with Andriy Kravchuck when he's in a better mood. He knows as much about Vivaldi as any man alive.'

'Which is not a lot,' Luca added. 'No one does.'

I shook my head. 'I'm sorry. I don't understand.'

'You will soon enough.' Mia again. 'Antonio Vivaldi may be one of the best-known composers in the world when it comes to his music. But as to who he really was...'

There was an image in the concert hall entrance, close to that haunting statue. A painting I'd seen so many times in Venice, a man in a white wig and red cape, violin in hand, music on a desk.

'That's him,' I said pointing at it.

Mia Haas nodded. 'Yes, that painting is everywhere. As to whether it's Vivaldi...' There were raised voices again somewhere. Her voice fell a tone. 'Enough for today, gentlemen. We have our agreement. You have your money. I, a tetchy musical maestro to contend with and a husband who will soon be hungry. Go home. Enjoy your good fortune, Arnold. Perhaps treat your friend to a drink or two. Luca turned down this commission and insisted you were better placed for it.'

'And Valentina?' I added.

She blinked. 'I'm sorry. Who?'

Luca nudged me with his elbow. 'No matter,' he said. 'A Negroni is in order. I know just the place.'

'You always do...'

Then it happened. A moment the world seemed to stand still, waiting on something it could never begin to imagine.

Someone was screaming. A woman. High-pitched, wordless yet somehow musical, getting closer, coming towards us.

The three of us looked at one another and I was aware of that damned wooden spectre watching from the door, the skinny Mary Magdalene in rags, eyes in sockets, boring down on us.

Ellen Kim, the violinist, the woman in the red silk dragon dress, burst in. She was running, stumbling, weeping. 'Marcus,' she whispered then stumbled to the ground, shaking, sobbing like a broken child. 'I'm so sorry...'

'What about him?' Mia demanded.

No words. Just more tears. Then a glance back towards the gardens and she raised her hand, delicate fingers stained with blood.

I ran outside, past the scaffolding and painters' sheets all around the palazzo.

The gardener I'd seen earlier was lounging on his spade in one of the half-dug flower beds, a cigarette in his mouth, looking bemused.

He pointed to the hothouse by the wall. 'Thought I heard something in there. Before that piece of skirt came out bawling.'

'Heard what?'

'Like a gun.' He grinned. 'This place, eh? Madness.'

'Thanks for telling people,' I muttered.

'Just the gardener, chum. Nothing more.'

Mia was there already. I caught up, asked her to stay back.

'I live here, you don't,' she said and strode ahead.

It was a long building, old iron framework, glass ancient, cracked in places and dusty and covered in algae. When I got to the door a sweep of exotic fragrances greeted us.

There was a sign on the glass: *Casa delle Orchidee*. The Orchid House.

Strange flowers, thick stems, glossy petals in livid colours, rose from pots hidden among palms and ferns, the path through them so narrow only one person could get through at a time.

I was determined it would be me, much as Mia Haas struggled to force her way in front.

The hothouse had to be a good thirty metres long and twenty wide, crammed with plants and flowers that flourished in the overheated, humid atmosphere.

After I pushed aside a thicket of fleshy palm leaves, we saw. There was a scarlet velvet couch against the far end of the hothouse, an old-fashioned one with leonine wooden arms and claw feet. On it lay a man, slumped back against the headrest end. Blood and bone from a wound above his left ear. Free arm falling towards the tiled floor where a handgun lay on a pile of curled dead leaves.

Mia Haas screamed, a heartrending shriek, wordless, and was there before I could stop her, one hand on her husband's chest, the other reaching for the gun.

'I'll call an ambulance,' Luca said and stumbled back outside, phone in shaking hand.

'What's the point of a damned ambulance?' she snarled, furious, tears streaming down her cheeks. 'He's dead. Can't you see?'

Marcus Haas. The man so few had met. The impresario, the financial guru, the lover of Vivaldi who'd spent so much time and money attempting to bring the Teatro Maddalena and its palazzo back to life in his memory. Mia began to weep, a steady, rhythmic movement of her chest marking every moan like the sound of a metronome.

'I'm so sorry,' I said, ashamed how inadequate the words sounded.

She turned and gazed at me, calm in the way disbelieving people sometimes can be at such moments. 'Leave me with him please.'

My mind was turning to what had to come after. An investigation. The police. Valentina Fabbri, I imagined. She'd already taken an interest in the place.

'You should put the gun down. Don't touch anything. People will want to look.'

As she placed the weapon back on the pile of leaves, she saw something on the floor, just beneath the couch. A piece of paper, half-scrunched up as if Marcus Haas had been holding it before he shot himself. Mia was shaking her head.

'What is it?'

'Someone kept sending him this.' She passed it over. 'It upset him. Why?'

Two crochets scrawled against five lines of a hand-drawn musical staff, slanted, crude, as if written in haste.

An odd thing for a dying man to clutch, I thought, as the siren of an ambulance boat echoed down the narrow canal.

Chapter Two

Largo e pianissimo sempre

A man dead of a gunshot wound in the orchid house of a half-restored noble estate on the edge of Giudecca. It was inevitable the Carabinieri would soon be crawling all over the place, a determined and ever-curious Capitano Valentina Fabbri at their head. The media took an interest too, Austrian as much as Venetian. Marcus Haas, it seemed, was a man of some notoriety in Vienna, a controversial business figure admired and loathed in equal measure for his ruthless, international dealmaking.

I was anxious his widow wouldn't face the necessary inquisition on her own. With her agreement I sat in on the interviews which Valentina conducted with her usual thoroughness. Such facts as emerged seemed to confirm a picture our capitano friend had half expected. Marcus Haas was a volatile man, a drinker and an occasional drug taker – cocaine was in his veins in quite some quantity when he died, along with booze.

The project to restore the Teatro Maddalena and the adjoining palazzo had overrun the original budget by two hundred per cent. He was, it appeared, one of those wealthy people rich in the money of others. In other words in hock quite beyond his means. Two weeks before, unknown to his wife, he'd negotiated a debt rollover that gave him enough money to finish the estate and bring in paying customers by the following spring. Even so, he was under pressure, from quarters Mia Haas said she didn't understand. Business was left to Marcus, the development of the theatre and hotel project to her.

Then there were the unavoidable questions about their private lives. They'd been married for eleven years, childless, mostly happy though she flatly refused to elaborate beyond that. A small apartment in Vienna – their main house in the smart district of Leopoldstadt had been sold to fund the development in Venice. No relatives on his side, so all Haas's complex stockholdings and business arrangements now belonged to his wife.

As to the tearful Ellen Kim... she insisted she'd no idea why Haas asked her to meet him in the orchid house that afternoon. To discuss musical matters, she presumed, as the two of them had done before. She'd assumed he was sleeping on the sofa and tried to wake him, only to have him fall against her just as she saw the gun.

There seemed little more to discover. Four days Valentina and her team of officers and technical experts spent examining the orchid house, the palazzo, and interviewing those of us who'd been there that afternoon. After that she decided, in her usual rather reticent manner, that Marcus Haas had, as seemed obvious, shot himself under the influence of cocaine and alcohol, unable to deal with the financial pressures of the foundation he'd set out to build from scratch.

Within a week the place was free of Carabinieri, of musicians, of builders too, Luca back at his desk by the Frari, me at a loose end once more. That only added to the strangeness. There was something so unreal about the grim end of Marcus Haas, so unexpected on that idle April afternoon on Giudecca, that it took a while to process the idea it was real. The whole, bizarre interlude had that slow, soft tempo that so often follows sudden mortality. As if time itself had decided to halve its pace, wondering at the oddness of it all.

I never knew the man, of course, nor would. Yet, in the days after Valentina passed her verdict of suicide, as we drifted into May, I sought out those members of his motley musical circus I could locate. Most were still in the accommodation they'd rented for the months ahead, uncertain what to do. You expect fallout from a sudden, unforeseen death, especially suicide. But there was real shock, genuine among the ragged band he'd brought together in the former convent of the Zitelle. Perhaps it was out of self-interest. They'd been treated magnanimously, paid well, promised months of work in a profession where employment was often brief and poorly rewarded. As had I.

Few, I came to discover, had met the man during their time working with Andriy Kravchuck, rehearsing, allowing the technicians to begin to adjust and perfect the acoustics of the rebuilt theatre where Vivaldi himself had played almost three centuries before. All, it seemed, were convinced this was the premature end of the Teatro Maddalena, his widow too, or so it appeared.

Mia Haas had vanished back to Austria, determined to arrange a swift funeral for her husband in the city of his birth, and seemed to want to stay there. A decision that puzzled a few given the uncertainty around the Giudecca project, though not me. I knew what abrupt tragedy felt like, how the survivors sometimes retreated inside themselves, incapable of making decisions even halfway rational for a while. I'd experienced that with my wife Eleanor who collapsed and died without the least warning which led to my moving – fleeing might be a better word – across Europe to what was meant to be solitary exile in Venice. Except Luca Volpetti and Valentina Fabbri intervened and dragged me out of my miserable state of mourning, placed challenges and problems on my lap and left me to come back to life to tackle them.

There was no antidote to death, only an anaesthetic to ease the pain of those still breathing. That soporific was life itself, activity, mindless or engaged, it didn't much matter.

There were few signs of that around the half-finished Teatro Maddalena. Without Haas and his elegant, ever-active wife, the estate hidden away on Giudecca seemed as dead as the man himself. No builders working on the palazzo and the theatre, no technicians erecting baffles to improve the auditorium's acoustics. Most of all no musicians, that lively carefree gaggle I'd seen only briefly, a colourful crowd who'd filled Haas's auditorium with gaiety and life.

Andriy Kravchuck, I gathered, was staying in an apartment near the Doge's Palace with Ellen Kim, refusing to come out. When I ran into Rupert Hazard outside a bar in Campo Santa Margherita, he was downright furious at the outcome, drunkenly telling me how suicide was the route of cowards everywhere, oblivious to the damage they did to others. Reggie Davies, downing spritz next to his Negronis, felt much the same way I suspected but put it rather more politely.

I had the last of a dead man's money in my bank account and nothing to do.

Then, after the middle of May passed, marked by the Vogalonga, the annual rowing regatta when the city was once more overflowing with visitors, I received an unexpected summons out of the blue.

'Arnold,' Mia Haas messaged me. 'I am back in Venice. We must speak. Please. The café by Zitelle, tomorrow, eight thirty.'

It was a warm and blustery day, angry anvils of storm clouds building over the grey Adriatic, mosquitoes and midges beginning to rise from the swirling waters of the lagoon. Spring edging ever more towards summer, a transition marked by the screaming swifts overhead. We took a table by the canal with that exquisite view over to the Punta della Dogana and San Marco.

It was hard to believe I was sitting down with the same woman I met almost a month before on that fateful day her husband died. Mia Haas looked quite different, thinner, her face understandably gaunt, older too. Her hair was now shorter, more natural. Her clothes plain and simple, a white cotton shirt and jeans. It made me wonder how much I'd changed after Eleanor died, and never noticed.

'You've been very kind,' she said, picking at a pecan plait. 'Very patient. I heard you'd been ringing round checking on people. Andriy. Ellen Kim. The other musicians.'

'It was nothing. Besides, you paid me for a job I haven't done. There's still a little of the money left if you'd like–'

She scoffed at that. 'Don't be so silly!'

'I mean it. I heard what you said to Valentina, remember. About Marcus and his finances.'

'The finances are... manageable. Until next spring. I've funds enough to complete the theatre and the palazzo, along with the grounds. If we do that and bring in some customers and a couple of sponsors maybe... just maybe this crackpot idea will fly. I don't need your money but thank you anyway. In any case... what else do I have to do? I need something to take my mind off what happened. Otherwise, I'll go crazy.'

I hesitated but said it anyway. 'When I lost my wife, I had people asking me all the time how I was. It became quite annoying in the end.'

That got a smile.

'Very tactfully put.'

I waited.

'I am... doing fine, thank you very much. Marcus had been out of sorts for quite a while. Something nagging at him, and he'd never say.' She reached into her bag and pulled out that scrap of paper found by his body. Something I'd quite forgotten. 'When I went through his papers in Vienna, I found two more of these. Do you know what they are?'

'I don't read music.'

'Me neither. I had to ask that odd cellist who always smells of drink. It's called the *diabolus in musica*. The Devil's Tritone or something. A nasty evil disharmony.'

'He received more than one?'

'He did. Someone, I think, was taunting him. Threatening him maybe. Unless...'

'Unless?'

'Unless he was the one sending them. To himself. He was a little crazy towards the end, maybe more than I appreciated. I've no idea to be honest.'

'You could show that to Valentina Fabbri.'

'Your Carabinieri friend? I think not. Marcus is gone. No bringing him back. I'd rather keep those people out of it if you don't mind. Also...' She stopped.

'Also...?'

'I wasn't entirely frank with her. Please don't pass this on.'

'I wouldn't dream of it.'

'Marcus and I were discussing divorce. He'd taken to being unfaithful. For rather longer than I knew. Boredom, he said when I confronted him. After eleven years it seems I'd become somewhat tedious.'

'You really don't need to tell me this.'

'I do! I apologise if it's a burden. But I need to tell someone. He had his eyes on that young violinist, Ellen. She was one more victim I guess you'd say. Or so he hoped. Whether it happened...' She sighed. 'I neither know nor care. He used to take his women to the orchid house when I was out, hoping I'd never know. I'm sure that's why she was going there that day. I'd seen them talking earlier. He wasn't picky. Could be anyone. It didn't matter. Marcus tried to tell me he was a sex addict, whatever that means. As if he wasn't responsible for his own actions.' She finished her coffee and ordered another. 'Perhaps he was right. He wasn't. The drink. The coke. The instability.'

This seemed so odd. 'He doesn't sound like the kind of man who'd want to spend a fortune creating a theatre and a foundation devoted to Vivaldi.'

She stared right at me. 'He wasn't. He wasn't much interested in music at all until I came up with the idea. We've always loved Venice. I go to La Fenice, to concerts. Vivaldi, Corelli. Anything from that era. Marcus never came along. I thought we needed to build something together. That the Maddalena might heal things. Not that I put it quite like that. He said yes. And here we are. Halfway through a strange journey I never foresaw.'

'If there's something I can do...'

'You can write your book.'

I laughed. 'I'd assumed that was a dead duck...'

'You assumed wrong. You signed that contract. The next instalment will go into your bank account shortly. I expect my money's worth. I told you. The Teatro Maddalena still lives and breathes. It needs your book. Soft launch at the end of the year, then a full one, hotel and everything in the spring. Every guest will get a copy. We sell them in the shop, online. It will be wonderful, I just know it. Readable. Controversial. Full of material people have never seen before.'

'What... what material?'

She hesitated. 'That I'm still working on. Marcus hadn't

completed the negotiations. All in good time. Reggie Davies briefed you, she told me. I'm assured she's an excellent editor.'

'But…'

'Your friend Luca Volpetti from the Archivio. He's expecting you there at ten thirty tomorrow. Andriy has to go to London for a while. Private business. When you're ready, he can be your guide here. He knows every footstep Vivaldi took in this place on his way to penury and death. Every note he wrote too. Any questions?'

'Well…'

'Good. One last thing. Please keep a case packed. I may need you to go to Vienna at short notice.'

That took me aback. 'Because…?'

Mia Haas didn't look me in the eye when she said, 'Because there, somewhere, lurks the most important part of the story you're going to tell. Those elusive papers my husband said he was going to buy. Now come with me, please.'

We walked the way I'd come that awful day, through the housing blocks where the same pensioners lounged in the sun next to their cats, on to the door and the wooden bridge. I'd last been on the estate of the Teatro Maddalena a week after Marcus Haas's bloody death. The place was empty then apart from that surly gardener who seemed to live in the same hut he stored his tools. He'd told me everyone was gone and grumbled about being paid.

Not now. The fellow was there with his spade, working on a bed of rose bushes, a few half in flower. Some of the scaffolding on the palazzo was down, the walls behind clean and fresh with renewed stonework and windows. The glass of the orchid house looked as if it had been recently washed too. There were technicians working in the theatre where Andriy Kravchuck sat in a chair, leading his group of musicians through a rehearsal, Ellen Kim to the fore. It was almost as if nothing of note had happened here. Mia Haas was right. The dream appeared alive once more.

'Come,' she ordered and for the first time I got a good look at the palazzo.

The hallway was brightly lit, what I took to be a Murano chandelier at the centre. A new and shiny lift was installed next to a sweeping staircase which rose, she said, four floors – too many steps for guests she expected to be paying a fortune.

Inside she pushed the button for the private quarters of the top floor. The lift opened directly into the hall of the sprawling apartment that occupied the whole lagoon side. The furniture looked luxuriously old-fashioned, a living room, a kitchen, two bedrooms, a dining room that led out to the terrace dotted with potted palms. The view was breathtaking, over the gardens, down into the orchid house itself, then to the glittering lagoon with the long finger of the Lido on the horizon. Though I struggled to take my eyes off the glasshouse. If he'd taken his lovers there for assignations, he must surely have known his wife might easily see.

Mia realised I'd noticed. 'I told you. I didn't mind. We were past that point. Once all this was up and running, Marcus would have gone back to Vienna to make more money, and I'd have stayed here to run the show. Then, unless matters changed greatly, divorce. He was generous that way. Come...'

On the other side of the floor was a large office, beyond it what I took to be the private quarters of whoever was meant to run it, bedroom and bathroom. Expensive fittings, a new computer with a gigantic screen on a swish modern desk next to a bookcase full of titles about baroque music, Venice in the early eighteenth century.

'This is all yours,' she said. 'As is...' She went to a door behind the desk and threw it open. Another apartment was there, finely furnished, quite compact, for staff I imagine. 'This. Move in for as long as you like. It has the highest speed internet you'll find, and I've signed you up with all the academic research subscriptions Volpetti recommended. They are limited to this one computer, I'm afraid. So, if you want to use them...'

'I'll need to work here?'

'Yes. Undisturbed as you see fit. I won't say I wouldn't appreciate the occasional company because you might feel that was untoward pressure. Even if it's true. I struggle with Kravchuck and his musicians. Out of my depth. Whereas you seem... easier to talk to.'

'Thank you for the offer.'

'Will you take it?'

'The office when I need it. For the rest... I have my little place in Dorsoduro. Things there. Habits. Old ones. Hard to break.'

She took that well, and perhaps it was expected. 'Just an idea. I thought you might like to live alongside your subject as it were.'

'A little distance would help. To begin with.'

'Your decision, of course. Kindly bear this in mind. I'm not made for mourning. I crave activity and fully intend to bring this project to fruition. Marcus is owed.'

'I'm sure you'll do him proud.'

I didn't know how she took that. To be honest, I couldn't wait to get out of there.

There was no music when I left. Kravchuck was handing out one of his loud lectures in that booming heavily accented voice of his. Or perhaps a rollicking aimed at none other than Rupert Hazard who sat upright on his chair, instrument resting between his legs, face florid and I thought furious.

Reggie Davies saw me, waved with her fingers and mouthed, 'Later.'

A quick thumbs up and then I fled.

~

First thing the next morning my phone buzzed. Luca. He didn't want to meet in the Archivio di Stato. Instead, we were to have lunch with Valentina Fabbri in a place we all knew well.

As regular as clockwork, newspapers and magazines carry a travel article dedicated to 'secret Venice'. Invariably the supposedly hidden gems they talk about aren't secret at all. Just spots known to regular foreign visitors, a little way off the well-beaten path that most tourists, here for a day or two, take – the Piazza San Marco, the Rialto, and all the teeming streets between.

Ugo Abate's tiny bacaro was different. Almost impossible to find without detailed directions, it lay at the end of a dead-end deep in a warren of alleys close to the tiny Scuola di San Giorgio degli Schiavoni with its gorgeous Carpaccio paintings. Untouched by the noisy world of commercial Venice, it was a welcome reminder that a local city still lived, just, beneath the surface of glitter and avarice that marred so many establishments closer to the mecca of the great piazza.

Ugo was seventy or so, long retired from the Carabinieri where he'd once schooled a young cadet Valentina Fabbri in the complexities of Venetian policing. Now widowed, he spent most days working in his minuscule bar, living above the shop in what was originally a couple of terraced houses built for the craftsmen of the Arsenale boatyards.

A genial man, always ready to pour wine and spritz, turn out all the classic Venetian *cicchetti: sarde in saor, baccalà, salumi,* happy to chat to anyone from behind his old red wooden counter, though if by chance they were foreigners, he would always beg them to take no photographs and never mention the place on social media.

He was also still a kind of mentor to his former pupil, though she'd now attained his old rank of capitano, much younger than he'd ever managed. Different days. When Ugo Abate first joined the Carabinieri the only women working in Valentina's San Zaccaria Station were secretaries.

An invitation to his little bar was always a pleasure, but usually business too. Rarely the occasional translation work I did for Valentina over some English fool who'd got himself into hot water. More the delicacies of law enforcement in a city where conventional serious crime was rare and misdemeanours could be dealt with more subtly than one might expect elsewhere.

I'd soon learned since moving to the city and making the acquaintance of Valentina and Luca Volpetti that Venice ran to its own rhythm, never willing to be rushed, rarely leaping to a quick opinion when a slower more considered one might be available.

It was Tuesday, just after one when I got there. The warmth of coming summer was on the city, and it showed in the delicacies Ugo brought out the moment I arrived – stuffed courgette flowers, fresh mantis shrimp from the lagoon, asparagus and a cheese from the Dolomites. All with a carafe of Pinot Grigio made by a friend who ran a small family vineyard outside Treviso.

Quite a spread. Valentina, immaculate as ever in her dark blue Carabinieri uniform, gave me a hug and a kiss. Luca, in Paul and Shark head to toe, white polo and pale blue trousers, was all smiles. I sat down feeling, as usual, underdressed in my jeans, old shirt, and worn cotton jacket. Wary too. A trip to Ugo's was rarely the simple pleasant social occasion it first appeared. For Valentina, it was a place away from the office where conversations might be had, ideas ventured, that never need enter the records.

'Cheers,' I said and raised my glass.

'Salute!' cried Luca, then Valentina.

'Now...' I added. 'What on earth are you two up to? What is it you want?'

They both looked deeply hurt.

'You're getting overly suspicious in your old age,' Valentina complained.

'Really? I was supposed to meet Luca at the Archivio this morning. To start work on this crackpot book project he's lumbered me with.'

'A simple thank you will suffice,' he declared with a wave of the hand.

'Thank you. I think. What do you want?'

Ugo came over with another round of snacks and took the empty seat at the table. 'Suicide,' he said. 'Do you believe that?'

I felt like screaming. 'Why put this question to me? Ask the capitano of the Carabinieri who's in print saying it was so.'

She nodded, head side to side the way Italians did, and sipped the wine. 'I did say this. I had no alternative.'

'Why?'

'Because it looked like suicide.' She nodded at Ugo. 'Did it not?'

He seemed to concur. 'I did the course. In Milan. How to tell. It would have helped if his wife hadn't touched the gun. Next time kindly remember to leave things as they are.'

'Next time? Next time?'

'Ugo means if you ever find yourself in similar circumstances,' Valentina said, as if that was a reasonable explanation. 'Which is unlikely in Venice, of course. As I have said on many an occasion–'

'The only murders you have are the imaginary ones created

by foreign purveyors of lowbrow fiction. Long may it continue. I'd like a spritz if you don't mind, Ugo. Campari. A strong one. This conversation is taxing my feeble brain.'

'No Campari for him,' she ordered. 'Arnold needs every last of his marbles as the English say.'

'I thought I was here to talk to Luca about this damned book.'

She found that funny. 'Oh come, Signor Clover. You didn't think we'd invite you just for that. The truth is there are undercurrents in this matter. I don't say I understand them. Only that they exist.'

'Could you please knock off the very Venetian cryptic act?'

'Marcus Haas was hoping for an affair with Kravchuck's violinist,' said Luca. 'Other women maybe too. Everyone was on top of one another in that place. You saw. No keeping secrets.'

Valentina stared at me very directly and asked, 'Did you have any idea?'

'I never knew these people until the day Luca dragged me there! Never met Marcus Haas at all. How would I know? How would you?'

Her expression told me she thought the question ridiculous. 'The violinist told me, of course. She claims she hadn't accepted his advances. But she was under pressure. I think, perhaps, considering it. Artists.' She scowled. 'Their private lives...'

Enough, I thought. 'You told the papers his death was suicide. Case closed. You said–'

'The place he died... that couch... it was where he went for his assignations,' she interrupted. 'The wife must have known. I find it inconceivable she didn't.'

'Then ask her. Not me.'

Ugo got up, went to the counter and came back with two Campari spritzes, one for each of us. He wasn't taking orders from Valentina.

'Austrians,' he said and raised his glass. 'At least they gave us this.'

'I believe the wife is from Croatia. And Campari comes from Piedmont.'

'Pedantry is an unattractive trait, Arnold. Still, point taken. Very well. From what I learned on that course in Milan, it does appear Haas shot himself while full of cocaine and booze. Nevertheless, something stinks. It's a funny business it seems to me. All that money, such a massive project financed entirely privately...'

'By a man known to be a cutthroat and distinctly disreputable operator, famed for flying close to the wind,' Valentina added. 'Someone who'd never had any connection with the musical world whatsoever until he began pumping his millions into that place in Giudecca.'

Luca pointed across the table. 'Fishy. The very word you used to me that afternoon.'

'I'll start thinking about going back to live in England if you continue in this vein. Is there a more serious a threat than that?'

Valentina reached over and touched my hand. 'Don't be ridiculous. We just wanted to meet up for a friendly drink and chat. To bounce around a few ideas. See what you think.'

'I think you're being quite deliberately enigmatic because you're forever suspicious, especially when it comes to foreigners.'

'What a shocking accusation,' she complained. 'I simply feel there are—'

'Dangling threads,' I interrupted. 'There. I said it for you. There are always dangling threads for you. I've never known it otherwise.'

She shrugged. 'Perhaps you're right. All will become clear. In due course. One way or another.'

A long and awkward silence followed. Finally, Luca broke it. 'The book...'

'I was under the impression we were to meet at the Archivio this morning to start work on that. Not throw around gossip and tittle-tattle over an excellent lunch of wine and *cicchetti.*'

'And which would you prefer?' Ugo demanded.

'I can answer that,' Luca cut in. 'Our little lunch here. By a long shot.'

'Because...?' I wondered.

'Because...' He grabbed his briefcase, placed it on the table, and flipped open the lid. 'As I've already intimated, I've nothing much to tell you. We really do have precious little concerning Antonio Vivaldi on file.'

I almost fell off my seat. 'Don't be ridiculous. Venetians are the greatest hoarders of documents I've ever encountered. There's scarcely a piece of official paper been thrown away here since god knows when. You've got government invoices going back to the tenth century.'

'A little earlier actually. Nevertheless.' He placed an old hardback on the table, *Antonio Vivaldi: The Red Priest of Venice* by Karl Heller. 'There's more in here than we have, far more. Though I should warn you it's mostly about the music, not the man. The waypoints of his career, his ups, and later, many downs. Then there's this...'

He threw a pamphlet on the table, one from a local music society, on the cover the portrait seen everywhere, a fair-faced man in a white wig and red cloak, a violin in his left hand, a quill over a piece of music in his right. The same painting I'd seen in the Teatro Maddelena.

'Everyone presumes this is Vivaldi, painted in the Netherlands it seems, when he would have been around forty-five,' Luca went on. 'Yet there's nothing to suggest the artist ever met the man. Who knows? And if you compare it with a caricature produced in Rome...'

I'd seen this one before too. A line drawing of someone who looked much older, with an exaggerated long nose and a very different kind of wig, curly and short.

'They don't look like the same fellow,' I said.

'The drawing's exaggerated, perhaps a little cruel, but I agree. And supposedly they both date from the same year. Which seems impossible.'

'Wait...' Hand on heart, I was beginning to find this fascinating. 'You're telling me there's no known, authenticated portrait of the composer of arguably the most popular piece of classical music in the world? No contemporary account of him as a man? What he was like? What people thought of him?'

'Enough!' he cried. 'Just because he's world-famous now, it doesn't mean the man's always been that way. Nothing could be further from the truth. You've much to learn.'

'The fact is,' added Ugo, 'were it not for that monster Mussolini we might never have heard of him. I remember hearing that story at school. Wasn't there some American poet who lived near Salute, a fascist...?'

My head was starting to spin. 'Mussolini. What on earth...?'

'The genius you seek is a ghost,' said Valentina. 'A myth. No one really knows him. Not that most people realise. If you'd mentioned his name here a century ago, not a soul outside a few obscure academic circles would have heard of him. Antonio Vivaldi was a forgotten shadow. Why do you think he was thrown into a cheap grave in Vienna without a mention on his death certificate he was a musician at all? Just a down-on-his-luck itinerant priest. Why do you feel Mia Haas is setting such store by your book? She claims she'll soon have access to new material that will put flesh on a man everyone – quite wrongly – thinks they know. If she's right, it could be a sensation.'

They were all looking at me and I couldn't work out how much was pity and how much expectation. I was caught, trapped. All the assumptions I'd made so glibly seemed questionable if not downright inaccurate. The idea I might be the one who could draw back the veil and see who Vivaldi really was... who could refuse?

'Anything else I can find I'll email,' said Luca. 'But I warn you... it's mainly a chronology of dates, appointments, journeys. This book's a gift.' He pointed to a coloured tag sticking out near the end of the tome he'd placed before me. 'There was a time he worked with Carlo Goldoni, when the writer was young, before he was famous. Goldoni wrote about that meeting. You should read it. That's the only worthwhile verbatim account of a meeting with Antonio Vivaldi I could find. It's a start, I guess.'

I remembered Reggie Davies's advice. 'I begin with his world. Here. Venice. The places he lived. The places that made him. Kravchuck knows them all. He's going to show me when he gets back from London.'

'When's that?' asked Valentina.

'I haven't a clue. Which you may take as my considered response to pretty much any question you wish to pose at the moment.'

'Plenty of time to start your reading then,' she added. 'Do please keep me in touch with how your detective work proceeds.'

A week passed with no news from Kravchuck and not a word from Mia Haas who, it seemed, had once more to returned to Vienna to settle some pressing problems with her late husband's estate. In the meantime, my monthly fee arrived, with an extra thousand and a note saying this was to cover the work I did talking to people in Mia's absence after the death of Marcus.

I'm not the most financially literate of men. All the same I couldn't help but notice this payment came not from an outfit called Wurdulac in Bucharest but an equally obscure company by the name of Bokor in Haiti. Dammit those names bothered me. All I got from the public sources on my laptop at home in Dorsoduro was gossip and hints. I took the vaporetto over to Giudecca, made my way into the empty palazzo and sat down at the desk with the PC prepared for me. The place was quiet, spacious and rather beautiful in its solitary green location at the edge of the island, a kind of little Eden, the peace only broken by the occasional banter and noise of builders. No Mia, no Kravchuck, no musicians either.

There I used a few professional academic sources to check the names of the mysterious accounts sending me what seemed quite large sums of money. Wurdulac was some kind of vampire or monster from Slavic mythology. Bokor, a Haitian voodoo god. Not that I could locate any businesses that used the names, though perhaps that was because none of the research sites available to me focused much on the corporate world, let alone firms based in Bucharest or Port-au-Prince.

It occurred to me then that Mia – or someone else – might easily be capturing what I searched for and typed on this captive machine. Perhaps an excess of suspicion on my part, but it was enough to send me scuttling home to Dorsoduro and the little old laptop in my apartment. There I was able to browse the documents Luca had set up for me from the Archivio, start on the book he'd provided, and embark upon a little sideways research of my own.

My friend was spot on. The life of Antonio Vivaldi was, for one so famous in modern times, remarkably devoid of fact and detail. How remarkable I could see from looking at one of his contemporaries, Johann Sebastian Bach, just seven years younger.

When the young Bach came to Vivaldi's work, the Venetian was arguably the most famous composer in Europe, in demand everywhere, a kind of continental rock star with concertos and operas in production north to south, east to west.

Bach was a great admirer of a composer who was stretching and inventing musical technique. He transcribed several concertos and used some of Vivaldi's ideas to develop his own work as it grew in ambition. On the side, he was determined to set down the talents of the Bach family and wrote a chronology of his ancestors going back several generations to his great-great-grandfather Veit, a miller who used to play the cittern, an early kind of guitar.

There remain plenty of contemporary accounts of the ill-tempered composer, covering his itinerant career and many arguments with his various employers, his family, his difficult relations with pupils, one of whom gave him a beating after being insulted about his bassoon playing.

Finally, the sad final years when his poor health was made worse by two cataract operations inflicted on him by an English charlatan who'd also blinded Handel with his quack cures. All that I could find in a matter of minutes.

And of Vivaldi, a far more famous figure in his time? As Luca said... precious little but gossip and speculation. The only contemporary account of the man I could find was in Keller's book, as Luca had predicted. The young playwright Carlo Goldoni was summoned to Vivaldi's home, to talk about rewriting a libretto for the opera *Griselda* and later recorded the meeting in a memoir. The brief account was more tantalising for what it left out than what it said. Goldoni, desperate for work by the sound of it, noted that Vivaldi was more often referred to by his nickname, *Il Prete Rosso*, the Red Priest, than by his real one and was living in the same quarters as the singer, Anna Girò.

This would have been around 1735, when Anna was twenty-four or five and the composer fifty-seven. She had been his muse, and perhaps more, since she became his student as a teenager, later a steady companion and preferred mezzo-soprano and contralto for his many performances around Europe. The relationship between master and pupil was, I felt sure, bound to be at the heart of the story I was meant to relate. But what was it?

Goldoni said Anna was agreeable, though not pretty, with a slim waist, beautiful hair, a charming mouth, great acting ability... and a thin voice.

Vivaldi, when the writer mentions this, flies off the handle and asks why Goldoni has insulted his companion. She is, he insists, good at everything and sings beautifully. The playwright, fearful of losing the commission, backs down and, after this awkward introduction, the two agree to collaborate, though not without further storms as the work progresses.

But of Vivaldi and the young woman thought to be his lover... nothing more. Except that Goldoni makes a point of describing how Vivaldi demonstrates his piety so visibly, clutching at his breviary and making the sign of a cross at regular intervals as he speaks.

'Monsieur,' the writer tells him at one point, 'I do not wish to distract you in your religious devotions. I will come back at another time.'

Was I reading too much in that last part? Did Goldoni, a clever, witty chap, perhaps hint that Vivaldi was professing his piousness a little too much when he was in the public presence of his charming young companion?

There was no way of knowing so I moved on. And the story became murkier yet in ways I could never have imagined.

~

The trajectory of Vivaldi's career was astonishing. At the age of twenty-five in 1703 he was nothing more than the violin teacher at the Ospedale della Pietà on the Riva Degli Schiavoni, a home for orphans, a good few probably the illegitimate offspring of Venetian nobles. Ten years later his name was becoming known for sacred vocal compositions and a series of operas, mostly first performed at the vanished Teatro San Samuele, the owner of which had commissioned *Griselda,* the work that brought Goldoni to the Venetian home Vivaldi shared with Anna Girò. By the 1720s, Vivaldi's fame had spread well beyond Italy, bringing him commissions across Europe for his compositions and acclaim as a violin genius given to spontaneous displays of fiery improvisation.

Then, in ways which seemed unexplained, tastes changed. Within a decade, he fell steeply from favour. His commissions dried up, his wealth with it, though the loyal Anna Girò seemed to stick with him until close to the end. He died a pauper in Vienna, buried in an unmarked grave, his death certificate that of an itinerant priest, no mention that he was once the most famous composer in Europe.

And after that... obscurity. No one played his concertos, no one performed the many operas he churned out for the Teatro San Samuele and elsewhere. As Valentina Fabbri had rightly pointed out in Ugo's bar, only specialists in the history of obscure Venetian composers would have heard of the man or his music a century before. Both Vivaldi and *The Four Seasons* might have remained unknown were it not for a remarkable series of events in the first part of the twentieth century.

After Vivaldi's death in Vienna in 1741, his autograph compositions – the original, handwritten music – remained in Venice, and then began a largely random journey scattered across Europe, through the libraries of a variety of collectors, none of whom seem to have done much with them.

In 1922, a large part was handed over to a religious boarding school in Piedmont which soon decided to find a buyer to fund some urgent building work. The director of the National Library of Turin and a local professor of music felt the collection worthy of a wider audience and found a benefactor who was willing to fund the purchase. Going through their rich acquisition, they realised it was just half of the original collection. Undaunted, the pair researched the lineage of the aristocratic families that had owned Vivaldi's papers over the centuries and managed to find much of the rest, acquiring for the Turin library ninety per cent of Vivaldi's autograph manuscripts, though not those for *The Four Seasons*.

Enter here the fascist poet mentioned by Ugo Abate, the American Ezra Pound, a vocal anti-semite and fan of Mussolini who lived in the Calle Querini in Dorsoduro with his lover, a fellow American and acclaimed violinist, Olga Rudge. The couple came to learn of the Turin manuscripts and decided to use Vivaldi as an example of the revival of Italian cultural heritage demanded by their beloved Mussolini. The pair edited and transcribed the music for performance and publication – Pound was a self-taught musician as well as a poet – and found sponsors for a series of concerts in Rapallo on the Ligurian coast.

Pound was in no doubt of Vivaldi's obscurity. Starting work he wrote, 'Nobody, in 1938, knows anything of Vivaldi. A few (less than six) scholars have approximately respectable ideas of his compositions. Not one of them has even read through all of his composition.'

The concerts were a modest success and attracted some of Italy's most famous musicians. Then came war, and a forgotten Venetian composer was the least of the country's concerns.

Vivaldi's faltering revival might have ended there were it not for three friends who, in 1946, set out for Turin from Venice intent on photographing the autograph manuscripts and using them as the basis for accurate transcriptions that could be published for performance. They travelled across a devastated country, begging photographic film from the hospital X-ray department in Treviso, locating expert copyists to deal with the work and, more than anything, searching for a sponsor to pay for their output to go to press since they had little in the way of money themselves. Their benefactor turned out to be an entrepreneur from Reggio Emilia, Alfredo Gallinari, whose first words when he was approached were, 'Tell me about this Vivaldi, about whom I know nothing.'

That was in November 1946. Within a year the Istituto Italiano Antonio Vivaldi was born and a contract signed with the publisher Ricordi to bring all the lost works back into print. As soon as editions came off the press, they began to be played across Italy. Technology came to the game, long-playing records, vinyl that could hold twenty-two minutes on each side, enough, just, to fit the whole of *The Four Seasons* on a single disc, firing a series of recordings by various orchestras around the world.

Then, in 1951, London marked the rebirth of the post-war world from the rubble of war with the Festival of Britain, in the newly opened Royal Festival Hall on the South Bank. The first season was almost totally devoted to the works of Antonio Vivaldi, the rediscovered genius of Venetian baroque music, now restored from obscurity to the pantheon of his contemporary peers, Bach and Handel.

I savoured every twist and turn of this extraordinary tale, much abbreviated here. It occupied me over the best part of two weeks, at home, out in the city, talking to Reggie Davies on Giudecca from time to time, and at that desk in Mia Haas's empty home where I had access to academic databases denied me elsewhere. Part way through I made one brief visit to the Istituto Italiano Antonio Vivaldi's present headquarters in the Fondazione Giorgio Cini on the delightful little island of San Giorgio Maggiore opposite San Marco, a short ride across the water to Zitelle. A charming place run by charming people, and of no real use to me at all. Any more than the rest of the story I've outlined here, fascinating and enjoyable as it was to unravel.

My brief was to uncover Vivaldi the man. All I could mostly find was his music, masses and masses of it, so much I had to wonder if he was like one of those authors who must write a certain number of words each day out of habit and necessity. That Antonio Vivaldi, perhaps watched by Anna Girò who may or may not have been his mistress – I'd no idea at all – would snatch at parchment and a quill and dash off part of a concerto or an opera between breakfast and lunch and curse himself if he missed the opportunity.

May was in full heat by the time I felt I'd exhausted every avenue available to me from Luca's research and the material I'd acquired myself. There was a sonnet accompanying each of the seasons in Vivaldi's most famous work, poems written by the composer himself or so most experts thought. I looked at them again and thought of the months ahead, the changes the year would bring to Venice where spring and summer, autumn and winter, were so marked in every way, the colour of the sky, the freshness of the air, the mood of the locals as they journey through the year.

He wrote – in words and in music – of how thunder and lightning would give way to silence while songbirds began their tunes once more.

It seemed a cheerful sentiment, from a cheerful man one imagines. But really, I was struggling in the dark.

Then, one Thursday just before the end of the month – the

end of spring, the start of summer – my phone buzzed with a message from Mia Haas.

> I will be back from Vienna this evening. I apologise for my absence. You must see me in Giudecca tomorrow at ten when I will address the entire company of the Teatro. If you are still on board with our insane adventure as I hope.

> In advance of our meeting, do not believe all you may read in the press. Those idiots know nothing.

Her timing was apposite. The next morning the news was full of stories about the late Marcus Haas, and I found myself wondering what, with a little prompting from Luca Volpetti, perhaps in consort with Capitano Valentina Fabbri. I'd let myself in for.

Chapter Three

Allegro pastorale

Marcus Haas was a criminal. That explained so much. The odd method by which everyone was paid, from a different source somewhere in the world each month. The strange atmosphere hanging over that out-of-the-way estate at the back of Giudecca. And, I had to admit, though with little in the way of surprise, Valentina Fabbri's curiosity about the whole thing.

Do please keep me in touch with how your detective work goes.

Indeed. I wish I could say it was the first time she'd tried to use me as an unwitting spy. The line between professional and private was always a little blurred there. But that was how she was, a law enforcement officer at heart, one who never truly went off duty. Luca Volpetti knew, of course, as he admitted reluctantly the following morning when, intent on dealing with this face to face, I caught him on his way into work in the great archives by the Frari church around the corner from my little apartment.

'Arnold!' he bleated.

I was delighted to see he looked embarrassed.

'I'd love to stop but...' He tapped his wrist where there was, as always, no watch. 'Time presses.'

'Not the only thing,' I said then grabbed his arm and diverted him to the empty stools outside the nearest café.

Two macchiatos, two pastries and a smile from the women behind the counter. We sat by the Frari's looming brick wall, silent for a couple of minutes while I enjoyed watching him squirm.

In the end I said quite blithely, 'I imagine you've heard the news?'

He flapped his arms about, as always. 'Such a shock. I'd no idea. Not a jot. I swear. Well... perhaps an inkling.'

It was everywhere. On the front pages of the Venice papers. *The Financial Times.* With much greater coverage in Austria, naturally, a whole page of it in *Der Standard,* Vienna's paper of record.

The intricacies of international finance are beyond me, I'm delighted to say. As far as I could understand, Marcus Haas was a master of them, up to a point. A former investment banker who set up his own complex network of companies mostly in tax havens around the world, handling all the many baffling tentacles of modern global finance, hedge funds, cryptocurrency, spread betting. Haas had stakes in conventional businesses, from telecoms firms to media outlets, but the core of his empire, the papers said, was what amounted to a clever but ultimately doomed Ponzi scheme, raising money from investors, some of whom should have known better, to pay earlier backers their promised unrealistic returns. Like all such frauds, his depended on the financial fillies he bet on finishing the race in front. It was a contest Ponzi schemers never won. In the end, there were always too many people demanding their money, and insufficient new mugs to fund the growing gap.

Haas, the papers said, had been under investigation in the US, Germany, France and the UK for more than two years. An indictment was due in New York the week after he died. He knew his number was up and had taken to liquidating what assets he still had, ferreting away the proceeds into a series of foreign accounts now being frozen by authorities around the world. They numbered one called Wurdulac in Bucharest and a Haitian outfit by the name of Bokor, naturally, which made me wonder if someone would soon be asking for their money back from all of us connected to the Teatro Maddalena.

But it seemed not. The Venetian papers were principally interested in whether this scandal would sink the Teatro and deprive the city of a new tourist attraction on neglected Giudecca, a long-deserved tribute to its famous composer son. As far as they could establish, that seemed unlikely. While some of the early funding had come from Haas's overseas companies, the theatre was, his widow assured them, quite separate from the businesses under investigation, a legitimate enterprise that would stand on its own two feet once the concert hall and the hotel were up and running.

Luca sat in miserable silence as I read this out from *Der Standard* and the local *Il Gazzettino*. When I'd finished, he tried to look cheery and said, 'Well, that's all right then.'

He was never comfortable when cornered.

'No, it's not all right. There was something suspect about this all along and you were well aware of it. You turned down that book deal yourself. Then kindly put my head on the block.'

'Pah! Nonsense! What block? I have a job. No spare hours to write a book. You, on the other hand, have all the time in the world. And...' I got the finger jab. 'You needed the money.

Valentina and I were agreed. You were the best man for the task. The only man if I'm honest. They wanted it in English, remember. A curious and obscure language I may speak but writing a book in it... well, I couldn't begin to imagine.'

'If you'd filled me on all this to begin with...'

'Then you'd have walked away with your English nose stuck up in the air. Out of pride. Or suspicion. Or plain bloody-mindedness. Besides, I'd no idea Haas was quite such a crook. We thought he was just a touch dodgy. There is a difference, you know? Between a bit dodgy and being an out-and-out criminal.'

'Only in Italy.'

He flapped a hand in my direction. 'Hilarious! Have you forgotten? You are in Italy, Arnold. You came here willingly. We don't do your stiff upper lip. Not that it's as stiff as it used to be. If you wanted to stay above all the odd murkiness of the real world, perhaps you should have remained in London.'

'Perhaps I should...'

'Please! You're my friend and I don't wish this to be an argument. The days when the English could look down their sharp noses at us and say "We're purer than driven snow and you're just a bunch of corrupt foreigners" are long gone. Or do you no longer read the news about your own country, only ours?'

A fair point. Italy, it seemed to me, was, for the most part, no more venal than anywhere else in the world. The idea that England alone remained untouched by graft and grifters was one for the birds. The same, it seemed, could be said about Austria and wherever else Marcus Haas did his dubious business.

'What now?' I wondered.

The question surprised him. 'Now you get on with what you're paid for. You write your book. If the papers are right and the Teatro Maddalena is above board and funded, what else can you do?'

'Mia's called a meeting there this morning. For all of us. Musicians, everyone.'

He finished his macchiato and looked again at that imaginary watch on his wrist. 'There you are. We had your best interests at heart, Arnold. Believe me. You were at a loose end. You were broke. You're not a slothful man. And...' He took my arm again. 'Believe me. This is a great opportunity. Write a good book. Mia Haas, it seems to me, knows how to sell things. Even if she doesn't, that's a fair old sum you've got in the bank anyway.' He smiled. 'Until Valentina and I find you something else.'

I grunted something wordless.

'Or,' he added, 'you could carry out your threat and go back to England. Is it still Merry Old England? Doesn't seem so from what I've read.'

'You're a conniving bunch of amiable scoundrels.'

The smile turned into a grin. 'We're Venetians. What do you expect? Now... the book.'

He was right, of course.

'The book. I've got the makings of the world. Andriy Kravchuck will fill me in on more of that when he has the time, I gather.'

'You've the events you asked for, too. All in that list I organised. A chronology, from cradle to grave.'

'Places and dates. Lots of them. But I don't have the man, Luca. Not a clue.'

He threw some money on the counter. As usual, I wasn't to pay. 'You're not alone there. Antonio Vivaldi died both broke and broken, then vanished into obscurity for two centuries. All that came back was his music.' He hesitated. 'I thought Mia Haas, or her husband, was in the process of acquiring something that might solve that. These mysterious papers...'

'She says I may need to go to Vienna...'

'The train! You'll love it.'

'Didn't you–?'

'Yes. On a wild goose chase. Haas assured me there'd be someone at the other end with a collection of documents he'd acquired for the Teatro. A new cache of Vivaldi material, recently rediscovered.' A shrug. 'I spent three days there, very pleasant ones, at his expense. No one called. No one came. A logistical delay he said in the end and off I popped back to Venice on the overnight sleeper.'

'I assume that means money.' I paused. 'What was he like? You said you only met him once.'

He waved a dismissive hand. 'The man took me to Florian's for coffee. After that a couple of phone calls and emails. Marcus seemed very rich, very sure of himself. Very confident he'd get whatever it was he wanted. It was all an act. I see it now. Marcus Haas was going to pieces. They're like that, aren't they? Living in a different world to ours. Is his wife the same?'

'Why ask me?'

'Because you've seen more of her than anyone I know. Because...' He paused for a moment. 'She seems to have her eye on you for some reason.'

'Don't be ridiculous. The poor woman's just lost her husband.'

'I'm aware of that. All the same...'

'She wants the book.'

'The book, of course,' he agreed. 'I really do have to go. Enjoy Vienna. You know where I am should you need me.'

Ten o'clock found me back in Giudecca, along with a full assembly of the musicians I'd seen the day Marcus Haas died, all of us waiting in the theatre, now half-complete from what I could gather. The box office was there, shiny walnut and polished glass, computers going behind the counter, geeky young men waving around cables. Andriy Kravchuck sat on his usual chair in front of the stage, a dark suit this time, very formal. Ellen Kim wore the same scarlet silk dress I recalled. The rest of them were in rehearsal mode, jeans, jumpers, old clothes, in the case of Rupert Hazard downright scruffy. Reggie Davies had on a brightly coloured sweater in rainbow colours, her hair not quite as lurid as I recalled.

The copy of Donatello's Maddalena was gone, and I have to say I didn't miss it. The thing was as disturbing as the original. Perhaps Mia Haas had realised there were better ways to greet her customers.

Outside, in the warm early summer air, the builders had downed tools and were taking a break on the terrace along with the gardener, an air of expectation all around. A memory flashed into my head, an unwanted one. The thuggish looking man with his forks and spades, that little hut in the grounds, and the way he'd seemed almost amused that dreadful day Haas shot himself. But before I could think more of it Mia Haas appeared from the palazzo, white shirt, smart jeans, no make-up, blonde hair tied back in a businesslike ponytail, composed, smiling briefly with a wan expression, the way one might expect of a widow. An air of sadness, of a burden about her I thought. No longer the catwalk model demanding caviar, blinis and Franciacorta, there were lines around her eyes, her mouth, I hadn't noticed before. A woman carrying a burden, and perhaps it wasn't simply the sudden violent suicide of her husband.

Her voice was lower, more serious too as she summoned us into the theatre and took the stage. It was an odd atmosphere. No one quite knew what to expect.

She began by thanking us, then assuring everyone their monthly fees would be paid as usual. This time from an account in the name of the Teatro Maddalena, with Intesa Sanpaolo, Italy's biggest bank, one most people surely knew.

'As I've told the media, the finance people, and the Carabinieri, the charitable status of the parent foundation is sound and perfectly legal. Our funds, our organisation, were ring fenced from my late husband's other businesses.' A smile, very brief. 'Of which I'm sure you've now read. All of them, I must admit, as much a shock to me as they were to everyone else.' She brushed back a few stray hairs from her forehead. 'This is awkward as I hope you appreciate. A private and personal matter with public ramifications. I want to assure you of my continued support. Both because I love the work you're all doing here, and because it now seems clear to me this represents a parting gift from Marcus. To me. To you. To Venice and the world. One he must have undertaken knowing the rest of his shaky empire was on its last legs. One he was determined would survive the storm he surely knew was to come.'

Mia glanced at the orchid house by the far wall, closed her eyes and for a moment we saw a shadow of pain.

'I'd no idea that was his intention. I was too busy, too caught up in...' She waved a hand around the auditorium. 'All this... Marcus ran everything behind the scenes while I did my best to be his public face. I'd not a clue what was going on in his businesses, as the police in Austria and the Carabinieri here now accept. I still don't, to be honest. It's all quite incomprehensible. No matter. That's behind me now. Behind you, if you wish to remain. Andriy...? You two have reached a decision?'

The conductor struggled to his feet and bowed. 'I'm going nowhere, signora. Great and worthwhile work is being undertaken here. This is only the start.' He nodded at Ellen Kim by his side. 'We're both with you for the duration, and intent on making the Teatro Maddalena another fine concert hall for this extraordinary city, dedicated to the most illustrious composer Venice has produced.'

'Thank you,' Mia said with a broader smile now. 'And the rest of you? If anyone wants to leave, you have my permission. I'll pay the balance of your contract willingly. I don't wish to trap anyone here who would rather be elsewhere. Arnold?'

Dammit, I should have expected that. 'Yes?'

'Your book. Our book. Well...?'

What to say... 'I'm making progress. There's still much to do.' I paused. 'I'll do it.'

Reggie Starkey stood up and looked around the room. 'We've already talked this over. I can speak for everyone. We're with you. No giving up now. Too much work done already. Too much promise to throw it all away.'

Mia grinned and clapped her hands like a happy child. 'Good. I'm delighted to hear it. Now you have work to do. And little time to do it. Your next public performance won't be in midwinter. Andriy...?'

Kravchuck laughed and turned to his players. 'We have a surprise. An engagement. Not half a year away. Not a month. A week even.' That throaty laugh again. 'Tonight.'

There was a communal sigh and a ripple of disbelief.

'I know, I know,' Kravchuck cried, waving his arms around. 'You're thinking... how is this possible? How shall we rehearse?' A chuckle. 'What on earth shall I wear? Fret not, my little band of musical warriors. It's time to give the public a taste of what the Teatro Maddalena can do. In the city. Somewhere Antonio Vivaldi and his father knew well. The only venue left that is as it was when they were here. A place few have seen. And none of you...' He pointed round the room. 'Have ever played before. There we'll give them something you know well. *The Four Seasons* in front of an invited audience. As they rarely hear it. Alive, vivacious, full of bright energy, not the jaded lethargy of a hack version played out of duty. Now... positions please. One final run-through then you have two hours to get your things together before we leave.'

They looked excited too, except for Rupert Hazard who seemed mildly annoyed he was expected to work for his pay, not bunk off as Mia's musicians had been doing at her expense for weeks.

As I left the hall I heard the sounds of rehearsal, familiar now. Instruments being tuned, snatches of music, the odd cough, a snatch of conversation, chairs being moved, Kravchuck trying to call his players to order.

Mia caught up and took my arm. 'Come with me, Arnold. We need a word. Peter and I–'

'Peter?'

'Peter Lombardo. The gardener. Have you not met him?'

That dark day, the way the scruffy looking thug had grinned at me, all came back again.

'Not to say hello.'

'Well.' She beamed at me. 'We have something for you.'

I'd never set foot in an orchid house until that dreaded day we found Marcus Haas. The very idea of them seemed to hark back to an England long vanished, a place of country mansions, upper class garden parties, trysts among the aspidistras, intrigue behind the frosted glass as frenzied costumed servants dashed to and fro with glasses of sherry and canapés.

Not so here. The place was large and humid, filled with glossy exotic plants and small shrubs, a forest of them reaching from the brick path at the centre to paned windows that rose to the elegant, curved panels of the roof. An antique from the previous occupier I imagined, restored by Marcus Haas who, it seemed, loved the place. His favourite refuge to think and work and make calls, Mia said, rather glossing over the fact he'd taken his life here with an illegal handgun a few weeks before.

The gardener was there already, feeding the orchid inmates from an ornate green metal watering can.

'If it isn't Arnold Clover, the historian,' he said, without looking my way. 'Got to get their nourishment, don't you know?'

English, not Italian. With a distant accent that took me aback. Glasgow, I'd say. Broad Scots anyway. This strange hidden quarter of Giudecca seemed full of surprises.

'Cat got your tongue, Clover?'

'For a moment. I'd always assumed you were Italian. Foreign anyhow.'

He frowned, put down the watering can, gazed at me and said, 'I am. Peter Lombardo. Half anyway. Dad was born in Milan. I grew up in Cambuslang. Got the passport now. Otherwise, they wouldn't be letting me in so easy, would they?' He grinned. 'I'd just be a little Englishman like you. Citizen of nowhere, as good as.'

'Not Arnold's fault,' Mia pointed out.

'Course not,' Lombardo went on. 'No man gets to choose where he's born. If you could we'd all be Italian.'

'I thought you said you were from Cambuslang.'

'Ever the English smartarse I see.'

He was a burly man, late forties or so, scruffy in a blue boiler suit, dark, unruly hair, bushy, unkempt beard. A tramp almost I'd have said, happy in his garden shed mucking about with the flower beds and this strange hothouse by the wall adjoining the lagoon.

All around orchids were coming into bloom, decorative palms waving in the light breeze wafting through the ventilation windows. Mia began to walk round, toy with their stems, sniff the blooms, give them names, Latin always, perfectly pronounced it seemed to me. And their origins. Her territory, obviously. *Cymbidium* from China. *Laelia* from Brazil. A Himalayan *Dendrobium*. An *Encyclia cordigera* from Mexico with the scent of vanilla and sweetness. The colours in the early summer sun were so bright they almost hurt the eye, the fragrances close to overpowering, sickly and somehow, in their power, almost sinister. Between the leafy branches of the palms a couple of birds kept dashing, squawking with fear, trying to find a way out. The orchid house of the former Palazzo Colonna-Ottoboni was not a place I'd choose to work. Or read. Or doze even. There was something unworldly, vaguely unnatural about this overly lush glass hideaway.

'You told him then?' Lombardo asked, a little familiar in the way he spoke.

'I leave that to you,' she said and walked to the end of the room.

The divan on which her husband had killed himself was gone. Even if she'd wanted to keep it, she said, the blood stains couldn't be shifted from the fabric. In its place was a wicker sofa, two chairs and a matching table, a jug on it, three glasses. Iced lemonade, freshly made from the trees in the garden. I took the one she offered, sat down and wondered what on earth came next.

Lombardo went behind the sofa to the back wall, solid or so it appeared, and began to remove a series of bricks there. An explanation followed. After Haas's death he'd felt it was time to deal with the orchid house, to tidy the place up, wash away the blood stains from the tiled floor and remove the soiled divan.

To care for the precious orchids too which hadn't been fed or watered for weeks.

'Not their fault the master took his life while, as they say, the balance of his mind was disturbed.'

Mia Haas gulped at her lemonade.

Behind the façade of bricks was a safe, square grey metal with an old-fashioned rotary combination lock.

'Shall I, ma'am?'

'Do it,' she murmured, then glanced at me. 'Marcus was a man of fixed methods. Fixed ideas. One of them was that we should have no secrets between us. I know...' She screwed her eyes tight shut for a second or two. 'I know now that was a lie. But not all of it. He always said we should share the essentials. Passwords. Logins. Codes.' She read out a series of numbers. 'Anything numerical was the date we first met in Dubrovnik.'

Lombardo turned the combination and opened the door. The rehearsal had started outside. The distant sound of the familiar opening to '*La Primavera*'.

'The password we shared was "Angelicaoo". The name of the daughter we lost a week after she was born. That was six years ago. Only you two know of this and I would be grateful if it wasn't made common knowledge. No one's business but mine.'

Another blink of those bright blue, glassy eyes. 'Thinking about it now I tend to believe Marcus was preparing me for the time he wouldn't be here. Knowing I'd need to do things, have access to accounts, to his business, that would have been impossible otherwise. At the time I thought he was just being sweet. Perhaps that's as well. Who's to know?'

The Scot groaned as if this embarrassed him, then reached inside the safe and pulled out a blue folder and a small laptop.

'We left them there so that you could see where they came from,' Mia explained. 'Maybe you can make more sense of this than me.'

Lombardo placed the things he'd found on the table, plonked himself down between us, finished his lemonade in one go and frowned at the empty glass as if he'd wanted something stronger.

'Arnold,' Mia said and passed me the blue folder. 'Can you at least give us some idea if this is really what it looks like?'

Five pages inside, out of an office printer by the looks of it.

Photos of leaves from an old book. The first, in large hand-written capital letters, '*La Storia della Mia Vita.*' Beneath, in a smaller, shaky hand, '*Antonio Vivaldi, Satlerisch Haus, Sattlergasse, Wien, 20 Aprile, 1741*'.

The other three pages appeared to be extracts from a journal in the same flowery, elegant handwriting. One contained a brief but heated complaint that Vivaldi had been abandoned by Venice, his original home of La Pietà in particular, and a similarly offended bleat that he'd been forced to travel to Vienna to seek assistance from the estate of his patron, the Hapsburg Emperor Charles VI. The second was a plea for Anna Girò to join him in Vienna, along with a demand that she leave her older sister, Paola, behind.

Mia tapped on a paragraph in the middle.

I desire your presence, darling Anna. I desire your touch, your warmth, your ecstasy in this bleak, cold city that treats your greying red priest as a pauper, unloved, lacking in his deserved adoration, nothing more than an impoverished, itinerant fool. Come smother me in your embrace, warm me with your lips, succour me with your darling breasts, bring your sick, old lover back to life with those secret talents you have honed between us all these years. I have masterpieces in my dreams and crave your passion to make them real.

'Marcus told me he had some dirt on the man,' she said. 'That he could prove the Red Priest was no monk. Not that I knew he had this.'

I kept quiet and turned to the last page. There, in the same shaky but elegant hand, was a short poem called *L'inverno.*

'You know this already, don't you?' said Mia.

'Of course.' It was one of those verses Vivaldi wrote himself.

This was the one for winter, divided like the rest into lines for each of the three movements. The first described the frozen landscape, and biting, bitter winds. The middle two lines, for the largo section, a slow and peaceful interlude, talked of being comfortable by the fire while those outside were drenched by freezing rain.

'You think these are his original notes?' Lombardo asked. 'I know bugger all about music, man. Mia here's struggling. What do you reckon?'

'I haven't finished...'

One more page. This was musical manuscript, old, ten staves in all, just as I'd seen in the autograph manuscripts in the Keller book. Notes scribbled across them at speed I'd say, furiously almost. At the top '*L'estate Concerto II Violino Principale*' in that same handwriting.

Mia called something up on her phone. 'This is the modern score. The one Kravchuck's using next door. I'm no expert but it looks the same.'

As if to cue the rehearsal had moved to summer now. I had the uncanny sensation of listening to Vivaldi's familiar music while looking at the very notes the man had penned when composing the concerto some 300 years before. Or so it appeared.

'We need the originals, Arnold,' Mia said. 'That's what Marcus was trying to negotiate. We need–'

'They're not the originals. At least, one isn't the same.'

I pulled out the verse for *L'inverno*. The difference wasn't obvious at first but the more I thought of it, this was telling. If the date on the documents was correct, Antonio Vivaldi must have been putting all this down for the record in Vienna a month before he died. Sick, penniless, missing the company and the comfort of Anna Girò. Perhaps bargaining with some unknown collector for a frank account of his life and his work in return for the money he needed to return home to Venice.

'What do you mean?' said Lombardo. 'Kravchuck can tell you. These are the right notes.'

'They appear to be. But all we have are photographs of them. To authenticate anything, I need to see the paper, the ink.'

'We know this, man! That's why you're here–'

'But this...' I tapped on the last line of the winter poem. 'The original is optimistic, happy, upbeat. *Quest' é 'l verno, mà tal, che gioja apporte.* It's winter! But it brings us joy for sure.' I pushed the page in front of them. 'That's not what it says here. *Quest' é 'l verno, mà tal, che la morte apporte.* It brings us death for sure.'

Mia flipped open the laptop and typed in a password. 'I need you to get to the bottom of this. No one else can do the job.' She handed the computer over, smiled as Peter Lombardo watched my every move. 'Please...'

The thing still had charge, and an internet connection. It was clear there was nothing on it that Mia, and presumably Lombardo, hadn't already seen.

A browser with a single page open at the website of a hotel in Vienna, one near Mitte Station, off the street, down an arcade it appeared. A place Marcus Haas had been looking at? One he'd been directed to?

I asked and she'd no idea. Lombardo had only found the secret safe two days before. She'd been racking her brains trying to understand what to make of everything there. And got nowhere.

The only other active app was an email client. It was for an address Mia said she didn't recognise: the username vivaldi1741 – the year of the composer's death – with a provider I'd never heard of. One based in Uzbekistan it appeared when I did a quick check.

There were two emails there. One dated the day before Marcus Haas died. It read...

```
Final offer. The equivalent of $100,000
in bitcoin to you know where, dear
Marcus. As to where we meet... The grave's
a fine and noble place but none I think
did Antonio there embrace. Poor mutt.
You're Viennese. You know what I'm
talking about.
```

'What on earth can that mean?' Mia wondered.

'It means,' said Lombardo before I could get in a word, 'he's a fan of mangling old English poetry.'

I said nothing and clicked on the second message. That was from three days before...

```
I've no idea if anyone reads a dead
man's email. But if they do, reply
swiftly, dear friends. My patience is
not unlimited, and there's more than one
buyer for a dead priest's risqué memoirs
and the original, the autograph score,
of the work we all know so well. Out of
respect for the deceased Herr Haas I
will maintain the price as before, and
the rendezvous. If you're so dumb you
can't work that out this precious
consignment is not for you. I wait... but
not for long.
```

Without asking them I hit reply and typed *Talk to me*.
Then we sat and twiddled our thumbs.

'Do you have the money, Mia? If they come back?'

She looked a little embarrassed. 'There are scraps of bitcoin that Marcus left lying around.' She pulled a shiny recent iPhone out of her bag. 'A wallet thing on his phone. I don't really understand it. But the money seems to be there. Maybe a bit more if needs be.' She peered at me. 'The poetry...'

'It's a bastardisation of a famous English poem–'

'Had we but world enough and time,' Lombardo recited, casting her a sideway glance. 'This coyness, lady, were no crime.'

'Very good. Your accent faded a little there,' I noted.

'Andrew Marvell was an Englishman,' he said, back to being the Scot. 'It seemed appropriate.'

Peter Lombardo was an intriguing man, much more than the scruffy, rough gardener I'd first thought.

'It's a poem called "To His Coy Mistress",' I explained. 'A very literate attempt at seduction through the argument of *Carpe diem,* seize the day, life proves short, too much so to hesitate. The correct line is, "The grave's a fine and private place, but none I think do there embrace."'

She shook her head, and a hank of her fine blonde hair escaped the quick and careless ponytail. 'This is all quite beyond me.'

I stared at Lombardo. He stayed silent, frowned, then shrugged.

Before I could say a word, the laptop beeped. A new message there...

And you are?

I typed:

An associate of Haas's widow acting on
her behalf. We have the money. We can
close the deal. How do we know these
items are genuine?

A moment then the screen filled with two lines of laughing,
weeping emojis. Nothing else.
How do we know? I typed again.
A series of angry faces then...

Dead Marcus knew and that's enough. Not
going through all that shit again, bro.
You wanna play, play. You don't I go
elsewhere.

Mia nudged my arm.
'Ask him where to send the money.'

Where do we send the bitcoin? After we
get the goods.

A long wait.

Sigh. This is like pulling teeth. The
deal's agreed. All money upfront. You
meet me in Vienna on Wednesday. You go
home with the goods. Nuff said.

Then a QR code appeared on the screen. I'd no idea what
this meant but Mia fiddled with the iPhone, took a snap of it,
called up some app I couldn't see. Hit a button.
Quick as a flash the message came back...

```
Good girl! Now you know where to send
it. Money by close of play tomorrow. You
know where to find me. Wednesday. Noon.
Ciao.
```

That was it.

'You're going to give a complete stranger a small fortune?' I said. 'In return for nothing?'

'What else am I supposed to do? Marcus left me those scraps and a wallet. To use in an emergency.'

'Is this an emergency?'

Lombardo chuckled then grunted. 'Sounds like one to me. If what he's offering's real, you've got your book, mate. A bestseller. Off you hop to Vienna then.'

Wednesday. Two days away.

'I can get your train tickets,' she said. 'Business class. It's the only way to do it, and a sleeper back on Wednesday night. You need to go to Vienna for the book in any case, don't you? Kravchuck said. Vivaldi died there. It seems to make perfect sense to me.' A pause. 'But only if you know where to meet this man. I still have no idea...'

I got to my feet. 'Tonight at the concert. You'll have my answer.'

The rehearsal was coming to an end. I recognised the closing movement, remembered the poetry Vivaldi surely wrote to accompany it.

Quest' é 'l verno, mà tal, che gioja apporte. This is winter but at least it surely brings us joy.

Or death. Did Vivaldi really come up with that changed line when he was sick, impoverished, slowly wasting away in a flophouse in Vienna waiting on his lover?

'Arnold...' Mia leapt up, clasped my arm and whispered. 'Please...'

'I'll see you this evening,' I said and left it there.

Kravchuck had chosen the venue for his private concert well. It was a church called San Lazzaro dei Mendicanti, by the side of the main hospital, on a canal leading from Campo Giovanni e Paolo to Fondamente Nove. I'd walked past the handsome façade of San Lazzaro many times and never entered. The place often seemed closed. There were so many churches in Venice, and too few hours to visit any but a handful.

I arrived late quite deliberately to avoid unwanted conversations, and slid into an empty pew at the back, well in the shadows. There was that quiet, expectant buzz in the audience, soft and echoey in an airy nave. The small orchestra was assembled and preparing for the concert. The church was half full, invited guests only. Luca was there in the front row alongside Valentina Fabbri and her husband, the restaurateur Franco Scamozzi. Some dignitaries from the city council and a few local art and music lovers I'd come to recognise from earlier events sat on the opposite pew. I'd no great wish to speak to anyone at that moment. Instead, I buried my head in the pamphlet I'd picked up on the way in. It seemed San Lazzaro was rarely used for concerts anymore, though the place had a formidable musical background which was doubtless why Kravchuck and Mia Haas had somehow talked their way in there.

The church once ran a hospital for lepers on a small island in the lagoon just off the Lido. Later, when that vile malady became rarer, the place was taken over by a religious order from Armenia and became the monastery where Byron was once a student, a role it still performs to this day, welcoming visitors on the occasional Number Twenty vaporetto. Somewhere else on my to-be-visited list. Even after a couple of years it remained quite long but that's just Venice.

Alongside its medical work, San Lazzaro was also a charity that took in orphans, and in the case of girls taught them music which they sang and played hidden behind the grilles that were still there around me. A religious duty but also a moneymaker, attracting paying crowds for weekend concerts. Vivaldi's father, Giovanni, taught violin here for four years while he was his son's tutor too, and surely brought Antonio to concerts in the same quiet space where I now found myself, explaining to him the makings of a professional musical career in busy Venice. How players were paid and, if they were good enough, taken on as salaried musicians by institutions like San Lazzaro. How, too, those with sufficient talent would win commissions for original musical pieces for these small orchestras and those lucrative concerts for the music-loving Venetians.

It was no great stretch to believe that the young Antonio Vivaldi's dreams of being, first, a virtuoso violinist, and later a famous composer, might have been sparked by concerts in this place three centuries before.

As I sat there hearing the familiar rousing opening of *La Primavera,* I had that familiar sensation of history coming alive, the past shaking off its dusty shroud, revealing itself as something still breathing, still pertinent to those of us struggling through a world as strange and angry as any of the lurking dead might have known.

Could I picture Giovanni and his son there alongside me? Not quite. The ghosts of Venice are elusive. They hide inside your head, heard but rarely seen. Besides, as I now knew, I'd no real idea what Antonio Vivaldi looked like. The two extant portrayals I knew were quite conflicting, one a caricature with an exaggerated nose and grotesque features, the other that familiar handsome figure in the red cloak, white wig, a fiddle in his hand. Which was accurate? Perhaps neither. The man remained an enigma infuriatingly out of reach even as his music began to seep into my thoughts, my dreams, my growing obsession with his work, his secret history, the tribute to his damaged genius half-built on Giudecca, its future perhaps hanging by a thread.

All the same his presence was unmistakable, there in Ellen Kim's fierce, intense focus as she entered the mental fugue that was required of the part, nothing else in the world but that storm of notes flying from her lightning fingers and bow. On the craggy face of her mentor Andriy Kravchuck, seated in the front row, eagle head bowed, chin on fist, listening to every note. In the eyes of the other players, even though many knew the parts they were playing by heart, committed to musical memory by rote and practice from all the times they'd played them before. Vivaldi's music was as much a narcotic as the city itself. It had worked its way into their veins, mine as well. Once caught, always captured.

I was trapped, ambushed beyond hope long before the third section, Allegro pastorale in E major, filled the body of San Lazzaro with all its sonorous strains.

A slight and fragrant figure slipped into the space beside me on the pew. Mia Haas, in an elegant purple silk dress, glittering diamond earrings and a matching necklace, a dark shawl around her shoulders, her blue eyes perhaps glistening from recent tears. A beautiful woman emerging from the fading light of a perfect early summer Venetian evening. Another time I might have felt odd, out of place, to have her next to me. But not anymore. There was, I felt, an arrangement on the table, an unspoken covenant in which I would indulge the many lacunae in her story while she, in turn, gave me the opportunity to spread my wings, chase this mythical lost history of Vivaldi's, write a book as a result, perhaps one that would earn me a little money and even a modicum of fame, not that I cared a jot about that.

She took my hand and briefly squeezed it.

I sighed, waited for the movement to come to an end.

'You know I'll do it,' I whispered in the breathless silence before *L'estate*.

Mia screwed her eyes shut for a moment and gasped, 'Thank you.' She reached into her bag and took out an envelope. 'I took the liberty of booking you a ticket. Business out, sleeper back. The hotel too. Out tomorrow. Back Wednesday night. It will be enough, I'm sure.'

'I'm sure it will.' I nodded, praying for the music to recommence.

'You'll be our saviour, Arnold. I can sense it.' Another squeeze of the hand, a longer one this time. Then she kissed my cheek, a peck really, very quick. 'In some odd way I've felt this all along. Since the first day we met. Your friend Luca seems a decent man too, though one who'll always be a Venetian, unable to see beyond the lagoon it seems to me.' Her fingers rubbed my palm then left abruptly. 'You're a man of the world. You've been places. London. You have a broader sense of life, and an innate decency I detected from the start.'

'You mean I'm a sucker?'

The smile vanished. I wondered if I'd broken the spell. I quickly added, 'Just joking. An English habit. Nothing to worry about.'

I felt guilty for being so flippant, so obvious. The covenant was in place. No need to complicate matters. They were hazy enough as it was.

The Four Seasons isn't a long piece. Forty minutes or so at most. When it was done and the long and well-deserved applause had died down, Kravchuck gave a short speech to his audience about the work's provenance, its connections with San

Lazzaro, and how its next public performance by the players of the Teatro Maddalena would be in its new home, the concert hall across the water hidden away in Giudecca.

Mia walked to the front, elegant and composed once more, and began to talk about the prospects for both theatre and its accompanying hotel, her dreams and ambitions, along with a few short words of appreciation to her late husband. I couldn't help but notice she held up her hand as she spoke and touched her glittering wedding ring.

I made a rapid exit as I saw Rupert Hazard heading in my direction, glugging an imaginary glass with his right hand.

Austria tomorrow. I had to pack. And think.

The next morning found me at Santa Lucia Station, watching the noticeboard, waiting for the platform for the OBB Railjet to Vienna. A journey of seven and a half hours which I could have done in a fraction of that if I'd caught a plane from Marco Polo. On reflection, it might have been a smarter move. More time in Vienna, since I'd now be arriving there at five thirty in the evening, with a few hours of daylight left to explore a city I'd visited only in books before. Then the following morning and my appointment at noon. But Mia had been insistent and so had Luca Volpetti. The train was an experience not to be missed, and I ought to have the opportunity to read.

As the long, sleek Railjet pulled into the station I walked up the platform to the front compartment, business, six seats, a place for quiet and work, both of which I would appreciate.

My phone buzzed. Mia.

> Arnold! I meant to ask last night but you ran away before I had the chance.

The compartment was spacious, my leather seat by the window comfortable, a waiter soon round with an offer of coffee and a bottle of water. Only one other passenger, a woman in a smart business suit who took out her laptop and phone, made a loud call in an American accent, then buried her head in what I took to be a library of spreadsheets.

I took my time then answered, *Ask what?*

If you know where to meet this mysterious stranger, of course! That poem! About a grave and a fine and noble place. What on earth can it possibly mean?

I laughed. Another reason I was on my way to Vienna. Something I'd been promising myself for years I ought to see.

I'll tell you when I return.

Then I switched off the phone.

A few minutes later we were crawling across the bridge that links Venice to *terraferma*. Ahead, beyond the ugly urban sprawl of Mestre, lay mountains, to the north the route that would climb high into the Alps skirting Slovenia, then eventually wind its way down towards the capital of Austria.

I pulled out Keller's book on Vivaldi with all its many paper tags for the parts I needed to reread, and a travel guide I'd picked up at the station. Soon there was little beyond the window but vineyards in leaf, serried lines of well-ordered green running off in every direction, Prosecco in the making.

It was the first of July. My strange adventure in Giudecca had begun weeks before on a chilly spring day, the hours still short, the ground still mostly bare, April, an in-between month in Venice. Now the Veneto was fully awake all around me, summer coming on fast, verdant, alive and boisterous. Following all the moods and rhythms a genius from Venice had set down in music almost three centuries before.

In verse too. How had his begun? I checked my notes.

> *In the harsh season, under blazing sun*
> *man languishes, flocks wither, pine-trees burn...*
> *the heavens thunder loud with hail-filled rain,*
> *cutting the heads from stalks of wheat and grain.*

Venetians are never enamoured of the heights of summer, many fleeing the place in August to escape the heat. That all lay ahead, a time of wind and storms. Perhaps not just the weather either.

The train ran on, past Udine, into the mountains where the houses became alpine, with wooden features that made me think of Switzerland. Shortly after Tarvisio, we entered Austria, snow still on distant peaks, the odd fairy-tale castle set on the lower slopes.

The familiar music from the night before kept running through my head, a ceaseless earworm. Something else, too. Those discordant notes of the *diabolus in musica*. The Devil's Tritone. Like the cry of a hungry hawk screeching behind Vivaldi's lush and lyrical hymn to the eternal rhythmic changing seasons, competing with the natural sounds he'd placed in his work, the bark of a dog, the murmur of a flowing stream, drunks dancing, a hunt in progress and bird calls, lots, all set to a specific species.

I thought of that fragment of what was meant to be the original score, a rush of notes scribbled down on notation paper with a quill and ink, the work appearing so quickly it was obvious Vivaldi was one of those rare individuals whose musical invention ran straight from his head, through his fingers onto the page. No translation there, nothing much in the way of correction from what I'd seen. His was a genius one might almost think divine, the ability to hear great swells of orchestral works in his mind and then be able to scribble them down in an instant, with little in the way of conventional thought or consideration.

There, I thought, with a start, *a personal insight into the man.* The first. They were coming. They would come. They had to.

When I got to Austria.

In a fine and noble place. One populated by the illustrious dead.

Intermezzo I

The wind had quickened on the empty beach at Alberoni. December sand kept flying around our deserted driftwood bar and stinging at my eyes. There was, though, a sensation of relief in talking about this curious year and its even stranger events and tragedies. Something cathartic in getting a few things off my chest.

'With the benefit of hindsight, of introspection,' my companion asked, toying with the gun, 'do you now feel a fool, Arnold? No blame attached. Perfectly understandable in the circumstances.'

Never rise to the bait.

'I'm not sure I agree with that last part. But yes, in a sense, I do. Still, that's nothing new. I go through life trusting others, hoping against hope I won't be disappointed. It seems to me the only way to conduct oneself. The alternative is to trust no one at all, and that's a miserable prospect. A lonely one, and loneliness is the scourge of the heart, a stony, disagreeable state of affairs that makes a man cold and unfeeling, as good as dead.'

'As good as dead...' A laugh then, though it was hard to detect any warmth there. 'I feel you do protest too much. You went along with everything knowing much was not quite right. You couldn't help yourself, could you? That burning curiosity...'

'Curiosity has been the defining principle of my professional life. My creed if you like.'

'Oh, come. This was more than professional, wasn't it?'

I wasn't minded to explain, certainly not for someone who seemingly couldn't stop playing with that damned weapon. Yes, much about the Teatro Maddalena appeared, to repeat a word my friend Luca Volpetti was wont to overuse, downright 'dodgy'. Not least in that smirking Scots-Italian gardener with the physique of a rugby player slowly running to seed, and knowledge of the seventeenth century metaphysical poet Andrew Marvell, a fellow Yorkshireman and Cambridge graduate whose work I'd loved since I was at school. Where, to my shame, I'd used *To His Coy Mistress* as a feeble chat-up line with a young girl called Rosemary Bairstow to no avail whatsoever since she took up with a class thug, Jim Carlton.

Funny how names from half a century ago, lost loves, hated bullies, still stick in the memory. But then things do, matters concerning Venice in particular. That, more than anything, explained why I blundered on with Mia Haas's mad treasure hunt when a more rational man might have shrunk back into the comforting shadows. My companion on that chilly winter beach was right. Events around the Teatro Maddalena had thrown up those infuriating doubts and mysteries Valentina Fabbri called 'dangling threads'. I was hooked on them. I simply had to know.

That was what led me to take that train into the Alps on the first day of summer, to marvel as the peaks and valleys and castles began to drift past beyond the window. The idea of writing a book about Vivaldi was no longer a novelty I found daunting. I'd learned enough of the curious man, a genius known to the world only through his work, to want to understand more.

Still, I'd spent my life in quiet circles, archives of old documents requiring understanding, preservation, insights into where they came from and what they might truly mean. Taking that train to Vienna meant I vanished from the quiet, insular, secure sanctuary of Venice and stepped out into the real world, a place of uncertainty and hidden dangers, far from the quiet, enclosed quarters of ancient ink and paper that had wrapped themselves around me for decades.

'It seemed,' I said, mostly to myself as the winter wind of

Alberoni dispatched more icy gusts our way, 'an adventure. Something I'd never before experienced.'

'Say that again, Arnold Clover,' came the quick reply. 'Fortunate you've survived at all.'

Part Two

L'estate, Summer

Chapter Four

Allegro non molto

We pulled into Vienna Hauptbahnhof on time, just after five thirty, and I experienced the immediate shock of being drawn back into the real world, a place I'd pretty much forgotten. Venice had been my delightful prison for so long. I never saw a bus or car unless I ventured over to the Lido. Traffic, commuters, busy roads and – outside San Marco and the Rialto – crowds were quite alien to me, so I sat back in the cab from the station to the hotel wondering at the commotion beyond the window. Trying to imagine what it was like for Antonio Vivaldi on that last journey of his. Leaving behind the unique place of his birth, the republic seemingly secure behind its watery walls in the lagoon, for a journey through the mountains, one that must have taken him a week or more.

Then the inevitable, busy chaos of the metropolis, a daunting place for a sick, old man, career vanished behind him, short of money, lost without that beloved female companion, Anna Girò. Dreaming of her presence, her embrace, if that teasingly partial extract from his papers was to be believed.

Vivaldi's last few months must have been miserable. Was it ridiculous to think he might have spent them waiting on messages and money that never came, scribbling down a rambling document recording his extraordinary life?

No. But that's not enough for a professional archivist. I wanted proof, ink and paper in my hand, something I could pore over, digest, call in experts when I needed them. Hard evidence against fakery and crooked dealing.

My head was still full of dispirited thoughts about Vivaldi when I walked down the cobbled alley to my hotel along from Mitte Station, a coach house once upon a time I imagined. There, standing at reception, tired, probably a little grumpy, I was checking in when a familiar voice rang about behind me.

'Lucky! Fancy meeting you here, old boy. A tincture first – bloody good beer in Vienna – then it's either a couple of sausages or a curry round the corner. What do you think?'

Rupert Hazard. Who else? A man who never takes no for an answer. What the hell was he doing dogging my footsteps?

I thought of making some ridiculous excuse. A headache. Exhaustion. But the truth was I felt my mood might be improved by company, even that of a garrulous cello player. And I was curious, of course.

Thirty minutes and a quick shower later we retired to the bar where an Austrian snack and beer were taken, and I realised there's no such thing as small portions in Vienna.

'Well?' said Hazard, tucking into his first Debreziner sausage. 'Rum thing the two of us turning up here. And the same hotel.'

'I don't suppose you were on the train too?'

He looked baffled. 'Train? Why take the train? First flight out from Marco Polo this morning. Here in an hour, and a twenty-minute ride from the airport to Mitte.'

Mia had insisted and I suppose I was glad of it. The journey was quite spectacular. 'I was ordered to enjoy the view. Going back by sleeper tomorrow night.'

'Ah. Lady Haas, I imagine. She does have you under her thumb. Doing anything special?'

I kept it simple. 'Research for this book I agreed to write. Vivaldi died here. I need to get a feel of the place. Can't write in a vacuum.'

He raised an eyebrow. 'You think you can fill that vacuum in just one day?'

'I don't know.'

'Big place, Vienna. Complicated. I've done three or four stints here over the years. Always takes me a while to adjust.'

'I appreciate your insight. Now you know why I'm here...'

He set his knife and fork to work chopping up the second sausage and dipping it in some spicy gravy. Put a big chunk in his mouth and said, 'I'm screwed in Venice. The Teatro Maddalena. Whatever the hell that is. Kravchuck's taken against me. No changing that old bastard's mind when he's set on something.'

'I never noticed anything like that.'

He stabbed the last banger with some force and snapped, 'I wasn't aware you spent much time at rehearsals. Did you enjoy the show last night?'

'I did. It felt... moving. Knowing that Vivaldi and his father must have been in that place once. Playing. Listening. It was clever of Mia–'

'It wasn't her idea. It was Kravchuck's. He thinks he communes with the late Antonio or something. Soulmates.' He guffawed. 'Though I doubt his relationship with the gorgeous Miss Kim quite matches that of our beloved composer's beloved Miss Girò. Much as he might like it.'

He surely hadn't caught sight of the snippet from the diary I'd seen.

'I'd always understood that was unproven, malicious rumour. About Vivaldi and the young girl that is.'

'Come on,' Hazard retorted. 'The two of them, all those years together. You don't think he'd take a pop at a pretty young thing? Who wouldn't?'

'A priest, maybe?'

'He was a priest in name only. Even I know that. Next, you'll be telling me everyone believes poor Marcus killed himself.'

I shivered. 'Why shouldn't they? The Carabinieri say so.'

'The Carabinieri! The Venetian Carabinieri! What do you think they know about crime? When did they last have to deal with a murder? A real one? A bunch of posers in fancy uniforms mostly.' He jabbed that last piece of sausage in my direction, dripping gravy all over the table, which got us a snooty look from the bartender. 'If I was going to murder someone, you know where I'd do it? Right there. In the Piazza San Marco itself maybe. They'd be too busy chasing tourists for sitting on the steps or feeding the pigeons to notice.'

'That's the local police,' I pointed out. 'I think you'll find the Carabinieri set their sights higher. Financial crime for one thing.'

Another laugh and it sounded rather cruel. 'Oh come, come. That's the Guardia di Finanza, don't you know? Then there's the State Police. And let's not forget the *Magistrato alle Acque*. The Magistrate of the Waters.'

My head was beginning to spin. 'Who?'

'Ah. Before your time. The Magistrato used to control most of the sea and lagoon of Veneto back in the days of the Republic. Then he was revived in modern times. Only to be shut down... I don't know, a decade ago, because of... well... what's the word?' He put a finger to his cheek. 'Oh, yes. Corruption. So rank and obvious people finally couldn't stomach it anymore.'

'I didn't realise you knew Venice so well.'

'Been going there on and off for a couple of decades. Had a fling with a young filly in the Fenice chorus once upon a time. Corruption, old chap.' He tapped the table. 'Rot. Never far away in that place. And so many different police or quasi-police organisations supposedly to deal with it. Venice is a beautiful old lady, but she never wears her knickers. Know how many of those fancy buildings in the Piazza San Marco, how many palazzi on the Grand Canal, are owned by furious Russians who can no longer visit them or pocket the rent?'

'No,' I admitted. 'I don't. It had never occurred to me. How many?'

He shrugged. 'Ask your Carabinieri friend, not me. Though I rather doubt she knows the real number. Venetian dirt is always swept beneath the carpet, you see. *Sub rosa*. Can't let it spoil those tourists enjoying their coffee in Florian's now, can we?'

'For a cello player you seem to be very familiar with the police. In all their many forms.'

He didn't like that. 'Anyone who works across borders is a fool if they don't. You were a civil servant all your life. A solid citizen in their eyes. I'm just an itinerant artist picking up a living where I can, when I can. Dodging the taxman and the bloody immigration people. You wouldn't believe the crap I went through just to be able to get a work visa now we've gone all Little Englander. But...' He brightened. 'Fortunately, I have one for Austria too. And Germany. Legacies of a life on the road. I don't have to take Kravchuck's shit. Spoke with a couple of people here today. More chats tomorrow. Rupert Hazard will be on the move soon, mark my word. More work here than there for one thing. You can play your part in that odd little pantomime on Giudecca without Rupert Hazard.'

I had to ask. 'You don't really think Marcus Haas's death was suspicious, do you?'

A wicked grin. 'God, you're easy to wind up. No idea. It just seems odd. Like that place. So much money getting thrown around, needlessly too. She's keeping on all those musicians on a retainer when any sane organisation would have told us to bugger off and come back when there's real work around. Why? Why have Kravchuck and his girl in a fancy apartment in San Marco all this time? Not out on the road somewhere else until Mia has her beautiful little auditorium all finished?'

He ordered another beer, a schnapps with it. I declined.

'Your problem now, Lucky. I hope you live up to your name.'

'It's not my name.'

'The pedantic civil servant still! Oh... are you leaving?'

'Tired. And I need to do some reading.'

'Should have done that on the train instead of gawping out of the window. Sure about that snifter?'

I was.

'Then...' he waved his hand. 'On your way. You do know where you're going tomorrow, I presume?'

'Just a few places here and there to tick off.'

A long silence, followed by a longer stare.

'Best jog on then, Signor Clover.' He slammed his schnapps glass down on the table which the barman seemed to know was a sign for another. '*Auf dich!*'

Of course I had an idea where I was going. I just wasn't going to let on to him.

You know where to find me. Wednesday. Noon. Ciao.

And...

The grave's a fine and noble place but none I think did Antonio there embrace. Poor mutt. You're Viennese. You know what I'm talking about.

More of that later.

First, I had to do the job I'd originally set out for myself. Trying to picture what it was like when Vivaldi turned up in Vienna and came to die.

I was out of the hotel at seven, case safely stashed behind the desk, desperate to escape without bumping into Rupert Hazard again. It was hard to believe the man would be an early riser the way he was knocking back the sauce the night before.

Breakfast in a nearby café, coffee and a pastry. My appointment was at noon. That left me a few hours to try to trace Vivaldi's footsteps in Vienna and build a picture of this elusive man during his last few months on earth.

As ever, there was scant hard information in the resources I had. Keller's book has him leaving Venice around May 1740 – in June that year he was summoned to testify in a court case, about what we don't know, but he failed to appear and was reported to be *fuori della terra*, outside the region. His movements for the next nine months are a mystery. Was he dodging his creditors? Begging for work wherever he might find it? Even writing his memoirs and penning desperate letters to Anna Girò, now working with a run-down opera company in Graz? There was no way of knowing. The man vanished from all existing records that May and didn't surface until there was a report of his presence in Vienna on 7 February the following year.

It seems certain he made for Vienna during 1740 in the hope of winning a commission from the ruler of the Habsburg Empire, Charles VI, the Holy Roman Emperor. A talented musician himself, Charles adored Vivaldi's work and in 1729, at the height of his fame, had given the composer a substantial sum of money and a knighthood for his talents. Another round of generosity, perhaps even an invitation to become director of the court orchestra, would transform Vivaldi's penurious position. A final role, surely, for an infirm man now in his early sixties.

Why had his career fallen so low and so quickly? One more mystery to add to the rest. Contemporary references talk vaguely of his style of music becoming unfashionable, in Venice and beyond. In the space of a decade, he'd turned from being the most famous musician in Europe, earning fabulous sums, to a hard-up itinerant hunting desperately for work. There were no firm reports of scandal, except for the odd rumour about his relationship with Anna, though a few comments at the time suggested he was a spendthrift who travelled everywhere with an extensive entourage and indulged in 'extravagance' – the details we can only guess.

Whatever Vivaldi's reasons for seeking his final fortune in Vienna – a paid position or money to write a new opera for the prestigious theatre, the Kärntnertor – he was to be disappointed. The music-loving Charles VI, a colourful character with exotic tastes in music, art, men and women, died in October 1740, either after getting drenched during a hunting trip or, if Voltaire is to be believed, consuming a meal of death cap mushrooms. Any chance Vivaldi had of reviving his failing fortunes through the Habsburgs were dashed. Austria was in dire financial straits after Charles VI's mismanagement of the economy, and by the end of 1740 engaged in a war of succession that would spread its bloody tentacles across Europe.

Reports of Vivaldi's last few months are sparse and depressing. We know he tried to tap up an aristocrat, Duke Anton Ulrich of Meiningen, for money, because Ulrich casually notes down in his diary how Vivaldi kept coming round begging for a meeting, only to be sent packing.

There was a rough address for where he was living. After

going through my research notes once again, I caught a bus into the centre to try to find the place for myself. I was disappointed yet again. I'd succumbed to the Venetian trap of thinking historic cities don't change much over time. Back home I could walk in Vivaldi's precise footsteps – and Casanova's, along with so many famous names from the past – and see the city much as they had centuries before. But that was part of the uniqueness of the city, one you took for granted after a while.

Vienna was much older, dating back to the Roman outpost of Vindobona where the emperor Marcus Aurelius died while on a campaign against the Germans. But little remained even from Vivaldi's time. A few exceptions apart, such as the monumental cathedral of St Stephen's and the streets around it, everywhere I turned I saw tall nineteenth-century buildings, imposing, a little impersonal it seemed to me, though that was doubtless because I missed the older, more elegant face of home.

Vivaldi took lodgings in a boarding house on the corner of Kärntnerstrasse near the Kärntnertor theatre, presumably praying he'd soon be invited inside there to work and play. But wandering around the busy city centre that warm summer day I could picture none of it. This may have once been the heart of Roman Vindobona. Now the whole area was part of the 'Golden U', a highly commercial, pedestrianised shopping area dedicated to chain stores, restaurants and cafés, and buildings everywhere that postdated Vivaldi's time. The home of Swarovski and Burger King, Apple and any number of souvenir stores. The city wall and the Carinthian gate through which he would have entered were long gone, as was the theatre and his boarding house, now buried beneath the exceedingly posh Hotel Sacher, home to the famous Viennese chocolate cake, the sachertorte.

The vast monument of the State Opera House opposite had a poster advertising a forthcoming concert of some of Vivaldi's less well-known works, but it was a place the man would never have recognised, built more than a century after his death. There was nothing here, not a plaque, not a single sign, that indicated one of the most famous composers in the world had spent his final months on this very spot, struggling to get by, perhaps in need of love and support as much as money and food.

I felt lost, my quest to find something that might help me picture Vivaldi the man slipping away with every step amidst the jostling summer crowds of visitors eating their ice creams and gawping at the shops.

It didn't help that a character dressed as Mozart, powdered wig, scarlet dress coat, tight white trousers and long socks, shiny buckled shoes, was staring at me from across the street.

Enough of this pointless meandering. It was close to midday already and the one site I knew I still had to visit would have to wait. I had an appointment with a dead Holy Roman Emperor.

The grave's a fine and noble place...

I couldn't get those words out of my head the moment I read them. There was only one hidden treasure in Vienna that could mean, somewhere with a link to Vivaldi too, which clinched it.

Twenty minutes to spare I wandered around the Domkirche, caught a coffee and a sandwich, then found my way to Neuer Markt. There, opposite the inevitable Swarovski, was a plain white wall next to a small church, a barn-like door and a sign, 'Kapuzinergruft'. The Crypt of the Capuchins, though this was much more than a burial place for friars.

Four centuries of imperial history lay here, the remains of the men and women who steered the Habsburg Empire through war and famine, plague and family turmoil. I'd read about the place in one of the many books I'd plundered for research over the previous weeks.

From 1618 on, this had been the family burial vault of the dynasty, somewhere twelve emperors and twenty-two empresses and queens were interred in ten vaults deep underground, along with more than 122 family members. As I wandered down the staircase a chill wave of modern air conditioning greeted me and – though possibly this was my imagination – the faintest whiff of decay. I couldn't think of anywhere else in the world where the bodies of a country's dead rulers were gathered in a location like this, one opened daily to the curious public, a few of whom sometimes headed there to escape the cruel summer heat.

I shivered walking those corridors, confronted by a maze-like, snaking succession of rooms filled with sarcophagi, some like large chests, others bizarre ornate monuments or simple urns. Writhing cherubs, grinning skulls, bouquets and simple posies, some fresh, some long dead, sat amidst bronze eagles, a display of bones alongside jewellery, weeping statue mourners behind their veils and more depictions of the crucified Christ than I could count.

I had a map but soon I was lost, wandering in and out of the different vaults, a few shadowy visitors alongside me, seemingly as disoriented as I was. In these bizarre underground caverns devoted to royal death there seemed to be no north and south, no left or right. I doubled back only to find myself where I began. It was a maze of bronze and bones, chilled by a constant breeze of air that felt as if it belonged in a modern hotel.

Interred here were corpses that rang out through history, aristocrats whose rule spread far beyond Vienna to Tuscany and Venice, Sicily and Portugal. Then there was Maximilian, the son of Archduke Franz Karl, who was talked into accepting the position of Emperor of Mexico, only to be deposed by a nationalist coup and executed by firing squad. Elisabeth of Bavaria, the eccentric 'Sisi', who slept beneath a mask of raw veal or strawberries to preserve her looks and was stabbed to death by an anarchist in Geneva. Next to her simple coffin, fresh flowers seemingly just placed there, lay her husband, the emperor Franz Joseph. Missing from the crypt – it seemed the poor man hated the place – was his son, Franz Ferdinand, whose assassination in June 1914 sparked the First World War.

I wandered quite oblivious to the passage of time, almost forgetting what I was looking for. Then, on one more circumnavigation of this deathly maze, there he was in front of me. Charles VI, the music-loving eccentric emperor who'd once gifted Vivaldi with gold and a knighthood. And died unexpectedly as the distressed composer made his way to Vienna to seek his aid.

Here, just a few feet away, lay the remains of an emperor who'd spoken with Vivaldi, loved the man and his music, raised him on high. The sarcophagus was much as I might have expected, beyond ornate, a massive casket of bronze with a crowned skull at each end, armour, weaponry, a weeping veiled maiden, a cherub mourning as he looked at an effigy of a scowling, bewigged Charles who seemed decidedly miffed at being dead.

This was the closest I'd got to Vivaldi in all the time I'd been chasing him, and a foolish idea ran through my head. If only I could ask the ghost that might once have hovered round this casket some questions. What did he look like? What did you talk about? How did he seem, voluble or quiet? And the mysterious Anna Girò. Did she appear more than a musical companion?

There was no ghost, and no answers. Then my phone went and it was such a shock I jumped. Dammit but there was wifi down there as well as modern air conditioning. A number I didn't recognise.

'Well, Arnold,' said that low, sly voice I'd heard the night before. 'How goes your adventure?'

'Rupert. I'd no idea you knew how to get hold of me.'

'You're losing it, dear boy. Don't you remember giving me your number back in Venice?'

No. I didn't.

'Well, anyway,' he went on when I said nothing. 'I thought I'd tell you my travel plans have changed. After your fulsome account of the views from your train I decided to take it myself. Tonight. You're on that one, aren't you?'

'There won't be any views. It's night.'

'It leaves at twenty to nine and gets in at half eight. You still there?'

'Yes. I am on that train. Mia booked me a shared compartment.'

'Did she indeed? You won't have to listen to me snoring. The cabins are sold out, sadly. I'm slumming it in a seat. Still, we can share a beer or two, can't we?'

'Have your auditions gone well?'

He laughed. 'Till later. Very brave of you to take all this on, you know. I'm impressed. Good luck chasing down old Antonio.'

Then he was gone.

Someone tapped my arm. A young woman of twenty or so, a student perhaps, casual dress, straight dark hair, a serious, worried face. She had a pamphlet in her hands.

'I don't need a guide, thanks,' I said without thinking.

She frowned. 'That's not what I was told. Am I right you're thinking about Vivaldi?'

There was a tiny bag slung across the shoulder of her denim jacket. That was all.

'You are. I thought you'd have something for me. This was the place I was told, rather cryptically, to come.'

Another frown. 'I know nothing about cryptic instructions, sir. All I have is a message. A man in the street gave me fifty euros to pass it on to someone he said would be standing by this odd monstrosity of a tomb, thinking about an Italian composer. He said you should leave this place now and meet him outside the Karlskirche. Somewhere a man interested in Vivaldi ought to see, or so he claims.' She grimaced at the tomb, and the cavern around us. 'I don't know why people obsess so much about the dead. It seems wasteful.'

A messenger, sent in from the street. I cursed my own slowness. Of course they wouldn't pass over precious material, perhaps something illicit, in a place like this. There'd be video cameras everywhere. A record of who came and what they did.

'Does he know what I look like?'

'I've no idea.'

'Then how...?'

She laughed and I got the distinct impression she couldn't wait to get out of there and spend her fifty euros in the local shops.

'You can't miss him. We get a few of them dressed up in wigs and all that, pushing concert tickets to the tourists. Not out by the Karlskirche. I'm pretty sure he'll be the only one you find there.'

'Who–?'

She sang a snatch of something familiar, a classical tune.

I shook my head. 'Sorry. I recognise it. But...'

'Oh dear,' she said with a sigh. 'From what he said I'd assumed you were somewhat musical. *Jupiter*. First Movement. Allegro vivace. Our own genius, Wolfgang Amadeus Mozart.' A quick salute, a fifty euro note in her hand. 'Job done. Money earned. Ciao, sir. Enjoy your day.'

~

I retraced my steps to the Opera House and walked on to the Karlskirche, fifteen minutes in all, and at the end found a quiet, beautiful space in the city. The church was as impressive as I'd expected, elegantly baroque with, for me, a touch of the Venetian Palladio in the Greek temple portico. A mix of styles with two pillars either side that clearly harked back to Trajan's column near the Forum in Rome. The green dome roof shone in the bright summer sun. Families pushed prams through the park and a group of children were enjoying themselves in a nearby playground. The air felt clean and fresh. It was hard to believe I was in the heart of a European capital.

A man dressed as Mozart looked as if he was drowsing on a bench by a coffee stall. Behind him was a broad pond where the pale reflection of the church glistened on water as still as a mirror. A tram nearby squealed and rocked as it passed.

I bought myself a large espresso and sat next to him. The same fellow who'd been staring at me as I lingered by the State Opera House and the Hotel Sacher trying, and failing, to come up with some mental image of the boarding house where, thereabouts, Vivaldi died.

He smiled, showing teeth slightly stained by lipstick, took a box of chocolates out of the huge shopping bag by his side, and said, in English, with a light and musical accent I couldn't work out, 'Signor Clover. Would you care for a taste of one of my balls? I have it on good authority they're luscious.'

I shook my head.

'Mozartkugel,' he announced, taking out a small sweet wrapped in silver foil, a rather crude portrait I took to be the composer on the top. 'Pistachio, nougat, marzipan from Fürst in Salzburg, so the real thing, not some cheap rubbish for the tourists. Here...' He found a small box and placed it on the bench. 'A gift for your return journey on the train tonight. But don't eat any till then. They'll spoil your appetite.'

'It seems you've been paying me a good deal of attention.'

'Oh please.' He indicated his scarlet coat. 'I'd be rather conspicuous, would I not? Legwork I leave to others, like that charming girl you met down with all the dead people. This is serious business. Seriously expensive business. It pays to be prudent when it comes to knowing who you're dealing with.'

'But I don't.'

I got that hard stare again. With all the make-up and the costume, it was difficult to imagine what he must have looked like when he wasn't got up as a pomaded theatrical version of a dead musical genius.

'You're dealing with someone who can help. What else would you need to know? Besides, Marcus and his fair lady always preferred to travel by train so it's fair to assume they would recommend the same to you. They thought air travel wasteful and poor for the planet. A couple with a conscience, you see, though with Marcus, as the world now knows, that conscience had its limits.'

I was starting to take a dislike to this glib, smirking stranger. 'You've something for me?'

'If you deserve it. Are you any nearer getting a picture of our mysterious Venetian yet? You've stood next to the bones of his long-dead patron.' He nodded at the pavement beneath our feet. 'We might be sitting over his own right here. Shame we can't ask him.'

It was extraordinary. This patch of pleasant open public space in front of the Karlskirche was where Vivaldi was laid to rest in a simple grave. There was nothing now to suggest it had once been a cemetery. Yet the details of his end were clear and known, much more than any firm facts of his life in many ways. He died in the long-vanished boarding house in the city centre on Friday, 28 July, 1741, according to the burial accounts book of the parish. A coroner recorded the cause of death as 'internal inflammation', whatever that means. He was buried the same day at a cost of nineteen florins and forty-five kreuzers, a modest sum it seems, hardly deserving of the description a 'pauper's burial' you find in some sources, though the cemetery was certainly for the impoverished, and called the 'poor sinners burial ground' in some documents.

Most shocking of all, the death certificate records him as 'the Very Reverend Signor Antonio Vivaldi secular priest'. Not a word to suggest he was lately the most famous composer in Europe. Not a hint he was even a musician who'd once been given a knighthood by the recently departed Holy Roman Emperor, ruler of Vienna and beyond, buried just a few months before in the Kapuzinergruft.

'I don't know enough to write a book. Which is why Mia Haas gave you a small fortune she can scarcely afford.' I held out my hand. 'We've done our part. Now do yours.'

He frowned. 'You're rather more forward, pushier than I expected.'

I'd no idea how he could know what to expect at all, and I wasn't minded to ask.

'This is tedious,' I said. 'I have to pack. I need to make notes about the places I've seen this morning. You've got your money. Now I'd like the goods.'

'Ah.' He yawned. 'The goods. Don't you know what they are?' He didn't wait for an answer. 'Vivaldi spent four months here after his patron, the Holy Roman Emperor, bit the dust. Selling off what music he had for a pittance. Twelve Hungarian ducats for sixteen compositions he had with him. That equates to about twelve lire per work, around half the sum he'd have got for the same in Venice from La Pietà, and a quarter of the price he was charging all-comers at the height of his fame a mere eight years before.'

This was hinted at in Keller but spoken now with a surprising degree of confidence.

'You seem very sure of your facts.'

'I am.' He patted the shopping bag. 'I read it. In his own words. It's all here. With the rest of his unfinished memoirs which give Casanova a run for his money when it comes to frankness. The *Prete Rosso* was a passionate man, which shouldn't come as a surprise to anyone who's heard his music.'

It was important to ask. 'And you acquired this... legally?'

'What do you care?'

'I care because I don't wish to go to jail for handling stolen material.'

That laugh again. I really didn't like him. 'Oh, my naive English friend. How can an item no one knows exists be stolen? What kind of thief possesses the psychic power to purloin something that, as far as the world's concerned, isn't there?'

A reasonable point. 'All the same...'

'Ever the pedantic archivist. I should have known. The truth is dreadfully mundane.' He tapped the bag. 'You'll find a full description of the provenance of these goods in here. I'll be damned if I'm reading it out loud for you.'

'Then...' I held out my hand, further this time.

'One last thing.' He pointed to a building on the corner, beyond the playground full of happy kids. 'I want you to walk over there, then come back and tell me what you see.'

It wasn't far, and from the look on his face there was no shirking the demand.

'Well,' he said, when I got back. 'What did you find?'

I showed him the photo on my phone. A stone plaque on the wall that said the citizen's hospital, also known as the Poor Sinners, was located here until 1789. Antonio Vivaldi, born in

Venice on 4 March, 1678, died in Vienna on 28 July, 1741, was buried in the same place. The plaque, from a bank, marked the 300th anniversary of his birth.

'Very good. You'll see his name plastered regularly on the Karlskirche,' the man dressed as Mozart said. 'His music, you see. But the man himself... that's all you'll find in Vienna where he died. As to Venice...'

I'd yet to start to look closely in the city. There hadn't been time.

'Point taken,' I told him all the same.

'I hope so. Try and do the sad, old fellow justice. Here...' He pulled a compact, leather valise out of the shopping bag. Very sturdy with a combination lock.

'I'll send the code that releases it to Signora Haas when you're on the train. Don't try and break into it yourself. You won't manage and if you did, you'd probably damage the precious goods inside.'

The case felt heavy when he passed it over and a sudden, ridiculous thought ran through my head. What if it was a bomb? What if all this strange escapade was something else altogether?

'There's a lot of material in there, Signor Clover,' he said, seeing my surprise. 'That's why it cost a lot of money.'

'I trust it will be worth it.'

'And this...'

He pulled out of his fancy jacket pocket a USB stick, a fat, silver one, with the word Mozart imprinted on the side along with a colour portrait of the composer.

'Which is...?'

'You'll want to test the paper and the ink, I presume. To make sure it's all authentic. It is quite delicate and does not enjoy handling. I took the precaution of photographing every page – memoirs and the score for The Seasons, a little surprise as well – so you can read it all safely, without having to touch the original. Once I send the code.'

I nodded. 'That is a good idea.'

'We are a full-service facility.' He picked up the chocolates. 'I would like to say it's been a pleasure doing business with you. But to be honest I've found it rather tedious. Don't forget your balls, will you?'

The man dressed as Wolfgang Amadeus Mozart held out his hand. I shook it. A strong grip, perhaps that of a musician playing a hefty instrument. Or a soldier.

'We will not meet again, Arnold Clover. Make good use of the material I have provided. There are bones beneath our feet that demand you bring their owner back to life.'

He left without another word. I watched him walk back towards the city centre, handing out leaflets from his shopping bag to a couple of tourists, as if he was just one more local pushing a concert. A good act. A man I should have thought about when I saw him earlier.

This was all new to me, the idea I had to watch my back, take care. Venice had left me soft. I made a mental note to try to remember that. But all it meant was I kept looking round on the bus to the hotel, wondering if I was being followed. The effort for that was so distracting I missed my stop. A piece of good luck. As I got near the passageway to the hotel, I saw Rupert Hazard march out into the street carrying a small bag, hail a cab, then drive off.

Time to go in and collect the things I'd left in reception, to sit in the bar we'd eaten the night before and jot down some thoughts in my notebook, about the city, the crypt, the complete absence of any record of Vivaldi's presence here apart from that small sign on a wall near to where he was interred. It disturbed me to think we were so close to his remains, talking about the man as if he were a piece of history, not a human being who'd lived and breathed and died not far away. The fact I was meant to be carrying his memoirs and the manuscript for his most famous piece of music didn't help. He was with me. He wasn't. I held a part of him but there was no way I could examine it, not without the numbers for the very heavy small briefcase that refused to fit in my own luggage, or the code that would unlock the memory stick with photos of the documents I was carrying. A thoughtful detail, it occurred to me, the work of a man who had long prepared for that moment in the park.

One hour left before the train and I decided to take a last look at the Karlskirche and that open space in front which had once been a graveyard. It was a delightful place, perhaps an appropriate one for Vivaldi to be laid to rest even without a headstone. Had he died in Venice few, it seemed, would have noticed. He might have been carted off to one of the city cemeteries – this was long before the graveyard island of San Michele, an invention of Napoleon after his invasion sixty years later – and unmarked there. The only composer I knew with a funerary memorial in the city was Monteverdi, remembered with a stone in the floor of the Frari round the corner from home.

I was looking for a cab to the station when Mia Haas called.

'Do you have it?'

I hesitated, wondering what to say. That suspicious part of me was beginning to think perhaps someone was listening.

'I have something. It's locked. He said you have the code.'

'I have nothing. What do you mean?'

'Then maybe he's about to send it. I don't know. Tomorrow, Mia. I'll see you on Giudecca.'

It was her turn to pause for a moment. 'I ask so much of you, and you do it without question.'

'I said I'd write the book. So I will.'

'You're quite valiant really.'

That made me laugh. 'Anything but. I'm just...'

Just what? I wondered to myself. I'd found myself in uncharted territory and I'd no idea what to make of it.

There was a man, lurking down the street, head in a paper. Just someone on the way home, surely. How was I to know?

'I look forward to seeing you tomorrow,' she said. 'We owe you so much.'

Then she was gone just as a taxi rounded the corner. We drove off and the man with the newspaper glanced up as the car drew past. As one would, I guess.

~

The OBB Railjet night train was quite different to the day service I'd taken on the way here. The two-bed couchette had a bunk on either side. My booking was for the left, while on the right was a smartly dressed young man pulling out a toiletry bag and sniffing some aftershave. He had the air of business about him, expensive looking grey suit, white shirt, red tie, dark hair neatly cut the way a company director might years back.

'Ah!' His eyes lit up and he said something in German I couldn't understand.

'*Ich bin Engländer,*' I explained.

'We all have our crosses to bear,' he replied in English with scarcely an accent. 'Sorry. I was being flippant.' He held out his hand. 'Gerhard Rauch. *Frankfurter Allgemeine.* We are bunk buddies for the night. I don't snore, at least if I do my wife's never mentioned it. Yours?'

'I don't think so. You're a journalist?'

He laughed. 'Merely a humble ad salesman.' He touched the lapels of his smart suit. 'The reporters don't feel the need to dress like this. And you?'

'Retired. I live in Venice. Fancied the trip.'

'I hope you enjoyed it. I must try to sell some space to the Venetian hotels. We have a special travel issue coming.' He looked at my luggage. 'You don't seem to travel light, Herr Clover.'

My name was on the label for the bunk. That explained it, I guessed.

Before I could say a word, a familiar face popped round the door. 'Lucky! My, you travel in style.'

Rupert Hazard looked a touch more florid than usual. I assumed he'd been on the drink already.

'A snifter in the bar, old boy. You can't want to be locked up in your little prison cell all night surely.' He smiled at Rauch. 'Bring your new friend.'

The train was moving, chugging slowly out of Vienna. Outside dusk was falling. Soon it would be dark. There'd be precious little to see. I wondered how much sleep I'd really get inside that small cabin, a stranger on the bunk opposite.

'The restaurant car won't open for a little while,' Rauch said. 'I am a regular on this journey and know its habits inside out.'

Hazard pulled out a silver hip flask that came with a couple of small beakers.

'Just as well I brought this then. Anyone fancy a drop of absinthe? Bugger me but there's a museum that sells this stuff near Meidling Station and boy does it blow away the cobwebs.'

I smiled and shook my head. Rauch said he'd try a sip and looked as if he'd regretted it.

'Well,' said Hazard, 'I'll go and find my seat. Meet up with you privileged chaps in an hour or so then.'

~

The sleeper service took a different route. After a little more than an hour we were only approaching Linz, and it would be another two before we reached Salzburg. Not till five thirty would we be in Italy at Tarvisio Boscoverde. I rather wished I'd taken charge of my own travel arrangements and booked a straightforward flight home.

The dining car was empty, Hazard garrulous as ever, Gerhard Rauch polite but obviously a touch embarrassed by the state of him. We picked at a selection of sandwiches, salads and meat platters, and I listened as they talked idly of the latest political shenanigans, of football and opera, and Rauch's opinion of getting money out of Venetians, never an easy task it seemed. I'd left my own case on the bunk bed and lugged the locked leather valise with me into the dining car where it sat at my feet. The USB memory key sat inside a buttoned-up pocket in my jacket. I wasn't letting go of either until I reached Mia Haas the following morning.

It must have been somewhere after Salzburg I first noticed. A buzzing in my head, a queer sensation in my stomach. I looked at my hands and saw they were trembling.

'You all right, Lucky?' Hazard asked.

'I wish you'd stop using that stupid fucking name,' I snapped, which was quite unlike me. They seemed to realise, and a sudden, awkward silence descended on our table as the train made its slow, rocking journey through the night.

'I'm sorry, old boy.' He looked mortified. 'I didn't realise it offended you quite so much. Never again. That's a promise.'

'I feel,' said Rauch, 'it's time for me to retire.' He put a hand to my arm. 'You too, perhaps, Herr Clover. I hope it wasn't your friend's absinthe.'

'I never touched that shit,' I mumbled and lurched to my

feet, grabbing the leather valise, patting my jacket to make sure that memory stick was still there.

I remember stumbling down the corridor back to the couchette. Falling on the bed, too, quite incapable of doing anything else.

There were noises in my head, strange patterns running across the ceiling. I thought I heard my dead wife Eleanor tut-tutting at me from somewhere and making one of those mildly caustic remarks she'd utter whenever I did something stupid.

The lights went out. There were voices, Hazard, cross, not drunk though, not anymore. And maybe never was. One loud yell in German, him or Rauch I'd no idea.

Then darkness, endless, a velvet black night, the only sensations I was aware of, my own heartbeat and the rapid, rhythmic pant of my breathing.

The next thing I knew I was throwing up over the side of a stretcher, above me the familiar roof of Venice Santa Lucia Station, to my right, the gleaming line of the night train from Vienna.

Valentina Fabbri was there, stern, worried.

'I'm fine. Where's the case?' I said or tried to. 'Where...'

I saw then. Another stretcher being carried by medics next to me. Carabinieri everywhere.

A pale white sheet over a body. The way they'd taken my Eleanor out of the house when she died. Though in her case there wasn't a lurid blood stain on the fabric.

After that nothing at all.

Chapter Five

Adagio e piano – Presto e forte

Someone was dead. But it wasn't me. Not quite. That, at least, I understood.

Not much else though. It was as if I'd fallen down a hole, found myself in a cavern where time seemed to pass but nothing happened. Dark spaces all around, howling sounds, distant, muffled voices, low, the way medical people spoke when they didn't know if you could hear or not.

I hurt in a way that's hard to describe. Not distinct, pinpoint pain, the kind you get when you're cut or maybe stabbed. More a background, dull thudding ache, one that ran all through my body.

Before long I was aware of a familiar presence. And though I couldn't turn to look I knew it was Eleanor there, my dead wife, sitting close, whispering in my ear.

Don't come here.

As if I had a choice.

After a period I couldn't begin to guess there were new voices. Live ones this time, sharp and clear and familiar.

Valentina Fabbri and Luca Volpetti, speaking Italian so quickly, so quietly I could barely catch a word. Then another woman arrived, and it took some concerted effort to put a name to her.

Mia Haas. Elegant, beguiling Mia to begin with, a more genial, approachable woman later after she was widowed. The one who sent me all the way to Vienna, insisting I take the train and enjoy the view.

Getting there was memorable. As to the return journey that was all fog and haze. I'd felt ill in the dining car while talking to Rupert Hazard and that slickly dressed ad salesman from the *Frankfurter Allgemeine*. Needing to lie down, I'd staggered back to the couchette, made it through the door, found myself falling headfirst for the narrow bunk bed. After that blankness until I was limp and sweaty on a stretcher being wheeled through what I dimly recognised as Santa Lucia Station, people staring all around. A body, bloody and twisted, being pushed along by my side.

All these things – my dead wife, the train, the ad salesman, the voices of Venetians I knew and loved – kept revolving round my head while all I saw was a whirling red blackness, the inside of my own eyelids I guess, made more vivid by my racing imagination. Yet in some odd way I wasn't really scared. Just puzzled, almost curious. Wondering when it all might come to an end.

That happened when a light came on, so bright I blinked and whimpered from the sudden shock.

Blue sky, blue-grey water beyond the window, the familiar shape of San Michele, the graveyard island, pinpoint cypress trees and white marble glittering in the sun.

'Oh my God,' said a voice near me. 'He's back.'

~

'The English do take their time,' Valentina Fabbri declared, glancing at her watch.

Mia Haas bent over me, pink-eyed, lips quivering. I found myself weeping too, swamped by so many sensations. The chill, air-conditioned atmosphere of a hospital room. The unique aroma of the medical world, chemicals and perfumes, somewhere the physical presence of humanity, doubtless me. All the while my mind running wild with memories or tricks of them. Not knowing what to believe.

'How long?' I asked in a voice so croaky I barely recognised it as my own.

'Three and a half weeks,' said Valentina. 'They said they had to put you into an induced coma and work out what to do. It's nearly August.'

The brain kicks in of its own accord sometimes. I found myself reciting out loud some of Vivaldi's verse for summer that had stuck in my memory.

> *In the harsh season, under blazing sun*
> *man languishes, flocks wither, pine-trees burn;*
> *the cuckoo's voice trails off, while turtledoves*
> *and finches sing impassioned in their turn.*

They were staring at me as if I'd lost my mind. Which at that moment, I probably had.

~

A fierce-looking woman doctor and a male nurse pounced and ushered them out of the room.

'Tell me how you feel,' she demanded.

'I feel fine.' My mouth was dry, my stomach rumbled. 'I'd

like to go home now, thank you. I'm sure there's someone who could make better use of this bed.'

'Well,' she said. 'That's morphine for you.'

'I can discharge myself.'

That amused her. 'And how, Signor Clover, do you plan to get out of the room?'

I lifted an arm. A line in it, something stuck to one of my fingers. Probes seemed to be attached everywhere as if I was a robot in some sci-fi cartoon.

'When then?'

'If everything goes well... if... we should be able to discharge you by Ferragosto. Provided you promise to accept daily care until I say it's no longer needed. Nor must you go mad with the drink and partying.'

August the fifteenth. That would be six weeks of my life gone, most of it to oblivion. And for what?

'Honestly,' I insisted. 'If you just took out all this stuff you've stuck in me...'

The words fell away. My eyelids drooped. Something kicked in, maybe a drug from the line that ran into my arm.

Back into the darkness I swam. Only to be shaken awake some time when the blackest of lagoon nights loomed beyond the window, broken only by the glimmering lights of passing boats.

A young nurse hovered over me with a hypodermic syringe in her fingers.

I never liked needles.

'What's this for?' I asked as she bent down to stab it into my shoulder.

'To help you sleep,' she said.

Hospital time and real time are quite different, even more so when you're hooked up to drugs, visited by a constant stream of doctors and nurses curious, perhaps surprised, to find you're breathing at all. Nevertheless, I was alive, conscious up to a point, if befuddled with medication and wont to spout to any passing nurse or doctor unlucky enough to hear.

My attentive carers took it well, even when I accused one of the more unsmiling medics of being out to finish the job and murder me. The hospital of San Giovanni e Paolo is a unique institution, being modern on the lagoon side with the beautiful fifteenth-century façade of the Scuola Grande San Marco on the other. The sounds are equally remarkable, the chugging of vaporetti cruising the lagoon, the occasional arrival of a helicopter on the roof, a regular chorus of sirens from ambulance boats, the squawk of gulls. Now and then a snatch of classical music, although perhaps I imagined that from the evening I'd spent in the nearby church of San Lazzaro dei Mendicanti the night before I headed for Vienna, listening to Kravchuck's small orchestra bring Vivaldi, or rather his music, to life.

Marta Neri, the woman doctor who'd taken such an interest in me, wasn't quite so fierce when she realised I was going to be compliant with her demands. Trapped in my bed by lines and sensors and the knowledge of the telling-off I'd get if I tried to move, it wasn't as if I had a choice.

One bright day, morning or afternoon I'd no idea, Doctor Neri came and sat by my side, stared at me and said, 'You hardly ever raise a question, Arnold Clover. I'm surprised. Amazed frankly. You seem remarkably uninterested in what put you here.'

'First things first. Right now, I'm more interested in the who than the what.'

'Ah...' She smiled. 'There I can't help. The who is the business of your Carabinieri friend, Capitano Fabbri, and any number of quiet men in suits who've been buzzing round this place ever since you arrived, asking questions, telling us nothing. All that concerns me is the what. And how to deal with it.'

'Which you did.'

She sipped a coffee as pigeons battled outside the window. 'If I can't prompt you to ask, I'll tell it straight. You were poisoned. Orally I'd have thought, though there was also a puncture mark on your left arm which looked like a careless and hefty stab of a hypodermic needle. Whatever it was, I can only imagine you had a small dose, however it was fed to you. Which is why you're still alive. It was a nerve agent. The kind you read about in spy novels and tales of murdered dissidents.'

'Good god. Are you sure?'

'Ha! If I wasn't, do you think we'd be having this conversation?'

The train. The dining car. Gerhard Rauch, the ad salesman, and the beery, garrulous Rupert Hazard. We ate. We drank. Not much on my part, which was perhaps just as well.

'Where on earth do you get something like that?' I wondered.

'Russia? Or somewhere on good terms with Moscow? That seems to be the likely source, I'm told. But these days... who really knows anymore? Those men in suits perhaps have an idea. If they do, they haven't shared the information with me. Though they did confirm my suspicions, so you can thank them for that. A laboratory in Berlin nailed it, apparently. A variant they haven't encountered before. Which may explain why you recovered reasonably quickly and with no apparent lasting effects. Fortunately, it responded to atropine and pralidoxime as I'd hoped. You're a lucky man.'

Lucky. Rupert Hazard's chuckle and that frequent taunt of his echoed around my head.

This whole thing seemed quite bizarre. 'Why on earth would someone try to murder someone as unimportant as me?'

A shrug. 'As I said. I'm only a doctor. As I also said, that is an issue for your friend from the Carabinieri to address. For my part, I am happy to say I expect you to make a full recovery, provided you're sensible, follow our advice, and ease yourself back into whatever this matter of Vivaldi and Giudecca entails.'

'I need to know what happened.'

'I'm sure you do.' She got up and fiddled with the line into my arm. 'But not now.'

And then the darkness came again.

After a while she agreed I could have my laptop which Luca fetched from my apartment and left at the desk. Nothing much to catch up on there, though I read the news stories about what was termed the 'infamous incident' on the night train from Vienna. One man dead. Another almost fatally poisoned. They had a picture of Rupert Hazard provided by the Carabinieri, not a good one I thought. Then, in the absence of developments and decidedly short of hard information, the story seemed forgotten. The dead man was German. The villain in the piece English, as was the surviving party, not that I was named. No local angle at all, I guess.

Mia emailed to say she was delighted I was feeling better and bereft that she was the cause. I tried to disabuse her of the last. Whatever happened on that train, it was in no way her fault. Her reply was brief. She'd been forced to rush to Vienna to reassure some financial contacts there that the Teatro Maddalena could continue. Then fly on to Berlin and London to try to find new sources of support to keep the venture afloat.

On doctor's strict orders, I was expected to complete my

recuperation in the top floor spare apartment I'd seen along from Mia's in the palazzo. Mia and the rest of the company were determined to help me get back on my feet, and – the telling fact, I guessed – Marta Neri lived nearby behind Zitelle. I was, in short, going to be allowed no privacy or time to think until I was deemed fit enough to move back to my own flat in Dorsoduro and care for myself.

There was no avoiding it. I lacked the energy to object and, besides, trying to disobey the command of a formidable Venetian woman, a doctor to boot, would be a battle I could never win.

One stormy morning, black clouds and torrential summer rain outside the window, dappling the leaden lagoon, Valentina Fabbri walked through the door, Luca Volpetti behind her carrying a bunch of flowers and a bowl of fruit.

'Well,' she said, pulling up two chairs then grabbing the bouquet and stuffing it into an empty vase by the bed.

'Flowers. That can only mean I won't be getting out of here soon.'

She smiled. 'You do look better.'

'Much,' added Luca. 'It's a delight to see. May I peel you an orange?'

They could lay it on thick.

'I'd rather someone told me what the hell put me here.'

'Don't you know?' said Valentina. 'You were poisoned. Surely you've read the newspapers? Marta told me she'd allowed you your laptop because you were doing so well.'

'They never mentioned my name.'

'Do you regret that? This is our way. Victims need protection unless they make themselves public. Which I know you, of all people, would hate.'

That was true. The last thing I wanted was reporters on my back.

'Thanks for coming, anyway. Took your time.'

She glanced at Luca. 'We wanted you to gain your strength. Marta was adamant that a succession of visits wasn't a good idea. We had to dissuade half the orchestra from Giudecca turning up and serenading you.'

'I've been stuck here for ages racking my brains. Trying to work out what went on.'

'Join the club. It's complicated. You wouldn't want me to tell you something that turned out to be wrong now, would you?'

Always the stickler for accuracy. Valentina never rushed to an opinion or offered one without good reason.

'A man died. Alongside me.'

'Your companion in the couchette. A salesman it seems. Gerhard Rauch. Austrian.'

'The newspaper said he was German.'

'Did they?'

'They said little else. No hard facts at all.'

'Good. Details in the hands of those who aren't owed them only complicate my job.'

'Was Rauch poisoned too?'

She brushed some dust off the lapel of her smart blue uniform jacket. 'No. He was shot. A Tanfoglio handgun complete with suppressor. Your fellow countryman, Rupert Hazard, left the weapon on the couchette floor. We have his prints on it. We also have him on CCTV fleeing the station.'

This seemed incredible. 'Rupert Hazard? A murderer? The man's a bit of an oddball, I know. All the same, I can hardly believe–'

'Believe it. We've been all over your little couchette. I

impounded the whole carriage for a week so forensic could do their work. It's clear there was a fight, between him and Rauch. Then the Austrian was shot.'

'I don't remember that.'

'Well,' she said, slowly as if I was being thick, 'you wouldn't, would you? As far as I can gather, you were unconscious by then. Hazard's there on CCTV rushing over to Piazzale Roma. He takes the tram to Mestre. After that... we're still looking. Do you have any idea where he was living?'

I had to rack my fuzzy brain for that. 'He was a few doors down from me in San Pantalon. Then he went to Mestre. I seem to recall he said something about moving to Santa Marta.'

She scowled. 'We're still in the dark about that. He was carrying a leather valise, nothing else. There was a backpack with a few of his belongings three carriages away which is why we have his fingerprints. I gather the valise was yours.'

I'd been waiting for that news all the time I lay in bed. The media mentioned nothing of any missing items. 'It had Mia's Vivaldi papers in it. That was why I went to Vienna. The whole project might hang on what was in there.'

'Then that,' Luca broke in, 'is your explanation. The fellow poisoned you, murdered your companion, and made off with the treasures meant for Signora Haas.'

My head was spinning. 'Oh, come on. Rupert Hazard was a walking disaster! Stumbling through life like the wastrel he was. The man was in Vienna for interviews for a new position. He told me Kravchuck didn't rate him, so he'd gone to look for work.'

'He may have told you that, but he had no interviews there,' said Valentina. 'We tracked his movements or tried to. He checked into the same hotel as you and never set foot out of the place until he left early for the train. He was there to grab that valise. I assume when he came for it, after knocking you out with some kind of narcotic, the Rauch fellow caught on. Unfortunately for him. That makes sense, don't you think?'

'Not a bit of it. Rupert was a sad old stick who didn't know where to turn. He was broke. His marriage had failed. From what he said, I think that affected him...'

She shushed me to be quiet. 'Fine. Let me tell you then. Whatever he was called, it wasn't Hazard. We checked his passport details in London. It was a forgery. No record of a man of that name at all.' She wagged a finger, which was never a good sign. 'A fake work visa for Italy too. That surely means he was up to no good. His details are on the Interpol list now, not that they've a clue who he is. Though I suspect he's no longer in any part of Europe we can reach.'

This was getting ridiculous. 'He was here before I even heard about the Maddalena, and the Vivaldi papers. You can't tell me he came knowing something was on the cards.'

It was Luca's turn. 'It seems he was nothing more than a petty criminal. A conman. An opportunist thief. Quite the opportunity in the case of the Maddalena.'

'Not just an opportunist thief,' I pointed out. 'An opportunist murderer. With access to some kind of exotic poison that nearly killed me. How could someone get hold of stuff like that? A gun as well?'

Valentina groaned. 'But he did. I told you. We have the weapon, his fingerprints on it. As to the poison... you'd be amazed what a villain can pick up if he has the contacts and the money.'

'He didn't have any money.'

'When faced with the obvious, and no other explanation, what else is there? Tell me.'

I couldn't. 'Very well. How could he possibly know my movements?'

'A good question,' Valentina agreed. 'Didn't you tell people you were going to Vienna?'

'Not that I recall.'

'Perhaps someone blabbed on Giudecca. Your friend Mia does seem quite talkative, I have to say. It wouldn't surprise me if she let it drop.'

'It would me. I didn't get the impression she was careless when it came to private matters at all.'

Luca picked himself a couple of grapes and said nothing.

'Still,' Valentina went on, 'it's not something I can address. We're in the dark when it comes to where Hazard went after he got to Mestre. There's no record of him hiring a car. Stepping into a taxi or a hotel. Or a bus. He simply vanishes, which suggests to me he wasn't working alone. Someone was waiting for him there. That would answer your money question too.'

'A man dead. Me nearly. All to steal some old papers supposedly of Vivaldi's. Not that we can ever verify them now.'

Luca sighed. 'Unless the thief intends to ransom them or something.'

'Does he?'

Valentina's eyes narrowed. 'If that's the case, Signora Haas isn't telling. I find the woman quite... enigmatic. Has she been to see you yet?'

'She's been through hell,' I said with some heat. 'Losing her husband. Discovering the man was a crook. Fighting to keep that dream of the theatre alive. Now you tell me these papers, which cost her a fortune, have gone missing. Besides, didn't you say the doctor was discouraging visitors?'

Valentina glanced at her watch. 'I see Hazard's poison hasn't damaged your intellectual acuity. Good for you. I gather she went to Vienna and on to London. Once we heard the happy news you were doing well.'

'Yes. She had business.'

She sniffed. 'What kind of business, I wonder.'

'Are you here to ask after my health or interrogate me?'

Luca took a deep breath and glanced at the door.

Valentina said, 'Do you remember any useful detail of that night?'

I tried to think. Was there something I should have spotted? Some sign that a rather tedious train journey would end in death and mystery?

'The three of us had a bite to eat in the dining car. I felt ill. The next thing I knew I was being wheeled out of Santa Lucia Station on a gurney.'

'That's it?'

''Fraid so.'

'Well...'

'Where are my things? My clothes. The little case I had with me that Hazard didn't take.'

'Somewhere here,' she said. 'As far as I know. They reunite you with them when you're discharged.'

'And when's that?'

'You need to ask–'

'Marta Neri. I will.'

They left after Valentina kissed my cheek, and Luca gave me a hug and a wink. Two more days of tedium followed then Marta Neri bustled in and said I could leave that afternoon. A good four hours later a wheelchair was shuffled into my private room. I was reunited with my case, my clothes, all neatly folded and clean. A nurse was sent to shuffle me down to a waiting water taxi to Giudecca.

I asked for some privacy as I got out of my hospital gown

into the outfit I'd last worn when I nearly died on that night train for Vienna. Alone, heart in mouth, I reached inside the small button-down pocket in my jacket. The USB stick I'd been given by a man dressed as Mozart, weeks before, was still there. Beneath it a small piece of paper. A scrap of musical manuscript, modern and handwritten in blue ink. I knew those notes by now. I'd seen them in the tightly clenched fingers of Marcus Haas, dead and bloody on the couch in the hothouse of the Palazzo Maddalena. The Devil's Tritone.

I hadn't put that scrap of paper there. It could only have been Rupert Hazard who'd slipped it in, surely. But not without seeing the silver memory stick labelled 'Mozart' with a colour image of the composer. Why would he take the valise and not that? Because he was in a hurry? Or he simply thought the thing unimportant, not worthy of his attention?

Why leave me the Devil's Tritone? What was the point of a warning to a dead man?

There were more mysteries here than the obvious ones. As Valentina and Luca doubtless suspected. Perhaps Mia Haas too.

I made the journey to Giudecca stretched out on the rear seat of a gleaming white and walnut water taxi, my first experience of one since it was a form of transport far too fancy and expensive for the likes of me.

A wonderful way to travel, though some of the locals I met complained vociferously about the damage these things did to the lagoon. All the same, at that moment, I was grateful I wasn't making the usual trip on a crowded vaporetto, hoping someone would make space for me in the seats for the elderly and infirm at the front. I felt as weak as a kitten, barely able to walk unaided, both exhausted and energised, and deeply grateful to be alive.

The journey reminded me why I'd found myself in this strange city, this unique enclosed world, in the first place. The boatman took me the scenic route, east, past San Pietro, rounding the corner by Sant'Elena, traffic everywhere, one great transport ferry lumbering towards San Nicolò on the Lido, vaporetti trekking right and left, a few yachts and private boats dodging the wake of their larger cousins.

Apart from the modern maritime traffic, Venice from the water always looks so peaceful, much as it did in the canvases of Canaletto three centuries earlier. None of the sweaty, bustling crowds of San Marco, or the grubby commercialism of the Rialto. Just the great sights that have set their stamp on the city over a millennium.

We edged past San Giorgio Maggiore, with its campanile a mirror image of the busier one in the Piazza San Marco across the water. That small island left behind, we passed the Cipriani hotel and headed for the Zitelle jetties.

Two figures were standing by the landing in front of the handsome Gothic palace of the Casa dei Tre Oci, the House of Three Eyes, a trio of curious large windows that gave out onto the lagoon. Mia waved, beaming at me from the promenade, blonde hair down, plain white shirt, pleated navy trousers. The young man with her helped me out of the boat and introduced himself as Toni as he led me to a wheelchair. He was to be my aide for as long as I needed him, she said, living in one of the downstairs rooms that would eventually be part of the hotel.

Through the back alleys, onto the wooden bridge. Beyond, the place looked deserted. The auditorium doors were shut, no music behind. The palazzo had lost all sign of renovation work and was now quite magnificent. The gardens too, filling with roses and bedding plants, a larger vegetable patch established by the wall alongside the orchid house. No sign of Lombardo, that curious workman, though. It was Ferragosto, a time when locals fled Venice for the beach and the hills.

The lift took us to the top floor of the palazzo. That looked changed too, more like a private home. Paintings on the wall, modern art, more furniture, and in my new bedroom a large vase of flowers by the window that looked out over the gardens.

Kravchuck and Ellen Kim were working in the US for the rest of August, Mia said. The small orchestra had dispersed and wouldn't return until the end of the month.

Toni came with food, sandwiches, San Pellegrino, a small bottle of white wine if I wanted it. I determined to stick with water for a while.

When he was gone, Mia helped me to the bed. 'If there's anything you need just call. Extension one.' She closed her eyes for a moment, the sign she was about to say something difficult. 'I want you to know something.'

'What?'

'It doesn't matter about the book.'

'Mia...'

She put a finger to my lips. 'Listen to me. You nearly died. Getting you better is all that counts. I can handle things here. By the time the musicians come back, I'll know whether we can go ahead. It's just...' She winced. 'Just a question of money. It always is.'

'They say Rupert Hazard stole the papers.'

'So I gather.'

'Has he tried to ransom them? Sell them back?'

She shook her head. 'I've heard nothing. And if I did, how could I trust the man? A murderer? I've already been taken for a small fortune with no reward. Nothing to show.'

My jacket, with the memory stick and that scrap of notation

paper, was still in my small case outside the wardrobe. She saw me looking at it.

'Do you want me to help you unpack?'

'Thank you. I can manage.'

'A stubborn Yorkshireman.'

'Who told you that?'

'Luca Volpetti. He said he got it from you.'

'Ah.'

She got up to go.

'The man I met in Vienna said he'd send you some codes.'

That seemed to surprise her. 'I forgot about that. There's only one. I imagine that means he wasn't part of Hazard's scheme. But who knows?'

'What was it?'

'Something obvious. 431678. Vivaldi's birthday. Not much use now, is it?'

'I imagine not,' I said and yawned.

She reached down and kissed my cheek once, very quickly. 'If you want anything, just ask.'

Yawning, fighting to stay awake, I managed to lug the case to the bed and began to unpack. The few things I'd taken to Vienna. The box of chocolates 'Mozart' had given me. Unopened. I wondered whether to hand them over to Valentina and ask her to check them for poison. Then cursed myself for being both so suspicious and so rash. Perhaps I'd been allowed too much time on my own to think, but by now I was decidedly mistrustful of pretty much everyone. My friend in the Carabinieri clearly had a murder case uppermost in her mind. Luca, as always, was anxious to avoid anything unpleasant. Mia... there, I just didn't know. Caution seemed the best way forward. I dumped the chocolates in the bin in the kitchen, poured myself some water, and set to work.

Finally, the memory stick, the only thing I'd gained from that odd journey. I'd assumed the fellow in Vienna had meant two codes, one for the valise, one for the stick on which he'd said he placed the entire collection of Vivaldi documents. But no. When I plugged the thing into my laptop and typed '431678', it opened straight away and there they were. A folder marked *Music* and another marked *Memoirs*, all full of photographs with simple labelling, *Memoir 1*, *Music 1*. This was going to take time.

In the first was a collection of original musical manuscripts marked *Il cimento dell'armonia e dell'inventione*, The Contest Between Harmony and Invention. The name meant something already. These were twelve concertos of Vivaldi's published in Amsterdam in 1725 by a French printer, Michel-Charles Le Cène, who specialised in music and had also distributed work by Handel and Telemann. The first four, dated 1722, formed *Le quattro stagioni*, *The Four Seasons*, missing in autograph manuscript form for centuries. Every version of perhaps the most famous classical music in the world came not from Vivaldi's pen but the transcription of Le Cène's workshop in Amsterdam.

Inside the second folder were 123 pictures of yellowing sheets of paper covered in a sloping, perhaps feeble hand, dark blue ink, almost black, against vellum that was curling at the corners. I could see why 'Mozart' advised against handling the originals too much, not that it mattered now.

There was a letter in the same folder in which Vivaldi commended the works to Le Cène and asked for them to be published, along with a dedication to none other than his late Habsburg patron, Charles VI, whose tomb I'd visited in Vienna. Vivaldi scarcely mentions money except to say that he wished for the sums raised by sale to be conveyed to him speedily through a financial institution in San Marco. None of this could have happened, I presumed. If it had, there would surely be some record of the book.

I was in no position to judge the scores. There were plenty examples of Vivaldi's autograph works around, some in Keller, others on the academic networks Mia had arranged for me. The man, it seemed to me, produced music much as he wrote his memoirs, in great haste. Everything – words and notation – looked scribbled down in an anxious hurry, as if the notes came to him out of nowhere and needed to be recorded the moment they appeared before they vanished as swiftly as they'd arrived.

I recalled a detail from Keller. A note Vivaldi had written at the foot of something he wrote for the Carnival in Mantua in 1719, *Tito Manlio... 'musica del Vivaldi fatta in cinque giorni'*. Music by Vivaldi, made – in other words, composed – in five days. A three-act, three-hour opera written in under a week. Another time he told a companion he could compose a concerto, with all the parts, more quickly than a copyist might copy it. I found it odd that such a man, as keen on money as fame, would tell the world how easy he found it to produce his work. If you could write such a vast piece of music as *Tito Manlio* in so short a time, how much was five days' work really worth?

Mantua was where he met Anna Girò, taking her in as his companion, muse, and preferred singer, even though many commentators thought her voice nowhere near as fetching as her looks. Time and again, he denied the relationship was anything but chaste, not that everyone believed him.

One thing at a time. We'll get there, I told myself then promptly fell asleep.

～

Mia was my most frequent visitor, with food and drink, and stories of how she was receiving promises of support to keep the project on an even keel until it could earn its keep the following year. I soon learned her favourite phrase when faced with a tricky problem... 'There's always an accommodation to be made.'

It seemed there was too, judging by the brightness of her mood.

Marta Neri popped in at the end of every afternoon, on her way home from the hospital, took my pulse and temperature, talked to me in that slightly condescending way doctors do when they're trying to ascertain if all your marbles are in place. Toni hovered around constantly, taking me down to the garden to enjoy the fresh air from time to time.

In a slow and puzzled procession, the musicians returned, and everyone went out of their way to see me, to say how sorry they were to hear of the incident on the train, how glad I'd survived and would soon be well.

One day, when I was lounging in the shade of the wall by the orchid house, Reggie Davies turned up with a loaf of Whitby parkin, that ginger and molasses concoction I remembered from childhood, a gift for any Yorkshireman, she said. And she was right.

'About the book...' I said, offering her the first chunk.

'Forget about that for now.' She took a bite. 'Mia told me it's of no consequence. Can I get you anything?'

'A few explanations would be welcome.'

She grinned. 'Venice, love. Explanations are rare and always come late in my experience.'

'But it is of consequence. The book that is.'

'That bastard Hazard nicked your papers, didn't he?'

'And killed a man. I still find the whole thing improbable.'

She wrinkled her nose. 'Odd fellow. I couldn't work him out.'

'You'd never have put him down as a murderer, would you?'

'Haven't met one before as far as I'm aware. How would I know? I doubt they wear a badge.'

'All the same...'

'As I said. An odd fellow. Take it easy, Arnold. Get better. You look bloody awful.'

'Thank you.'

'Candour's important in this life. You'll find out if you ever get round to writing that book and handing it to me to edit.'

That I didn't doubt. But I think I nodded off at that moment and by the time I came to she was gone. There was just Peter Lombardo standing there, in new blue overalls, a hoe in his hand.

'You've been leading an adventurous life, I gather, Mr Clover.'

'Too adventurous for my liking.'

'Well... you've got a manservant now. And Signora Haas to wait on you hand and foot.'

'I have to say... you seem an unlikely gardener.'

'Really? Done a good few things over the years. This suits me more than most.'

'How did you find your way here?'

He leaned on the hoe and stared at me, walnut skin, wrinkled, blue keen eyes, the unshaven face of a rogue, a pirate from a kid's movie maybe. I couldn't work out whether Peter Lombardo was a man I wanted to like or fear.

'I answered an advert. You?'

'It seems I was... chosen.'

'Oh dear. That doesn't sound good. Do you like gardening, Mr Clover? It's very therapeutic. I could start you off on some weeds.' He ran the blade of the hoe along the foot of the wall. A couple of small lizards ran out. 'No need to worry about those little chaps. They're harmless though sometimes the English take fright the way the English do. We do get them in Venice, nasties. The occasional small tarantula.' He ran the blade deeper into the earth and something scuttled away towards the orchid house. 'Saw a black widow once. Now those buggers you do steer clear of. Put you back in hospital, one of them. Though...' He leered at me. 'It's only the females you need to fear. Nasty pieces of work. They scoff the male right up once he's serviced them. Did you know that?'

'No.'

'Now you do. Good day.'

Ten days or so that went on. I wasn't minded to count. I could feel my old self returning steadily. After a while I didn't need to nap every hour or two. I was able to walk around unaided, take myself down to the garden, listen to the musicians chatter and play, without Kravchuck's guiding hand, of course. Toni went back to the agency that had provided him. Mia was now my carer, breakfast, lunch and dinner always carefully prepared.

I'd put off taking an analytical look at the material on the memory stick for a very practical reason. I needed my wits about me just to begin to process everything. Perhaps it was this new suspicious me, but I wasn't keen to face that challenge until I felt I could approach the text with a clear mind, and sufficient intellectual heft to be able to gauge what it all meant.

There was also the issue of the volume of material on offer. It was overwhelming. No wonder that leather valise had felt so heavy.

The music I had to leave to someone else, Kravchuck preferably when he returned. The memoirs I would have to tackle directly, though I found some of the Italian difficult, and the handwriting close to illegible in places where he appeared to be writing like a man determined to scribble out his will before the chapter of his life came to a close.

It was now the end of the month. The end of summer, September, autumn making itself known in the shortening of the day beyond the window, the attenuation of the August heat, the sloughing off of all that high summer lassitude among the musicians, and in Mia too.

Where to start?

By doing what I always hated when it came to any kind of book. Sifting through the mass of photographed pages there then going to the last one.

I blinked, I felt a headache coming on. I stared at the page trying to come to terms with what I was seeing.

This was the surprise 'Mozart' had talked about surely. A different hand altogether, one that was shockingly familiar. It was in French, the writing elderly but clear, leaning drunkenly to the right, as did each careful line.

> *I finish by swearing before God that every word in*
> *L'histoire de ma vie, every tale, however amusing, however*
> *damning, happened as I wrote it. This page alone I demand*
> *Camillo keep from the account I wish to see published since*
> *it records the one lie I have told, that of my parenthood. In*
> *this I was deceived, first by that cunning rascal Michele*
> *Grimani, the theatre owner who could scarcely keep his*
> *hands off any young woman who trod his boards. And*
> *second by my own conceit, since a gentleman must remain*
> *a gentleman in the eyes of all, and the cost of falling from*
> *that position of grace is all too painful as I, eking out my*
> *final days as a mere librarian, appreciate more than the*
> *common herd.*

In truth I was sired when my flibbertigibbet mother succumbed to the arms and loins of a more talented individual, not the patron, a man of 'commerce', who claimed me to his chums.

This I discovered when, as a young man needing remuneration, I returned briefly to San Samuele and played fiddle in the orchestra. Though not as well as my true father, naturally, since I was taught by another, less talented fellow. That being Doctor Gozzi, whose sister Bettina was my first passion, promised me most every pleasure only to deny it and choose that dolt Candiani instead.

But providence works for the best. I had a higher calling than lingering impoverished in an orchestra pit sawing bad opera for fools. San Samuele served its purpose, in more ways than one. It was there I stole my real father's private papers from the office of Grimani himself after he acquired them from Vienna. There, in the small room the old fool had found for me, I read them in private and learned so much about the world, about art and aspiration, about women and the joy and pain they may bring.

Nevertheless, for the herd I will continue to claim Michele Grimani as my father, a wealthy noble, long dead, remembered fondly by those who did not know him well. For the sake of my conscience – I have one, whatever the dolts and doubters may say – I assign the verity of my lineage to this private memoir, to be kept for posterity should posterity think it pertinent. That I doubt, which is why I am happy to leave the hoi polloi to believe an old Venetian theatrical fathered me.

Who, after all, would want to be known as the offspring of an itinerant cleric, buried like a pauper, far from the home which no longer recalls his name? A hypocrite whose work is now as dead as he.

I read it twice, determined to make no mistake. Then, exhausted, I lay back on the bed and fell asleep.

It was seven by the time I came to. Outside the long windows dusk was falling. Mia must have heard me moving about. She knocked on the door with a tray loaded with panini, *cicchetti* and a bottle of San Pellegrino. I thanked her then walked to the open balcony at the front of the palazzo and took a chair by one of the tables. Soon, if she had her way, this would be the territory of wealthy tourists, keeping her place alive, the auditorium next door too. We all have dreams, though sometimes they're best unrealised. A goal to aim for, rather than a target reached.

'Arnold?' she said. 'May I join you?'

'Of course.' I smiled. 'This is your home.'

'Yours now.'

'No.'

'You can stay as long as you like. The apartment you're in...' She blushed, went back inside, and returned with a bottle of chilled Soave Classico and two glasses. 'Here.' She poured me half a one. 'You look up to it. You seem your old self.'

'The apartment–'

'It was meant to be mine. Marcus and I had been sleeping apart for almost a year. I think it was only this...' She nodded at the garden, the theatre, the little wooden bridge. 'The idea of it that kept us together. So really, you're welcome to keep it. For nothing. By way of reward for your work. Volpetti said you were short of money.'

'I'm not a pauper.'

'I didn't mean to offend you.'

'I know. But I need to go home. Tomorrow. I'm well enough. I've enjoyed your hospitality, your kindness, your company. But at heart I'm a solitary man and happy that way. Also... if I'm to work on this book–'

'I told you already. The book's irrelevant.'

'No. I've started on it, and I'm not someone who likes to leave tasks unfinished. Nor can I work here. It's too...'

'Too what?'

'Too... not me.'

'But we don't have the papers, Arnold!'

I remembered Reggie's advice. 'All I need is a world for the story. Got that. It's Venice. Some characters to fill that world. And events to bring both to life. Don't give up hope.'

'I'll miss you,' she said and touched my hand.

I locked the bedroom door. Perhaps it was just my memory, or something from a dream, but I thought I heard a gentle touch as someone tried the handle during the long, dark night.

The next morning we walked together to the Zitelle vaporetto stop and had coffee and pastries before I took the Number Two to Zattere. There didn't seem much to talk about. She felt I was abandoning her, I thought. Nor did I have the means or the evidence to convince her that was the last thing on my mind. Except to say I would deliver the book she wanted, one way or another. And the Teatro Maddalena would come to life, just as she wished. Kravchuck would be back soon. The auditorium would resound to the little orchestra playing Vivaldi under his direction.

Just without a murderous crooked cellist who'd called himself Rupert Hazard and stolen the most precious set of papers I'd ever come across, right from under my nose.

Mia stood on the cobbled pavement and watched as the vaporetto headed out.

With luck, I'd bagged a seat in the open area at the stern.

I waved.

She waved back.

Twenty minutes later I opened the door to my small apartment near San Pantalon for the first time in the best part of six weeks. Chiara, my cleaner, had been in as I'd asked over the phone the day before. The place was spotless. Empty. Without warmth or character, I saw now. The way I'd always wanted it.

For a moment I missed Mia Haas's plush apartment on the top floor of her Giudecca palazzo. Missed her too, and wondered about what might have happened had I left the door unlocked the night before. Though maybe that was a dream. Was I ever to know? Did I want to?

I had my home. My books. My laptop. My privacy and a space at the desk by the window over the narrow stretch of water behind the bedroom.

Finally, somewhere I was free to think.

I lay on my familiar old bed, closed my eyes, glad to be home, even gladder to be alive.

The next thing I knew I was waking to the sound of the Frari's bells. It was eight in the morning, and I'd slept like an infant, twelve hours or more.

I waited till nine when Luca would be at work. Time to call.

As I reached for the phone it rang. Number withheld.

'*Pronto*,' I said, expecting an Italian.

'Good lord, Lucky.' A familiar English voice, one that made my heart miss several beats. 'You have gone local, haven't you?'

I couldn't speak.

'You still there?' The man who told me he was Rupert Hazard sounded the same as he had that night on the train from

Vienna. Cocksure of himself, rascally. 'Now listen and listen carefully. Time, as they say, is of the essence. I trust you've read the taster of my material now and appreciate its worth.'

'You left me the Devil's Tritone too.'

'Of course. I wanted to you to know I hadn't missed that memory stick by accident. If you lived. I'm glad you did. Honestly.'

'That's rich, given you tried to kill me.'

'Oh please...'

'Didn't you?'

'Not now. We'll talk about that anon.'

'To hell with this, Rupert. Or whoever you are. I'm calling the Carabinieri.'

He laughed. 'For God's sake... why?'

'Because you shot a man! Tried to murder me. Stole the very things I went to Vienna for. What kind of a mess do you think Mia Haas is in now?'

He waited a moment. 'A bit of a pickle, I'll agree. But then this whole business is rather like that, don't you think?'

'I'm cutting this call. The Carabinieri can deal with you.'

The laugh again. 'First, they'd have to find me. Not very good at that so far. Really... is this the avenue you wish to pursue? Do you believe the lovely Mia will avoid skid row if you keep whining to your mate, Capitano Fabbri?'

That took me aback. How on earth did he know Valentina's name?

'Listen, Arnold. There are more things in heaven and earth than you could begin to dream of in your meagre philosophy, chum. Roll with it or lose the game. You've seen what's on that stick. You know you want those papers. Your beautiful friend needs them more than anything in the world.' He hesitated. 'Just as she needs her amanuensis, the learned Arnold Clover.'

'Why should I believe a word you say—'

'This is tedious, Lucky!' he bellowed. 'You believe everything you're fed, don't you? Why should I be any different? Enough. Think of the treasure on offer here. You've got the rest of the day to come to your senses. I will call when I feel like it. You choose.'

Chapter Six

Presto

I was scarcely off the call, wondering what to do, how to process what I'd heard, when the doorbell rang. There, to my discomfort, was Valentina Fabbri, elegant as ever in her neatly pressed navy uniform.

'Are you all right?' she asked, eyes narrowing.

'Of course. You don't think your doctor friend would have let me out of Giudecca if I wasn't?'

'I didn't mean that. I know exactly what Marta Neri thinks of your condition. I meant... you. In yourself. You look... flustered. Which is rare.'

'Work,' I said. 'Trying to get back into it.'

Something was going on outside. There were men there, in uniform, a few doors down close to the end of the little alley where I lived. The last house before the narrow canal.

'You're still going to try and write that book? I assumed...'

'Assumed what?'

'Since the papers are missing... where's your material?'

Always fishing... 'We'll see. Thanks for popping round.' I glanced behind me. 'Lots to do...'

She took my arm. 'First, follow me please.'

It struck me then. Her team, at least four of them from what I could see, were clustered around the door to the small terrace where Rupert Hazard – I could only think of him as that – had lived until a few months before.

'I don't know why you're bothering. He moved out ages ago.'

'Did he?'

There was an athletic-looking officer outside the bright red front door, next to a couple of large plant pots full of dead flowers. In his hands was one of those battering ram things you see on TV. He was swinging it, getting ready to deliver the first in what I assumed would be a series of blows. Venetians did like their locks. I'd never met a front door that had fewer than two, and some ran to as many as four.

'Might be easier if you ask the landlord for the key?' I suggested. 'Hazard told me had to move out because he was down on the rent. It was going to be another tourist flat.'

She harrumphed. 'The landlord is a company in the Cayman Islands. True ownership entirely opaque. CCTV around the corner caught someone who looked very like your friend walking down here last night.' I got the hard stare. 'I don't suppose you've seen him?'

I was aghast or tried to look it. 'I think you can assume I'd be on the phone to you in an instant if the man who tried to murder me, who killed someone in the same train compartment, was hanging round my street.'

Another harrumph. Then we watched as the hulk started to beat down the door. Four locks this one. It took umpteen swings and a good deal of Venetian cursing. Someone in the Caymans was going to get a hell of a bill at some stage.

They stood back to let Valentina in first, and she beckoned

me to follow. The place was a sight tidier than I expected. Narrower than my own home, a single bedroom to one side with a window over the canal, a living room and kitchen combined, a small bathroom. All modern and recently refurbished.

There was a pizza box on the table. Fresh, the crust still left there with a few scraps of what looked like spianata from Calabria, Tropea red onion and gorgonzola.

'That,' I said, as I watched her pick up the bill, 'is what's left of a Barababao from Al Profeta in Calle San Barnaba. One of my favourites. I remember I told Rupert about it.'

She held the receipt in front of me. Timed at eight thirty the night before. 'You're sure he didn't invite you to share?'

I folded my arms and stared back. 'I was fast asleep. Weren't you watching the place?'

'We can't watch everywhere. There's something very curious going on here. You seem to attract the curious, don't you?'

I made what I hoped was a very Italian gesture of exasperation with my arms.

'I don't like being in the dark,' she went on. 'As you may realise by now. I want this man Hazard in custody. I want to find out who's been playing games.'

'Deadly games,' I said.

'Quite.'

The officers were busy around us, gloves on, opening drawers. After a little while one came back with a large manila envelope, in it six different passports, two Irish, two UK, one Canadian, one New Zealand. All with different names, all with a different photograph, each clearly the man we knew as Rupert Hazard.

'Why wouldn't he take them?' I wondered.

Valentina went through the pages. None of them stamped. 'All counterfeit. Perhaps he hoped to come back here. Perhaps he has others. How am I to know? The man seems to be one step ahead of everyone.'

Another officer wandered over. He had a box of ammunition. Shells, what kind I'd no idea. It was half full.

'A harmless, solitary cellist,' Valentina said, picking through the bullets and holding one up to the light.

'As far as I knew. Shouldn't you be asking these questions of Andriy Kravchuck? He picked his musicians, didn't he? He must have employed the man.'

'Andriy Kravchuck has yet to return to Venice, as you surely know. But when he does...' She nodded at the door. 'You can go now. We've work to do.'

I didn't move. 'Why exactly did you want me here?'

No answer.

I was at the threshold when she called out, 'Arnold! If you hear anything, anything at all... I demand to know.'

'Of course,' I said and that was that.

Should I have told her about the phone call I took half an hour earlier? Perhaps.

Would matters have worked out differently?

Who's to know? Not me. Not Valentina Fabbri. Certainly not the man I still thought of as Rupert Hazard.

In truth I was sick of being cajoled and manipulated and treated as if I was a pawn in the play of others. Besides, if there was a chance I might get hold of those papers I was going to take it. As Hazard knew full well, that was a treasure too precious to refuse.

Back home, I called Luca and listened to all the usual questions I realised I was going to get for weeks to come.

How are you?

Are you taking it easy?

You know there's no need to rush?

Except, when it came to that last one, there was. In my old job in the National Archives, I'd handled papers signed by monarchs, penned by statesmen, great and evil, touched manuscripts that had changed world history. But nothing like the memoirs I'd spent hours poring over in bed in my sick room on Giudecca. The most extraordinary documents I'd ever come across. Ones that changed our perception of accepted history in ways I'd yet to grasp to any great degree. The one problem being we no longer possessed the originals, only the photos the man posing as Mozart somewhere near Vivaldi's hidden grave outside the Karlskirche had provided. The pages themselves were still out there with Rupert Hazard, a man I thought I'd known but clearly didn't. Without them... could I really believe what I was reading was genuine?

Even after a lifetime surrounded by vellum and parchment, I'd no idea. I needed help. I needed advice. I needed someone proficient when it came to deciphering the scribbles in archaic Italian on those pages.

'We must meet,' I told him. 'Now.'

'What is this? I have work. I can't just–'

'Make an excuse.'

'But–'

'I know why Hazard stole those papers. I know what they're worth. I know...' I stopped myself. I was about to say I knew why someone might kill for them. But that was a step too far. 'Please, Luca. Indulge me this once. Just you and me. And...' This was important too. 'Tell no one. Not even our Carabinieri friend.'

Dammit. She was just a few doors down from me and I'd no idea how long her officers would be there.

Silence. I imagine he didn't like that.

'Change of plan,' I said. 'Coffee. Ten minutes. The usual

place. Hear me out and if you think I've lost my mind I'll never mention this again.'

'I suppose I could use a coffee...'

When couldn't he? 'Just between the two of us for now. If you can't agree I'll have to exclude you. And believe me you'll regret it.'

'That sounds like a threat. Not like the Arnold Clover I know at all.'

'Someone tried to murder me. He killed the man in my compartment. I'm lucky to be alive. You think all that just vanishes? Water off a duck's back?'

'No,' he murmured. 'But for what? Tell me. I need reasons.'

'I've been going through photos of those papers the fellow in Vienna left me on a memory stick.'

'You never mentioned any memory stick.' He sounded annoyed.

'I wasn't sure I could get into it. But I have. There's a page there seemingly written by someone you know very well. Someone you hate.'

He kept quiet at that. Luca had told me time and time again how much he loathed the man, and the way he was now lionised.

'If this is for real,' I went on, 'Antonio Vivaldi didn't just know the young Giacomo Casanova. He was his father...'

'Impossible!' Luca cried.

But, as we'd both come to learn over the last few years, this was Venice, a place where the narratives of players, notorious and unknown, crossed and crisscrossed one another relentlessly over the centuries, a tangled web of relationships, enmities and ambition, much of it still to be uncovered.

'Isn't it?' my archivist friend asked more meekly.

'Coffee. I'm buying.'

'That sounds rather public, surely. I could come round to your place.'

'That's not possible right now.'

He groaned. 'Very well come here. I'll find us a quiet place no one can see.'

The State Archives of Venice. A warren of corridors, offices and storerooms that ran all the way around the side and back of the great church of Frari. There was a run-down empty space overlooking the neglected courtyard at the back. We'd used that before. It would, I told him, surely do.

'Agreed. Pick up those coffees on the way, macchiato for me and an almond cornetto.'

I snuck out without being seen. As I was paying at the café a message came in from Valentina.

> We may have found his ammunition, some of it anyway. There's no sign of a gun. I thought you ought to know.

~

The Archivio di Stato. It was a sound suggestion of Luca's that we should continue our conversation there. The pages I had on that memory stick were just the kind of material that might once have found their way into its compendious collections, by the Frari and in the overspill annexe on Giudecca, not so far from the Mia Haas's budding concert hall.

The question in front of me was the perennial one when faced with the apparent discovery of important new material. Was this authentic? Could the story these photographs tried to tell really be true?

I had much experience in analysing historical documents, and, since arriving in Venice, a little in trying to decide if they were fake or not. Luca was far more experienced in the latter, and had some proficiency in palaeography, the study of hand-writing in old documents. If anyone could help me determine whether these supposed memoirs were genuine, it was him.

We settled down to the task in a stuffy, scruffy, empty room at the far end of the archives overlooking the deserted, weed-strewn courtyard, a counterpart to the smarter one attached to the Frari itself. He'd brought the largest laptop he could find so that we could read the images clearly. After my explanation of what appeared to be on them, we decided to start logically, not by trying to analyse the words and what they said, but through the simple test of the calendar. Could the claim, apparently written by an elderly Casanova, that Vivaldi might be his father fit with known events?

If this turned out to be impossible, then the whole collection of documents contained in those images was surely suspect, part of a concerted and clever attempt to defraud the late Marcus Haas.

Casanova makes not a single mention of Antonio Vivaldi in his memoirs, written in French in old age when he was a lowly librarian in Bohemia, working from a memory that was, perhaps, coloured more by wishful thinking than fact. His escape from the rooftop cell of the Doge's Palace, for example, was one of his tall tales that Luca found exceedingly hard to believe. Conman, crook, seducer, intellectual, a writer of genius and spy, Casanova was born in Venice on 2 April, 1725. His mother, Zanetta Farussi, was seventeen at the time, a performer in the troupe at the Teatro San Samuele, married to a fellow actor there, Gaetano Casanova. By all accounts, Zanetta was both beautiful and flighty, pursued by many, among them the owner of the theatre, Michele Grimani, Casanova's real father according to his notorious published memoirs.

The year after Giacomo's birth, Zanetta and her husband

left to perform in London where she became pregnant with her second son, Francesco, whose father, gossips had it, was none other than the future king, George II. The infant Giacomo, in the meantime, was raised by his grandmother in a terraced house in what is now the Calle Malipiero close to the site of the vanished Teatro San Samuele.

In 1725, Vivaldi was forty-eight, at the peak of his fame after the publication that year in Amsterdam of *The Four Seasons*. He had recently been commissioned by the French ambassador to write a serenata, a dramatic vocal piece, for the wedding of the fifteen-year-old Louis XV. This was premiered in the grounds of the French embassy on 12 September that year, music we still have as an autograph score since it was among those documents discovered in Turin in the 1920s.

Going through all this, I started to feel a familiar, disconcerting sensation, that of the city of old coming back to life and haunting my own imagination, entering the present world, colouring the experiences I had of it today. The old French embassy was in the Palazzo Surian Bellotto on the Cannaregio Canal, a place I visited from time to time for Laguna Libre, a restaurant, and its associated jazz concerts. The ghosts of the illustrious and the unknown, the saintly and the damned, are never distant hereabouts.

In autumn that year Vivaldi went back to working for the Teatro Sant'Angelo, a smaller, more recent rival to Grimani's San Samuele a short walk away. The two men must have known each other. Zanetta Farussi surely moved in the same circles. The idea Vivaldi could have had an affair with Casanova's mother was, then, feasible, if quite unproven or even hinted at by any proven records we knew.

That, at least, takes care of 1725. But what of the later claim that Casanova discovered the papers and the music in the Teatro San Samuele some twenty years later while working as a musician? Again, Luca knew this part by heart. He'd spent months studying Casanova's *L'histoire de ma vie* for an exhibition at the Museo Correr. Casanova had, indeed, learned to play the fiddle. He must have been at least competent. When he turned twenty-one, five years after Vivaldi was buried in that unmarked grave in Vienna, Casanova returned to the Teatro San Samuele and persuaded Grimani, perhaps thinking he was the lad's father, to give him a job as a violinist in the orchestra pit.

Luca went through the relevant passages, cursing at regular intervals. The world may see Casanova as some kind of romantic hero, but a closer reading of his memoirs reveals a far darker individual. Around this time, Casanova records how he and his chums used to run riot in the city, one time committing the gang rape of a poor woman in the Do Spade tavern which still exists behind the Rialto. A rather fine place in my experience, but one Luca refuses to enter for no other reason than the outrage that happened there 300 years ago. And it's true, there's no sense of regret in Casanova's account of this episode. Far from it, he almost feels the woman should be grateful for their attention.

All the same, there was the truth. Both chronologies, from 1725 and 1746, worked. Vivaldi might have been Casanova's father. Casanova might have stolen his papers when he returned to play at the San Samuele as a young man.

And someone might have forged this whole thing as a gigantic hoax, a fraud designed to fool Marcus Haas into forking out a small fortune.

We needed to delve deeper, this time into that strange art Luca alone understood, palaeography.

First, we went out for more coffee and some panini to take back to the office – this was turning into quite a task – before peering closely at the handwriting of the documents themselves. Or rather our pictures of them. The autograph score supposedly of The Seasons we decided to leave to one side. I was no musician, and Luca neither. Those pages would have to be placed before Kravchuck for an opinion once he returned.

As for the rest – that brief document supposedly by an ageing Casanova and the bulk of the images, Vivaldi's private 'memoirs' – I was dependent on Luca's expertise. Did the handwriting in both appear to match examples of both men's penmanship in existing documents proven to be their work?

This is a field I find both fascinating and baffling. In normal circumstances, we had physical evidence to examine too. Ink to be analysed, parchment to be dated and its provenance sought. These are established scientific procedures which can deliver hard answers. Old manuscripts are increasingly difficult to fake now experts can say with some certainty what year paper dates from, and often what part of the world. The same with ink and even the kind of pen used by the author.

But, thanks to the elusive Rupert Hazard and that deadly incident on the night train from Vienna, all we had for the moment were photographs of the material we were trying to judge. Again, Luca was ahead of me there, pulling up something called EXIF data. It was gibberish to me but with a few quick searches he had something. The pictures, it seemed, were taken with an iPhone 16 over a period of four days, ending a week before I arrived in Vienna.

'No location,' Luca murmured.

'Sorry?'

He tapped the screen. 'Ordinarily I'd expect a phone to include location data. Where these shots were taken. But…'

'It was deleted?'

'Possibly. Or the photos were taken indoors where there was no phone signal, no internet, nothing to help.'

'Four days,' I said. 'It would have taken quite a while to photograph all those pages.'

'Quite. Equally, whoever did this would know we'd think that. If we saw the EXIF and it all happened in an hour or so... something was up.'

'I couldn't do any of this without you, Luca.'

'I haven't done much. All we know is there's nothing so far to say this is anything but genuine. It doesn't prove a thing.'

He hit the keyboard again and pulled up an example of Casanova's handwriting from the manuscript of his memoirs in the Bibliothèque nationale de France, alongside the page from the memory stick claiming that Vivaldi might be his father.

'Well?'

I didn't know what to say except, 'They look very similar to me.'

'Yes,' Luca agreed. 'They do. Let's deal with our composer.' More hammering of the keyboard. Then, the Casanova pages dismissed, he pulled up an astonishing whining letter written by Vivaldi, complaining of ill-treatment and fraud to do with a musical event in Ferrara in 1736.

'He comes across as quite unhinged,' I said.

Luca scrolled down and discovered the cause of the argument, a disagreement with a scenery painter, Antonio Mauro, over money and theatrical management. 'Certainly doesn't sound much like a priest, does he? Let's see what else we have.'

Another letter, this time to someone whose name I recognised, Cardinal Guido Bentivoglio, scion of an aristocratic clan, again from Ferrara. A place, I recalled, that had rejected Vivaldi over suspicions his relationship with Anna Girò was not as platonic as he claimed.

And here it was. Written in Venice on 16 November, 1737,

at the point where Vivaldi's career was beginning to fall apart. He'd been told by the Apostolic Nuncio, a Vatican diplomat, that he would not be allowed to mount a planned opera in Ferrara because he was a priest who never said Mass, and a 'friend of the singer Girò'. The composer complains he's in debt for a sizeable sum for the production already, that only Anna can sing the part, and warns that he won't allow the opera to go ahead without her. What troubled him most, he says, is the 'stain' attached to Girò and her sister. He'd appeared with them throughout Europe, and their modesty was admired everywhere. As to saying Mass, he hadn't done so in twenty-five years because of a chest ailment that meant he couldn't leave the house without a carriage or gondola, and a retinue of four or five helpers.

'I don't know about you,' Luca said, scrolling through more letters, 'but he sounds a complete pain to me. All the fellow does is whinge. Either that or he's sucking up to anyone he thinks can help or threatening the impoverished scenery painter he's hoping to sue.'

It was true. The tone was unpleasant.

'His life was falling apart,' I said. 'He was sick. His career would soon be over. In five years, he'd be dead.'

'You haven't seen these before?'

'Of course not. I never knew they existed.'

'Apologies. I found them a few days ago during an idle trawl. You need to read this. It's one of the last.'

Another missive to 'his Excellency' Cardinal Bentivoglio. This one from January 1739, when Vivaldi had two years left to live. Ignored by the theatres and opera companies that a decade before had adored him. Now clearly on his uppers, complaining that he will be in a 'wretched state' without Bentivoglio's help. His reputation had been 'scourged' so much in Ferrara that the opera *Farnace,* which he'd rewritten completely, had been rejected. A final boast... his name and reputation were known throughout Europe, for the ninety-four operas he'd composed. Then a barely veiled threat that he would do something terrible to reclaim his reputation.

It was depressing stuff. A man at the end of his tether, aware he was on the brink of disaster.

'These,' Luca said, 'we know are real. As to this...'

He pulled up the pages from the memory stick. They were in chronological order. It wasn't hard to get to 1739, January again, the same month he'd written that desperate plea to Bentivoglio for help a year after he'd lost his long-held post as maestro de' concerti at La Pietà, the position that had first fired his career. Why he was fired no one knew.

Here was a short but vitriolic note about the perfidy of men from Ferrara, Bentivoglio, once his saviour, now the chief culprit, a devious individual, more a politician than a churchman.

'That rings true,' Luca said. 'From what I recall. But the handwriting...'

He zoomed in and looked closely at the cursive script. Then, seeming lost in the scrawls in front of him, he pulled up the Casanova pages again and compared the two, the sloping, hurried hand of Vivaldi, the elegant sweep of Casanova's French.

'What do you think?' Luca asked.

'These are two different people. It's not the same hand. Or the same pen. The paper looks different too.'

'I agree.'

Luca pointed out individual characteristics to each page, how letters were formed, the angle of the script, the way lines rarely ran horizontally. 'They look very convincing. Though...'

He stopped there.

'Though what?'

'AI. I've seen experimental programmes that have been designed to mimic old handwriting. They do it very well.'

I found this incredible. 'You can't possibly mean a computer might have written this?'

He laughed. 'Not all of it. But some. If it's been given the right source material.'

'Then...'

Luca sighed and pushed back his chair. 'I have a meeting. I'm sorry. If you wish you can stay here and browse a little more. Let yourself out. I'll tell security.'

'You're done?'

'I am. It seems to me all these things could be real. Equally, it's possible they're the work, the very clever work, of a forger. Someone who wrote the script for these fakeries then used some kind of AI mechanism to make them look original, trained with the real men's handwriting and parchment.'

'We need the pages,' I murmured.

'If they exist. It's not beyond all possibility they were never printed in the first place. That someone simply generated these photographs of yours from whatever computer he used in the first place.'

That didn't add up.

'The EXIF. The code that told you when they were supposedly snapped using an iPhone?'

'It's the modern world, Arnold. Anything digital can be faked. The only real proof is—'

'The originals. Yes. I have the message.'

'Exactly.' He got up, stretched, cast me a weary gaze. 'Don't knock yourself out, will you? I don't think you look as perky as you're making out. This is a very large rabbit hole, and a very deep one if you ask me. Tread carefully, and with Mia Haas. The pickles you get yourself into sometimes...'

'I was rather under the impression you got me into this

particular pickle. The day you persuaded me to take the vaporetto to Zitelle.'

'Ah,' he said, raising a finger. 'Yes. Do please drop off the laptop in my office on the way out.'

'Wait...' I tapped through the Vivaldi images, going backwards in time. 'There's a passage you need to see.'

As an example of the trials an artist must face, I can only relate the time I was employed by the French Embassy for my serenata. I played, naturally, and felt quite pleased by the performance. Imeneo, the god of marriage, praising the institution for the glorious King of France. Good money for flattery I must say. There was only one unpleasantness. Upon leaving I was beset by a pestering young filly Farussi, newly married to an actor of little regard. Just seventeen, she'd given birth to a brat named Giacomo. Work, the girl declared, must take her and the husband on the road. Then who will pay for the child? The grandmother must look after him, but money, it seemed, was short.

I pointed out to the near-hysterical child that it was for many, but all must rise to the challenge. Then she bearded me with the most ludicrous accusation. The boy, she cried with a vicious leer, was not her husband's, he was mine.

I knew not whether to laugh or cry. Here are the facts as I recall them. The girl, as beautiful as she is vacuous, hung around the San Samuele theatre looking for an opening for months. I encountered her just the once when she took me to one side in the privacy of a dressing room, lifted her skirt, and offered herself in return for a role in my company at the Sant'Angelo. A man being a man, one wishes to test the goods before acceding to such a request naturally. But the little minx was no fool when it came to bargaining for her beauty. Though a mere sixteen, I seem to recall she was careful to restrict my attentions merely to the porch of her sweet temple, never granting me entrance to the sanctuary itself.

This, I pointed out in no uncertain terms when she demanded coin. Give in to such blackmail, and I would be paying for the rest of my life.

She threw back her head, glared at me and announced, 'Sir! You misremember. I was yours that night in full. You demanded it and I was happy to comply. Your seed was within me and now its fruit bawls and mewls in my mother's house. And with ginger hair!'

I was speechless for a moment. Was I mistaken? Perhaps. There were so many pretty young things after my attention at that time. The housemaid was in one of her moods, denying me regular access to her charms. My darling Anna was still fourteen, a little young for me. That was a delight to come. As to fathering a child. I never wished for one. Never would acknowledge one. Nor pay for the brat year after year.

I told her straight. 'You opened your legs for Grimani, your employer, far wider than you opened them for me. Tell him the boy is his and feed on the man's bottomless purse. He's an aristocrat, rolling in it. I am an artist, a musician, who, like you, must live from hand to mouth.'

And there the matter ended. The husband was a miserable creature who would, rumour had it, be cuckolded often in the years to come. Farussi, it seemed to me, was trouble, beautiful, alluring trouble, and a tiger beneath the sheets no doubt. Not that I recall our ever meeting that way myself.

Luca stared at the extract quite rapt. Then he began sorting through the records on the laptop until he found a copy of Casanova's memoirs.

'There,' he said, when he found the entry. 'I knew it.'

It was in an account of one of the man's many erotic encounters, an attempt at lovemaking that was, for once, unsuccessful, with a galley captain's wife he called 'Madame F'.

With greater control over herself than women have generally under similar circumstances, she took care to let me reach only the porch of the temple, without granting me yet a free entrance to the sanctuary.

Luca ran through the words with his finger. 'Well. What a conundrum.'

'They're fake, aren't they?' I said. 'Someone's copied Casanova. Or the computer's trained on his memoirs or something.'

He made that very Italian motion, his head moving from side to side, lips pursed, that spells... possibly.

'Unless, of course, it's actually proof.'

'Proof?'

'Yes, proof. The story claims Vivaldi is Casanova's father. And Casanova came to steal his memoirs from the Teatro San Samuele then, one assumes, held on to them for the rest of his life.'

I was being slow. 'The alternative is that Casanova took after his father. Not just when it came to women. But when he wanted to write his own memoirs too. Even down to mimicking his style from Vivaldi's own.'

'In which case,' Luca noted, 'we can add plagiarism to his list of sins. Oh my...'

'Enough for now,' I said and closed the laptop. 'I need a drink.'

~

I ambled towards home, puzzled, disgruntled. There was something disturbing in the way the jigsaw pieces of Vivaldi's life, so opaque and barely known, seemed to fit into that of Casanova, a man who had seemingly chronicled every year of his own. Yet Casanova had made it plain in his memories that some aspects of his story he'd left out quite deliberately. Given the admissions he'd included – rape, larceny, an obsession with the very young among them – I could only wonder what those omissions might be. The fact that a composer – quite forgotten by the time Casanova was dying, a lowly librarian in Bohemia – was really his father, not the aristocratic theatre impresario he claimed?

It was – the word that dogged me – plausible. And quite unprovable one way or another without the contents of the valise stolen from me, almost along with my life, on the train from Vienna.

Too fed up for a cheering spritz in one of the local bars I turned the corner to my cul-de-sac and almost bumped into Valentina Fabbri. She looked just as miserable as I felt.

'Find anything?' I asked. As if she'd tell me.

'Not much. You?'

'Doing my best to come up with what Mia wants. She needs it to keep that dream alive.'

'Very good of you. I suppose.'

'What does that mean?'

She looked around, trying to make sure we weren't over-heard I felt. 'Has anyone been speaking to you?'

'A rather uncharacteristically vague comment if you don't mind my saying.'

'What I mean is... has anyone leaned on you? Tried to make you push this idea of hers one way or the other? Tried to scupper it, perhaps?'

'Now you've gone from being vague to downright obscure.'

'You know what I mean.'

'But I don't, Valentina. I'm trying to put together a biography of sorts. One of a man we simply don't know, famous as he is. To say that's a struggle given the paucity of source material would be something of an understatement.'

From the look on her face I realised. This was a prompt.

'Has anyone been asking that of the Carabinieri, then?'

A brief, shadow of a smile and a shrug. 'Perhaps.'

'Who?'

'None of your business.'

'Then...'

She saw the last of her men coming out of Hazard's front door, waited till he'd said goodnight and was gone from earshot before she continued.

'I can only assume your... patron has friends in high places. I have been informed in a way that does not brook misinterpretation that the Teatro Maddalena is a project the city wishes to see succeed. That the fact it relies on private funds, not civic ones, makes it even more attractive. That any lingering interest I may have in its many mysteries – the suicide of its originator, the oddities of his financial background, the fact we found a dead man on the night train, and you nearly expired next to him – all these events are matters for others and the project in Giudecca must go on undisturbed. Though who those *others* might be I've no idea.'

'Not the Carabinieri, you mean?'

That brought out in her the sweetest of smiles, which always gave me pause for thought. 'If only I knew. Except I'm not supposed to.'

'A man was murdered on the train. That ad salesman.'

'By Hazard. Or so it would appear. Nevertheless, I'm informed that the culprit is now outside our reach and may well have fled to distant pastures. The Gulf. The Far East. South

America. It seems no one knows. The trail is, as they say, dead, though if I'm honest it was never much of a trail at all. At least as far as I was aware.'

I did my best to look baffled and a little stupid. 'I have to say what I told you before. He never seemed that kind of fellow at all. You talk as if he's some kind of international man of mystery. Not a rather impoverished hack musician with a drink problem. As I'd assumed.'

'That...' She tapped my shoulder. '...is where we part company. Assumptions. They're not much use to me.'

'If there's anything I can do to help...'

'Then I'm sure you'll do it, won't you?'

I watched her wander off towards the canal where, I imagined, her Carabinieri boat was moored. Then she changed her mind, returned and held out something in her gloved hand. 'All we found was a selection of these...' A scrap of musical manuscript bearing the Devil's Tritone written in blue ink. 'Look familiar?'

'There was one with Marcus Haas. When he died.'

'I know. Do you think the man who called himself Rupert Hazard sent it? Still...' She scowled, a rare look of exasperation. 'What business is any of this of mine?'

Quite a lot, I thought as she headed off to the boat. Valentina Fabbri was not a woman to give up, however much others might want it. Sooner or later, I felt, I was going to find myself back in her office in San Zaccaria, seated opposite my Carabinieri friend at her desk, going through the slow and patient torture of the clinical interrogation only she could perform.

No point in worrying about that now. I was, it seemed, planning to meet a man who'd tried to kill me. Who'd absconded with the very precious material I needed to authenticate the Vivaldi memoirs one way or another. And now for some reason was begging to see me.

At six a simple email came through from a gobbledegook address even I could see was fake.

```
Tronchetto  at  seven,  Lucky.  Don't  be
late.
```

~

Tronchetto.

A place few visitors to Venice ever see. Somewhere the city couldn't do without. If I recall correctly Venice takes in twenty million visitors a year or more, and sometimes it feels as if every one of them is crammed into the streets between the station, Rialto and the Piazza San Marco.

Catering for all those masses is no small exercise. The infrastructure behind it lies to the right as you enter the city from the bridge: an artificial island next to the moribund cruise liner jetty, two modern concrete creations that most of us can happily ignore. I'd passed by many times on the Number Two vaporetto, marvelling at the busy commerce on both sides of the waterway: Amazon parcels being unloaded, fish consignments headed for the nearby market where most Venice restaurants bought their wares, not at the famous one at the Rialto. On Tronchetto itself, a vast car park, cheaper than the more convenient one at Piazzale Roma and always busy.

I had forty-five minutes to get there and no clear idea how to do it. Walk round to San Tomà for the vaporetto? Or stomp to Piazzale Roma and take the People Mover, a shuttle from Tronchetto to the city originally built to bring in the thousands of cruise ship passengers landing there.

Out of interest I banged back a reply to that obscure email address.

`Running late.`

Straight away I got a response: undeliverable, recipient unknown.

Well done Rupert Hazard, whoever you are.

The People Mover was out. No idea if it was running or not, or how to use it. Which left me with just the vaporetto, a thirty-two-minute journey with a meander round the Grand Canal.

This was going to be tight. I dashed out of the door, past the Frari, down the narrow lanes to the stop, just caught the boat as the railing was about to close. The heat was dying. I could feel September slipping closer, shorter days, cooler nights, the promise of autumn fog.

Not that any of that dismissed from my head the image of Valentina Fabbri at our last meeting. That look on her face, anger at being pushed off the case, and puzzlement too, which a woman like her would find equally infuriating.

I'd lied to her, for the first time I felt sure. Though there'd been a good few occasions when I'd simply avoided telling the truth which is, perhaps, just the same. One thing always followed though... Capitano Fabbri kept on digging till she found out what she wanted. It was in her nature, her genes, one reason I admired the woman even though her persistence occasionally came at some personal cost. To me, rarely her.

I found an empty right-hand seat near the front by the open window and watched the city I'd come to regard as home edge past like a moving postcard. All the familiar sights. The chaos at the Rialto, tourists fighting to get on board. The handsome façade of the Ca' d'Oro, the plain frontage of the station of Santa Lucia. All the while wondering what the fallout might – would – be when Valentina discovered I'd deceived her.

That I'd agreed to meet the man she thought, with good reason, had tried to take my life.

'Well, Arnold,' I said out loud, to the bafflement of the tourist in a cheap and very unseasonal mask sitting next to me. 'You didn't come here for the quiet life, did you?'

No.

Just as well.

~

The squat old Number Two rounded the corner past the commercial market and headed for the jetty.

I got up and walked to the open section of the boat behind the cabin, the spot where passengers got off on both sides. The vaporetto had emptied at the station and Piazzale Roma, locals going home to the mainland after a day's work. Only a handful of tourists were left inside, fighting over the open space at the stern. The *marinaio*, the assistant who ran the cabin, opening and closing the railings, running a rope to keep the vessel tied at each jetty until the passengers were on or off, was where he usually was between stops, chatting with the captain in the wheelhouse.

Just me then, scanning the concrete promenade of Tronchetto for a sign of Rupert Hazard, a man I thought I knew but clearly didn't.

Maybe this was a joke, a blind, a farce. One more trick the man seemed intent on dispatching in my direction for reasons I couldn't begin to comprehend.

The only people waiting at the stop were a woman with an infant in a pushchair and an elderly man tugging a shopping trolley.

'Damn you,' I whispered. 'There has to be a reason...'

I so wanted those pages he'd stolen. I so needed to be able to prove Mia Haas's dream one way or another.

Then I heard it. A shout. A yell. English, I thought, a curse, inarticulate yet distinct. We were slowly curving in towards the jetty. I leaned over the side to look and saw the ever-attentive *marinaio* watching me from the cabin. He'd be out in a minute to deal with the passengers in any case. Someone else came behind me, then another. Locals heading to their cars I guessed.

Still no sign of Hazard. Then I heard those voices again and dashed to the other side of the boat. He wasn't on the jetty at all.

In the middle of the grey canal was a stationary speedboat, glossy white, pricey I imagined, open cabin, leather seats, hefty rear engine. Midships Rupert Hazard stood, two men with him, big men, angry men. The three of them in the midst of an argument.

Hazard had something in his hand. I recognised it immediately. The case I'd been given by a man in Vienna dressed as Mozart at the start of that extraordinary summer.

'Rupert!' I yelled.

Nothing. Either they were too far away, or he was too engaged to hear.

The vaporetto docked. I could hear people getting off, those two locals coming on. No one else seemed to notice this small drama taking place between the car park of Tronchetto and the abandoned jetties where vast cruise ships once disgorged their thousands of curious passengers.

The *marinaio* slammed the railings shut and we set off again, on towards Santa Marta and the Giudecca Canal. The speedboat with Hazard and those two men was behind us. I couldn't see what was happening anymore though it was clear any meeting with Hazard, an explanation, any chance of getting those pages back, was surely gone.

An engine fired up, a high-pitched powerful noise. I could just catch sight of the boat by leaning out of over the rail. Something that got the attention of the attendant who was swiftly over telling me to get back, tugging at my arm.

The sleek speedboat had come to life and was bobbing on the low waves, propelled at speed, a stranger at the wheel, no sign of Hazard anywhere. It cut in front of us, making the vaporetto skipper sound his horn, shriek a curse, hit reverse to slow us with a sudden, physical tug.

'What is this?' the young *marinaio* asked.

If only I knew.

There was what looked like a fight going on in the well of the boat, next to that familiar valise. Then my heart was in my mouth. Rupert Hazard was on his back, flailing helplessly with fists that connected with nothing, a look of abject terror on his face. The man over him had a gun, a black pistol, obvious now.

Two loud cracks, a cry of pain and shock, and the speedboat hit another gear, nose lurching towards the dimming sky then falling onto the grey water with a retort even louder than the weapon.

An elderly aunt from Rotherham once told me a shiver went through you when you saw someone die, that it was their spirit trying to hold on to you as it fled into the darkness. A ridiculous superstition I'd always thought, but at that moment I wasn't so sure.

I'd watched someone I knew, someone I felt sorry for in many ways, come to his end in a violent altercation on a fancy speedboat lurching along the canal outside Tronchetto, the most unlikely place for a man to die.

The vaporetto was stationary as we watched the slick vessel head out towards Giudecca and the vast expanse of the lagoon. The *marinaio* was shaking and murmuring a prayer. I wondered if I might faint.

A long moment after I saw the skipper was on the radio.

The oddest of things come into your head at these moments. Just then it was those verses that accompanied The Seasons. Written in the same hand that supposedly I'd seen already.

September was a day away. The arrival of autumn. I recalled the last of his words to go with the concerto of the season.

> *The hunter at the break of dawn goes hunting,*
> *With horns, and guns, and dogs keen on the trail;*
> *The animal runs off, with them in tow;*
> *In terror and half dead from the commotion*
> *Of guns and dogs, the beast, now wounded, tries*
> *To flee, but harried and exhausted, dies.*

I'd tried to find the beast.
I'd failed.
Watching that speedboat bob its way out of view I took a deep breath and called Valentina Fabbri.

Intermezzo II

All I knew of a Beretta 92 was the little I'd gathered from a YouTube video of a large Texan in a T-shirt blasting tin cans into tiny pieces in his backyard. Now one sat in front of me on the table of a deserted beach bar at the foot of the Lido, a winter sky descending, full moon, strips of grey cloud running like rips in a black velvet shroud.

Alone at that point. My companion had vanished behind the bar to make a call. On the dark horizon a vast ship, a tanker or some other commercial vessel, slipped slowly north to south. There were bird sounds nearby, gull squawks mingling with the hoots of waking owls in the woods behind the strand. A reminder that, dead and empty as this place appeared, it was all an illusion. Feral animals scuttled through the sand dunes, cats and foxes and wild dogs. Birds scavenged for carrion along the tide mark of the shore. A single small boat with a lamp was skirting off the coast, fishing I presumed.

There was life hiding everywhere. Behind in the brackish lagoon where locals trod through mud and shallow water seeking crabs and mantis shrimp, small creatures with a snap to their claws that could break a finger. Then, across the narrow strip of land on which I sat, in the Adriatic lay the mussel farms of Malamocco and vongole, clams, buried deep in the soft sand, waiting to be found.

The year before, one warm April day, I'd taken the boat to Treporti north of here and walked to Lio Piccolo after a tip from Luca. A good one as always. There, with not another soul around, I'd sat and watched a flock of flamingos tread like ballerinas through the marsh, dipping their inverted beaks into the water for food.

On my own then, wondering what the rest of that day would bring, I found myself regretting every lost moment, every day I'd stayed at home reading, being idle, making excuses instead of exploring every unknown inch of this place until I was sated and could take no more. Was that even possible? It was hard to know if you didn't try. Luca and Valentina had ensnared me in all this because they were worried I was becoming indolent, detached, sinking into the selfish, solitude of retirement, a place from which I might never return.

Though not when it came to the Vivaldi papers. They'd occupied me for most of that year, took me close to death, close to people I still didn't understand, people whose trust I needed though I doubted whether that was deserved. Close to places I would never have been had I stayed safe in London, a widower in quiet Wimbledon, days filled with little at all.

Life, it seemed to me, depended upon challenge, difficulty, threat, jeopardy. It was either that or slip slowly away into nothing.

I was lost in thought, listening to the unseen birds, the distant engines of the fishing boats on the water, the hum of a plane descending towards Marco Polo airport.

Then, with a suddenness that made me jump, a hand slammed on the table and a battery lantern came on.

'A successful call?' I asked.

'Oh yes,' came the reply.

'When, may I ask, do we leave this place? The concert—'

'The concert?'

'Yes,' I snapped. 'The concert.'

'Ah.' I was offered another glass of wine, which I declined. 'No concert for you, Signor Clover. I'm afraid you're otherwise engaged.'

Part Three

L'autunno, Autumn

Chapter Seven

Allegro

I awoke the morning after the Tronchetto incident in Santa Maria Maggiore. If this were Rome, an important pilgrim basilica, 'Our Lady of the Snows', named after a miracle when snow supposedly fell in August back in the fourth century, burial place for Napoleon's sister Pauline, several popes and the sculptor Bernini, the man who created so much of the city we see today.

Its Venetian equivalent is somewhat less grand, a wreck of a church, long abandoned, on the waterway bearing its name below the car parks of Piazzale Roma, not so far from Tronchetto, the place that put me there. The one modern legacy it's left us is the Casa Circondariale Santa Maria Maggiore di Venezia that envelops the site on all but the crumbling canal frontage. The city jail, not that most visitors realise there is one, a sizeable prison too, supposed to hold 160 male inmates though when I was banged up there, in a cell with a pickpocket from Mali and a Mestre drug dealer, both very chatty and pleasant fellows, the population had surged to something like 270.

The cell was hot, the bunk bed hard, the food passable, the puzzlement on my part overwhelming. I'd expected Valentina to be furious when she realised I'd headed off to meet Rupert Hazard on my own. I'd not foreseen she would turn up mob-handed with three accompanying police boats, order one of her minions to take me into custody, then run me round to Santa Maria Maggiore where a reluctant prison officer would, on her strict orders, confine me to a cell.

Not a word was spoken along the way. I was, it appeared, under some kind of arrest or unspecified detention, though for what I'd no idea.

Two days followed in complete ignorance and then it was September. The beginning of autumn, the third movement of Vivaldi's work. The composer's words for the season came back to me again...

> *the beast, now wounded, tries*
> *To flee, but harried and exhausted, dies.*

Poor Rupert. I'd never seen a man killed before, and it hurt and nagged at me, however much I had reason to detest the fellow.

On the third morning, after receiving endless advice from my cellmates about my rights and which lawyer to choose, the door swung open and I was ordered to go to the visiting room. There was Mia Haas, back in jeans, navy shirt and red linen jacket, golden hair in a ponytail, oscillating between apology and outrage.

'How can they do this to you, Arnold?' She sat on the other side of a metal table in a room empty save for a bored guard.

This was not, I suspected, a normal visiting session. Surely there would have been more people there for that.

'I was rather stupid,' I admitted and told her. Hazard had called and seemingly offered the Vivaldi papers. I decided to go along with the idea.

'You should have told me. I would have gone.'

'There wasn't time. As I said... the man sounded desperate. And besides I'd never have allowed it.'

That got me a severe look. 'I'm not a child in need of your protection. I was in Dubrovnik when there was a war on, a siege. We lost relatives in the fighting. They're not...' A shadow crossed her face and that made her look rather vulnerable for once. 'They're not the only ones either. You come from a part of the world that doesn't know much about life when everything falls apart. Count yourself lucky.'

Was that a reference to Marcus, the husband who put a gun to his head in the orchid house of the Maddalena? I wasn't sure.

'Anyway...' She looked a little apologetic for that outburst. 'When will they let you out of this dreadful place?'

'I've no idea. Did they say I'm being charged with something?'

'Ask your friend in the Carabinieri – she is your friend, isn't she? All I know is I got a call asking if I'd confirm you were still working for me. Something to do with a residency check to make sure you're not illegal. You are under scrutiny, you realise that, don't you?'

It felt as if I had been ever since Luca lured me to Giudecca that April.

'I am? Still working for you, that is?'

'Of course! I want that book. I need that book! Kravchuck will be back from America any day. You can start by picking his brains–'

'The papers are sensational. They say Vivaldi was Casanova's father. That he was just a much a womaniser as his son.'

She gasped, wide-eyed. 'How can you possibly know? We don't have any papers. That bastard stole them when he nearly killed you.'

Clearly, I had some confessions to make. I told her about the USB stick I'd been given in Vienna, how Luca and I had sat down and gone through the contents, a little of what we'd found.

Mia glared at me. 'You tell me this now?'

'I didn't want to get your hopes up. In case it was a blind. A joke. One more trick. Nothing of use.'

'And is it? Can you tell from what you have?'

The million-dollar question as they say. 'I honestly don't know. Any more than Luca. We can run checks on the hand-writing again, the contents. The language used. From what we've seen it looks authentic. Or perhaps the most convincing forgery either of us is likely to encounter.'

She folded her arms and waited.

'The only way we could be sure is if we obtain the originals. The papers.'

'Which seems unlikely, doesn't it?'

Dammit. If only I'd got to Tronchetto earlier. Hazard might still be alive. I might be in possession of the key to this whole mystery. 'Mia. Who knows the papers were stolen?'

A shrug. 'You. Me. Your Carabinieri friend. I haven't adver-tised the fact we've lost what might be the most important docu-ments concerning Vivaldi anyone's ever seen. Why would I?'

'Then keep it that way. Let's make vague noises about the discovery of some extraordinary historical documents that will change the way the world will think about Vivaldi forever. Leave it there.'

'Are you sure?'

'Anything but. I'm dancing in the dark.'

Mia reached across the table and took my hand. 'You're not dancing alone...'

'Please. Just do as I ask. I'll share the score with Kravchuck and ask for his word he'll keep all this secret. Between us, Luca, me, him, perhaps someone I haven't thought of, it may be possible to verify the material to an acceptable degree even if we never find those pages.'

She took her hand away. 'I don't deserve this. I don't pay you enough for all you've gone through. The train. Now...' She glanced around the bare room. 'Jail, for God's sake...'

The guard's phone trilled. He took the call, listened, then looked at us. 'Signore, you need to go back to your cell,' he said. 'You, signora, must leave.'

'I was promised an hour!'

'I'm sorry. I have my orders.' He opened the door. 'The Carabinieri are on their way. They wish to interview the prisoner. You must go.'

Thirty minutes later the same guard was back and told me to collect my things.

'What things?' I wondered.

He grunted something inaudible, I said farewell and good luck to my baffled cellmates, the drug dealer and the pickpocket, and there ended my first and, I trust, only spell in the clink. That was a side of Venice I had no wish to meet again.

Outside, on the doorstep of the jail few but locals know exists, I blinked at the sunlight. The prison was just around the corner from the Rio Terà dei Pensieri, a charming little street where I frequented the small twice weekly organic market. Back then I'd noticed a guard rail running along the wall a few metres out and signs warning people to stay back. Now I knew why.

September. But still hot. Was this autumn? The seasons played tricks these days.

Valentina was on the deck of a sleek Carabinieri launch, arms crossed, face stony.

'I can walk, thank you,' I said, trying not to sound hurt.

'No, you can't. Get in.'

'Am I a free man or not?'

'Get in. Don't make me any more cross than I am already.'

Two officers up front, I took the leather bench seat inside opposite her. 'Am I to be charged then?'

'With what?'

'You tell me! You're the one who threw me into prison.'

She snorted. 'No less than you deserve. You swan off directly after we've talked and go to meet the man who tried to murder you. If idiocy was a custodial offence, I could have you locked up for that.'

'But it isn't.'

'Lucky for you.'

The boat rounded the corner into the Giudecca Canal. Home wasn't so far away. Or the Teatro Maddalena. I would have taken either at that moment.

'Then why? You barely gave me a chance to explain.'

Another sigh, then she took an iPad out of her briefcase and turned on the screen. Venice is covered with CCTV cameras, far more than most people realise. It's also scanned for mobile phone signals constantly. Few cities have such intense surveillance, all supposedly to monitor tourist numbers.

'You recognise this man?'

I could see myself walking past the Frari to pick up the vaporetto. She pointed out a figure in the busy crowd around the basilica, dark T-shirt, sunglasses and a black baseball cap pulled low over his face.

'Should I?'

No answer but then she switched to me striding through Campo San Tomà. Finally, the boat. He was with me all the way.

'You'd no idea you were being followed?'

'Of course not. Why would anyone follow me?'

She put a finger to her lips, a sarcastic gesture. 'Perhaps to find out where you were going? Just a guess.'

'They knew where I was going. They had hold of poor Hazard by the time I got there.'

'True. But perhaps they didn't when you set off. Alternatively...'

This had occurred to me already. 'Alternatively, they wanted to seize me if I got hold of Hazard's case.'

'Quite. In which case you might be dead too. For real this time. Arnold, you presented me with a deeply awkward situation. It was very clear a man had been stalking you and perhaps he was still around. The fellow got off at Tronchetto, but we lost him after that. I had an investigation to assemble and you standing around looking lost for words and very embarrassed, with good reason I might add. So, for your own safety...'

'You threw me in a cell with a drug dealer and a pickpocket.'

'It worked, didn't it?'

'And was not in the least way a kind of punishment?'

'What an outrageous suggestion. Do you think I'm that vindictive?' She reached over and tapped my knee. 'I wanted you out of harm's way until I could work out what on earth was going on.'

'And?'

'Still thinking about it.'

'I'd really like to go home.'

'Did Mia Haas tell you anything when she came to visit?'

'Only that you'd been checking up on me. Making sure I still worked for her.'

She grimaced. 'The immigration people were asking. I've put that one to bed. If you were convicted of something criminal here that would affect your residency.'

'I'm not a criminal and have no intention to embark upon that career at this late stage of life, thank you.'

'Just as well.'

We were past Zattere, Zitelle on the other side of the canal. I could see that alley I'd walked down with Luca in April and found myself enmeshed in the mysteries of Vivaldi, of Mia Haas and the Teatro Maddalena.

'You can go home in a little while. There's something I want to show you.'

We rounded the Punta della Dogana and that famous view of the city lay in front of us. Most days it never failed to raise my spirits. This time, not so much. The boat kicked up a gear and powered on. I had an inkling where we were headed. The marina on Sant'Elena near the football ground. I'd seen Carabinieri activity around there before.

'We found it,' Valentina said.

'What?'

'The speedboat you saw.'

'What about Rupert Hazard?'

She shrugged. 'They went out to sea. Our radar tracked them across the lagoon, but only as far as that. This was all planned. They must have met someone. The speedboat was stolen from a very unhappy hotelier. An expensive and recent one. It was scuttled off Malamocco, half sunk, a hole punched in the side with a pickaxe or something. Where they went, north, south, I've no idea. But we are looking.'

'I asked about Rupert Hazard.'

The look on her face told me this was a question she didn't want. 'If they'd dumped his body overboard in the lagoon, we'd have it by now. Most of the water is shallow, and in lots of places there's not much current to take away anything of size. But they didn't. The Adriatic is not a large and brackish puddle, part marsh, part mudbanks. If the tide is kind, perhaps he'll be washed our way. On past experience I'd say that's unlikely. Your friend has vanished, and all his secrets with him.'

'I do wish you'd stop saying that. He wasn't my friend.'

'No? Then I'm sorry.'

'And now, I imagine, you're back on the case?'

It was never easy to read Capitano Valentina Fabbri. When she heard a question she didn't want to answer, all she did was ignore it.

'I'll fix a ride home once we're done. Let me be blunt... you're badly in need of a shower and a change of clothes.'

We docked near the football stadium and walked to a small secure jetty by the side. The fancy speedboat I'd seen that night was there, fancy no longer. There was a name on the bows, 'Aurora' and the logo of one of the city hotels. It now looked a wreck, the leather seats stained with sea water and weed, torn, ruined. A couple of men in boiler suits, forensic officers I assumed, were clambering over the hull, taking pictures, prodding with tools.

The sight of the thing brought back a host of unpleasant memories. The look on Rupert Hazard's face as he struggled against his attackers. The sound of two gunshots. The ferocity of the fight as I stood helpless on the vaporetto as it docked at Tronchetto. Violence was rare in Venice, as Valentina so frequently said. Even among drunken tourists who would other-wise behave abominably, with no respect to the city or its inhab-itants, fisticuffs seldom happened, only noise and nuisance.

I was tempted to think it was time to abandon writing and music altogether, and the increasingly fanciful idea of piecing together a life of the mystifying composer Antonio Vivaldi out of very little at all. Save for those photographs of pages that may or may not have been genuine. A louder, more determined part of me said – no screamed – that now more than ever I had to go on. Three men were dead, Marcus Haas, that charming ad man on the train, a shady musician who had tried to take my own life. I'd run to Venice in the first place after Eleanor's death, lost and a little fearful. I was going to run no more.

'You're not asking any questions,' said Valentina.

'Such as?'

'Such as... have we found anything?'

I stared at the deck. 'I don't imagine there was blood.'

'It spent half a day sunk in the Adriatic. What do you think?'

'Is there nothing? No trace of the man at all?'

Another pained sigh. 'If you wish to remove all proof of your presence at a murder, I can think of no better way than dumping the scene of the crime in the Adriatic. Where we only chance upon it by accident when a fishing boat reports the thing's there, half submerged. Can you?'

'It's not an area where I pretend to have any experience.'

Valentina laughed and touched my arm. 'Sorry. I shouldn't find that funny.'

'Then why–?'

'You're remarkably sly for an Englishman at times.'

'No, I'm not.'

'Ha! It's one reason you never told me you were going to

meet Rupert Hazard. You wanted to solve this for yourself. You seek the glory.'

I shook my head. 'Rubbish. I don't give a fig about glory. It's simply that I have a job to do. I told Mia Haas I'd do it, and I don't like taking people's money for something I don't deliver. I wanted those pages. The way Hazard spoke, it sounded as if he was desperate for me to have them.'

'You mean he was scared?'

To be honest, I wasn't entirely sure. 'Possibly. It was a brief and unexpected conversation. I realise people in your line of work believe civilians should remember every word people say and the inflection with which they were spoken. Life isn't that simple.'

'So not scared? Simply anxious?'

'Yes. Now, I imagine we understand why.'

A squeeze of my arm then. 'At the risk of repeating myself... you might have died too. If you'd got there sooner. These men who came for him had you in their sights too.'

It was nearly four. The heat was falling the way it did when summer afternoons edged towards autumn. I felt exhausted – sleep was not easy in a cell – and more than a touch grumpy. Valentina was playing some kind of game, I felt sure.

'You brought me all the way here to tell me this?'

'Quite an important lesson, don't you think?'

'One you could just as easily have delivered in jail. Why am I here?'

She turned to one of the forensic officers. 'Gianluca! Go fetch.'

He went into the cabin by the jetty. I caught my breath as he came back out. In his hand, much as it was when I'd last seen it two nights before as Hazard and his attackers wrestled over the thing, was the leather valise from Vienna.

Gianluca walked over and placed it on the jetty.

'Wait,' I said. 'I know little makes sense here, but this really takes the biscuit.'

'Biscuit?' Valentina wondered. 'Why the hell are you talking about biscuits? What on earth would make these men you saw want one?'

'It's... it's a turn of phrase. An English one. We can speak Italian if you like.'

'I prefer English for times like this. It's easier to see when you're being evasive.'

'I am not being evasive! Anything but. Hazard summoned me to Tronchetto to hand this over. The men who murdered him... I assumed that was what they came for.'

Valentina nodded. 'You do?'

'What do you want of me?'

'The case is locked. A number code. We can force it, of course. But I did wonder if you might know a better way.'

A stray thought occurred to me, a ridiculous one surely. Was the Palazzo Maddalena bugged? Did Valentina know already I had a code from Vienna?

'I can try,' I said, then picked it up and selected the same numbers that had unlocked the USB stick, 4 March, sixteen seventy-eight, 431678.

The latch flicked up.

'You are a source of surprise at times.'

'*Prego.*'

We both gazed at the contents of the case, drenched, curling at the edges, ruined.

'Well,' she continued, 'I imagine we know now why they never took it.'

There was nothing there but reams and reams of blank pages, the kind an office might use for a printer. And a bundle of scraps of notation paper, an identical smeary set of notes in blue ink on each. It was hard to tell exactly but I recognised the look of the Devil's Tritone by now. The man I knew as Rupert Hazard appeared to have died in the presence of the same strange auguries he'd been sending others.

'And why,' I added, 'they killed him.'

'Because...?'

'Because Rupert Hazard was far too wily a man to walk around with the real treasure at the end of his arm. He must have used it as bait. And refused whatever offer they made.'

A smile. 'Very good. You must not talk about any of this now.'

'What? What? A man was murdered.'

'Was he?'

'I saw it. So did the *marinaio* on the vaporetto.'

She shook her head. 'We interviewed him. He confirms there was some sort of violent disturbance on the boat. Then it sped off. Nothing more.'

'There were two shots.'

'I know you think that. But the vaporetto assistant was quite unclear on that point. Look at the boat. There are no signs of a bullet.'

I was getting mad. 'Would there be if someone got shot?' A frown, a shrug. 'Someone's told you to cover this up.'

'Don't be conspiratorial. It's not like you. The media reported what is known. There was a disturbance on a boat near Tronchetto. Nothing more. Please don't go round spreading rumours saying this Hazard man has been killed. There's no solid evidence to support that and as far as we're concerned he remains on our wanted list.'

I was speechless.

'You can go home now,' she added.

'Thanks a bundle. The lift?'

She was staring at her phone, clearly displeased by what

was there. 'We have to go elsewhere. You know the way to the Sant'Elena stop from here, I'm sure. And...' The Fabbri finger wag, close and in my face. 'The next time a criminal wishes to meet you, make sure I'm informed in advance.'

'I very much doubt–'

'Who's to know? Remember this. You won't get out of jail a second time so easily. Remember, too, what I said about your residency status. I'd hate to have to repatriate you back to London. As much as you'd detest that idea yourself.'

And so autumn began. With a dead man I wasn't supposed to mention, a stolen wrecked boat, and a leather valise full of nothing but soaking blank paper. Oh, and the nagging, inescapable conviction in my thick head that, come what may, I was going to deliver Mia Haas's book, penetrate the fog of mystery surrounding Antonio Vivaldi, and reveal the man for who he truly was.

Never had I thought of myself as an obsessive man. It's Venice that does that to you, or so I plead, m'lud. There's something about this strange, unique city, its culture, its history, those dark secrets lurking in the inky shadows, that draws you in so slyly then refuses to let you go. I'd walked out of one jail in Santa Maria Maggiore into the lovelier, more inescapable prison that was now my home.

Time for sustenance. I stopped off at my favourite bar for a much-needed Negroni followed by a chicken kebab from a spot in Calle Crosera. No one lives off pizza and pasta alone. This was work food and drink, and work, I understood, was what I was going to face for weeks if not months to come if I was to crack this curious conundrum.

Whatever Valentina Fabbri claimed, Rupert Hazard had

surely died for it, as she well knew. However hard I racked my tortured head, I couldn't begin to understand why, or fathom what he'd intended that night he'd summoned me to Tronchetto. Had he intended to cheat me with his valise full of blank pages? How? I'd nothing to offer, no money, no escape from the forces who were surely hunting him.

Perhaps he thought I might take the case for nothing as an unexpected gift, without checking the contents till later. Perhaps – and this sounded both convincing and depressing at the same time – he knew other criminals were watching him, and, by passing the supposedly precious papers on to me, he might throw them off his trail. Which might well mean I was the dead man for real this time, not him. There was a kind of sense to that idea. All the same a nagging feeling refused to go away. Rupert Hazard made a passable impression of a rogue in the brief time I knew him. Despite all the plentiful evidence, I still struggled to see him as an outright villain capable of murder.

And where might those original pages – if they existed – be now? Valentina and her team had been all over the small apartment four doors away that Hazard had kept on – and visited – unknown to me. There was nothing there, or so she said and on that, anyway, I'd no reason to doubt her. Hazard, from what we'd learned earlier, wasn't working on his own. Someone had helped him escape Venice in the first place. The men who shot him on that stolen boat? Had he cheated them as he seemed to be about to cheat me? Yet it seemed clear they didn't possess the pages either. If they did, why pursue poor, doomed Rupert in the first place?

No. If the mysterious treasure trove I supposedly picked up outside the Karlskirche existed, he must have hidden it. Or placed the things in the possession of another party connected to this strange tale, someone he trusted. But who? He'd never mentioned any acquaintances in Venice, one reason he was always pestering me to join him for a drink. If anything, it was in the small orchestra of the Teatro Maddalena that he had anyone who might have passed as a friend. Reggie Davies, perhaps. The woman who was contracted to edit my book if ever I came to write it. Someone who surely stood to benefit if I could make it as sensational as Mia Haas hoped.

Or Mia herself.

Or Peter Lombardo, the curious gardener who seemed scared of setting foot outside Giudecca.

Or any one of the other players in Andriy Kravchuck's little orchestra.

I soon found myself drowning in conspiracies and suspicion. All of which went nowhere at all.

This was a two Negroni problem if ever there was one. It was late, but I needed to get out. The bar was busy with university students mostly, happy young things from Ca' Foscari around the corner, all in their early twenties, embarking on the rest of their lives without so much as a care.

Giorgio, the barman, caught my mood. 'Another? Really?'

'Yes. Really.'

'No need to be snappy. You've been leading a busy life from what I gather.'

My ears pricked up at that. 'People have been talking?'

'Luca. The man from the Archivio. He was in last night asking about you. How you were. He seemed concerned. He was worried. He said he couldn't find you.'

'Of course he couldn't. I was in Santa Maria Maggiore. The prison.'

He nearly dropped his tray. 'Are you serious?'

'A case of mistaken identity. All settled now.'

He went away and came back with the drink. 'That's your last one for tonight.'

~

The next morning, I met Luca for coffee and a pastry at our usual table. He looked pleased to see me if a little evasive.

Before I could speak, he waved a hand and said, 'I spoke to Valentina this morning. Now I know all about this nonsense with the jail. Let me say from the outset... she overstepped the mark. Uncharacteristic of her. She's usually much more measured. It was shameful. I told her myself, quite directly.'

'How did she take it?'

He grimaced. 'You can imagine, I'm sure.'

'Was it bad?'

'Well...' He stirred a second sachet of sugar into his macchiato. 'She didn't throw me into a prison cell. Though perhaps it was a close thing. No wonder that husband of hers works most nights in his restaurant. Much as I love and admire our mutual friend, she can scare the living daylights out of you. I think she relishes it too.'

'She said she did it for my safety.'

'Oh.'

'She didn't tell you that.'

'It's Valentina! She's never going to tell anyone a thing unless she wants to. All she said was that there'd been an unfortunate misunderstanding. One that's now dealt with.' He hesitated. 'She didn't elaborate except to say you did something stupid. Something you shouldn't.'

No point in hiding it, and besides I wanted to see his reaction. 'Rupert Hazard called me and said he had the Vivaldi memoirs. He seemed keen – no, desperate – to give them back. He wanted to meet me by the Tronchetto vaporetto stop.'

He gasped. 'Wait. The papers said there was some kind of violent incident in Tronchetto. The Carabinieri are looking into it.'

'Some kind of violent incident? I saw two men shoot him. In a boat they'd stolen from some hotelier.'

'Good god!'

'He was murdered. Not that I'm supposed to tell anyone. Valentina is pretending nothing really happened. Didn't the papers say much...?'

'Haven't you looked?'

'I've been banged up in jail for one thing. Since she let me out, I've had a few other things on my mind.'

'All they said was what I told you. Those car parks can be a bit dodgy sometimes. But you're sure... murder?'

No body. No one arrested. Just a boat half sunk off Malamocco and a case full of blank pages ruined by seawater. Not much of a story if you left out my part of it. 'I know what I saw.'

'And he had the Vivaldi papers?'

'No. At least not with him. Or so it seems.'

'Very strange.'

'You could say that.'

We got two more coffees then he asked, 'So what next?'

'I give up on the whole thing. The Teatro Maddalena. Vivaldi. Writing a book. It's not for me. Never was. Also, I did not enjoy spending time in jail.'

He stared at me wide-eyed. 'But Mia Haas? I thought she was counting on you. And the money, Arnold. She's been paying you quite a lot, hasn't she?'

I'd thought this through already. 'That's true. But I can't cope. There are hundred and twenty-three pages supposedly written by Vivaldi on that memory stick. They need translating. It's not easy Italian. Quite beyond me.'

'Your grasp of the language is very good and getting better by the day.'

'That's not the point. Someone tried to kill me. I saw the man they think responsible murdered in front of my eyes, and I'm supposed to believe I didn't. Do I really want to continue dipping my toes into these shark-infested waters?'

'Hmmm.'

'Is that it? Hmmm?'

'What is it you're really asking me?'

'I wasn't aware I was asking anything.'

'Stop this!' For once, Luca looked quite cross. 'It's not like you to be evasive.'

'Why not? Everyone else is round here.'

'But not you! Dearie me. You've changed since you became embroiled in this Vivaldi business. I used to think you were the only chap I knew who needed to go on an anger management course to find some. Now it seems you can get snippy at the tiniest of remarks.'

I jabbed a finger at him. 'Since you embroiled me.'

He squirmed a little and glanced at his watch. 'I rest my case. There's a meeting I need to attend.'

'Cheerio.'

'If you give up on the book, you give up on Mia Haas. You realise you probably condemn the whole idea to its doom.'

'I repeat. Someone nearly killed me. I just saw a man murdered.'

'Some people, the English in particular I was always led to believe, would see this as more of a reason to continue than give up.'

'Perhaps I'm becoming Venetian then.'

Luca took some cash out of his pocket and slapped it on the bar. 'Very well, my friend. How many pages?'

'I said. One hundred and twenty-three. You've seen what they look like.'

'Send me half...'

'No. I send you the lot. You translate all those scribbles into

English, or normal Italian if you prefer, and push them back to me.'

'While you?'

'Fact checking. Lie checking. Call it what you will. If the dates and places add up, then everything is genuine. Or we have a master forger on our hands.'

He said nothing.

'And when I manage to get Andriy Kravchuck to myself, I ask him his opinion of the music. Whether he really feels we're in possession of a genuine draft of The Seasons in Vivaldi's own hand.'

Luca hesitated. I had him.

'This will take weeks,' he said.

'We've waited almost three centuries. Is that so much to ask?'

It was three days before Luca's transcriptions started to turn up, and then only in a trickle. In the meantime, I'd concluded I was sick of being driven by the actions and needs of others. There's a simple truth in life. You're on the way up. Or the way down. The idea you can simply stay somewhere between the two, idling, is nonsense. Stasis is for dreamers.

Luca's remark about anger management, and how I was changing, was a reminder. It was time to rise above the sorry mess I'd found myself in. I called Mia and kept it brief, telling her I needed to dive deep into my research material. This meant I would be offline for a period I couldn't at that moment esti-mate. She was puzzled and begged me to come to the palazzo to discuss it over lunch. There was a chef being tested to see if he could start a restaurant there and a *cicchetti* bar attached to the Teatro. Matters were moving, with Kravchuck and Ellen Kim back in harness, and musicians – quite a few new apparently – starting to fall into shape with occasional concerts for pensioners in the neighbouring public blocks.

She never mentioned Rupert Hazard and seemed quite unaware anything connected me with the soon-forgotten story of a violent incident at Tronchetto. When Valentina wished to kill a story, she made very sure it stayed stone dead.

With a polite refusal, I set about a concerted period of malingering, thinking, reading, imagining, phone switched off, email on autoresponder with a vague reply for everyone who tried to contact me saying I'd get back to them when I could. I kept away from San Pantalon as much as possible since I'd no wish to deal with a knock on the door.

The weather was fine, with none of the August heat. Ideal for navigating the lagoon on any vaporetto I fancied. On Torcello I reacquainted myself with the apocalyptic devils on the walls of the cathedral. Around Treporti I found old forts and batteries and Roman remains I'd long promised myself I'd one day see. One Wednesday I took the fast Number Six to the Lido and then a bus to Malamocco, stared at the grey Adriatic thinking about a wrecked stolen speedboat and a man whose death seemed unremarked, quite forgotten. After that, I ate some local mussels steamed with pepper, since Malamocco is famous for the things.

Desperate to stay away from home and all attention, I splashed out fifty euros on a Friends of the Museums of Venice card and set out to explore the odder outposts, beyond the usual Doge's Palace and Museo Correr. On Burano I learned about lace. In the Palazzo Mocenigo I sniffed the ingredients of perfume, discovered the complexities of scent, and how far musk and spice and exotic flowers travelled to fill the boudoirs of women across Europe. The best part of an afternoon passed in the Museo Fortuny, once home to the

Spaniard Mario Fortuny y Madrazo, a polymath who painted, took exquisite photographs, was both fashion and stage designer, and an inventor of advanced stage lighting techniques.

In short, I buried myself in parts of Venice I'd heard of but never found time to enjoy, always dismissing them as visits for another day, one that might never arrive due to my growing indolence as I settled into a comfortable, solitary retirement. A lazy state of mind now banished by events, few, if any, planned.

Each night I hooked up the laptop to the internet only briefly, enough to download Luca's daily delivery of translated pages. The trickle of emails – from Mia, a fishing expedition from Reggie asking if she could see early pages, and the usual rubbish – all ignored. In the end, Mia pushed a note through my letter box while I was out watching locals delve in the mud for gobies off Burano. She sounded hurt and worried so I dashed back a quick reply saying I was making slow but steady progress, and would be in touch soon.

Then, on the first of October, the best part of a month spent in delightful discovery of sides of Venice I mostly never knew existed, and a good deal of thought about Luca's documentation of the Vivaldi papers, I emailed her again.

The next day I would be back in the Palazzo Maddalena, working there much of the time, in need of the office she'd so kindly provided and some time with Andriy Kravchuck.

The hunter at the break of dawn goes hunting...

After which I called Valentina Fabbri and in as calm and apologetic voice as I could muster said, 'I'm back in business, capitano, working on the book. I'm sorry for any awkwardness my foolish decisions may have caused you. I promise that won't happen again.'

There was a long pause and then she asked in a distinctly puzzled voice, 'Are you all right?'

'Never better. Must rush.'

Head clearer than at any time since Vienna, I caught the Number Two to Zitelle. The Maddalena estate was quite transformed. Lombardo, that odd gardener, must have called in reinforcements. The flower beds were blooming with roses, geraniums and lilies. The vegetable patch showed a tiny row of what I assumed to be artichokes rising for the spring, lettuce and carrots alongside them, and a small patch of thistly cardoons.

A red and gold banner now fluttered from a flagpole in a newly cobbled square between the theatre and the palazzo, the lion of Venice, waving gently in the soft marine breeze. The auditorium was empty. No one there I thought until I saw a bobbing head of lurid purple hair emerge from the foyer and a voice called out, 'Bloody hell, Clover. Where do you think you've been?' Reggie Davies was on me like a shot.

I lugged my shoulder bag around me and steeled myself for the storm. 'Hello,' I said. 'How's things?'

'Hello my arse. We've a book to get out and you've gone awol for weeks. I want to see early copy. I demand it. I'm your editor. To think I gave you free Whitby parkin too.'

'Ah.'

'What do you mean... ah?'

I'd prepared for this, not that I expected to be bearded by her quite so soon. 'You see I've been looking into this writing thing. It seems to me there are two sorts of author.'

'If only...'

'Those who need editorial support, a comfort blanket if you like. Advice on how to start, how to continue, how to correct the way the ship is steering when you're off course.'

She folded her arms and gave me a stern look. 'And?'

'Those who prefer to get it all down in one go then return to the beginning and fix things.' I smiled. 'With a great editor's assistance of course. I've decided I'm the latter variety.'

'You've never written a book in your life.'

'True. But I've read lots. And you gave me such admirable guidance at the beginning. A world to enclose the story. Characters to populate it. Events that bring the narrative to life. Matters are in hand.'

Reggie growled. 'Have you written a single word?'

'I repeat. Matters are in hand.'

'And this new material Mia was hinting at? The historical documents, whatever they are?'

'Don't you know?'

'Ha! I'm in the dark. I haven't the foggiest.'

This was a struggle. 'I'm assembling a good deal of research. It's taking a while.'

'You're dodging the question.'

'Yes.' I smiled. 'I am. Not now, Reggie. Please.'

'When do I get first look at some copy?'

'By February.

'The first.'

'In an ideal world. I prefer to think of it as a target for the month, rather than a particular day. How about that?'

'How about when you've written the first chapter?'

'I refer you to my previous answer. Were I to show you the first chapter I'd be asking your opinion about something I'd doubtless want to change once I'd finished the last. It's your time I'm thinking of. Honestly.'

Mia Haas was calling my name from the balcony of the palazzo, looking delighted, asking me to come in.

'It seems,' I added, 'the boss needs me.'

'What happened to your curious friend Rupert Hazard?'

That was the last question I wanted. 'I don't know what you mean.'

'Oh, come off it. He was a decent enough cellist, but I never had him down as a criminal. Now it seems no one knows where he's gone. Or why. What this business with that dead man at the station was. That's all been swept under the rug, hasn't it? I know the chap was supposed to be an Austrian but all the same...'

'No, no. Rupert Hazard was an acquaintance. I barely knew the man.'

'Lucky, he called you.'

'Which I never liked.'

'I did say. Never trust a man who speaks in E-flat minor.'

'You did. And what key am I?'

She wrinkled her nose. 'Good question. I had you down as something simple and monophonic. Like a plainchant. Now I'm not so sure. Not at all.'

'Pleased to hear it, Reggie. And you?'

She chuckled. 'Me? I'm any damned thing I like. Anal Seepage in Barcelona, if you recollect. A photocopier of manuscripts in publishers. A workaday musician thereafter. On the side, editor to a chap who's never produced a single book let alone shown me a single sentence he's actually written.'

To my relief, Mia intervened and cried out, 'Arnold! Are you coming up or not?'

Reggie's eyes narrowed and she muttered, 'Never mind. Your mistress calls.'

The lower floors of the palazzo had workmen in them, all the accoutrements of a hotel in the making. Beds and bathroom fittings, chairs and lighting. Mia showed me around the level beneath her apartment. Eight suites finished, all very fancy with views of the garden where Peter Lombardo was busy in a flower bed outside the orchid house.

'Looks lovely,' I said. 'And expensive.'

'It is. Sadly, budgeting isn't my strong point. However...' She cheered up and clapped her hands. 'We have our first customers. Two rooms reserved! I've set the date for the opening concert. New Year's Eve. Andriy is agreeable and the musicians all have it in their diaries.'

'I won't have a book by then.'

'I know, I know. Come upstairs for a drink.'

Her quarters had changed. New furniture and flowers everywhere. The sign of a woman determined to stamp her own identity on a home that was, before, shared with the husband she'd lost. She poured two glasses of Soave Classico, and we went outside and sat on the balcony beneath the shade of a gigantic parasol. Out of the wind, in weak October sun, it felt quite warm.

'Valentina Fabbri has been asking questions again. Though I imagine you know that already.'

'Yes.'

'She said she needed something on paper to show you were being paid here. I sent proof off straight away, of course. It's probably none of my business... why she wanted to know, that is.'

'She's not happy I went to meet Hazard without telling her.'

'She's not the only one. It seems rash. Which isn't you.'

The wine went down too quickly. She dashed inside and came back with a refill and a plate of fruit, peaches from the garden.

'Please don't keep things from me again. You do trust me, don't you?'

'Of course.'

A pause. Then she frowned and said, 'That came easily. A

very English response. The way you always say when asked about a meal you've eaten or a book you've read... it's fine. Even – sometimes especially – when it's not. You can speak the truth. I prefer that.'

On the spot.

'I trust you. Why wouldn't I?'

She winced. 'Lord knows I think I've given you plenty of reasons. The whole mess this place was in for starters.'

I said nothing.

'You vanished, Arnold. I was worried.'

'Busy.'

'With the book?'

'I've nothing else right now.'

There was an awkward silence then, one I didn't know how to break. Mia did, of course. I could imagine she once worked in public relations. She was very good at filling in awkward gaps in conversations, talking to strangers as if she knew them, mixing, engaging with people. Schmoozing I guess some people would call it. Everything I was terrible at.

She took me through the marketing plan she'd assembled with an agency. A handsome logo for hotel and theatre, a violin imposed against a silhouette of the portrait with the wig. Adverts for the international media. A press release announcing the New Year's Eve concert and invitations for local dignitaries. The dream was starting to become real, or so it seemed. There was even a rough cover for my book, though no title for it yet. That, Reggie Davies insisted, could only come once I'd delivered the manuscript.

We walked the grounds before I left and she told me her plans for the gardens, how Lombardo was bringing in specialists to plant some exotic species that would come to life in spring and last through summer.

'The seasons,' she said with a broad smile. 'Don't you love

them? This place felt dead when we moved in. Even back in April, I think. So much to do. So much uncertainty. But now...'

'You've transformed the place,' I said.

'No. We've transformed it. Peter Lombardo. Andriy and his little orchestra. You with your patience and your curiosity, and your book which I know will be a marvel. We all did it.' She rushed forward and took me by the shoulders, beaming, damp eyed. 'I believe it now, Arnold. We're nearly there.'

Chapter Eight

Adagio molto

Slowly the months slip from season to season, barely noticed until the day you open the front door and find yourself going back inside for a scarf to keep out the sudden razor-like breeze. By the middle of October, the city was well on the way towards its midwinter slumber, fewer visitors, the Biennale winding down, no great cultural events, spaces on the vaporetti where, six weeks before, one had to squeeze into a grumpy crowd and stand.

The days grow ever shorter, the weather more uncertain. Rain and mist slip over the lagoon in a grey shroud, harbingers of the denser fogs to come. The colours on the market stalls change from the vivid shades of summer fruit to the soft yellow of finferli mushrooms, the chestnut brown of porcini, the golden skins of squash, prized, expensive treasures turned into gnocchi and spread across pizzas.

Every month is different in Venice. Vivaldi, a knowledge-able local, understood this intimately, which is why his words and the music for *The Four Seasons* ring so true. Even if some of the verses clearly refer to the mainland, *terraferma,* probably observations from his time in Mantua where, from 1718 to 1720, he was employed as maestro di cappella, chamber music director for the court of the music-loving Prince Philip of Hesse-Darmstadt, viceroy there for the Austrians.

There. You see how examining so closely the chronology of his life was beginning to seep into my thoughts, month by month, year by year, from existing proven sources like Keller's book and the images left for me on a train next to a dead man while I struggled for breath by his side.

Long days spent going through Luca's steady but desperately slow stream of translations, poring over them, making notes, filing them carefully as only an old archivist would. Then taking the Number Two over to Giudecca, slipping into the palazzo and trying to get to the office without anyone noticing. Mia Haas most of all. Her presence was delightful, enticing, made me feel alive in a way I hadn't in quite a while. The last thing I needed at that moment.

I took in my laptop, copied the information I needed from the academic sources she'd arranged, then hotfooted it out of there as quickly as I could. I'd set myself a goal. By the end of the month, with Luca's help, more reading, and the databases I had access to in the palazzo, I would decide, once and for all, whether the documents I had could be regarded as genuine, without the original pages or not.

A foolish ambition perhaps, but one forged of necessity. If I was going to write this book – and it seemed to me I must – then I had to start soon. To begin, I needed to appreciate the length and breadth of Vivaldi's extraordinary career, from the existing sources and what I had begun to think of as The Stick Papers. It was quite a challenge. As the delivery of translations from Luca grew, I began to doubt I would ever get to grips with the full weight and detail of the correspondence on hand.

There was one other reason behind this obsessive behaviour. By burying myself in the minutiae of Vivaldi's career, real and perhaps imagined, I was able to blot out all the misgivings I had about the pages, the project, about Mia more than anything. No thoughts of Rupert Hazard or an incident on a speedboat outside Tronchetto, both of which seemed to have slipped the mind of Valentina Fabbri. All I heard from that direction was an invitation in the middle of the month to join her on her day off at Ugo's bar in the outer depths of Castello where we had the usual *cicchetti* and spritz, and for once made small talk about the weather, a small local scandal involving the administration, and how her husband's restaurant was faring amidst the continuing rise in the price of food.

She was fishing, of course, but I had nothing to place on her hook of any moment. At least it appeared I'd been forgiven for the way I'd failed to tell her about my appointment with Hazard at the end of August. Forgiven, never forgotten. That, I had come to realise, was Valentina Fabbri's way.

We chatted, parted company with an embrace, and it was back to The Stick Papers, Mia Haas's office, and the now large database of documents and notes I'd assembled in a research app on my laptop.

One rainy evening in the second week of the month Luca delivered the last batch of translations with a grudging note saying he'd found the task, and the raw material, unusually taxing. How much he believed what he'd translated he never revealed.

There was only one thing for it. He'd got me into the mystery of the Teatro Maddalena through that boozy meal in Ai Pugni.

It was time to return the favour.

I called him, aware I was probably interrupting an evening

with one of his girlfriends. But no, he was on his own and sounded pensive.

After fulsome thanks for all his work, I said, 'Please give me two days to analyse these last pages. Then I owe you lunch at our favourite table. It's booked. I'm paying.'

He seemed surprised. 'My turn, surely?'

'It's always your turn. One way or another, you've been keeping me since I came here. I have my own money now, Luca. Thanks to you.'

'Ah. Very well.'

'And take the afternoon off. We have work to do. A decision to make on my part, one on which I require your opinion.'

The back part of the bar at Ai Pugni was another place that mirrored the changing seasons in the daily dishes on offer to the modest number of lunch customers the place could serve. It was the end of the month, the Friday before the annual madness of the Sunday marathon, when Luca and I gathered over a rich mushroom pasta and two glasses of good Raboso to mark the last of his translations.

A celebration I'd hoped, though something in his normally cheery face told me this was not the case. It had been a long and difficult process as I'd expected, made more onerous because in the middle he'd had to deal with some sort of managerial crisis within the Archivio to do with funding, something the institution always found pressing. Money was almost always short in the heritage establishments that depended on the state. I could appreciate why the city appreciated it when wealthy individuals came along and paid for art projects themselves.

All the same I found myself looking at my lunch companion, dressed flamboyantly as ever in a dark velvet jacket, a gaudy neckerchief at his throat, a blue pinstripe shirt beneath, and felt the words, the very annoying words, my Yorkshire mother used on such occasions rise towards my lips.

Cheer up. It'll never happen.

Thank goodness common sense kicked in before that and I said, simply, 'Is everything all right, Luca?'

'No,' he said, taking a generous swig of his glass of red. 'It isn't.'

'I'm sorry. Work then...'

'Not work, Arnold. Those damned pages you sent me. I'd no idea...'

His voice trailed off as the barman came over for a chat, then spotting the atmosphere, rapidly retreated.

'I'm very grateful you helped me out.'

He groaned. 'Did you actually read what I sent you?'

In a way, I explained. I wasn't looking to think closely about the prose, the sentiments, the stories the pages told. That seemed irrelevant just then. What mattered was the basic question of authenticity. Was there something, an inaccurate date or some obviously false event, that would ring alarm bells and expose the whole collection as fake?

'Lucky you.'

His glass was empty. I ordered a couple more. This was not like him at all.

'Then...?'

'I can't get it out of my head.' He almost looked ready to weep. 'The voice. His voice.'

'Vivaldi's you mean?'

'If it was him. You tell me.' He went through some of the tests he'd run on the quiet in the Archivio. It seemed they had access to computer tools designed to detect the use of AI. Luca had secretly applied them to the images I'd sent him, deleting the files immediately afterwards for security.

'You can't be mistaken?'

'Listen, I ran those tests because I had to. For my sake. There's a human being behind those words, my friend. A very real one. Someone consumed by their emotions. Unpleasant ones too. You must have noticed! The ambition to be better than everyone else. The envy of anyone he regarded as a rival. The lust. The way he used women, young women for their bodies, older women for their money as well. I felt as if I was reading the confessions of a devil, not a man who'd once been a priest. It...' He pushed his plate away, half eaten. Delicious it was, as usual too. 'It disturbed me. It still does. There's something about the tone. Something cynical and cruel. I'm taking a break next week. A holiday with Silvia in Sicily. I need it.'

'Silvia?'

'Silvia Casciano. The librarian from the Cini Foundation on San Giorgio Maggiore. You've met her?'

'No.'

'She helped me a little. A lovely woman. Very knowledge-able. I think it affected her too. Honestly, whoever wrote that material... they're not someone you'd ever want to meet. There's such... such outright contempt for humanity. Men. Women. Fellow musicians and artists. It makes out Vivaldi to be a man without an ounce of feeling, or empathy, for anyone but himself.'

'And yet,' I pointed out, 'he wrote beautiful music that's loved around the world. There was joy in him, surely. Perhaps that's an indication this is all some kind of scam.'

He toyed with his glass. 'Perhaps. But we must always separate the artist from the art, don't you think? Caravaggio was a murderous bastard. Benvenuto Cellini too. Plenty of them around today if only the rest of us knew.'

A reasonable point. All the same, there was such life in Vivaldi's work. *The Four Seasons* in particular. The obvious pleasure he took in the changing weather and popular mood, in music and in the verses wrote. Even bleak winter with its final words... *Quest' é 'l verno, mà tal, che gioja apporte*. It's winter! But it brings us joy for sure. Though in the version we had, supposedly amended towards the tragic end of the composer's life, 'death' was, of course, substituted for 'joy'.

There was darkness in the material I'd glibly passed on to Luca with a demand he translate something that was vast and quite beyond me.

'To details,' he said, noticing my sudden reticence. 'Practicalities.'

With Silvia, his new friend from San Giorgio Maggiore, he'd gone over the images in some depth, looking for evidence they were generated, not written. There was nothing there to suggest this, no obvious repetitions of exact style in the handwriting, no telltale signs they came from an algorithm not a pen. The possibility he'd been exploring I understood already. Someone had written a version of the pages, Vivaldi's and that short entry from Casanova, and had them transcribed into handwriting of the period using AI trained on the composer's existing personal letters and Casanova's memoirs.

'You mean these weren't from a computer?' I asked.

'It's not as simple as that. The problem of verification I have is the same as yours. While you look at dates and events, I search for glitches, flaws in the handwriting and the language. I can find none.'

'Then...?'

'Then we're back to square one. This is the work of someone with access to technology that's very clever indeed. And lord knows there's enough of that around right now. Or it really is what it appears. A hidden side to our reclusive composer no one has previously heard of or guessed at. Along with the revelation – quite a sensational one I'd say – that he may well have been father to that monster Casanova.' He went for his glass once more. 'You have quite a story on your hands if that's the case. A bestseller. A sensation. That alone might put the Maddalena and Mia Haas on an even keel.'

Fine, I thought. That side of the investigation was closed. Or rather as they say in Scottish law, not proven.

'Am I done now?' Luca asked, wide-eyed. 'Please say yes.'

I called for the bill and snatched it from his fingers the moment it appeared. The last thing I wanted at that moment was losing his advice, his insight, his company.

'Of course. I can't thank you enough. I never will be able to...' I waved a hand around the Pugni and one of the bar staff waved back. 'Not least for taking me here when I felt lonely and lost.'

He smiled for the first time then. 'It's always been a pleasure. At least mostly. I do hope I didn't lead you astray with this one.'

As if.

I left a hefty tip.

'Now off with you,' I said as we strode out into the grey day by the vegetable boat that always sat in the canal, amusing visitors. 'Take to your heels with your Silvia and put Antonio Vivaldi quite out of your mind.'

~

There's a logic to analysing old documents. Processes to follow, checks to be made. I'd left Luca to handle the linguistic part of all that, at some cost it seemed from his downcast mien as we said goodbye on Campo San Barnaba, a fair amount of Pugni red running warm around our veins.

He'd done his best to locate holes in the handwriting and the prose of The Stick Papers. And, perhaps to his surprise, could find nothing incriminating, nothing out of place, nothing to suggest they were, as we both feared at first, clever counterfeits designed to part Marcus Haas from his money.

My job now was to marry what I found in his translations with the known events of Vivaldi's life and see if there were any suspicious lacunae there. It was no simple or swift task.

The first entry in Vivaldi's 'memoirs' was dated 4 February, 1715, though obviously written at a much later date, probably when he was at a loose end in Vienna, desperately searching for work. This much was clear from the handwriting which was consistent throughout. In this entry he boasts of improvising a cadenza on the fiddle at the end of an opera in the Teatro Sant'Angelo, one, he records, the audience found so astonishing, 'I was approached afterwards and asked by so many for a repeat of the performance, and perhaps the music!'

There was another discovery. The man wasn't simply a formidable composer, but a violin virtuoso too, with the kind of improvisational talent one would later associate with someone like Paganini. It took only a quick look through my reference material to see this was based on a real event. A German scholar, Zacharias Conrad von Uffenbach, an inveterate traveller and diarist, was in Venice at the time and witnessed the performance, saying it was unlike anything he'd ever heard before, though more 'artifice' than pleasant music. A show-off in other words.

This was an extremely obscure reference. Yes, a forger could have come upon the same material I was using. But why go to such lengths? Mia Haas had handed over the 'ransom' without seeing the originals. He – or more likely they – could have had their money for those blank pages Hazard seemed to be carrying when he died.

One new obstacle to verifying the material soon appeared. I'd spent most of my time thinking about marrying Vivaldi's entries to real world events, not so much the content of his material. When I did, it became apparent that these were rambling, occasionally incoherent recollections, not lucid, organised memoirs set out in chronological order. Quite unlike Casanova's account of his life. Vivaldi was writing for himself, often trying to justify his actions, his arguments with promoters and fellow musicians, his relationships with women which went far beyond the affair with Anna Girò.

And there was the problem. Because he was talking to himself most of these events were quite without context. I never heard the other side of the row in November 1737 that resulted in Cardinal Tommaso Ruffo refusing him entrance to Ferrara for a planned opera, a ban that started the composer's spiral into debt and misery. Money? The continuing relationship with Girò? There was no way to tell, only Vivaldi's spiteful and deeply personal remarks about the cardinal and his acolytes in the church there. I was, as the days passed, growing closer to an understanding of what appeared to shape Vivaldi's life, and take him from the glory days as Europe's most acclaimed musician to that miserable, self-pitying end in Vienna. But who he truly was... what drove him other than ego and an astonishing talent... I'd no idea.

The dates and the places were there, though. As November approached, I'd come pretty close to checking every one of them. Nowhere could I find a point where the entries failed to match the known records for Vivaldi's work, commissions and travels over the last three decades of his life. A few were so small and seemingly insignificant I could only believe they had to be real.

An example. In the spring of 1733 he records an argument about money with an instrument maker called Domenico Montagnana, one that led to Vivaldi storming out of Montagnana's workshop in the Calle degli Stagneri declaring he would henceforth buy his fiddles from a rival, Sanctus Seraphin.

I read this at eight in the morning, a chilly grey day, winter in the air. I knew that street, a narrow alley near the Rialto, because Rupert Hazard had persuaded me to go there on Saturday to watch Manchester City, his favourite football team, on the TV in the Irish pub, The Devil's Forest, while he downed pints of Guinness. It's an area for tourists, a Disney store, a Captain Candy. But that morning I reminded myself that the Venice of old surely continued to live beneath all this shallow surface glitter and bling.

It was time for a walk, so I set off through Santa Croce, past Campo San Polo, to the lanes around the market, across the bridge, empty at that time of morning, and stood by the statue of Carlo Goldoni in the square. Goldoni, the author who'd had that difficult conversation with Vivaldi in which he'd cast aspersions about the singing talents of Anna Girò. Something that never got a mention in The Stick Papers at all, perhaps because the composer refused to set down any criticism of his favourite companion.

The statue of the playwright loomed above me on his plinth, tricorn hat, curly wig, stick in hand, legs apart as if ready to stride off into the distance, perhaps to the nearby theatre now named after him where once his comedies filled the stalls year after year. There was a broad smile on his pleasant face, a reminder that history often remembered cultural figures the way we wished to recall them, not as they were. The truth was Goldoni fell out of love with the city and its tastes in his fifties and moved to Paris, never to return.

I walked on, into the Calle degli Stagneri. A mistake. It had obviously been a busy night around the Rialto. Behind the iron railings of the windows of buildings that dated back to before Vivaldi's time I saw beer cans, wine bottles, burger boxes and other rubbish stuffed there as if this somehow disposed of them. The place had the stink of urine and bad drains. This was the modern city, though perhaps the odours were the same three centuries before.

Could I imagine Vivaldi having a row about money with an instrument maker here? All too easily. The narrow street had the look of a place where once an artisan might have set up a workshop, close enough to the Rialto to be accessible to customers, far enough away for the rent to be cheap. Montagnana was a real man too, one whose work was regarded as being on a par with the more famous luthiers of Cremona such as Guarneri and Stradivarius. A 1733 cello of his, known as Petunia, made not far from that pub where we watched Manchester City, is owned by Yo-Yo Ma.

Even in that dark alley, surrounded by the detritus of the modern world, the past could still come out to swamp me. I stopped for a moment and wondered at the journey I'd made from Zitelle that April to now, whether it was worth it, how this strange adventure might end.

My phone went. It was Ellen Kim. Finally, I was summoned. Andriy Kravchuck had heard I'd obtained what was purported to be Vivaldi's original score for The Seasons.

'He wants you here now, Signor Clover,' she said in a singsong voice, half oriental, half New York. 'This very moment.'

Kravchuck shared a two-bedroom apartment with Ellen Kim along from La Pietà, on the first floor of what I took to be one of the original buildings of the religious *ospedale* for musical orphans – and the illegitimate offspring of Venetian nobles – who made up Vivaldi's first orchestra. He looked well, not as frail as he'd appeared in the auditorium that spring. Ellen Kim was bright and sprightly too, fetching coffee for us then leaving the room.

'Well,' he said, glaring at me, 'I must say I'm disappointed.'

'By what?' I wondered.

'By the fact you keep me in the dark. How am I to help you with something I don't even know about?'

'Um...'

'The papers, Clover. You have the papers. Mia told me when I was leaving last night.'

'Ah...'

'For an articulate man you seem remarkably tongue-tied.'

An awkward moment. 'You seemed busy enough. I didn't want to waste your time.'

'Waste time seeing an original score no one has set eyes on in centuries?'

'I've been trying to make sure the material I have is genuine. It's not easy.'

That didn't please him one bit. 'Dammit, man! I know Vivaldi better than anyone alive. Why do you think Mia Haas asked me to take on this job?'

'How did she find you?'

Kravchuck seemed oddly put out by that question. 'Find me? I'm a world expert on Vivaldi. Besides, we've known each other off and on for years. Lives intertwine.'

'Perhaps you should be writing the book then.'

'I know music. Little else matters. You really think you have the autograph score for The Seasons? The one he sent to Le Cène in Amsterdam?'

'Possibly...'

He threw up his hands in despair and I couldn't help but look at the disfigurement on his right hand, the fingers ending in stumps by the palm.

'Good god, man. Either show me what you have now or I'm off back to London and a semblance of sanity. Taking Ellen Kim with me. I've no time for these games.'

I pointed at the laptop on the dining table. 'If I may...?'

Everything I had, the original images and Luca's translations, was stored on a secure server attached to one of the academic accounts Mia had arranged. I wasn't leaving it anywhere obviously public. A minute was all it took to locate the music pages on my phone then dispatch them to Kravchuck's personal address.

I placed the laptop on the table by the window. Straight away he shuffled over, took a pair of half-moon spectacles out of his waistcoat pocket and began to look.

'You are still writing this book then? Despite the problems? This incident on the train? The deaths...'

I'd no idea what he meant by that. How much he really knew.

'I am.'

He grunted. 'You're not the only one who'd like this material, but I imagine you appreciate that by now. Go away, Clover,' he said with a wave of his hand.

'But...'

'Go away! Ellen is waiting outside to give you a tour of the places Vivaldi lived. The traces, such as they are, that remain. Buy her lunch – nothing cheap. Then come back here when I say, and I'll tell you whether what you have is real or not.'

I was taken aback. 'You can do that? Just from looking at something on a screen.'

He took off the glasses and gave me the kind of look a teacher might offer to a pupil who was being slow and stupid.

'I've lived with Antonio Vivaldi in my head for most of my adult life. So, yes. I can. Now kindly leave me alone.'

The tour of Vivaldi's Venice began. We stood outside La Pietà, a place the tourists were told was his though, as anyone who can read will soon establish, the original church was demolished and replaced decades after he died. Then we walked around the corner into the quiet square of Campo Bandiera e Moro, the point at which the San Marco crowds begin to thin out, thinking there's little to see. As always, they are wrong. Here, tucked into a corner, lies the small church of San Giovanni in Bragora where he was christened, in haste, his parents, only recently married, thinking he might be short lived. The elaborate font in which the infant Antonio was baptised still sits in its niche, next to it his birth certificate displayed in a frame.

Ellen had little to tell me I didn't already know and seemed almost resentful of her role as guide. It was clear Kravchuck had taken her on a such a tour of the city, and all she was doing was recounting what he'd said. We walked to Vivaldi's houses, the place in Campo Santi Filippo e Giacomo, now part hotel, part restaurant, not a plaque on the wall. Then to the Ponte del Paradiso, the terrace with a Turk's head on the front around the corner from Campo Santa Maria Formosa.

After that we made a long trek to the Rialto and found his final home in Venice, the place he returned to in 1730, saying he would stay in the city for the rest of his life. With Anna Girò now a constant companion. Here, according to my detailed chronology, was where, in 1735, he met the young Carlo Goldoni when the writer was less than fulsome about the woman's singing abilities after he was tasked with writing the libretto for *Griselda*.

Vivaldi was to leave for Vienna a virtual pauper just five years later, selling his papers and scores for a pittance to anyone who would buy them. This last residence was somewhere I knew already, next to the Palazzo Bembo, another historic palace full of stories that resonate from past to present in ways only Venice can manage.

It must have been a busy, noisy place in his time. Even more so today with one of the Rialto vaporetto stops directly in front of his old house, scores of tourists hanging round, staring at maps, trying to decide where next to go.

'There's nothing to say he was here,' I pointed out.

'Why should there be?' Ellen Kim wondered. 'When he died, most people had forgotten about him anyway. Tastes had moved on. They always do.' She laughed. 'The amazing thing is they returned. And here we are. Antonio Vivaldi, maybe the most famous Venetian there is.'

'Buried in an unmarked grave in Vienna.'

'So what?' She shrugged. 'Do the dead care?'

I wished Ellen Kim's short tour of Vivaldi's Venice improved the picture of the man in my head. In truth, that was more and more set by the vivid and often heartless tales I'd read in those purported memoirs. True or not, there was something in those pages that spoke of a real man of talent and the price he paid for that. A price that perhaps explained why the presence of this most famous Venetian was barely marked on the walls of his native city at all.

'Andriy said you'd buy me lunch. I'm starving.'

I looked at the bridge, teeming with visitors as always, cameras and selfies everywhere. I knew just where we'd go.

Do Spade lay in a shady *sotoportego* behind the Rialto markets. The place was on the tourist trail now but seemed unwilling to acknowledge the fact. It was old, barely lit inside, dark, stained wood everywhere, a counter full of dishes that might have been much the same in Vivaldi's time, *sarde en saor*, *baccalà mante-cato*, *calamari*, mantis shrimp from the lagoon.

I knew I had to come here after reading Casanova's account of how he and his gang of young thugs had led a young married woman into the tavern, plied her with drink, then raped her in an upstairs room. A joke, Casanova seemed to think. Nothing more than a juvenile prank. The Stick Papers made no mention of *Do Spade*. The sexual misdeeds of the character portrayed there appeared to take place in fancier locations, theatres mostly, or private apartments, and principally concerned young women willing to offer themselves in return for a chance to join Vivaldi's various companies. Some things, it seemed, never changed.

Ellen Kim picked at her food with the occasional frown.

'Don't you like it?' I asked.

'I thought we'd be going to a restaurant.' She looked around the old walls. 'Not somewhere like this.'

'You don't come here to dine. You come somewhere like this to eat.'

A thin smile then and I realised Ellen Kim was doubtless a young woman of great talent, photogenic and a natural for publicity. But not, I felt, someone I could begin to warm to at all.

As if to confirm the fact she reached over the table, dumped the remains of her baccalà on my plate and said, 'Do you think she killed him? Mia? Marcus I mean. Well, that was my first thought. After the shock.'

I stuttered some nonsense I don't recall.

'I'm so sorry, Arnold. You're close to her, aren't you? Forget I ever said it.'

'That's quite something to forget.'

'Well...' She pushed away her pickled sardines and wrinkled her nose. 'Strange food they have here.'

'It's Venetian food.'

'Thanks for the warning.'

'What on earth would make you say such a thing? About a woman recently widowed?'

'Not that recent, is it? Besides, she doesn't look as if she's in mourning. In fact, I'd say she's positively brightened since Marcus kicked it. The Teatro Maddalena seems much improved. None of the chaos and uncertainty when he was around.'

'I don't...'

'Marcus was terrified of her! He told me so himself. A few drinks down, maybe a few snorts too, I don't know, he could hardly stop going on about it. As if she'd somehow got him hooked on this Vivaldi idea. He wasn't remotely musical, you know. There's not the slightest chance he would have embarked on this if it was just down to him.'

'Talked to him a lot, did you?'

It just slipped out and from the sudden sharp look in her eyes I could see she read rather more into that than I wished.

'He wanted an affair. I told the Carabinieri. Marcus liked women. Women liked him. When he was halfway sober anyway. Money. Good looks. Charm.' I got eyeballed head to toe. 'Excellent dress sense. Understandable. To most people anyway.'

I tried to tone down the heat. 'Men sometimes belittle their wives as a way of starting an affair. Or so I'm led to believe. "My wife doesn't understand me..."'

Her eyes widened. 'You don't say! I've never heard that line. Not once.'

I motioned for the bill, anxious to be back with Kravchuck to see what he made of the music. To be spared this woman's company too.

'I know when married men want an affair,' she went on. 'I know when I'm willing. I wasn't just then. In different circumstances, maybe. As I said he was good looking, moneyed or so I thought. There was something wrong between the two of them, something more than the usual jaded boredom most marriages seem to descend into. I kept him at a distance, which wasn't hard, actually. He seemed to think it was part of the game. That one day I'd give in.'

'The day he died? Was that it? Was that why you went round the Orchid House?'

She giggled. 'Oh my! You are smart, aren't you? Yes, I was thinking of telling him that perhaps we should try and find an excuse to get away together some time soon. But...' A frown that was halfway to a sneer. 'I told that policewoman. I thought he was sleeping. Downright rude. So I tried to shake him awake.' A wince, a shudder. 'Got blood on me. You saw.' She edged forward, elbows on the table, hands on her chin, stared at me and winked. 'What do you think? Is it possible the lovely Mia had a hand in all that? Or are you so blind to think she's above that kind of thing?'

'Mia Haas is employing you, and your mentor, Andriy Kravchuck.'

'He's not my mentor. He's my teacher, who's been paid damn well for it over the years. By an elderly financier of immense wealth who lives on Central Park as it happens. A true gentleman. One with an eye for beauty and the arts.'

Kravchuck rescued me at that moment with a single message: *come.* I got up from the table, paid at the counter, walked out into the shadows of the sotoportego. The temperature seemed to have dropped a couple of degrees while we were having lunch. Or perhaps it was just the company.

'I think, Ellen, you should keep your opinions to yourself on that subject.'

She grinned then and I wished I was anywhere else on earth. 'You didn't answer the question. Did I touch a raw nerve?'

'It was unworthy of an answer. Unworthy of you.'

Nothing else was said on the vaporetto back to San Zaccaria. In the apartment she went into her room without another word. I found Kravchuck still hunched over his laptop. He looked up, adjusted his half-moon glasses, and told me to take a seat.

I sat and watched and waited, eyes on the tall campanile of San Giorgio Maggiore across the water, and the edge of Giudecca, the Teatro Maddalena hidden from view. Finally, he held up his right hand. Those cruelly severed fingers.

'You think you know how I came to have these, don't you?'

'They told me you never want to talk about it.'

'Did they? He brandished his stumps again. 'Well, it's true, most of the time. Not now. The work of a man called Vasyl Archaki. Someone I once foolishly called a friend. Until he did this.' He grimaced, glanced at the door to make sure no one was listening. 'And much more for others less fortunate. Much worse.'

'I'm sorry,' I said. 'I thought I came here to talk about Vivaldi.'

Andriy Kravchuck nodded at a drinks cabinet. 'You are. But first I have a tale for you, one you may find educational given your recent experiences. Pour me a brandy. I cannot tell it without a drink.'

In 2014, Andriy Kravchuck was musical director of the Crimean Symphony Orchestra based in Sevastopol, a job he'd held for five and a half years. It was a prestigious post with a prestigious organisation. A role given to him by Vasyl Archaki, a minister in the Crimean parliament.

'A man two decades younger than me, of little talent when it came to music, which annoyed him no end,' Kravchuck said, retreating into the shadow of the wall by the window. 'I first met him when he was a lowly cello player in an amateur outfit I mentored in Simferopol. He was a minor councillor in the administration at the time. Not for long. Soon, Vasyl rose through the ranks. I encouraged him. I felt...' He took a sip of drink. 'I felt he was the kind of young Ukrainian we'd need in the future. When the Russians – Putin to be more accurate – decided to cause us trouble.'

That February, Ukraine fell into turmoil. The Maidan uprising saw the pro-Russian president Viktor Yanukovych expelled from office in Kyiv, while in Crimea rival protestors began to take power, backed by undercover operatives linked to Moscow, and, later, direct and bloody intervention from Russian spetznaz, the special forces.

'Do not think for one moment any of this was political on the fellow's part. Vasyl was an opportunist. Had Kyiv come to win the fight for Crimea, I don't have the slightest doubt that he would have been there, waving the flag for the Euromaidan constituency. But when the wind changed and began to blow from the north...' Kravchuck knocked back the drink. 'Matters turned worse. Soon we were effectively back in Russia, just as we were during Soviet times. It was important to show your support. Costly if you didn't. One day he came to my office and demanded I line up the orchestra in a concert for the new regime, all Russian music, naturally. Not that I had anything against that in principle.'

A laugh, dry, ironic. 'But this wasn't about music. It would be a patriotic event, he said, a celebration of our return to the arms of Mother Russia. Yes, he used those words. Patriotism meaning accepting serfdom to our new masters. I told him. Even if I was willing, and I wasn't, my players would never go along with the idea. Some were Crimean Tatars, with relatives who were already beginning to vanish and would never be seen again. Others, including some foreign nationals, were simply appalled by the idea of bending the knee to creatures of the Kremlin. And so...'

He waved his damaged hand. 'In that case, Vasyl said, you'll never play the fiddle again.'

'They told me he broke your precious violin.'

He guffawed. 'God, the stories that do the rounds. You think a man like Vasyl Archaki would snap a precious Guarneri, worth a million dollars or more, into little pieces? No. He sold it to someone in Moscow. I've seen her in a concert they televised there not long after. I'd know her anywhere. She was like a child to me.'

I tried to think of something to say but the words weren't there.

'Anyway,' he went on, 'I was confined to a cell for a few days, left to stew. When I was unmoved, he returned and used a pair of agricultural shears to remove three of my fingers then offered me them in a plastic bag. I was lucky. The players who remained either gave in or were taken into custody and disappeared. The women...'

Andriy Kravchuck scowled, and I saw the hatred in his face. 'I don't want to think what happened to them. There was one, Elena, a lovely woman from the Balkans. Good looking woman in her forties or so. Archaki had his eye on her. She was fierce, not the sort to submit. They dragged me back into an interrogation room after they'd taken my fingers. She was there, stony-faced. She didn't say she wasn't giving in to them. She didn't need to. Men came in, Russians, bad men. They dragged her away while I sat there weeping with my bleeding stumps. My fate was supposed to move her, I imagine. They didn't know Elena. What happened after... god knows... I daren't think about it. Rape was a weapon for men like that, as much as a gun. A woman who didn't relent, who fought back... I wouldn't want to imagine how they behaved. Shit...'

His hands were trembling, the glass shaking in them, spilling drink onto the carpet. 'What's there to say? They kicked me on a bus west towards Kyiv, along with the foreigners in my orchestra who they were too scared to harm. And here I am.'

I took a deep breath and looked at my own hands. 'Andriy, you don't have to tell me this.'

He shook his grizzled head. 'But I do. It's relevant. More so because you English grew up in a world where there was a semblance of safety. A place where there are no wolves. But there are always wolves. Always. It's just that you think they cease to exist simply because you cannot see them. I was allowed to live as an example to my fellow countrymen in Kyiv, a warning of what was to come. Most weren't. It was Vasyl Archaki who dealt them their fate.'

I waited. It took a while.

'He's a complex man. Turncoat, traitor, a thug looking for the next rung to climb, the next victim whose corpse he might step on to get there... all those things and more. The fellow's a special kind of robber, of people, their dignity, their souls and talent, anything they hold dear. A relentless thief of cultural artefacts as well, anything he can lay his hands on, like my Guarneri. I'd begun to hear rumours before the end came, stories that gave me pause for thought.'

Kravchuck raised his damaged hand and gazed at the stumps of his fingers.

'It was maybe why he sided with the Russians. Kyiv was going to clean up our act, try to get rid of the corrupt and the venal. For the Russians, corruption and venality were feathers in one's cap, proof of your superiority. Vasyl seized so much, through threats, through violence, through murder I don't doubt. Paintings. Jewellery and ancient statuary. Before long, he had a holiday mansion by the sea in Yalta, another in Russia, Sochi. So much money. So many places to keep his loot.'

There was a book by his chair. A biography of Beethoven. He picked up it up and brandished the thing in my direction.

'He thieved historic documents as well. Manuscripts. The draft of a novel by Tolstoy he claimed, poetry by Pasternak. Some he sold on. Others, I think he wanted for himself. I don't know, and after he put me on that crowded, stinking bus to Kyiv, I hoped I'd never hear of him again. Vasyl Archaki was a name from my past, one I never wished to recall. Though after the last disaster, when Putin came for the whole country, I read he'd moved on again, upwards naturally. It was the only trajectory he wanted. To Moscow as one of the tame Ukrainians there, waiting on the monster in the Kremlin to put them back in power in Kyiv one day. Or so they hoped.'

'Historic manuscripts,' I said, starting to see where this was headed.

'Quite.' He nodded. 'You grasp the possible connection? He loved Vivaldi. That much was genuine, not a pretence. He was always asking me about the man, who he was, what kind of individual could write such music, so much of it, and remain a mystery. Whether he and Anna Girò were lovers... that fascinated him too. Something about the work seemed to touch him. I can't honestly say music calmed the savage beast, but it certainly whetted his appetite.

'There was a fellow in the woodwinds, Czech, I think, couldn't stop talking, rubbish mostly. He came from somewhere in Bohemia and was telling stories. He claimed someone back home had hidden a cache of secret Vivaldi papers, music, memoirs maybe, from the Nazis when they invaded. No one knew where they were now. I remember Vasyl saying he'd kill to see them.'

Kravchuck emptied his glass with a scowl. 'The words

people utter, and you don't really listen. I thought nothing of it. Why would I? What was this to me? But to Vasyl...' He finished the glass. 'Some men become obsessed with women. Or money. Or power. Some, like him, seek them all. But mostly, I think, it was about ownership. Possession. He was like a man who buys a stolen painting, so famous it can never go on the market, never be exhibited in public. But that doesn't matter. A fellow like that can admire the thing he owns in private, show it to impress the closest of his friends. There. That is why you should have informed me the moment you were attacked.'

I shook my head, astonished. 'I didn't realise you knew. It's not supposed to be public knowledge. The Carabinieri...'

He laughed, and it was genuine this time. 'The Carabinieri told me nothing. It was Mia. I had to drag it out of her.'

'They told me I was fortunate to survive what happened on the train.'

'If it was the work of men in the employ of Vasyl Archaki you were fortunate indeed. I blame myself. I should have realised that if such material was on the market, the chances were Vasyl would hear of it. The bastard will do whatever he wishes to get what he wants. Murder. Torture. Bribe and poison. Nothing is beyond him, and if he's where I think in Moscow, deep within its foul web of spies and assassins, heaven knows what means he has to hand.' He pushed the glass to one side. 'Of course, I could be completely wrong.'

'Poison,' I whispered.

'And yet you lived. It seems your fellow countryman Hazard, well named it appears, was part of the plan. Did that shock you?'

Shock? It still seemed ridiculous, despite all the evidence to the contrary.

'Very much so. Rupert followed me to Vienna. He said

you'd taken against him. He felt sure he was going to be fired and was looking for another position.'

Kravchuck shook his grizzled head and once again I was reminded of an old, grey eagle, sharp-eyed, cunning. 'I never said such a thing. Or had such plans. He was a competent player. Nothing special. I would never have put a particularly difficult piece in front of him. A journeyman musician. We need them.'

'He never struck me as a man capable of murder.'

'Neither did Vasyl Archaki. He still doesn't have these papers, does he?'

I nodded at the laptop. 'I was given copies, photographs. That's all I have. Where the originals are... we've no idea.'

'Hmmm.' He said nothing more.

'Andriy, the score...'

'I should have seen something was wrong here from the start. That so-called gardener Marcus Haas employed. The one who never stops watching when you arrive, when you leave.'

'Lombardo?'

'If that's his name.'

'What of him?'

'Oh, the English! Blind to wolves even when they appear in broad daylight. The man may well spend his days hoeing and weeding but he's security. Marcus hired him. I wouldn't want to mess with the fellow. Would you?'

'I've never messed with anyone in my life.'

'Oh dear. What a pair we make. Me a violinist with no real fingers. You a kind of historian discovering the real world isn't quite what you thought. What do you propose, Arnold Clover? With this miraculous work you've found?'

'I came here to ask if you thought it was genuine.'

He slapped his forehead. 'This score? Of course it's genuine! Didn't I say?'

'No.'

'Well, then... I say it now. This, I don't doubt, is the original in Vivaldi's own hand. The script. The way he writes. The speed with which he composes. You can see that from the fluidity with which the notes, the ideas, flow. Few could work like this. Vivaldi was always in a fury, a mental fugue when he began to write. As if the fire of God was running through him, and that – something divine, something of the earth, the seasons, life itself – was what poured through his fingers onto the page. I've seen plenty other autograph scores of his for other work. This came from the same man. I don't doubt it.'

'Unless there's a very talented forger somewhere.'

He waved a hand at me. 'I don't see how anyone could forge something like this so accurately.'

'There are computers, it seems. Artificial intelligence.'

Another wave. 'Does a computer know the fire of God?'

He was clearly immovable on the subject.

'Thank you for your insight.'

'And the little tour of Venice with Ellen?'

'Thank you for that, also.'

'I suspected the two of you wouldn't get on. She's an artist, Clover, and her art is more important to her than mere people. We all live in our own little worlds. Yours, the ordinary one, can often seem rather dull.'

'I wouldn't describe the events of my life since I came upon the Teatro Maddalena as dull. Not for one moment.'

'That, my friend... is because you've abandoned your world and entered ours. Welcome. One never quite knows what lurks around the next corner. Just pray it's not Vasyl Archaki.'

He glanced at the door. The interview was over.

'Now what?' he asked.

'Now,' I said, 'I write.'

Chapter Nine

Allegro

The last week of October. Three months to deliver the first book I'd ever written, and at that point I'd barely produced a single worthwhile paragraph. There was always something that seemed to get in the way. Or perhaps this was what happened to writers who were uncertain about how to proceed. They sought diversions, distractions, excuses, anything that might make you feel it was fine to put off the hard work of setting down one word after another until another day, when the ideas might come more easily, and the mind would find it easier to focus.

Excuses I'd had aplenty since I first stepped through the gates of the Maddalena estate. Doubts about the people I was surrounded with. A paucity of material until Vienna. The violent death of the project's founder. The shadowy presence of the Carabinieri at so many turns. And the plain fact someone had tried to kill me. Not many authors could boast of that I imagine, if *boast* is the right word.

Somehow, Andriy Kravchuck's unexpected revelation about

his past, and Ellen Kim's ridiculous aspersions about Mia, prompted me to get down to the job at last.

Though not, primarily, at home in San Pantalon, a busy solitary worker bee with a laptop and a strange collection of photographed manuscripts at my disposal. No, the day after seeing Kravchuck I decided it was time to face this issue directly, in the Palazzo Maddalena, watching what was going on there, becoming a part of what was obviously a team, a family almost, gathering around the music in the revived theatre, and the smart hotel coming to life beneath Mia Haas's delicate and refined touch.

There was an ulterior motive to all this, naturally. More than one if I'm honest. But let's begin with the most important. I'd decided that if we were to lie about our confidence in the veracity of the Vivaldi memoirs, it was now time to start to lie big, with purpose and ambition.

For that I needed Luca Volpetti on board.

Three days before the end of the month, with Mia's support, I invited him over to lunch, a single table in the empty restaurant still being kitted out, the menu the work of a second chef she was trialling for a job. It was a grey, cold rainy day, typical for the end of autumn. All the same, Luca was never going to turn down free food and drink.

Still, he looked nervy when he crossed the bridge and walked through the tidy gardens so beautifully created and tended by the man called Peter Lombardo. Who was in his small cabin by the canal, watching every step Luca took, leaning on a wall by the door smoking a cigarette. Kravchuck surely had that man down to a tee. While I merely found him curious, the Ukrainian saw him for what he was: subtle security, both practical help and a hired hood. There was the difference between growing up in a world in which wolves were regarded as extinct, and one where they still prowled, or so the old man would doubtless have it. The implications were intriguing but, like so much at that time, hard to elucidate.

From the very beginning, Marcus Haas had wanted a bodyguard for the wrecked palazzo and theatre he was renovating in a backwater of Giudecca most people never knew existed. But why? Because he was playing fast and loose with the rules of international finance, and doubtless making enemies along the way? Or was it something to do with the Maddalena? The search for the mysterious Vivaldi papers which only came to light, as much as they did, after he was dead?

No asking him now...

The restaurant was half of the ground floor on the theatre side of the palazzo, an elegant room, modern yet traditional, with contemporary artwork, paintings and what I took to be Murano glass sculptures dotted around the walls and alcoves. Mia's taste, I didn't doubt. It looked expensive.

There was little going on in the auditorium at the time, just Ellen Kim and her mentor along with a pianist – new to me – and some pieces of music I didn't recognise. Kravchuck's gravelly voice came through from time to time, quite loud, not fierce but uncompromising, the way a serious teacher often was.

Odd that here when he was in public – I suspect his time in the Teatro always counted as such – he spoke with a marked accent, not heavy but clearly audible. Though when we met in his apartment his voice was quieter, perhaps more uncertain, and he might have passed as an Englishman who'd once spent time abroad. The difference being, I felt, the context. In the Teatro Maddalena he was, like Vivaldi before him, master of ceremonies. Alone in his apartment on the Riva degli Schiavoni, he was just an old man, a little frail, memory maybe not as good as it once was, beset by dark memories that refused to leave him.

For the first time since I arrived in Venice, I'd bought new clothes. A plain dark blue suit, white shirt, no tie, smart shiny shoes, all from the sale in OVS on the Lido. Time, I felt, to appear serious. Mia looked lovely in a plain fawn jacket and matching dark skirt, hair tight back which made her face look narrower than usual. I wondered if she'd lost weight over the time I'd known her. Hardly unexpected given the tumultuous episodes she'd been through.

We were seated at what I imagined was meant to be the finest table in the house, by the window overlooking the gardens, close to a bed of fading roses, near enough to hear the music, far enough away for it not to be disturbing. Luca looked edgy as we made small talk about the weather and local news while picking at a communal plate of lagoon delicacies – mantis shrimp, the first of the season's moeche, soft shell crabs, the usual *baccalà* and *sarde* and some rather rubbery cuttlefish chunks. Mia pulled a face at the last and the chef, who served us personally, grimaced, apologised and took them away.

'I think he'll do,' she said when he was out of earshot. 'For the opening. So long as he listens to what I tell him. And doesn't serve cuttlefish like that.'

Luca smiled and said he agreed. 'So how are things? Coming along I gather.'

'They're on course,' Mia said. 'Kravchuck and I are agreed. It's pointless – and expensive – to keep bringing in his players to rehearse something they can play well enough as it is. These concerts for the local pensioners are all well and good, but they won't pay the bills. The Teatro won't be ready until December – well, it will, but the council won't get around to approving it until then. But that's a given. We can announce our intentions very shortly. A website is being built, posters and marketing plans are being assembled. Our first concert will be on New Year's Eve. Not a full opening, of course. Some of the accommodation won't be ready by then. Or the full music schedule. That will happen for Carnival, I hope. February. So many people around. It couldn't be better timed.'

'But...' He looked surprised. 'La Fenice has its concert on New Year's Eve.'

I took up the tale. 'Venice is a big place, Luca. La Fenice has nothing to worry about. All we need here are a couple of hundred people.'

'And theirs will be over by six,' Mia added. 'We start at seven. Just a one-hour programme then drinks. After that, they can head off to the lagoon and get ready for the fireworks. It'll be as much a social occasion as a musical one.'

'And...' His eyes were on me. 'The book?'

'Ah yes,' I said as Mia glanced at me. 'The book.'

It was time for the primo: spaghetti alle vongole with clams from Pellestrina.

'I'd hoped for something a little more adventurous,' she commented. 'But it's well done, don't you think?'

Luca nodded. I said, 'Very.'

Talking while eating spaghetti is not one of my talents. It's not a pasta the English – well this one anyway – find easy to eat in company. I struggled with a fork and a spoon while they gave me funny looks. Then, in desperation, I slashed the pasta to pieces with a knife – blasphemy, I know, but I was past caring – and did my best.

'I must teach you to eat spaghetti,' Luca said, with an uncharacteristic tone of harshness. 'It's remiss of me not to get around to it.'

'That's because the Pugni usually serve stuff you can eat without needing special skills. To return to the book, I need to ask for your opinion on an important matter. Your advice. Your... support.'

He looked nervous.

'Before we go any further,' Luca began, 'as I believe I've

made clear before, while the city council wishes your venture here the very best–'

'We're not asking for money,' Mia cut in.

'Oh.' He looked surprised. 'You're not?'

'No.' My turn. 'Though heaven knows the city should be grateful. They're getting a major new cultural venue without having to fork out a cent. One that's going to generate a lot of publicity. Attract the kind of visitors the mayor wants. Cultural ones who spend money. Not day trippers after a cheap gelato and a gondola ride.'

He looked mollified, up to a point. 'I'm sure the mayor will be delighted to hear it. Nevertheless, we're unable to become directly involved in any way, apart from event listings, of course. I'm sure you'll get a good show from the city tourism office.'

'Too kind,' Mia noted.

He glanced at her. 'The unpleasant news coverage earlier in the year has not gone unnoticed.'

She bridled at that. 'My husband's suicide didn't go unnoticed either, not by me. Nor are his lousy financial affairs anything to do with the theatre, as we've made abundantly clear.'

The secondo arrived. Chunky bass fillets in a lime and fennel sauce with a side of Sant'Erasmo cardoons. Mia told the chef to switch the wine to a Gavi she liked, and I wanted to pinch myself in my new smart suit. This was not the life I was used to leading.

Time, I thought, *to come to the point.* 'We're of the opinion, Luca, that the Vivaldi material we've shared with you is genuine.'

He said nothing and picked at his fish.

'Andriy Kravchuck,' I continued, 'one of the world's leading scholars concerning Vivaldi, has examined the score of The Seasons we found, bar by bar, note by note. He's adamant no one could have faked something like that with such accuracy. So many common elements match perfectly with the existing works, proven to be autograph scores composed by the man himself.'

Luca shook his head and put down his knife and fork.

'Furthermore,' I continued, 'we've agreed that, while it's impossible to put on show the original documents, there is a means round this.'

Now he looked worried. 'What means?'

Mia patted his hand. 'Don't look like a rabbit in the headlights. None of this concerns you directly.'

'Then why am I here?'

'To keep you in the loop,' I assured him.

'The originals...'

'The originals are very probably lying at the bottom of the Adriatic right now,' I said, which was a downright fabrication, not that he was to know. 'Beyond recovery. Beyond everyone.'

'So...?'

'We use the images we have and produce prints on suitably aged paper. On New Year's Eve, as well as our concert, we put on show Antonio Vivaldi's original score for the most famous of his works. Andriy and his small orchestra play it. When this place is fully open, we launch the book. It will be a tight schedule...' An understatement to say the least. 'But I've all the material I need now, and with Reggie's expert editing I'm sure we'll get there.'

Luca looked aghast. 'Let me get this straight. You're going to tell the world Vivaldi was Casanova's father? Without having the actual documents themselves?'

I tapped his arm and said, 'Calm down, please. In a way we have them, don't we? Besides, we'll tell the world that was what Casanova wrote, and that Vivaldi seemingly verified elements of that claim in his own private memoirs, even if he disputed the facts. It's not our job to decide a paternity case three centuries old. However, we can lay out the known facts and let people choose what they wish to believe–'

'Oh, come on, Arnold! You can't get away with that "what people choose to believe" nonsense here. This is history, not politics. Academic history. And you are an academic historian.'

'No.' I shook my head. 'I'm a humble archivist who's been gifted some important material that both of us have tried to pick to pieces and declare fake. And we've failed. Therefore...'

He looked at us both, horrified. 'Even if you're right – and we've no way of knowing – you can't just print this stuff on old, fake paper and make out people are seeing something genuine.'

'Of course not,' I told him. 'If someone queries it, we'll say the originals are far too precious and delicate to go on public show. These are very accurate facsimiles. If they ask. Otherwise...'

'We can sell them framed copies,' Mia added. 'At a suitable price.'

'This is fraud!'

Mia growled and read the menu for dessert: tiramisu. Not, I suspect, what she was expecting.

'What would you have us do then?' she asked. 'Pretend this material doesn't exist? That all the pain and expense we've been through, Arnold more than anyone, add up to nothing?'

'I-I didn't...' he stuttered.

'You said it yourself,' I went on. 'We've both spent weeks analysing every word. Nowhere can we find any reason to question the veracity of the documents. No slip-ups in the writing, the language, the style. I can't find a single instance of a wrong date or event. Everything matches, even down to the luthier he had an argument with near the Rialto. What kind of forger would come up with a detail like that?'

He waved his arms about. 'A very clever one! None of this

makes those documents real. I told you before. There are some very capable conmen out there, and they have access to some very powerful computers.'

'And,' Mia added, 'as Arnold pointed out to me earlier, there's the small matter of the Turin Shroud.'

Luca looked ready to explode. 'What on earth has that got to do with anything?'

My turn. 'Quite a lot I'd have thought. An object some think holy. A linen cloth supposedly bearing the image of Christ after the crucifixion. Which others are convinced is a medieval fraud. A relic invented by a conman. Who knows?'

'Quite,' he said. 'Who does know?'

'But millions of people think it's real, don't they? Are you the one, an unbeliever, to tell them they're wrong?'

'If need be... yes. The Turin Shroud's a physical object. They have something they can work with, something they can try to date. While you... you seem to think your originals may lie at the bottom of the ocean.'

'Just a guess,' I said. 'You do know the forensic examination of the shroud that claimed it dated from the Middle Ages is now being questioned? It's decades old. There are newer results from different scientists that say it dates from the time of Christ.'

The dessert arrived. It was quite a concoction and looked like no tiramisu I'd ever seen, more like a pudding invented by Salvador Dali.

'Yummy,' I said, after a spoonful. 'In spite of appearances.'

Luca glanced at each of us in turn. 'You're determined to do this, the two of you? Even though it might land you in jail?'

That was too much.

'I've seen quite enough of jail for one lifetime, thank you. If we make the claims in error, then all it means...'

'All it means is you've been lying to the public. Defrauding them to all intents and purposes.'

'That,' said Mia, 'would require someone to prove these things are forgeries. Without the originals, how is that possible? You two failed and lord knows you tried.'

Luca groaned. He looked mad. He stared at me with hooded, narrowed eyes. 'This is insanity. I can't believe I'm hearing it.'

'Perhaps,' I said. 'But we've decided. This is what's going to happen. The concert on New Year's Eve. The unveiling of the documents. Three months later, no more, the full opening of the theatre, the hotel and the book comes out. My book.'

'I'll have no part in it.'

'We're not offering you one. It's very simple. All we want of you is one thing.'

'Which is?'

Mia took his hand and gave him her sweetest smile. 'Your silence, Luca. Your agreement that when we reveal all this you won't shoot us down at the outset. If others do so, then feel free to join in. But give us a chance. Please. Let Arnold enjoy the opportunity to launch his book. Give me... the Maddalena here... the chance to open with a bang.'

He nodded, not that I quite knew how to take that. 'If it all goes belly up, a hell of a bang that'll be. I'm starting to wonder if I really know you, Arnold Clover.'

I laughed out loud. 'On the day you dragged me here, you ordered me to stop being so lazy. Well now...'

He thought for a moment. Then a sheepish grin crept onto his amiable face. 'True. I did. Blame Luca Volpetti as usual. That makes a change.'

He reached out and took us each by the hand, squeezed our fingers. 'It seems your mutual capacity for bluster is as good as your food. Yes. I will join you in your insanity. You have my word. My silence. On one condition.'

'Which is?' Mia asked.

'I want two tickets for New Year's Eve. Front row. I've a feeling the Teatro Maddalena is headed for a debut to remember.'

∼

That night I spent at home, gravitating between the keyboard, the documents, the unanswerable question of authenticity, and – something I couldn't avoid – searching for information on the man Andriy Kravchuck had mentioned. Vasyl Archaki. Once a lowly Crimean politician, now an important figure among what most would term the Moscow political mafiosi.

An elusive man, mentioned by the media but never in detail. Wealthy as many an oligarch, sanctioned naturally, unable to leave Russia for anywhere in Europe. A yacht under construction in a Sorrento marina had been seized, two villas, one in Tuscany, another outside Siracusa.

There was only one picture I could find, a sour-faced man of middle age in a dinner suit at the Bolshoi, a beautiful woman, unnamed, on his arm. Just a snatched photo. It's wrong to judge anyone on a single image, of course, but seeing that hard, aggressive face, the grimace, the dark, threatening eyes under heavy brows, a head of hair that seemed too slick, too stiff to be real, I found myself shivering as I recalled the encounter Kravchuck had described. The threat – do as I say or suffer – and its consequence. The ready resort to grim, cruel physical and mental violence.

It occurred to me that Archaki must have known the maestro he'd once looked up to would refuse his demands. That he'd already decided on the punishment he'd inflict, perhaps even organised a place for the wounded, miserable Kravchuck on that bus back to Kyiv. Cruelty is second nature to some, almost an automatic act that comes as naturally as a smile to the rest of us. I would not wish to meet Vasyl Archaki. I did not enjoy the thought that one of his lackeys might have been on my trail for months.

One stiff Negroni round the corner with a plate of free chips from Giorgio. I had need of Dutch courage. Then I walked outside and on a dark and chilly night, spattered with occasional drizzle, I stood beneath a tree in Campo Santa Margherita and made the call.

'Arnold,' Valentina Fabbri said. 'It's late and I'm off duty.'

'You're never off duty. Don't pretend different.'

'Nonsense. I'm in the kitchen sorting through the washing. You've no idea what it's like being married to a chef. It's impossible to know what he'll come home stinking of next.'

'I must admit that had never occurred to me. Tell me about the Russians.'

A long pause. Then, puzzled, she said, 'I don't understand. What about them?'

'How many are here in Venice? How important are they?'

'You want to know because...?'

'Because I think one of them may have an interest in the Maddalena.'

'A financial one?'

I never meant that. Stupidly put. 'Not exactly.'

'Do you know where Marcus Haas got his money?' she asked.

'How would I? He was a crook, wasn't he?'

'A fraudster, yes. Do you have any idea where his widow has found the means to continue with this project of yours?'

'Talking to me about money is a waste of time.'

'True. But I had to ask.'

'Are there many Russians in Venice?'

'Not so much anymore. They can't come, can they? There'll be a few businesses in the Piazza who feel the pain because of that. Not that we have a choice in the matter. Nor would desire one.'

'But some must live here.'

'Of course. This is an international city. We have all sorts. I can assure you that any whose name came up on the sanction lists fled long ago, before we found them. Those that are left are residents. Émigrés. Mostly decent people who daren't go back home for fear of what might happen. Dissidents, political maybe. Or just ordinary citizens who hate what's going on there and feel powerless to do anything about it. We have a list. Names to keep an eye on. They know we know, and they understand how to get in touch if they feel something is amiss. That someone is perhaps stalking them.'

'The way I was stalked.'

'There's only one way to stalk people. Don't be over dramatic. The line between crooks and Kremlin hoods may be a blurred one, but I've no reason to believe I need add you to that list.'

'Even though someone tried to kill me. With a poison that probably originated there.'

'Hazard. Now dead himself. I'm not about to make any progress on that, I'm afraid. Had you told me the night he called...'

'Yes, yes, yes. I am suitably scolded. Again. What about the Russians who can't come any more?'

'What about them? This is a question for the Guardia di Finanza. For politicians too. Not me.'

'Do they own much? Do they still have interests here?'

I heard a long, disgruntled sigh down the line. 'Do you really want to know?'

'It's why I asked.'

'The last time I met an officer from Finanza who handles

this kind of thing he said... lots. Not that it was easy to gauge, since they hide these things through so many offshore companies, obscure trusts, tax havens... you name it.' She hesitated. 'From the gossip I hear at least one property in the Piazza San Marco – a restaurant, the apartments above it – belongs to an oligarch who can't set foot in Europe or take rent from it, in theory anyway. The money must go somewhere else. One of their better-known conductors has somehow acquired a palazzo on the Grand Canal, not that he can visit anymore. That's for starters. I know this isn't a business that concerns you, but trust me, it's complicated. If you really understood how little of Venice is owned by Venetians you would, I suspect, be rather surprised.'

I said nothing.

'Now a question for you. Why do you ask?'

'Because I think a rather unpleasant man called Vasyl Archaki may be able to explain some of the mysteries we've encountered.'

A long pause and then she said, 'Never heard of him.'

I wasn't sure I believed that. 'He was the monster who cut off Andriy Kravchuck's fingers.'

'Oh.'

'I gather he's obsessed with Vivaldi.'

'Really? He's not alone in that, surely. Wait...'

I heard footsteps. Then the clattering of a computer keyboard. 'Sorry. I've nothing on the man.'

'Have they taken you off the case again?'

'You do ask the most ridiculous of questions at times. Am I supposed to answer that?'

'No need.' I laughed. 'You did.'

She laughed too. So often dealing with Valentina was like playing badminton. You shot a shuttlecock in the air, watched it float lazily across the net, and wondered what might come back from the other side when, after what seemed like ages, it finally fell.

'And you,' she added in the end, 'have subtly informed me a man like Vasyl Archaki is someone I should take an interest in. A name for my list.'

'Nothing was further from my thoughts.'

'Naturally! Goodnight, Arnold. The washing machine calls. And remember. The next time you fail to inform me of something I should know, I'll drive you to Marco Polo airport myself.'

The following afternoon, after another long day at the desk in the palazzo, found me at a café just a few steps away from the naval station of the Guardia di Finanza next to the Cipriani hotel. Valentina had made me think about this arm of the law enforcement world dedicated to taxation and smuggling and financial affairs. Not that I knew anyone there who might answer any questions about Vasyl Archaki. Or that I might have expected answers even if I did manage to ask a few. I was out of my depth when it came to matters of international criminality and the fringes of espionage.

Back in London, working in the National Archives, I'd seen enough intelligence documents to fill several lifetimes, a few necessarily kept secret, most withheld from the public on the grounds of national embarrassment, nothing more. I was familiar with the visits of various spooks from MI5 and MI6 explaining why we couldn't possibly allow some report about a dead politician or an outed traitor slip into the public domain. They were never people I felt comfortable with. But I noted their manner, their quiet persistence, the way they issued threats without seeming in the least bit menacing. A kind of steely charm was common among the most adept of them.

They also had the ability to appear quite ordinary and unremarkable, which was an essential part of the job, I imagine, since without those qualities how could one appear invisible? Real spooks, it occurred to me, were nothing like the ones you saw on the screen. They were men and women who could fade into the background at will, quiet, unremarkable, faces and voices you'd struggle to remember. I could do ordinary and unremarkable too, as Luca and Valentina Fabbri had, on occasion, noted. In fact, it required no subterfuge on my part at all.

I sat alone at my table by the grey waters of the Bacino San Marco. No Venetian would have braved the cold outside on a bitter day like that, the light rapidly fading, darkness falling as if an unseen hand was drawing down a hazy curtain on the day. Only an Englishman would be fool enough to endure the dying afternoon, as the look on the waiter's face told me when he brought out a decent spritz, complete with olive and lemon, and a bowl of crisps to go with it.

I closed my eyes and took a long draft. Well earned. There was a good reason to be there as I'd discovered during my reading. In Vivaldi's day a church stood where the chasers of smugglers and tax avoiders now moored their fancy vessels. San Giovanni Battista it was called, long demolished.

In 1676 a woman called Camilla Calicchio had hurried there from her home across the water in Castello, accompanied by her lover Giovanni Battista Vivaldi, a barber and a musician, both desperate to be married, but not seen to do so by their neighbours in their own parish of San Giovanni in Bragora. The unmarried Camilla was pregnant with a daughter, Gabriella Antonia, who would live for a year and a half, dying when her younger brother, Antonio was just three months old.

Somewhere behind the old brick wall of the Guardia di Finanza a marriage took place that would give us the musician whose mysterious life now consumed me. So much work, so much energy, so much constant activity. So much fluff and rumour to be dispatched before I could sit down and try to write what I believed to be the truth.

First. Dispel the myths. There was a fanciful story that the day Antonio was born Venice was hit by an earthquake, one so severe it set the church bells ringing, chimneys tumbling to the ground, locals fleeing into the street for their lives.

That Camilla held her infant son up to the turbulent sky and promised God she would make him a priest if only the Almighty allowed him to live. Just the kind of portent that would mark the arrival of a great Venetian, and a tale that would explain his early career in the church. Except there's no record of an earthquake then at all, and Vivaldi was pretty much a priest in name only, complaining constantly that a 'constriction of the chest' meant he was unable to take services.

I finished the spritz and, as I wondered about a second before catching the boat back to Zattere, I realised. There. I had my beginning. The tale of a pregnant young woman crossing the Bacino San Marco to be married somewhere her neighbours, perhaps aware and critical of her morals, could never see. Sex, Mia Haas wanted that. And a myth. Heaven knows there were enough of them to go around. At least the fairy tale of an earthquake greeting Antonio Vivaldi's birth was one I could disprove.

Worth a second drink, I thought, feeling rather proud of myself. Then my attention wandered. A figure had emerged from the narrow passageway by the Zitelle jetty that led to the Maddalena.

Peter Lombardo, the gardener, handyman and hired security guard, or so Kravchuck believed. His tall, muscular frame was bent, a little hunched, and he had a black baseball cap pulled low over his face. One quick look in both directions, so swiftly he didn't notice a nondescript Englishman a good hundred yards away, and a furtive

Lombardo was off, stomping west towards the next vaporetto stop. Redentore, the name of the Palladian church that was the focus of the hectic festival every third Sunday of July when the lagoon was lit up by fireworks, a temporary bridge built across the Giudecca Canal, and you could hardly stand anywhere for the crowds.

Vivaldi and his family vanished from my thoughts. I was suddenly back with those grey men from the security services badgering me in Kew to kill documents I knew represented no threat to the nation, only their own private reputations and those of men and women they wished to protect.

Once, out of interest, I'd followed a particularly obnoxious fellow from MI6 to the station, just to see if he'd notice. Of course he didn't. I was Arnold Clover, a mere archivist, a civil servant, not of his world.

Peter Lombardo had always seemed reluctant to set foot outside the Maddalena, perhaps for reasons of work or more personal ones he wasn't minded to reveal. And here he was striding along the waterfront.

I threw a note on the table and began to follow at a distance. It didn't take long. When Lombardo got to Redentore he took another quick, and I thought lazy, look around then stepped through Andrea Palladio's doors.

It was dark now. Night seemed to have fallen on a sudden burst of gravity. I pulled the collar of my duffel coat around me, thought of dragging up the hood too, though of course one could never do that in a church. I'd be drawing attention to myself, not away from it.

Be invisible, Arnold, I thought, and scuttled through the tall Redentore doors then hurried to a seat in the shadows by the corner.

Lombardo had come here to meet someone. I stared at them, faces clear in the candles and lamps near the altar. Two men locked in serious conversation. A shock at a sudden unwanted memory sent a shiver down my spine.

In the shadowy nave of Redentore I sat and listened. They spoke in German, rapidly, too much for me to understand more than the odd word. Lombardo was a chameleon, that I realised already. Perhaps he wasn't English – or Scottish – at all.

Watching their faces illuminated by the yellow light of the altar, I found myself back in Vienna, sitting on that bench outside the Karlskirche, wondering whether Vivaldi's lost bones might be somewhere beneath our feet.

The wig was gone, just a business cut of real hair now. Clean shaven, unsmiling round face, chubby cheeks, a mouth that looked almost feminine. The man I'd encountered outside the Karlskirche dressed as Mozart. The one who'd given me that case with the papers and the USB stick that had proved so vital these last few months. I knew it the moment the candlelight fell on his features. Then, finally, he slipped into English, and I heard that light, musical, slightly sardonic tone he'd used playing with me in Austria when he'd grinned at me outside the Karlskirche and said, 'Would you care for a taste of one of my balls? I have it on good authority they're luscious.'

I slipped through the shadows to get nearer, enough to hear more clearly though not, I hoped, be seen. They were back in German then, talking rapidly. I couldn't understand a word.

Then Mozart slapped Lombardo on the shoulder and embraced him the way one would an old friend or work acquaintance. There was something about the gesture, the look in their faces, that told me a decision had been made. A corner turned. But what?

They got to their feet quickly, men who'd made a decision. I stayed where I was watching them march outside. A conversation back at the palazzo was on the cards. Mia had placed so much trust in this man, inherited it from her dead husband I guessed. And here he was talking to the mysterious individual who set us on this path in the first place, and seemingly had taken a small fortune from her in return for the precious papers that might be anywhere, at the bottom of the Adriatic, in the hands of the men who killed Rupert Hazard... I'd no idea.

But Peter Lombardo surely did, and if he hesitated for one moment before talking to us, I'd bring in Valentina Fabbri and all the might of the Carabinieri. They wouldn't let him free until he talked.

Naturally, as I was struggling to formulate the words, the actions, the threats we might use to keep a man like Lombardo engaged until he'd shed some light on what he'd been doing all these months, reality intervened.

I stood at the top of the Redentore steps watching them walk down to the broad promenade. Lombardo would turn right, back into the warren of alleys that led to the Palazzo Maddalena. Mozart... I'd no idea.

The two stopped by the lagoon, black and oily in the lamplight beneath a cloud-filled sky that allowed not the least moon to shine through. For once there was a smell from the lagoon. Diesel spilled somewhere, and voices from nearby, cursing one another.

They were still talking, not that I could hear. A Number Two was heading into the public jetty, rolling on an unruly autumn swell.

'Climb on that, Mozart,' I told myself. 'And leave Peter Lombardo, whoever the hell he is, to me.'

The boat arrived. The two men dashed for it, so late the attendant had started to close the railing as they raced along the jetty. Just in time. He was a generous *marinaio* and opened it again. I watched Mozart and Lombardo step into the empty open space behind the cabin. Peter Lombardo looked back in my direction. Maybe admiring Redentore I thought in my innocence. Until he smiled and waved... farewell.

A sudden brain fog descended, along with the realisation I was terribly out of my depth in these strange, deep waters. Then the dawning truth. Lombardo hadn't vanished to brief Mozart on what was happening on Giudecca. He was walking out altogether, leaving Mia on her own in the empty palazzo. Unguarded.

I swore, began to run. Along the waterfront, into those alleys. The gate at the palazzo bridge was wide open. In the hot house where Marcus Haas had died two shapes moving, and then I heard a high-pitched angry scream.

There was a light in Lombardo's shack, the door unlocked. Clothes on the floor, drawers open. A handgun resting on the kitchen table. He'd never have got through airport security with that. I scurried in, grabbed the thing, ran across the dark garden, stumbling against the flower border walls, yelling something I don't recall.

I could just make out two figures at the back of the orchid house near the wicker sofa and the hidden safe. The place we'd found the laptop that set me on the way to Vienna and my meeting with the man dressed as Mozart, now on a vaporetto with Lombardo, the two of them doubtless fleeing Venice as quickly as they could.

A bulky man in a grey suit had his back to me, Mia in front of him, terrified and furious as his hands wound around her throat. The orchid house no longer smelled fragrant and exotic. It was wintry, cold and damp, and stank of decay and death.

He was yelling at her in a language I couldn't understand. A threat. A demand. Hard to tell. As I marched closer, he slapped her hard around the cheek.

Enough. I leapt on him, smashed the gun into his skull, watched him let go, fall to his knees.

I'd not the faintest idea how to use the weapon. There had to be a safety catch or something.

The thug looked up at me, baffled, felt his head. There was blood there and I was glad of that.

'Who the fuck are you?' he asked.

'Might ask the same question.'

'Arnold...' Mia said. 'Don't do anything stupid.'

'I'll try not to. Call Valentina Fabbri. Let's leave this to the Carabinieri.'

He looked up at her from the stone floor, grinned and said, 'She won't do that. Will you?'

On the side of the gun was what looked like a kind of latch. I flipped it, aimed the barrel just above his head, pulled the trigger and found I'd fired. Glass shattered, an orchid's dead flowers were reduced to shreds, the smell of cordite or something filled the air, and my arm ached from the sudden unexpected recoil.

The man laughed, got to his feet, began to walk for the door.

'Don't,' I said. 'You're staying here. Don't...'

I fired another shot above him and broken glass rained down on us from the roof.

He waved a hand and kept walking.

'Tell Vasyl Archaki to keep the hell away,' I yelled.

That made him stop. He turned to face us, puzzled I thought.

'Arnold,' Mia said in a quiet, determined tone. 'Let him go.'

'Of course he'll let me go.' That grin again. 'How on earth would a clown like him stop me?'

I raised the gun again.

He nodded in Mia's direction.

'You heard her, didn't you? I know you, Signor Clover. I

know that everyone's taking you for a fool.' He pointed a finger, the gesture of a gun. Said 'pow' as if it was a shot in my direction. 'Being an idiot ingénue is dangerous in the circles you find yourself. Bear that in mind.' He shrugged. 'On this occasion I must go home empty-handed. This is a disappointment to me and my friends.' He bowed. '*Buona Notte.*'

Before I could do a thing Mia closed on me, pointing at the weapon in my hand. There was a red mark on the side of her face and tears, furious ones I thought, smeared beneath her cheeks. 'For God's sake, Arnold. What do you think you're doing? Put that thing down.'

I did, on the small coffee table by the wicker sofa. Somehow the blasted gun went off, sending another bullet through the glass pane just a yard or so away.

She shook with laughter or tears or both.

'I thought I was helping.'

One quick step and she threw her arms around me, and I felt her warm tears against my cheek. 'You always are, love.'

I told her Lombardo was gone. Vanished into the night with the man I'd met in Vienna, the mysterious Mozart.

A nod then. 'Nothing surprises me anymore. I don't know about you, but I need a drink.'

We sat at the window of her dining room, overlooking that long stretch of dark and mostly empty water running over to the Lido and Pellestrina. Two tall glasses of Scotch and ice and water. I never touched the stuff normally. Just then it tasted like heaven. The night was so black, just a few distant lights on the lagoon, it was hard to believe we were still part of the city. The palazzo Marcus Haas had attempted to rescue was as solitary as it could be. A deliberate act on his part. I didn't doubt that anymore.

I told her about Lombardo, the man I knew as Mozart, how they'd spoken in German in Redentore then vanished together in the night. The mess in Lombardo's shack, the signs he'd decided to get out quickly.

She shook her head and said nothing.

'If he's headed to Marco Polo, or wherever, Valentina Fabbri could find him.'

That got an immediate response. 'I'm sure she could. Then what? A man walks out on his employer. It's not a crime.'

'He left you unprotected. Deliberately, it has to be. He must have known that thug was coming...'

'That thug...' she murmured.

'I couldn't tell what you were saying.'

'That's because it was Croatian.'

I took a deep breath. 'You knew him?'

It came out then, some of the story anyway. Before she was married, she'd worked for a suspect Dubrovnik gambling outfit at a time when Croatia was quite wild, a place where criminals made little effort to hide.

'We had all kinds. Men who'd roll up in Ferraris and throw away fortunes on the tables, wads of dollars, thousands, and never blink an eye. There was so much going on. Smuggling. Trafficking of all kinds. Drugs and people. The money they had...' A grimace then. 'It turned a lot of heads. Mine for a while. You don't know what it's like to be poor, do you?'

'Not seriously poor,' I admitted.

'Then there's no explaining. When someone's desperate they're... desperate. You don't look too hard at what's on offer. You're just glad something is.'

'You knew that man?'

The Scotch vanished. 'No. I recognised him. Back then he was a soldier for one of the gang lords. I don't remember his name. There were so many.

'One day Marcus drove down from Vienna in his Rolls-Royce. Parked outside. Stayed in the hotel. Lost a little money. Hung around looking lonely. A little lost. We talked.' She looked ready to cry. 'That was it. Nothing more. All the others couldn't wait to get me into bed with some offer that was never going to happen. Marcus was different. He knew those people, for sure. But I didn't think he was one of them. He was there two weeks and never really hit on me. Which was a shame. I so wanted him to. I guess he noticed. When he was about to leave, he asked me if I wanted to see Vienna. I never went back.'

'Never?'

'There was nothing for me there. My father was dead in the war. Difficult times, I told you. Marcus rescued me. He was a kind man. A weak man I know now. Manipulated by others.'

'This Croatian wanted the Vivaldi papers?'

Mia Haas nodded. 'The originals.'

'If I hadn't turned up–'

'I'm grateful, honestly. But I'd have dealt with him. I know these people, their sort. You don't. They don't harm anyone without a reason. I told him we didn't have them. But maybe one day we would. And when that day happens... There's always an accommodation to be made. I'm good at that.'

A smart way to try to get out of it, I guess.

'He didn't seem much convinced when I burst in there.'

'I'd have talked him down.' Her face fell for a moment, became hard, remote. 'It's not the first time.'

'I still think Valentina–'

She reached out and touched my hand. 'Arnold. Please. The last thing we need right now is trouble from the Carabinieri. The city council still haven't given me a permit to open. Bringing on some kind of criminal investigation could only make matters worse. Marcus...'

'Marcus what?'

'There are things he did, deals he cut, they still haven't found out about. I'd rather it stayed that way. If we can just get this thing off the ground...'

An awkward moment and she recognised it. 'Oh dear. I've placed yet more trust in you. Don't worry, love. It's nothing you need worry about.'

'I do worry. Lombardo was your security here.'

'I'll hire someone else. One of the agencies.' She looked me straight in the eye. 'Will you stay tonight? I don't want to be on my own.'

'I wouldn't dream of leaving you after this...'

She raised a finger. 'And promise me you won't touch that gun. You're not a man for firearms.'

No arguing there. 'Does the name Vasyl Archaki mean anything?'

Puzzled, she shook her head.

'You said that. No.'

I told her what Kravchuck had revealed to me. The grim story of how he lost his fingers, and the man responsible. How Archaki was obsessed with Vivaldi, perhaps to the point of wanting the papers he must have believed we'd obtained.

Again, she looked baffled. 'Someone would go to all that trouble?'

'Kravchuck seemed to think so. He said Archaki was dangerous. A violent man. With connections.'

'Oh.'

'Would your visitor from Dubrovnik know someone like that?'

She thought for a moment. 'He's Croatian, not a Serb. They're more likely to hang around with Russians. But... criminals. Who knows these days? My husband was one and I didn't have a clue.'

'They might come back.'

She picked up the empty glass. 'I doubt it. They know me. Or rather they know my kind. They appreciate I'd give them anything to stay alive. Even something I really wanted. I'll deal with it. Don't worry.'

I didn't know what to say.

'Enough. Are you hungry? I am.'

I was on my own before I could answer. A few minutes later she was back with a plastic water bottle filled with Pinot Grigio from a local wine shop, a can of tuna, a bag of Conad salad, a pair of blue silk pyjamas.

'I found them in the wardrobe. Marcus rarely wore pyjamas. Don't worry. They're clean. There's a wash bag in your bath-room. If you need anything else just ask.' She grinned as she opened the can of tuna. 'Not the fancy restaurant downstairs, is it? You're seeing how I actually live. The real me.'

We enjoyed one of those meandering talks people some-times have over dinner, no direction, no real purpose except company, which is sometimes the best purpose around.

At the end I turned down the offer of a supermarket tiramisu and went back to the apartment where I'd recovered from the poison on the train, mostly in a daze, thinking about Vivaldi and the story I'd been gifted, one that painted a myste-rious genius in dark and troubling tones.

A few taps on the computer. No emails. No messages on my phone. I showered, climbed into the pyjamas of a dead man called Marcus Haas and fell gratefully into the soft double bed.

Too tired to lock the door, of course. Or perhaps that was my subconscious making decisions I found too hard.

I was trying to nod off, not having much luck, when I heard soft footsteps come close to the bed. I didn't open my eyes. It surely couldn't be another intruder.

'Are you asleep?' she asked, quite loud.

'Not anymore.'

A hand patted the bed, like a parent scolding a child with the lightest of blows. 'You weren't anyway. Stop pretending.'

When I opened my eyes, there she was, inches away, leaning on one elbow, her face calm, interested, wide awake in the dim illumination of the nightlight.

'How may I be of assistance?' I asked.

'Don't talk like that. You're not a servant.'

'True.'

'Don't you ever get lonely?'

A question widowers get asked with an irritating frequency, not that I was about to show it. 'After a year like this? Are you kidding?'

'Not for a moment.'

'On occasion,' I admitted. 'Doesn't everyone?'

'Probably. What do you do?'

A moment then I said, 'Sometimes nothing. Sometimes I nag Luca to go out for a drink. Or Valentina. A walk. See an exhibition.'

'You meet your Carabinieri friend for a social drink?'

'Yes. Why not?'

'She's a dragon.'

'No. She puts on a dragon act. The truth is she's a caring, warm, lovely woman, who just happens to wear a uniform that may make her appear dragon-like at times.'

'Hmmm.'

'What does that mean?'

'You're so generous with your words. But you never get close to anyone, do you? When we meet here... all the things Italians do without thinking... a hug, a peck on the cheek... never you. It's as if you're afraid of physical contact.'

'Rubbish.'

'I hope you don't mind my saying. But it's true.'

'I'm English. Doesn't that explain everything?'

'Not at all! I know plenty of Englishmen who can't wait to lunge in for a quick grab. Too many to be honest. Not you.'

'I just–'

'It's very noticeable. That may be one reason Luca and your Carabinieri friend are so worried about you.'

'They're not worried about me!'

'That's not what Luca said when he asked me to hire you.'

She edged closer. I was becoming a little uncomfortable and determined not to show it. Somewhere outside there was the sound of a boat manoeuvring down the narrow canal, beneath the bridge into the estate. It carried on until the engine faded into silence. I was glad of that. The security of the palazzo still concerned me.

'I'm still waiting for an answer.'

Mia was wearing an exotic perfume, one that reminded me of the orchid house in bloom. I doubt I'd ever been this close to a woman so elegant, so composed, before. Eleanor was much like me: plain, straightforward, uninterested in embellishment.

'Okay,' I said. 'I'm not just English. I'm from Yorkshire.'

'What on earth does that mean?'

'Barry Horner.'

'Pardon?'

'Barry Horner! He was my best friend at school. Well, the only friend really.'

'Is there a point to this?'

'Yes. We grew up in this dead-end northern town, no hope, not much in the way of money, little chance of escape. I struck lucky. I got to Cambridge on a scholarship.'

'And Barry Horner?'

'He became a bus driver.'

'Did you stay in touch?'

'No. Different worlds. North and south. Middle class and working.'

'I still don't understand–'

'One time someone was ribbing us about how men where we came from never hugged. Barry said…' I wasn't sure this was a wise thing to come out with. I'd never even told Eleanor. 'He said that in our bit of Yorkshire hugging was only socially acceptable as a prelude to sex. And since no one ever had sex there, what was the point of hugging?'

She stared at me hard for a moment. Then burst out laughing. 'You should have stayed in touch with your friend. He sounds funny.'

'He was. Long time ago. Lot of water under the bridge as they say.' I knew she wanted me to ask. 'What about you?'

'What about me?'

'Do you get lonely?'

'Oh yes. I did when Marcus was alive. It was that kind of marriage. Now he's gone… it's odd. By now we'd have been in the throes of a divorce. If that hadn't affected the great project.'

'Is there no one?'

'I told you. My father died fighting the Serbs.'

'And your mother?'

'I was brought up mostly by my grandma. Long gone.'

'I'm sorry.'

'People die, Arnold. Not much you can do about it most of the time. I miss Marcus more than anyone, since he's the most recent I guess. The company. The laughter, infrequent as it was towards the end. I miss his presence. His pointless little tantrums and the fact that, however much we were drifting apart, there was still love in there somewhere. Battered, misshapen love, but love all the same.' She took a deep breath then said, 'I miss sleeping with him. The closeness. The way something physical and largely mindless takes away everything for a while. All the worries, the pain, the struggles.'

A gull shrieked somewhere. It was the end of October. Winter would be here any day.

Winter.

The final concerto in *The Four Seasons*. The movement that closed out the tale.

What was it Vivaldi wrote to accompany the ending section of the work?

> *We tread across the ice with careful footsteps,*
> *Paying attention not to slip and fall –*
> *But turn and crash down on the earth and sleet;*
> *Then, rising, hasten on across the ice*
> *In case the surface cracks beneath our feet.*

That was me, my life, my ridiculous, errant wandering through this strange, eventful year. Careful footsteps racing across the ice above an unseen, perilous fate. Wanting that danger, the excitement it brought.

Mia rolled over, kissed me once on the cheek, scrambled up and said, 'Goodnight. Busy times ahead.'

I waited till she was gone then pulled out the thing I'd surreptitiously liberated from her apartment that afternoon. The laptop belonging to Marcus Haas they'd found in the Orchid House, the one that set me on the path to Vienna.

The original email exchange with the figure who called himself vivaldi 1741 was still there.

Without a second thought I sent off another message.

```
Tell Lombardo he's a useless shit. Tell
'Mozart' he's a fool. As to your master...
I have what he wants. A price as well.
```

Intermezzo III

It was dark at Macondo. A biting breeze wafting in from the Adriatic. The calls of night birds, the rattle of the fisherman's *capanno da pesca*, the creaks and groans of the brazier burning down to its last embers. Time, I felt, running out.

'Did you have to bring me all this way to try to kill me?' I asked.

Laughter. 'My. You are the drama queen at times.'

I picked up the wine bottle and placed it over the scrap of musical notepaper to stop the Devil's Tritone blowing away.

'Why send me this then?'

A pained groan. 'For the same reason I left you the gun. To get you here. To bait that endless curiosity of yours. It worked, didn't it? If you thought I was out to harm you... why come?'

'Everyone wants to know the way a mystery ends. How everything pans out.'

'Curiosity killed the cat, Arnold.'

Nothing else. Just a rifle through the remains of the food and the discovery of the last cracker.

'I asked—'

'I'm not deaf! You make far too many presumptions, all too rapidly.' A smile. 'Besides. What have you got to complain about? You've a new friend now, haven't you? Keeping a widow happy in her grief, not that it was so great I'd have to say. Very thoughtful of you.'

Throwing punches was never my thing. But that, I felt, could change.

'Gone all quiet, have you? Tell me about the lovely Mia? Is this a sunset romance? How very touching if a tad unexpected. And... I'd have to say unrealistic. On your part that is.'

'Meaning?'

'Meaning she's the reason you're here.'

Not a single fishing boat on the horizon now. Anything could happen in a place like this. No one would know.

'No questions, Signor Clover? If you wish to talk about the lady–'

'I do not. It's none of your damned business. A spy like you should surely have more important matters on your mind.'

Two hands came out suddenly, grabbed the gun, did something with the magazine. Checked it had bullets maybe. How was I to know?

The last of the wine went. Not into my glass either. The scrap of musical notation vanished with the wind, fluttering over the darkness of the beach like a leaf fallen from a paper tree.

'How long am I supposed to wait? I have a concert to attend.'

'I said. No concert for you. That's off the agenda.'

'After all the work I've put in? All the pain?'

'I doubt Mia Haas was painful. Be patient, please.'

I got to my feet. 'Enough of this... I'm going for the bus.'

'Sit down!' The gun waved at me. 'Don't be so stupid. There is no bus. It's New Year's Eve. At seven a boat will pick us up. Straight to Zattere for you, then, I'd suggest, home. A quiet night in. Grateful you're still alive, I trust. Lord knows that's a miracle in itself.'

'Oh.' I grabbed the bottle and tried to squeeze the last drop of white out of it. 'You have your man then. Vasily Archaki. The great ruse – Vivaldi, the papers, the trickery and Vienna – they worked. I trust you think it all – the deaths, the lies, the subterfuge, so much money and effort – worth it.'

There was a long silence. Then, 'I so wish you hadn't said that. Excuse me. I must make a call.'

Straight round the back of the bar and I heard a low, concerned voice and a couple of curses.

There was a napkin in the hamper. I picked up the empty wine bottle, wrapped the cloth around the neck, went and stood in the shadows, hidden by what in summer would be the busy serving hatch.

Perhaps it was stupid of me to let him know I'd finally started to see through the labyrinth of lies and misdirections thrown at me that year. Or hoped I had.

Perhaps if I'd acquiesced everything might have worked out differently, for the better. Life has its own direction at times, regardless of any way you wish to push it. There are occasions when it's pointless to agonise over which fork to take in the road ahead, left or right, up or down. There may be no wrong decision, no right one. Just a choice to be made over the timid and craven alternative of apathy.

Dammit I was going to be there that night to see whatever climax they had in mind when Vivaldi's music returned to the place the maestro once played and conducted three centuries before.

Footsteps. I moved back into the shadows.

An angry voice, English, gruff, all too familiar. 'Oh for God's sake, don't play these games now. There's nowhere for you to go. All you have to do is wait. Seven, I told you... Christ, Lucky...'

Lucky.

Unseen I stepped out from the dark then hit the man I knew as Rupert Hazard as hard as I possibly could.

Part Four

L'inverno, Winter

Chapter Ten

Allegro non molto

Winter began with swirling fog, the heavy grey shroud of the lagoon, and the Maddalena estate finally bursting into life.

As the days passed, I could see the sketchy idea first described to me that April begin take physical form in a way that, for once, was greater, grander, more impressive than any architect's drawing. There was a new professionalism about the place. A larger security firm were supplying two uniformed, armed guards day and night, demanding ID for everyone who came and went. A necessity after the disappearance of Lombardo, a man Mia seemed to dismiss as unworthy of consideration. I soon gave up asking her to bring in Valentina Fabbri to chase the fellow and the chap with him, my mysterious Mozart from Vienna. Nor was there much point in wondering why these two unlikely acquaintances knew each other in the first place.

When we talked about this Mia thought the answer obvious. The seller of the goods had somehow placed Lombardo in their midst to keep an eye on affairs. Then the papers went missing, perhaps stolen back by them, or others. Quite who the Croatian thug was working for we didn't know, couldn't guess.

Vasyl Archaki? She shrugged and said again she'd never heard of the man. When the place was open, when there was money available, they'd be in touch and – that phrase she loved – an accommodation could be made. Perhaps simply an acceptance on their part that the papers really were gone, beyond retrieval. It was a problem, she insisted, for another day. What mattered was the project, the auditorium, the palazzo, the tribute to Vivaldi. Here and now, things we could touch, affect and hope to control. Nothing else.

In any case, if I'd finally persuaded Mia to bring in the Carabinieri, what would Valentina say? I'd just be asking for another fierce telling-off for failing to inform her the moment Lombardo vanished and that Croatian made his brief entrance. Nor was there any obvious crime to be investigated. As Mia insisted, a member of staff had bunked off. Nothing was missing, and a threatening conversation with a Croatian thug she couldn't name hardly amounted to a criminal investigation.

Besides there were such distractions, not just Mia, a woman quite unlike any I'd ever known, brimming over with ideas and enthusiasm, never still, always filled with a constant almost nervous energy. She was now the mistress of the Teatro Maddalena and its swish hotel, approving menus, furnishings, making me listen to Kravchuck's players and pass an opinion about the changing acoustics of the auditorium as a team of specialists moved around baffles and fittings to improve the sound.

Outside, new gardeners had arrived from a commercial horticultural company and turned Lombardo's simple flower beds into elaborate showcases of winter shrubs and a host of colourful ornamental cabbages. The seating and box office of the auditorium were all in place. In the palazzo, the first-floor rooms were finished and a few travel writers ushered through by Mia, a practised publicist as she'd said, in the firm hope of garnering some copy and bookings for the following spring. The restaurant was pretty much up and running too, offering inexpensive light dishes for lunch to Kravchuck's busy musicians as the menu took shape.

San Pantalon was forgotten. Seven days a week I spent either at my desk in the palazzo or insisting Mia take a break from her busy schedule and relax in the city beyond Giudecca. I realised that, with all the time she'd spent on the Maddalena, she'd never found the opportunity to explore Venice much beyond its walls.

There's a special, private joy in discovering you can act as a guide, a cicerone, for the uninitiated, opening someone's eyes to corners of a world they thought familiar but never really knew. I led her to the quiet places I'd come to love, the Scuola degli Schiavoni with its Carpaccio knights and saint and dragons, the same painter's Ursula cycle in the Accademia, to little-known churches and a few private palazzi where Luca Volpetti's name opened doors that would otherwise be closed.

We ate ice cream on the Zattere at Nico's, pasta at Ai Pugni where I so often sat with Luca, that winter speciality *moeche,* soft shell crab, at Al Mercà in the old market on the Lido.

All the time the unveiling of the Teatro Maddalena grew closer, as did she.

The twenty-first of the month was the Festa della Salute. A weekday but I insisted Mia abandon work for once and we took the vaporetto across the Bacino to San Marco then walked round to the temporary bridge built across the Grand Canal every year, to make a direct route to the basilica at the foot of Dorsoduro.

It always amazed me how Venice's engineers could erect the thing overnight, allowing boat traffic to pass through pretty much unaffected, then, from early morning till the evening, so much of the city's dwindling population would gather to cross the sturdy structure that in a couple of days would be gone.

Mia was impressed, naturally, and I told her the story of its origins. How in 1630 a terrible plague had wiped out a third of the city's population and the baroque wonder of Salute was built to celebrate its eventual end. How, for the locals, this was a day to remember those they'd loved and lost, and light a candle in their memory in Baldassare Longhena's great basilica.

We climbed Salute's fifteen steps representing the mysteries of the rosary then, inside the shady interior, I bought two candles, one for my lost Eleanor, the second for Marcus. The atmosphere of that place, of the silent contemplation of all the people around us, young and old, moved us both as we stood in the tenebrous octagonal nave listening to the hymns of a choir we couldn't see. A moment that needed no words. That waving sea of flickering candles around us marked both love and loss, life and death, for us, for all the others who'd crammed into the church that day.

After, there was another small ceremony, tracking down the little restaurant I knew near San Giacomo dell'Orio where I first tasted the unique dish Venetians ate for the Festa della Salute. Castradina, smoked leg of mutton with cabbage, a recipe originally made from meat brought in from Dalmatia and Albania, the only outside food that Venice obtained during the height of the 1630 plague.

We sat by the narrow rio in the wan light of a dying autumn day, the Ponte Del Megio in front of us, our presence amusing a gaggle of gondoliers hawking for trade who couldn't believe two foreigners were eating local. An acquired taste, a meaty cross between a rough stew and soup, simple to the point of being crude. But it was the Festa della Salute. Traditions mattered, and, as always in Venice, they marked the seasons.

'What do you think?' I asked.

She pulled a face. 'We won't be putting it on the menu.'

'You can't. It's for Salute only. Besides, not everything needs to be elegant and sophisticated. This is something Vivaldi would have eaten when he was here.'

'You're sure of that? Does he mention it?'

'No.'

'Does he mention food and drink at all?'

I had to think about that. 'Not that I recall. Just music. Money. Travel. Arguments. His ego, his achievements. Women, naturally. Many, many women.'

Mia pushed away her bowl of castradina, half-finished. 'I grew up surrounded by music. A lot of it his. It ought to sound different now, knowing what he was like. But it doesn't.'

'Why would it?'

'I've no idea. If the man in those pages is him...'

That was a subject we hadn't touched on for weeks.

'If...' I agreed.

'What happens should we turn out to be frauds, Arnold?'

'Maybe I write a book about being defrauded. And you sell more tickets to the Teatro Maddalena.'

She stared at me. 'That doesn't sound like you. Being cynical.'

'I was trying to be... positive.'

'No turning back now, is there?'

'None whatsoever.'

She reached across the table and took my hand. 'I don't deserve you.'

That made me laugh. 'You deserve so much more.'

'No.' She wouldn't take her eyes off me. 'I really don't.'

Mia walked inside, paid the bill before I had the chance, stood by the canal and blinked at the bright grey sky. She was crying and I couldn't for the life of me work out why. The gondoliers had gone quiet, embarrassed. One glanced at me and pointed a finger in her direction.

Not that I needed it. I got up, went over to the canal, held her, tried to wipe away a tear trickling down her cheek.

'It's okay,' I whispered. 'The first time I lit a candle for Eleanor, I cried too. It's Salute. The ones we lose come back for us, for a little while anyway.'

A short, grim shake of her head. 'You think it's that? Marcus? He's gone. He ran away and killed himself, leaving me to clean up his mess.'

'Then...'

I had my arms around her. She held me. We stood by that old bridge and that narrow canal and kissed, the way new lovers do, both tenderly and tentatively, wondering where any of this might lead. Behind us came a round of applause from the gondoliers and one ribald comment I wasn't minded to translate.

November. Everyone in town seemed to be at Salute. The rest of Venice appeared deserted. We had the open stern of the 4.1 vaporetto to ourselves, that curious itinerary, through the commercial areas behind Piazzale Roma, out to the open waters of the Giudecca Canal, then across, stop by stop, to Zitelle.

No words. Just company and comfort and closeness.

We rushed through the grounds of the Maddalena without stopping, not minding who looked, who wondered what they saw.

Then to bed. Mia was asleep in my arms by ten or so, the estate empty except for the guard in Lombardo's old hut beside the bridge, only the sounds of the lagoon, a night breeze, the odd bird call, a boat going down the canal.

There'd been a noise I'd heard from along the corridor. The beep of an incoming message on my laptop. Gingerly, I managed to unwind myself from her, slide out of bed, then walk back into the office.

There it was on the screen finally. A reply from vivaldi1741.

```
You are either brave or rash or both
Arnold    Clover.   One   day   we   must
find out.
```

There were no messages after that, just bustle and writing and the awkward, uncertain beginnings of love. By the start of December the name Vasily Archaki, the attack in the orchid house, pretty much everything dark from the past was gone from my mind. There was too much to do in the race to bring the theatre alive in time for Capodanno, to open the rooms for Mia's first guests in the palazzo, and to finish the book.

It was no secret we were now a couple. Reggie Davies acknowledged it in a quiet way and looked pleased. The same with Kravchuck. Ellen Kim simply gave me a side eye that I ignored.

In the first week of the month the recreated pages from the memory stick arrived from a specialist printer in Padua. They were placed in glass display cases in the finished foyer of the auditorium, four sheets from the score of The Seasons, two pages detailing Vivaldi's denial he was Casanova's father, and the page in which Casanova insisted he was.

The work the printer had done was exceptional. The yellowed vellum paper, curled at the edges and seemingly stained by age, looked, under glass, authentic, as did the penmanship of that swirling hand I'd seen in Vivaldi's proven letters and scores. The same with Casanova. Each sheet bore a label in Italian and English describing the contents, with a translation of Luca's in English. Nowhere was there mention of the provenance, or that these were copies of anything. We simply left that unspoken for now. The truth behind the texts could be revealed when finally my book was published, if the deception managed to last that long.

On 8 December, the Feast of the Immaculate Conception, the beginning of Christmas in Italy, Mia unveiled a small *presepe,* a traditional nativity scene, in an alcove on the canal wall next to the bridge, illuminated figurines of Mary, Joseph, the infant Jesus in a crib, farm animals and the three wise men. A crowd of locals from the neighbouring streets in our corner of Giudecca came to watch the ceremony, and were then, to their surprise, welcomed into the grounds. Kravchuck led the small orchestra in a concert of religious music with a Croatian choir Mia had invited over from Zagreb. I sat entranced by everything, the music, the quiet, sanctified atmosphere that harked back to the theatre's origins as a church. Then came free Prosecco and *cicchetti* from the restaurant kitchen, now almost complete. Mia had won the hearts of her neighbours for sure.

To my surprise, Luca was there in his customary winter tabard and long scarf, his friend Silvia from the Cini library on San Giorgio Maggiore by his side. We'd not spoken in ages, nor had I heard from Valentina. I felt bad about that. Scarcely a week went by usually in which we didn't meet for a coffee and one of those spiky conversations I'd come to love.

I'd seen him with quite a few different women in the past. He had an easy, engaging manner they found entertaining, one I could never hope to emulate even if I wished it. A serious man who hid his erudition behind a façade of pleasant, carefree chat. He was also someone who'd always prized his independence. But now, with his new friend from the Accademia, things seemed different.

At the end of the concert, while Mia mingled among strangers, charming them, perhaps selling a few tickets and hotel reservations, I edged over to talk. Silvia was charming, articulate, elegant, very Venetian, learned but light and funny with it, a perfect foil for my good friend's occasional flippant pomposity. As we chatted Mia came to join us and I found myself in a situation I'd never expected again, two couples making amiable small talk, about the weather, the dire state of the world, the coming holiday season, and, naturally, the Teatro Maddalena. Though when it came to the pages on display in the auditorium Luca kept quiet and cast me nothing more than a smile and a quick glance.

Silvia expressed an interest in seeing inside what was once the Palazzo Colonna-Ottoboni. She knew a little of its history from an exhibition she'd worked on in Rome, to do with Cardinal Pietro Ottoboni, patron, some said lover, of Arcangelo Corelli, a supporter of Scarlatti and for a time Vivaldi as well. A notoriously extravagant and sensual figure of the church, born in Venice, lover of both sexes, father to between sixty and seventy children among a veritable flock of mistresses. Nephew to the Pope, which helped.

'You must have him in your book, Arnold,' she declared. 'I can't wait to hear what Vivaldi wrote about him.'

I fumbled for an answer and found none.

'He did write something, didn't he? They must have known one another well.'

'Mostly he writes about the people he argued with.'

'Oh…'

Mia took the opportunity to lead her off to the palazzo.

'She's quite something your new friend,' I said when they were gone. 'You're a lucky man.'

'I am,' Luca agreed. 'Also, I'm getting old. I turn fifty next year, believe it or not. Am I too old to wed? Be honest, Arnold. What do you think?'

A married Luca Volpetti. There was something I never expected to see. 'Not that I'm an expert, but I'd say no one's ever too old for love.'

'This is all quite beyond me,' he admitted. 'Passion, the fire of the moment, is one thing. But when it turns deeper, into friendship and something gentler, more... indefinable, I'm at a loss.'

'I'm at a loss most of the time. You get used to it.'

'If it happens... will you be my *testimone dello sposo*? What I believe you call the "best man"? To make sure I get to the altar? Drag me if need be?'

I laughed and shook his hand. 'It would be the greatest honour. I look forward to the day.'

He hugged me and kissed my cheek once. 'They say that love makes a fool of you. If so I'm a happy fool. As are you by the looks of it. I couldn't be more pleased for you, Arnold.' He raised his glass. 'For us. Here's to autumn love.'

'Winter in my case,' I said without thinking. 'I'm a little older, remember?'

He was barely listening, just staring at the palazzo, its Istrian marble façade now tastefully illuminated by subtle spotlights.

'Strange there's no mention of Ottoboni. A Venetian too... Though it seems the Vivaldi you've uncovered is nothing like the man we expected.'

'Christmas,' I said, keen to change the topic.

'What about it?'

'Will you be here?'

'No. I promised to go with Silvia to see her mother in Bolzano. Valentina's lot are off to see Franco's grandmother in Milan. You'll be on your own this time, I'm afraid.' He tapped my elbow. 'Just joking. I'm sure you'll both be fine. And then there's Capodanno.'

He raised his glass.

～

By the twenty-fifth there was just the two of us rattling around the Maddalena estate, a happy couple, along with a single security guard in his hutch. Mia made sure he was fed and happy, triple time too, and produced lunch for us from the fishmongers by the vaporetto stop. Oysters, lobsters, a selection of fish *cicchetti* – no meat – and a bottle of the best Franciacorta.

After that, even on Christmas Day, it was back to work. She began processing the flood of bookings for the opening concert, and the trickle of reservations coming in for the rooms, now almost finished, in the palazzo. I wrote and wrote and wrote, rewrote and reread.

A week later, New Year's Day, we were up at six, preparing to throw the Teatro Maddalena open to the world. *The Four Seasons* with our resident small orchestra under the direction of Andriy Kravchuck, one of the foremost Vivaldi experts in the world. A new auditorium, using the latest acoustic technologies, the concert to be streamed live for free to anyone who wanted to watch and listen. Those display cabinets with the pages, Vivaldi's handwriting and Casanova's. A spectacle, a pageant to match all the other splendours of Capodanno in a festive Venice.

Kravchuck and Ellen Kim had returned from London and New York respectively. They'd joined the musicians the previous day for a final brief rehearsal, this time in concert dress, black and formal which somehow made the sound deeper and more moving than before. It was soon apparent the event would be sold out, with a fair number of VIPs, the mayor, city dignitaries, a senior official from the Culture Ministry in Rome among them. It would be a short event, The Seasons only along with a brief opening speech by Mia, followed, inevitably, by the mayor who had to have his say – a condition of his attendance.

When the music was finished, and after a brief reception in the palazzo, the audience would be urged to head out to the promenade along the lagoon for the fireworks. It all sounded so easy. Kravchuck's constant sessions in the preceding months had made sure his musicians were primed to perform at their peak. All the last-minute tweaks to the auditorium were done, every last chair and furnishing in the public areas complete. Mia had decided the copy of the Donatello Maddalena deserved to be reinstated near the lobby and ignored all my objections. That monstrosity apart, the Teatro and the palazzo looked, to my untrained eyes, tasteful, elegant, restrained and very Venetian, a tribute to Mia's taste for design.

My manuscript had reached 90,000 unrevised, very raw words. I'd deliberately held off reading much of it closely since every time I did, I saw some fault, a stupid error or typo. Get it down and fix it later was my plan. Reggie's advice about the necessity for structure had proved invaluable. It gave me a framework for the whole project and an idea of how to divide it into sensible sections and chapters. Since this was a map of Vivaldi's life from cradle to unknown grave, chronological order seemed essential. Out of the blue one day while working in the office, listening to one more rehearsal in the neighbouring theatre, it occurred to me to borrow the structure from the source. The book would be divided in the same way as Vivaldi had arranged his most famous work, spring, summer, autumn, winter. Except here they would be the seasons of his strange, itinerant, hitherto unexplained life.

Spring for the young man growing up when Venice was a republic grandly fading, Canaletto making a small fortune setting it down on canvas, visitors coming from all over the known world to wonder at its beauty. Antonio learning the violin from his loving father, playing in churches for money, training for the priesthood with a tonsure shaved in his ginger hair. In 1703 he's ordained as a priest, working first at San Giovanni in Oleo, later at La Pietà, where he assumes the role of *maestro di violino* and, for three years becomes chaplain before music turns into his sole employ.

Summer for Vivaldi starts when his prodigious output begins to be recognised, his concertos published in Amsterdam in 1711, his first opera in Vicenza two years later. The same year he's both impresario at the Teatro Sant'Angelo and *maestro di coro* at La Pietà. The ladder to fame is steep and swift, and over the next fifteen years, Anna Girò by his side, he rises to become the most acclaimed composer and virtuoso violinist in Europe.

Autumn. This I date to 1730, when Vivaldi's work is still popular, but something is amiss. He returns to Venice, declaring that, after his travels to Austria and beyond, he will never leave his native city again. But months later he's journeying to Germany in search of work and money and slowly it becomes clear his career has peaked, that tastes have changed, that Vivaldi, perhaps due to his combative nature, has few friends in the world. In 1735 his *Griselda*, with the libretto by Goldoni, premiers at Teatro San Samuele, and he returns, begrudgingly the memoirs say, to La Pietà in the role of *maestro de' concerti*.

Winter begins in 1736. Vivaldi's father, Giovanni Battista, dies, and the composer is heartbroken. His discussions about work in Ferrara turn vituperative and edge towards disaster. The following year he's banned from entering the city due to rumours about his relationship with Anna Girò, dashing his plans for a Carnival opera. One year later the governors of La Pietà vote not to renew his contract and his opera, *Siroe re di Persia*, now lost entirely, proves a commercial failure. The genius is unwanted, the star has fallen.

In 1740, after four final concerts at La Pietà, Vivaldi announces he's leaving Venice and sells more than twenty concertos to the church to fund his travels. At the beginning of the following year, he's in Vienna, desperately seeking the chance to beg work from aristocrats who do not wish to see him. By July, he's dead, an unknown, impoverished itinerant priest, buried in an unmarked grave, no mention of his musical career at all.

A life described in seasons, from bright, youthful spring to glorious summer, fading autumn and a final bleak and sickly winter.

The night before I'd finally plucked up the courage to pass my draft to Mia. She locked herself in her room with the laptop and told me to sleep next door. She wanted to focus on what I'd given her and seemed delighted by what appeared to her a privilege – I had to point out she was paying. Then, for the first time since Redentore, I went back to my old bedroom and slept like a log.

First thing the next morning, before the musicians and the staff began to assemble for the coming concert, I found her still reading spread-eagled on the bed in her pyjamas. I steeled myself and made us coffee and breakfast in the kitchen.

'Well?' I asked when I came back.

She wrinkled her nose, looked mildly disappointed for a second or two, then laughed and kissed me quickly.

'Well?' I repeated.

'You're getting there, love. You did say this was your first time.'

'For lots of things.'

'No. Not lots. Sometimes you forget what you know. Who you are. What moves you. Here...'

She liked the structure, the seasons. 'The story's all there. All the right parts. All the right order. It reads well.'

There was a note in her voice then.

'But it can be improved?'

'Of course! You don't need to sound so dry, for one thing. You're not naturally that way. Think of your audience. Write the way you talk, not the way you think you should put down words on paper. Maybe we can get an audiobook out too. You reading it. You have a nice voice.'

'Thank you. My audience?'

'Ordinary people. People like me.'

'You're not ordinary. Anything but.'

She blushed. 'You still don't know me, Arnold. The point is... people don't want to be befuddled by technical musical terms we won't understand, or a stream of dates and events. We want a story, an understandable narrative. The tale of a musical genius who rises to great heights then falls from grace. A man with a secret rather sordid private life who destroys his own legacy through what? Egotism? Arrogance? A haughty, inflexible nature? Or just plain bad luck?'

Nothing in the proven material supported that. I recalled what Luca's new friend Silvia said. It was odd a fellow Venetian, Cardinal Ottoboni, an important man Vivaldi knew and accepted work from received no mention in the memoirs at all. I'd checked meticulously for dates and places against known records. But it had never occurred to me to wonder about omissions, lacunae in the tale that seemed strange. Perhaps it was as I suggested to Luca. In Vienna, at the end, as he scrawled out these desperate recollections, it was only the bad memories that lingered, not the good. It certainly felt that way. The man who wrote this was unkind to women, ungenerous when it came to praise for his fellow musicians and only allowed flattery to come into his letters when begging for money from those who possessed it. With a tone very close to that of Casanova himself, supposedly his son.

Perhaps...

'You're looking sceptical, love,' she said.

'I suspect I usually do.'

'Of me too?' she asked, wide-eyed.

'No,' I said straight off. 'Not you. This year... made me feel alive. Engaged. As if I mattered, and I'd given up on that really. You do when you walk away from everything. Luca was right to send me here. I've watched you build something extraordinary.'

'With no small amount of help from you.'

'Every minute was a pleasure.'

'Not on that train, Arnold! It nearly killed you.'

'You've rather made me forget about that.'

She kept her eyes on the laptop, not me for a second.

There was a sound outside. A single instrument, a cello, two notes. I thought they drifted from the harmonic into the Devil's Tritone, but perhaps that was simply my febrile imagination. Something about Mia's frame of mind was odd.

'Now,' she said firmly. 'To more immediate matters. What do you plan to wear?'

'Wear?'

'A duffel coat and a lumberjack shirt won't work, will it? Do you own a serious suit?'

'For funerals and weddings mostly. At my age normally the former.'

'A white shirt? A tie? I can't keep pulling stuff out of Marcus's wardrobe. It doesn't really fit.'

'Um... Somewhere. Back in San Pantalon.'

'Well...' I got a finger wag that would have done Valentina Fabbri justice. 'It's back home then. I want you smart tonight. There are people to meet. Influential ones with money. I want you at your best.'

~

There was one last look at the manuscript, where I saw immediately that Mia was right. The tone was too dry and academic in places. Easy enough to fix. It was almost ten when I left the palazzo. By that time the Maddalena estate was looking busier than I'd ever seen it. Kravchuck was there with Ellen Kim, the two of them close in conversation by a piano in the auditorium, clearly not wishing to be disturbed. Caterers were bringing in plates and glasses, getting their orders from the kitchen staff. Strings of fairy lights hung across the winter garden, glistening beneath the winged lion flag of Venice.

I walked out across the bridge, open now with two security staff checking people in and out. It was the first time I'd left the place since before Christmas. There was scarcely a soul around in the adjoining streets. The waterfront was empty too under that bright, thin winter sun. Across the water, cormorants perched on the bricole, wooden markers for navigation that looked like sawn-off tree trunks, stretching their wings in gratitude for the warmth. This was the turn of the year in Venice, a time I'd always loved since I moved here. For its quiet and solitary nature, the way you could walk into the Basilica San Marco without a queue. The absence of people, a city laid bare in all its quiet beauty.

Stepping outside the Maddalena felt strange. Like returning to a known, familiar world after living inside a dream. Still, I couldn't get Vivaldi and those memoirs out of my head.

The Number Two was pulling into the Zitelle stop headed for San Marco. The boat looked pretty much empty, except there, seated by the window, smiling at nothing at all, was Silvia Casciano, Luca's new love, wearing a puffy black jacket and a fake fur hat. Next stop San Giorgio Maggiore. Going to work? On New Year's Eve?

I needed to know and dashed to get on. Two other passengers only, and an old man wrapped up for winter who stayed on the open deck for some reason. Still, the *marinaio* looked grateful for the company.

'Arnold!' She was waving at me as I climbed on board.

'What are you up to?' she asked as I sat down. 'Don't you have work to do for tonight?'

'I have to go home and get some clothes. Smart clothes. Mia insists.'

'Quite right too. This is an occasion to remember.'

'Silvia...'

'I'm meeting up with some colleagues first. Working lunch. Then we're all coming over to the Maddalena to wish you well.'

'Fine. But...'

She hesitated. A perceptive woman.

'What is it? What's wrong?'

A long shot. The vaporetto had already crossed the narrow channel past the Cipriani and was docking under the shadow of the church.

'Is there anyone there from the Vivaldi Institute? Today?'

'Why yes. Gabriele. Didn't you talk to him earlier? I thought you said you'd visited and found little of use for your work. Understandable. It's the music that interests them.'

'No. It was a young woman. She wasn't particularly helpful.'

'Ah... An intern, I imagine. They don't really know much if I'm honest. Did she put you in touch with the staff?'

No. And of course I hadn't pushed it, assuming there really was nothing to find.

We got off and began to walk towards the Cini buildings. Much more like it. Silvia moved very quickly. Before long we were in front of the maze dedicated to the writer Jorge Luis Borges, behind the magisterial building of the foundation library.

'Have you tried it?'

'Sorry?'

'The maze. Our garden of forking paths. You should. Not now. It's easy enough to escape if you keep your head. If you don't someone will come and rescue you.'

A simple entrance, choices about which way to go. No obvious exit. A memory came to me of something Borges had written in that story, about a 'labyrinth in which all men would become lost'.

Somewhere in that curious year I'd chosen a path ahead of me, one that led me into a maze from which there seemed no escape. And like every maze, there was never the chance to see beyond the route I'd picked. Or had picked for me.

Ottoboni should have been in the memoirs. It was obvious.

'Is Gabriele here?' I said.

He was. A tall and skinny academic with a grey beard, shoulder-length hair and that black tabard so popular among middle-aged Venetian academics in winter.

We stood outside the dining room where lunch was being prepared for the Cini staff.

One question.

'Gabriele. Was there someone here earlier, a year ago perhaps, asking questions about Vivaldi's background? Looking for material.'

'*Sì.* There was.'

'And...?'

'And I told him to get lost. The fool just seemed interested in gossip. Did we have anything that showed Anna Girò was Antonio's lover?' He laughed. 'As for the most ridiculous idea he had...'

'That Vivaldi had something to do with Casanova?'

'Were they related? He asked that! How ridiculous. There's nothing, not a scrap of material we know of, that puts the two together. Do you imagine Casanova wouldn't have put that in his memoirs if it was the case.' He pulled out a large smart phone and started going through some records there. 'It was last January, just after Epiphany. I gave him an hour of my time and then told him we had nothing to offer. The man... He was quite pleasant about it, I must say. When I appeared offended by his line of questioning, he said he was simply trying to write some kind of popular novel. A scurrilous story of the time. I suggested his attempt at fiction might best come from his imagination. Not here.'

I held my breath for a moment then said, 'A name?'

'He was English. Middle-aged. Quite heavy. I didn't take his name.' A thought. 'I believe he was some kind of musician. He mentioned playing an instrument himself.'

'A cello?'

'A cello. Yes. Do you know the man?'

'Possibly.'

I marched back to the vaporetto stop, wondering how long it might take to get a boat on a day like this. One was meandering across from San Marco, rolling on the gentle swell.

My phone went.

'Are you home yet?' Mia asked.

'Taking a while.'

'Sorry. Rather busy here. Hope you get there soon. Can't wait to see you in a suit.'

I stepped on board. Two more stops on Giudecca then Zattere and the ten-minute walk to a home I'd barely seen in weeks.

'Soon,' I said.

There were three people on this boat, two men, one woman, all wrapped up in their winter coats, faces hidden by hats and scarves. I wondered about the chap I'd seen when I first got on the vaporetto to San Giorgio. About the security guards on the gate by the bridge who always said a friendly hello, unlike their surly predecessor, Peter Lombardo.

For months, perhaps the whole time I'd spent involved with Mia and the Maddalena, I'd been surrounded by people who weren't what they appeared. Individuals part of a plan that was taking faint shape in my head. A ploy in which I was an unknowing participant. One that almost killed me. It was difficult to work out who I was most furious with. Them or myself for never realising, or, more accurately, facing up to my doubts and suspicions instead of burying them in an ocean of wishful thinking. And lately the arms of Mia Haas.

It was almost midday when I got off at Zattere. Everywhere was closed, the cafés, Ai Pugni, the supermarket and the local deli. Venice was a city of ghosts, waiting on the signal to wake for the great night ahead. Then another year. A fresh start. The midpoint of winter though for Vivaldi this was surely more like the end.

Quest' é 'l verno, mà tal, che la morte apporte. It brings us death for sure.

I walked down my little cul-de-sac and entered my apartment for the first time in weeks. The heating was still on low, the place damp from the humidity of the neighbouring canal. As soon as I turned on the light, I just knew someone had been there, and recently.

When I walked into the living room it became obvious. There on the dining table was a scrap of music paper, those two notes separated by a rest, all in blue ink, the same ones I'd seen foreshadowing death and danger all year long.

And a message...

> *It's time for the final act in this long performance,*
> *Arnold Clover. Macondo, 1430. Don't be late.*

Next to it a handgun, black, cold to the touch.

Two hours away.

I sat down and tried to think straight. Took a picture and searched the gun on the internet. After that I looked up Macondo. I'd just make it with a vaporetto to the Lido then, with luck, a bus.

My phone buzzed. A message from Mia.

> All OK? You found your suit?

What to say?

> Sorry. I may be delayed.

> Oh Arnold, love. I will keep a seat for you.
> Always.

With that I headed for the door.

Chapter Eleven

Largo

Rupert Hazard went down to the gravelly sand in a crumpled heap.

As he groaned, half-conscious, I sifted through the pockets of his winter coat. A flick-knife. A Canadian passport, his photo, the name 'Jeremy Sellers'. An envelope stuffed with money, a thick wad of US dollars. Two phones.

I cut a length of rope from the bar roof, came back, dragged him round, tied his hands behind his back. Pulled him upright against the beams of the veranda. Looped more rope round his chest so he was pinioned there, seated on the cold ground, back to the timber beam.

His eyes opened and he groaned. Blood was trickling down his cheek from a wound above the temple.

'You ungrateful bastard.'

Time to get the gun. I raised the barrel in the air, pulled the trigger. Nothing.

'Thought so.'

'Arnold. For pity's sake untie me. We wanted you here for your own sake. Not ours.'

'Seize Archaki at the concert. Fine. I don't care. I'll be happy to see him up for war crimes in The Hague. I'd welcome it.'

He said nothing. I carried on, all the questions that had been nagging me for months.

'It wasn't you who tried to kill me on that train, was it?'

He threw back his head and laughed. 'I saved your life, pal! That bloody German poisoned you. He was after those papers. On behalf of you know who.'

'An ad salesman?'

'Don't be so naive. When I realised what was going on I managed to beat out of him the fact he carried a syringe with an antidote. In case of accidents. Standard practice for that lot it seems. You were out cold. I gave you a jab and hoped for the best. A brief word of thanks would be appreciated. You lived.'

'The German didn't.'

He sniffed. 'An unfortunate lack of cooperation. People like that don't give in easily. They know the cost back home. His masters might have done the same if he'd come back empty-handed.'

'His master being Vasyl Archaki?'

'If you wish to see it that way...' he mumbled.

'There's another?' The fog was starting to clear, or so I thought. 'He was there to steal the papers, thinking they were real. You were there to grab them because you knew they weren't. Just a bunch of blank pages. If I'd returned with that briefcase the whole thing would have fallen apart.'

Hazard grinned and I didn't mind there was blood on his teeth. 'Good going, Lucky. I told them you were smarter than they reckoned. Sending that email saying you had the real thing, though. Honestly. What were you playing at?'

'I was hoping for a reaction. Praying it would come my way not Mia's.'

'Such a gent. You really should have played the sap, you know. That was the part we'd reserved for you.'

Nothing more.

'How on earth did you fake all that material? It must have taken ages.'

'Good job, wasn't it? Convincing.'

'Apart from the Casanova part. Possibly.'

'Pedant. For the record I wrote a bunch of stories I made up. Mixed it with stuff I picked up with a little research. The row with Montagnana, Sanctus Seraphin. I'm pretty good at music, you know. 2:1 from New College, Oxford. Good cover. No one ever suspects a fellow with a cello.'

'And then?'

'They fed all that and Casanova into one of their new-fangled AI systems to make it look and sound like dear old Antonio alongside the dates and places we knew. Lots of clever people in Cheltenham. I tidied up what Mr Robot came up with. Fun job, actually. Don't ask me for precise details. Even if I knew them, for your sake I'd stay shtum.'

'All the same you couldn't make it real. Make it physical.'

He found that amusing. 'Course not! Every page would get rumbled the moment you put it under a microscope or something.'

I pulled up a plastic chair and sat beside him.

'There's still some prosciutto left, old boy,' he said. 'Shame to let it go to waste.'

'Not hungry.'

'I'm bleeding.'

'Seen worse. I'm sure you have too.'

He sighed. 'Arnold. This is important. More than you can begin to guess.'

'The performance at Tronchetto... you wanted Archaki to think the papers were still around somewhere.' No answer. 'That I can understand. But Lombardo and whoever your Viennese Mozart was... getting them to leave Mia exposed like that... just to play the game again.'

'I think Signora Haas is quite good at playing games. Don't you?'

'The one I met. The Croatian. He might have killed her.'

He shook his head and scowled. 'Unlikely. A low-level hood in Moscow's pay. Killing her wouldn't have got them the papers, would it? Maybe meant they'd never find them. Pointless. Nothing happens in this business without a reason, old son. We're not bloodthirsty thugs for the sake of it.'

I thought back to the chilling description of savagery I'd heard earlier that year. 'The man you're planning to capture cut off Kravchuck's fingers out of spite. That sounds pretty bloodthirsty to me.'

'As I said... most of the time.'

It was five thirty. No chance I could get back for the start of the concert. 'And Mia?'

He had a sudden sheepish look about him. 'What about her?'

'Did she know all along?'

'Do you really want me to tell you? Honestly? You looked a right old sad sack when we first met. I gather that's no longer the case. Just stay here, be a good little boy when it's all over. Who knows? Maybe you can stay lucky, Lucky. Listen...'

I waited. It was obvious he wanted to keep me there. A story was as good a way as any. In a halting, overblown fashion, it all came out, or as much as he was inclined to share. How Marcus Haas was recruited in the first place, offered an amnesty for his financial misdeeds, if he cooperated with the British secret service and helped them snare a senior Kremlin official.

'Shaky bugger,' Hazard said. 'Not a good choice. It all got to him in the end when the bloody Americans decided they were going to charge him.'

'Wait. You mean they weren't in on this?'

I got a hard stare for that. 'Don't you read the news? This was a strictly European operation. I wouldn't trust those scheming sods in Virginia an inch right now. Anyway, Marcus panicked, topped himself, the way cowards do and left us all in the lurch. We offered his missus the same deal. No alternative, for us or her. Keep the show on the road and we'd help her shrug off her late husband's misdeeds. A sensible woman. A smart woman. You did well there.'

Something still didn't add up. 'He really would have risked coming here? Risked getting caught? Just for those papers?'

'The original score for *The Four Seasons*? Some snappy risqué memoirs no one suspected even existed? That would look good in a museum in St Petersburg, wouldn't it? Along with all the rest.'

'Instead, he'll end up in The Hague.'

Silence.

'I said–'

Rupert lost it then, turned angry. 'Oh, for God's sake! Just when I think you're cottoning on, you come up with crap like this. We started off as a honey trap with those lures. We wound up an extraction. Vasyl Archaki's no idiot. He rumbled us after that business on the train. Realised what was going on and offered himself up instead. Provided we could help him convince the goons around him all this was for real. He'd fly out, pick up the papers, then bring them back to Moscow and offer the prize to the Hermitage or something. Or so they thought.'

'Dangerous,' I said.

'The fellow wanted out. He knows that place is going to fall like a house of cards one day. When it does all manner of shit hits the fan. One minute you're in. The next you're flying out of the window. Literally. Vasyl wanted an escape plan. We gave him the means. So long as no one in Moscow got wind he was fleeing for good. Everything after that – Tronchetto, Lombardo, that visit from the Croatian – was a piece of *commedia dell'arte* for the benefit of his masters. Something he could sell to spook central and convince them he was making a brief covert visit to pick up some goodies and bring them back.'

'With me as a witness?'

He shrugged. 'Who better for the job than a tired old academic with no skin in the game? We needed someone to convince them the papers were genuine. That performance when you thought I'd copped it was icing on the cake, too good to waste on some gawpers on a vaporetto alone. We'd a story to tell, Arnold. All the world's a stage, mate, and all the men and women merely players: they have their exits and their entrances; and one man in his time plays many parts. Except you. Arnold Clover had but one and boy you played it well.'

I was starting to get a cold, sick feeling in my stomach and it wasn't just the icy Adriatic evening. 'Archaki's a war criminal. A murderer. He should face justice.'

Hazard cackled at that. 'Justice? Who gives a damn about justice? Life's about transactions. You give me something, I give you something back. Not do-gooder ideas about what's good and what's bad. Fat use he'd be to us behind bars in The Hague.'

'It's where he belongs.'

His faced turned ruddier, angrier and I realised I was finally seeing the man himself, not the seedy buffoon he'd pretended to be.

'Pin back your ears, matey! Vasyl Archaki's been in the middle of running their foreign infiltration programme. He knows where the money went. What the kompromat is. Honey traps. Bribes. Shell corporations. Money laundering networks.

Misinformation campaigns, shitposting, all the other assorted scams they've been throwing at us for years. Arnold...' His voice grew quieter. 'Think about it. With him on side and blabbing we can take down all the bastards they've been using to screw our world for decades. The politicians. The media hacks. Europe. America. America especially. Why do you think we're keeping them out of it for now? The stakes here are as high as any I've ever seen. Having Vasyl Archaki in our mitts gives us a win for once. Just when we need one. Is any of this getting through?'

It was and it didn't help.

'Does Andriy Kravchuck realise the man who stole his talent because he had none of his own is headed for a cosy life of anonymity, not jail?'

He didn't like that question. 'Don't get supercilious. Of course not. No one knows anything outside the loop. Except for Lady Haas. That idiot Lombardo blabbed when he warned her the Croatian was on his way and handed her the script. Anyway...' He smiled. 'What does it matter? It's done. By now we'll have relieved him of his accompanying goons at the airport. A taxi to Giudecca. He really wants to listen to that concert.'

'To gloat at Andriy Kravchuck.'

A shrug. 'Don't know. Don't care. This isn't about senti-ment, anything personal. After the concert it's back to Marco Polo and a private jet to parts unknown. The project begins. The interrogators can deal with it. I need a bloody holiday. This has been a hell of year.' He closed his eyes and groaned. 'No more questions. I'm done.'

'Only one. Why did Mia ask you to get me out of the concert? Lure me all the way here?'

He hesitated. 'Are you sure you want to know?'

'That's why I asked.'

'Your choice. Sorry, old chum. When it comes to love, you're not lucky at all. She said she felt ashamed, embarrassed. You were bound to realise what had happened if you knew Archaki was there, what was going on. She couldn't face telling you herself.' For once Rupert Hazard looked a little downcast. 'I was to pass on the bad news. She used you. Fun while it lasted, I hope. All over now.' A scowl. 'Didn't enjoy that part. But I was asked to set things straight. Come on, Arnold. Kindly take off these ropes. I'm freezing. My head hurts. I'm done. We're done. Time we sat here, took out this hip flask in my jacket pocket, knocked back some fine Scotch together and waited for the boat home. Game over, son, for both of us.'

He looked at me, right through me if I'm honest. 'We'll be grateful provided you do the decent thing and keep your trap well shut. A little money to make up for the absence of that book you've been working on. Not that it was ever going to sell anyway. And if it did in all honesty, you'd owe me and some geek at GCHQ half your royalties.'

I was cold. Miserable. Weary. I looked at that desolate stretch of beach and said, 'The Devil's Tritone. Those scraps of paper. Blue ink. You sent them to Marcus.'

'Yes, Sherlock. Me.'

'What a way to treat a damaged man.'

'Oh, do fuck off.'

'It was heartless.'

That loud, cruel laugh again. 'Heartless? Listen to yourself. Feeling sorry for a crook who'd have turned you upside, shook every last penny out of your pockets, and never thought about it twice. Heartless? Some jumped-up Viennese conman? Rich as Croesus? Him with that gorgeous wife any man would kill for? Living in the lap of luxury? While muggins here scrapes a living on the say-so of some teenage fuckwit in Whitehall, shit pension, shit contract, dropped as easy as a fucking Deliveroo driver who'd screwed up his round? And as for you in your bloody duffel coat and threadbare jeans. Why the hell should you care?'

I felt calmer than I had in weeks. 'You sent him those scraps of paper to keep him onside.'

He spat out something bloody and I wondered if it was a tooth. 'You never want your chumps comfortable. You weren't. And you...' He laughed. 'Christ... you were as big a chump as I ever met.'

'Marcus Haas knew nothing about music. He certainly couldn't read it.'

Silence and perhaps a brief look of shame.

'When he got those scraps of paper, he took them to you, the one who sent them... and asked what they meant. So did Mia. All they got was a pack of lies from the man who was tormenting him. The bullshit about threats, someone watching, something to nag at him, day in, day out.'

'Well done. So what?'

'You're not just the reason he went over the edge. You pushed him over. It was you in those pages, those phoney memoirs. All the hate, the envy, the bitterness, the contempt.'

He beamed. 'Spot on. And what a favour I did you. How is the delicious Mia between the sheets? A memorable fuck? A lost love to pine for? Where would you be without your old pal Rupert?'

I was glad the gun didn't work. I might well have used it then.

'Listen, chum,' he spat at me. 'Listen well. Your safe and cosy and decent world's an illusion. Welcome to the real one. A farce. A pantomime. In which you played the fool. Rather well too.' He bowed his head. 'Congratulations.'

I turned to leave.

'Arnold! Where the hell do you think you're going? There's nothing you can change now. Get back here!'

'Enjoy the boat,' I said, not looking back.

The beach was mostly pebbles. My geography here was hazy but I suspected that was going to be shorter than making my way back to the bus stop and the long circular road to civilisation.

Shorter maybe but it was hard work on the pebbles underneath a moon that kept vanishing behind scudding clouds.

No phone signal either, not until I reached the dead resort built by Mussolini to keep the Venetians fit. Almost Alberoni by then.

Mia was on voicemail.

So was Valentina Fabbri.

I didn't see the point in calling Luca.

The village seemed dead. Not a light on in the golf resort as I passed. Only a couple of houses looked occupied. By the bus stop on the lagoon side a café was open. I marched in, breathless, got astonished looks from a gaggle of locals seated around plates of *cicchetti*, bottles of Prosecco, and glasses of spritz.

'Any chance of a taxi to the Lido?'

They all laughed.

'Sir,' said the woman I took to be the owner, 'it's Capodanno. What do you think?'

I took out Hazard's wallet and slapped a wad of notes on the table. 'I think if any of you are sober enough to steer a boat you'll get five hundred US dollars for a ride to Giudecca. The Zitelle stop.'

There was an astonished silence. Then an elderly man, grizzled beard, shoulder-length grey hair, faded blue boiler suit, staggered to his feet. 'When you say sober...?'

'I said "sober enough".'

He looked around at the rest of them then said, 'I'll do it. For our new English friend.'

'Thank you.'

'For six hundred US dollars.'

There was just enough in Hazard's stash. He scooped it up.

'Is your boat fast?'

The whole room burst out laughing.

'Faster than swimming, signore,' the man said. 'Since you seem to be in a hurry, shall we continue this conversation along the way?'

It was an old fishing skiff. Space for three men at the most, nets packed untidily in the bows. A large gas lantern, for squid at night he said. No need for one to navigate. Tommaso, it turned out, was a lifelong lagoon fisherman who spent most days and many nights out on the water. He knew every channel from Chioggia to Burano, every shallow to be avoided, every spot where a catch might lurk.

'You seem,' he said, 'a man in a hurry. This is unusual on a day like this.'

I sat in the middle on a cold damp wooden bench as he stepped to the stern and tugged the outboard to bring it to life.

'Business.'

He grabbed the tiller, turned us away from the Alberoni jetty, towards the distant city lights. The temperature dropped a couple of degrees on the water, and there was that unique lagoon smell, seaweed, brackish water and fuel.

'Business? On Capodanno? Surely not. This is a time to

reflect, signore. A new year. A new start. In six days it's Epiphany and La Befana will fly across the sky dropping presents to my grandchildren. We take a break and then we begin again. The days are growing longer.' He waved a hand at the sky. 'Soon it will be spring and everything begins to live once more.'

'The seasons...' I agreed.

The little engine ramped up to full.

'They guide our lives, year in, year out. Beginning to end. I'm seventy-two which, in Alberoni, counts as mid to late winter. It's when those you've known years, sometimes loved, sometimes not, begin to head into the ground. Life, it seems to me, is marked by loss, at this stage anyway. About giving things away. That's much more rewarding than getting them. Here...' He reached into one of his deep pockets and took out the money. 'I don't want this. Don't need it either. You look like a man who does. Besides...' He grinned and pulled out a silver flask from the same pocket. 'I'm a little drunk already. You'll have a drop of grappa with me? Damned cold tonight.'

It tasted like firewater, crude, fierce, welcome on the squally lagoon, the wind battering us from all directions as we approached the channel that fed between Giudecca and San Giorgio Maggiore.

'And the money,' he insisted, holding it out.

'The money's not mine. I took it from a man who owed me a debt. I don't want it. Please...'

The breeze picked up and two lines came back to me.

'Through bolted doors we hear the winds compete, Sirocco, North Wind, all the winds at war.'

'Who wrote that?'

'A man long dead. Antonio Vivaldi. *The Four Seasons*. Winter.'

'Can't have meant it about Venice. We don't get the sirocco

at this time of year. November, yes. That's what used to give us the hell of *acqua alta*. Though those clever engineers who put up that giant contraption where I used to catch a fine *spigola* from time to time seem to have dealt with most of that. For now.'

The boat bucked. I had to hold on to the side. We fell silent for a while, and then, more quickly than I'd expected, we were almost there, the Cipriani to our left, the lights of San Marco's giant Christmas tree reflecting in the water by the Piazzetta.

'Are you a happy man, signore?'

'At times.'

'But not this particular one?'

'Why do you say that?'

'Because... I don't know. There's a look about you. That of a man facing something he'd rather not. Forget your business, whatever it is. It doesn't sound such a good idea. I've got all the time in the world. That bar in Alberoni won't shut till three. I can drop you anywhere. San Marco. Wherever you want. Or we can just chug slowly down the Grand Canal while I piss off all the rich people in their fancy taxis by putting this old tub in their way.'

I was tempted. Then I heard it, drifting on the icy night breeze. Strings and the final concerto in The Seasons. One I knew now almost by heart, along with the surprises Vivaldi placed in there. Notes that called up chattering teeth, snow and ice, and howling winds that battered his world just as they did mine.

I believed in the bitter, angry, dying invalid depicted in those fake memoirs because I wanted to. For Mia's sake mostly, but also for my own. Luca was right. I needed the challenge. I'd no idea how great it would prove, no more than him. Had I taken the time to sit back and think, I'd surely have realised there had to be an intense humanity in the man to come up with the music and words he did. However tragic his lowly end in

Vienna – and that we would never know – the voice in those pages was a combination of Casanova reworked by computers, and the sly, insidious real-life additions of Rupert Hazard. The fellow with a cello I never once suspected until it was too late.

'That's very kind of you, Tommaso. The Zitelle jetty please.'

The music kept getting louder. Somewhere close to the Cipriani, a firework exploded, loud, violent, filling the sky with a searing brightness that hurt the eyes.

'The money,' he said, holding out the wad of dollars. 'I don't need it. I don't feel good about taking it.'

'Thanks for the ride,' I said and stepped out onto the greasy stone step.

Giudecca was alive with people for once. Crowds lining the waterfront in anticipation of the evening's fireworks. Winter coats and hats, plastic glasses of spritz and Prosecco in one gloved hand, phones at the ready in the other.

When I crossed the wooden bridge there were lights everywhere, a host of locals in the garden, wandering round, happy, excited. The palazzo looked regal, bathed in tasteful spotlights. The Teatro too where the doors were open, the place so full the audience had spilled out into the foyer and the entrance. Mia had brought life back to the place as she'd promised. At what price I couldn't guess.

The winter concerto was sailing through its final bars. I pushed my way through, constantly saying, '*Scusi, scusi...*' ignoring all the complaints.

The back row of seats was as far as I could manage. As I got there the closing notes sounded and the theatre burst into wild applause. Ellen Kim stood at the front triumphant in her scarlet dress, the rest of the small orchestra beaming behind her.

Luca was in the front row, his friend Silvia on one side, Valentina on the other. I couldn't see Mia anywhere. Or Andriy Kravchuck. I'd no clear idea what Vasyl Archaki looked like. A man who kept out of the spotlight as much as possible. Maybe he'd scuttled out of there already and was on his way to the airport. Rupert Hazard was doubtless free of his ropes by now, cursing me out on the beach by Macondo, heading back here, furious as hell.

Something nudged my elbow and there she was. Mia in a silk dress, turquoise, her hair up, a bag over her shoulder. She looked just like the woman I'd first met that April, imperious, important, someone who'd never think twice about someone like me.

'Arnold?'

'Surprised to see me?'

Silence.

'I got the message,' I said. 'When you sent me home.'

'Message?'

'Those notes on a piece of paper. A gun.'

She groaned. 'I didn't know anything about a gun.'

'It wasn't for real. None of this is, is it?'

Her eyes glistened. 'Things are complicated. I can explain. Only later.'

'You didn't want me here.'

'True.'

'Why?'

With that she reached up, kissed my cheek, squeezed my hand. 'You're a kind and decent man and I've treated you terribly. Wait for me outside. Please.'

'Why...?'

'Outside,' she insisted. 'There's someone I need to talk to and–'

There was a cry then, a voice I knew. Loud and hard.

Kravchuck somewhere at the front, yelling in a language I couldn't understand.

'Damn,' she muttered and vanished from my side.

The audience was moving, leaving their seats. She'd plunged into the crowd, elbowing her way through. I couldn't see Luca and Valentina anymore. But Kravchuck was there, on his feet, yelling still, an outstretched hand pointing to the side of the audience.

Then I heard it... 'Archaki! Archaki!' And what sounded like a stream of curses.

I pushed through as hard as I could, against the momentum of the mass of bodies leaving the theatre.

They were at the front. The musician being held back by Ellen Kim and Valentina, Luca there looking puzzled, trying to help. A good six strides away the object of Kravchuck's ire was obvious. A tall man, black hair, shiny, dyed, a cruel face, smirking, the smile of a victor. There were three others with him, unsmiling spooks I guessed, suits and hard expressions trying to bundle him out of there.

But Vasyl Archaki was having none of it and it struck me then: this was why he came to Giudecca and the Teatro Maddalena. Not to hear the music, or for Vivaldi. But to taunt the man who'd once befriended him, the brilliant violinist whose life he'd ruined. Envious of such a great talent. Determined to let Andriy Kravchuck know he'd lost twice over. Those severed fingers that represented his genius, along with the hope the man who took them might one day pay the price.

I forced my way through, joined them holding him back. Strong for an old man, but fury does that for you.

Ellen Kim stood there looking lost and stupid, hand to her mouth.

'Andriy,' I said.

'They're letting him go. He threw it in my face. He said those bastards are setting him free. What kind of world is this?'

A complicated one. I thought of what Rupert Hazard told me at Macondo. If they were right, Archaki's testimony would help them take down so many traitors in the west. Where was the wrong in that? Where was the right?

'You think you've won Vasyl!' Andriy Kravchuck bellowed.

'I know it, old man!' Archaki shouted back in broken English.

'Then...' Kravchuck threw up his hands, stopped struggling against us. 'Enjoy your trip to hell.'

A silence. The musicians began to move. From the corner of my eye, I saw her striding out from behind them, something in her hand, a black shape against turquoise silk.

'Mia...' I whispered knowing what was about to happen, what a bloody fool I'd been.

She marched straight up to Vasyl Archaki, shot him once in the chest, once more in the head as he went down. The goons with him looked as shocked as the rest of us. One of them had his gun out when I threw myself in front of her, took the weapon from her hands, sent it scuttling across the marble floor of the Teatro Maddalena.

After that something heavy crashed into my skull and the last thing I glimpsed was the last thing I wanted to see.

That terrifying copy of Donatello's Maddalena that Mia had placed by the exit.

Her spectre loomed over me, old wood glittering with torn gold, hands together in prayer, as I fell into a darkness the colour of blood.

Chapter Twelve

Allegro

'Good morning, Signor Clover. You seem to like it here,' Marta Neri said with the faint smile I'd come to know a few months earlier. 'Perhaps we should make a permanent reservation.'

Not that I was in my old room from summer, the antidote Rupert Hazard had stabbed into me saving my life from an assassin's venom. Just a public ward, not even a view out of the window.

'I trust I'll live.'

'You will for now,' she replied. 'Though if you keep on getting yourself into trouble like this in future... who knows? I'm only a doctor. Not a fortune teller. Nor do I cure death.'

'What's wrong with me?'

'On a physical level, nothing much that I can find. You got hit on the head very hard from what I understand. The butt of a handgun I believe.' I felt my scalp with tentative fingers. 'Don't touch it and don't fiddle with the dressing. Come back here tomorrow and we'll take another look. We had to keep you in to check for concussion and brain damage. There you've come out clean. As to the side of your personality that seems to get yourself into such scrapes...'

'Thank you, doctor. When can I leave?'

'As soon as I get the last scan results. If they're fine.' She took out the copy of *Il Gazzettino* under her arm and threw it in my lap. 'In the meantime, here's some reading. Capitano Fabbri will be around shortly. I doubt you're surprised she wishes to have a word.'

'The dead man. What's happened to him?'

She looked surprised by the question. 'I deal with the living. Murder victims are out of my field, thank goodness. Talk to Capitano Fabbri about that. Now...' She glanced at her watch. 'If you don't mind I'll continue my rounds. With the normal patients.'

'*Grazie mille,*' I said with a salute.

'The English...' she muttered as she headed towards someone three beds down.

I'd been taken to hospital from Giudecca in an ambulance boat, not that I remembered a thing of the journey, bludgeoned unconscious by one of Archaki's handlers as I tried to protect Mia. It was highly unlikely I'd ever find anyone to acknowledge this, but the thug responsible was doubtless a colleague of Hazard's from the British security services, there to keep an eye on Vasyl Archaki. Not that there was such a man according to the remarkably brief story in the paper. A Bulgarian visitor attending the opening night of the Teatro Maddalena was dead, murdered in the crowded auditorium by Mia Haas, the widow of the financier who had begun the project. Two shots, one to the chest, a second to the head, had killed him outright.

The paper named the man as Nikolay Grozdanov, a

financier from Sofia who had flown in that same day. There was speculation that he'd been a partner of Marcus Haas in the past and the murky business activities of both men might have led Mia to believe Grozdanov was somehow responsible for her husband's suicide. But that was pure speculation. The Carabinieri were being unforthcoming about the case, and no one in Bulgaria, it seemed, had anything to say about a man called Nikolay Grozdanov.

Mia was in police custody in the Guidecca women's prison a kilometre or so away from the theatre and hotel she'd founded. She'd neither offered an explanation for her actions, nor spoken to the investigating officer – Valentina Fabbri naturally – much at all.

I grabbed hold of my phone – and had a sudden stab of pain in my head as I moved. That man guarding Archaki had really taken me down. There was an email from Luca, offering his sincere wishes for my recovery and what appeared to be a muted apology for involving me in the Maddalena project in the first place.

I called him, found him at the airport, about to depart on a New Year's Day flight to Sicily with Silvia. Embarrassed to hear my voice.

Before he could splutter another word, I said, 'There's nothing to apologise for. I went into this with my eyes open and willingly.'

'But it's so awful. How are you?'

'Bad headache. Keen to get home, happy to have a quiet life for a while.'

'I'll be back for Epiphany. We must watch the Regata della Befana at the Rialto as usual. You. Me. Valentina. Silvia. A quiet life. A normal life for all of us from now on.'

Yes, a bunch of old men dressed as witches racing their boats towards a giant sock strung from the bridge. Normality in

Venice. It was now almost a year since I'd stood there with Luca and Valentina watching the spectacle and he'd mentioned casually there was something exciting on the horizon to do with Antonio Vivaldi and Vienna. What a year that had been.

'I'd like that very much.'

'Just when it looked like everything was finally coming good. Why did Mia do it? To kill a man like that. Whoever he was. I saw the look on her face. She seemed quite triumphant. Vindicated somehow.'

'I've really no idea.'

'Not even a clue?'

Clearly no one knew about Vasyl Archaki. Presumably they weren't supposed to.

'Enjoy your break with Silvia. I look forward to sharing a glass of warm and spicy vin brulé with the two of you. *Buon viaggio.*'

And that was that.

Valentina was at the ward door talking to Doctor Neri.

I shuffled off the bed, waved with a big smile and cried, 'Morning, people! I'll require my clothes now, thank you very much.'

There was a blood stain on my duffel coat that wasn't going to vanish with dry cleaning. Time for new clothes I realised as I dressed behind the curtains. Time for lots of changes.

'Any chance of a lift home in that fancy boat of yours?' I said when I walked out to find the two of them standing there tapping their feet, a look on their faces rarely found outside Venetian professional women in something of a mood.

'You're discharged,' Doctor Neri said. 'If you could spare us your company for a little while I'd be grateful.'

The Carabinieri launch was outside with a smartly uniformed officer at the wheel. Valentina said not a word until we climbed in.

'Zattere will be fine,' I told her as I took the bench seat inside the cabin. 'Thanks very much.'

'Giudecca first,' she said. 'The women's prison.'

~

We retraced the route I'd taken that hot summer day they released me from the hospital after the poisoning. Though this time, at least, all I had to contend with was a headache and Valentina's mood. Which, for once, was more confounded than cross.

What she told me amplified a little of the story in the paper. A man carrying a Bulgarian passport – fake it turned out, to no one's surprise – died instantly in the Teatro Maddalena when Mia shot him in front of the stage. A very public death. No one in Sofia or anywhere else was claiming the body. No motive could be established since Mia Haas refused to say a word when she was first interviewed, and during later attempts after her incarceration in the women's prison. She'd been charged with murder and would appear in court within a week or two. Given the strangeness of the case, she was being kept in solitary in prison, and under armed guard.

'You know who he is,' I said as we turned the corner at Sant'Elena.

'I know who you think he is.'

'Vasyl Archaki. Ukrainian, something important in the Kremlin. This whole show was devised to lure him out of Russia. Or to enable him to escape. It seems more like that in the end.'

She looked at me, interested. 'Who told you that?'

'The man who called himself Rupert Hazard. He was in the orchestra. He wrote the basis of the fake memoirs. British intelligence, secret services. God knows what.'

She nodded and I couldn't work out whether this was news.

'And why would the British do that?'

'I don't think it was just the British. I suspect it was European. Your people too.' It needed to be said. 'That's why you were warned off the whole thing early on.'

'An interesting theory.'

'Archaki was going to give them the Holy Grail. The names of all the politicians, media figures, business people, the Kremlin have been bankrolling all these years. One reason they wanted to keep it out of the hands of the Americans, to begin with anyway. It was, shall we say, sensitive.'

'I imagine information like that would be. Do you think she killed him for that reason? To stop him? That Mia was on the other side, as it were?'

'I haven't the faintest clue. Though it seems unlikely.'

Valentina Fabbri smiled and touched my hand. 'Everything about this does, don't you think? And what was the part you were meant to play?'

'Pulcinella. The fool. I was the clown given a script that would provide the bait. The discovery of an original manuscript of Vivaldi's memoirs. A salacious document. And the original score for *The Four Seasons*.' I hesitated. 'I imagine I was meant to offer some kind of academic heft to the whole farrago.'

San Giorgio Maggiore loomed in front of us. The Maddalena estate was just out of sight. The bloody memory of the night before rose, unwanted, in my head.

'Pulcinella is never a simple fool,' she said. 'You read that wrong. It's an act. He plays the fool. In truth he's cunning, always on the side of the weak against the powerful.'

True. I remembered now.

'All that's beyond me. What will happen to her?'

That familiar shrug. 'Cold-blooded murder. Clearly premeditated, otherwise why would she carry a firearm into a concert? Why? She won't say. If that continues, perhaps they'll believe it was a political assassination.' Another shrug. 'Years. Years and years as things stand. Unless we trade her back to Moscow for one of ours.'

'No, no, no. I don't believe that's the reason.'

'Was she truthful with you, Arnold?'

It was my turn to shrug. 'People lie for all sorts of reasons. Sometimes ones they fail to understand themselves. If she blamed Archaki for her husband...?'

She waved a gloved hand. 'Stop there. We've no means of identifying the man as Vasyl Archaki. The Russians deny all knowledge of him. There's nothing in the way of documents. No physical means – fingerprints, DNA, medical records. As things stand, he'll go down in the morgue files as a murder victim, name and nationality unknown. Unless Mia Haas has information to the contrary–'

'The intelligence services! The British! Your own! They must know...'

Valentina sighed. 'Oh, Arnold. I'm merely a capitano in the Venetian Carabinieri. Do you think they'd tell a little woman like me?'

We passed Zitelle, closed on Redentore. I'd been to the women's prison once before. It was in a former convent on a small rio behind the main canal. An odd place, occasionally the site of a Biennale exhibition involving the inmates. Every Thursday they held a small market outside its walls, selling the produce from their garden and some scents and toiletries they made. Not that Mia would be taking part in that from what I'd heard.

'What makes you think she'll talk to me?' I asked as the launch turned off the main canal after the Palanca stop.

'Because I feel she came to like you. A lot. To admire you. That the way you two began, she seeing you as a means to an end, was not how it ended. For either of you.' Valentina's hand came out to mine again. 'She didn't want you there when it happened, did she? She didn't think you should see. There has to be a reason for that, and I can only think of one. She genuinely cares for you.' A squeeze, a quick, faint smile of sympathy. 'As you still care for her. Find me something I might use to help her if you can.'

We stopped just beyond the wooden bridge on the Fondamenta de le Convertite. The Italian flag was flying next to a security camera over the modest door to the jail, another former religious institution now given over to incarceration, as unlikely as the larger men's prison Valentina had locked me in months before.

'If Mia won't talk to you,' she added, 'I fear she's lost. Though that decision is beyond my reach.'

The jail was much as I remembered from my last visit to a woman who'd found herself there, though happily in that case, only for a while. Cold, bare, stark, but with staff who seemed gentler than any I'd encountered across the water in Santa Maria Maggiore. I waited thirty minutes in a reception room then an officer on duty told me Mia refused to see me.

'Tell her, in that case, I will stay here in any case and wait.'

'Signore...' the woman said. 'It is her right.'

'Tell her please. Tell her I feel I'm owed a little of her time. To say goodbye if nothing more.'

Another half hour and then I was ushered into a small room with a window out to a vegetable garden frozen in the white rime of winter frost.

Mia wore a plain blue prison uniform, hair back, face

thinner than I'd ever seen it. Beautiful as ever in her obvious misery.

I sat down and said nothing.

'I didn't want you here,' she told me.

'I know. They said.'

'Then... why?'

'As I said. I'm owed.'

She took a deep breath. 'I'll make sure you get the balance of the book deal even though it's not going to happen–'

'For pity's sake! I wasn't talking about money.'

'Ah.' She laughed for a second. 'I'm sorry. My head's not quite right just now. You were thinking about us.'

'Mostly I was thinking about you. About what happens now.'

She scowled and said, 'Isn't it obvious? Now I go to jail for a long, long time.'

'If you talk to them... give them some explanation.'

'It'll make no difference.'

I couldn't begin to work out what she was thinking. 'Archaki was defecting. They believe that maybe you were working for the Russians.'

She did laugh then, and never said a word.

'If you won't talk to them...' Nothing. 'If it was Andriy Kravchuck with a gun I'd understand. He had a reason.'

'And I didn't?'

'Marcus? Money? Tell me. If it's the last thing I ever hear from you.'

She turned to the guard and said, 'Is it possible we could have coffee, please? Two?'

The woman thought for a moment then nodded and left the room.

'I will say this once and once only, Arnold. And you won't pass on what I say to a soul.'

It began in Vienna two years earlier. Marcus had money then, hopes, kept away from the drink and drugs, from some of the shady people he'd dealt with before. Mia had introduced him to Venice where they'd come across the abandoned estate on Giudecca, going for a song since no one wanted it. She talked him into the idea of establishing a small hotel and a concert venue there, a tribute to Vivaldi, a project that would take him away from the dubious financial world he'd come to inhabit. Something they could share. The deal was done. The work began.

'Andriy Kravchuck was an obvious choice to lead the musical side. A charming, talented man. A fine mind, a great violinist until that bastard Archaki took his fingers. We assumed everything would work out. Then...'

She stopped.

'Then...?'

'Someone came to Marcus from the security services. Yours I believe. With a threat and an offer. They'd made the connection between Andriy and Archaki. They had a plan in mind to lure him out of Moscow.'

The picture was starting to clear.

'You could have said no.'

'Impossible. They had something on Marcus. Criminal charges. Accusations that would have ruined us. Put him in jail. It was either do what they wanted, or we lost everything. He never told me the details. They installed that Hazard fellow in the orchestra to keep an eye on us. Lombardo, the gardener. Maybe there were others I never knew about. We didn't have any choice.'

I thought of Hazard, the man's meticulous preparations hidden behind a front of incompetence and sleaze.

'Quite a scheme.'

She smiled. 'I guess. Rupert Hazard told us what he thought we needed to know. They'd lure Archaki out of Moscow with the promise of some fake memoirs. A counterfeit score for *The Four Seasons*. All they needed was someone to put a spot of academic imprimatur on the project.'

'Corroborative detail, intended to give artistic verisimilitude to an otherwise bald and unconvincing narrative.'

That surprised her. 'Quite. Who said that?'

'W.S. Gilbert. *The Mikado*.'

Another smile. 'You're so clever. So knowledgeable. So decent.'

I laughed and said, 'I was an idiot. Blind to everything.'

'Because I used you. I was meant to be your blindfold. The fact I had no alternative is neither here nor there.' She reached over the table and took my hand. The guard returned with the coffees. An end to that moment of physical contact.

'If I'd any idea they'd try to harm you, I'd never have agreed to any of it. Believe me.'

'I do. Why did Marcus kill himself?'

Her eyes closed for a moment at that and a single slow tear leaked out from each. 'He was a decent, kind man when he wanted to be, when the drink and the drugs weren't around. But there was always that shadow. Money and how he earned it. Or stole it I guess. He couldn't take the pressure. From the spooks who were on his back. Hazard and Lombardo watching his every move. From some of his shady crook friends who wanted their piece of him. Those stupid pieces of paper turning up from time to time.' She was lost for words for a moment. 'We'd climbed on board this rollercoaster. There was no climbing off.'

'You knew? What really happened on the train?'

'Lombardo told me when I flew at him after I heard. They

were all terrified you'd see through the whole thing. Realise it was a setup, a pack of stupid lies.'

If only, I thought. *Though what then…*

'As I said, I was to be your blindfold. It started off as a duty. A necessary and pleasant one. The more it went on… the more I hated myself for deceiving you. There was a feeling growing between us. That was impossible.'

'Because…?'

'Because I deceived you. Time and time again. Even if you can forgive that, love, I can't.'

All the same there was still something missing. 'You didn't have to shoot Archaki. They would have dealt with him.'

'Dealt with him?' she cried. 'They were supposed to put him in front of a judge. Send him away for the rest of his miserable life. Lombardo told me the truth before he vanished. Before he let that hood into the palazzo to try to convince Archaki's masters he really was just picking up a stolen prize he wanted. Lombardo said I wouldn't come to any harm. All my unexpected visitor needed to hear was that we had the real thing, the actual memoirs. And one day, when Archaki arrived, we'd pass it on. I didn't expect that. I knew something had changed.'

'It wasn't a trap anymore,' I said. 'It was an extraction. Hazard told me. They'd got to Archaki. Made some kind of deal. He threw off his goons at the airport.'

She scowled. 'They lie and lie and lie and make the rest of us do the same. You never saw Archaki at the end of the concert. He got up and walked right in front of Andriy, grinning at him. As if he was saying… look at me. I'm free now. And you, just an old man who can no longer pick up a fiddle. I couldn't take it.'

No. That wasn't good enough. Should I say it? The lines from Vivaldi flitted through my thoughts.

We tread across the ice with careful footsteps,

Paying attention not to slip and fall

'You went there with a gun, Mia. You knew you were going to kill him.'

Her eyes flared and turned on me. 'He was a monster. It was nothing less than he deserved.'

'Did you want to kill Archaki for what he did to your old friend?'

She kept quiet.

'Or what he did to your mother?'

There was the start of tears in her eyes, shock and anger too. 'What...?'

'Andriy said he'd known you for years. You told me how much you loved music. How you grew up surrounded by it.'

'I never spoke of my mother.'

'No,' I admitted. 'I found that odd at the time. Andriy talked to me of a woman who'd suffered dreadfully under Archaki and then seemed embarrassed he'd mentioned it. She was called Elena–'

'Stop it! For God's sake stop!' She was yelling, rising from her chair to confront me across the table.

The guard was on us in an instant.

'Signora,' she said. 'If you cannot be calm, I must bring this to an end.'

'No, no, no...'

'It's fine,' I said. 'We're fine.' I paused, smiled, passed over a tissue for her tears. 'These are difficult times. Please...'

She seemed a sympathetic woman and retired to the door.

'Mitigating circumstances,' I said. 'You need to tell Valentina Fabbri.'

Mia glared at me, and I thought there was a fragment of hate in her eyes. 'I heard them talking. Those British men in their dark suits who never looked as if they were there for the music. I hung around and listened. They were laughing about whose job it would be to choose a new name for him, a new home. It was insufferable.'

'Stand up in court and say it.'

'I don't need to justify my actions to anyone. If they were going to arrest him as they'd promised I wouldn't have done a thing. That wasn't going to happen.'

'You can say that too.'

She laughed and cried out, 'You believe they'll allow that?' Then more quietly, 'Surely by now you know the kind of people we sold ourselves to?'

'Then I'll do it for you.'

'No. You won't.' She shook her head. and I couldn't take my eyes off her. In all the time I'd known her, I'd never seen Mia Haas so strong, so powerful, so confident in herself. 'My mother's memory is mine alone. No one else's. If you intrude on that private grief, I promise I'll never talk to you again.'

'And if I don't...?'

No answer.

The guard's phone rang. She looked at the two of us and said the meeting was at an end.

'If I don't...' I said again.

Mia Haas closed her eyes, leaned back, folded her arms. 'I'm sorry. For everything. No...' She winced. 'Not everything.'

The guard tapped me on the shoulder. 'Signore. You must leave.'

'At least,' Mia said with a wan smile, 'you lost your fear of hugging. Oh, Arnold...'

I leapt to my feet and there we were, in each other's arms, the guard tapping her toes, embarrassed, too decent to intervene.

'You worry too much,' Mia whispered in my ear. 'Kindly stop.'

It was cold outside. Valentina's boat had vanished. When I looked there was a message on my phone, asking me to call.

Later, I thought and walked along to the Palanca stop and the bar there for a drink.

In January, I hardly left my tiny house in San Pantalon except for shopping and the occasional spritz. The weather was bright and icy, too cold to spend much time outside. It was a day or two before I answered Valentina's call and when I did, I told her nothing of Mia's revelations. I'd promised. It was what she wanted. There had to be a reason, not that I could guess what it might be.

Besides, I got the clear idea Valentina would be happy to leave the messy story of the Teatro Maddalena to the past. Maybe she'd been ordered not to take too close an interest in the case. Forces greater than a local Carabinieri station in San Zaccaria were at work, ones that brooked no interference.

It was easy to keep my head down. When it came to the sixth of January, and that gathering we'd planned by the Rialto to watch the witches' regatta, I pleaded a cold.

The city was moribund after Epiphany, so many places closed for a few weeks off ahead of the resumption of commercial life with the arrival of Carnival. I reread my finished manuscript based, for the most part, on the invented memoirs of Vivaldi and a single fake page of Casanova. Spat out by a computer in Cheltenham, GCHQ I guessed from what Hazard had said that chilly day in Macondo. All mangled from real material by AI alongside some invented passages he'd written himself. It made a good tale, even if it was mostly fiction. I marked up the passages I thought might be useful in future, then put the manuscript to one side.

I'd been researching and writing constantly for the previous nine months or so. They were habits it was hard to lose, so I started something new. Something true, this time. As much as I might make it. The real story of what had happened in Guidecca that year. As much for my own sake, to get the tale straight in my head, as anyone else.

By the start of February, when tourists were stalking the chilly streets shivering in their gaudy rented costumes, I'd reached thirty thousand words, about a third of the way through I guessed. The thing had momentum which meant I couldn't stop. When the Carnival crowds eased a little, I felt sufficiently confident to venture out. Luca had been pestering me for weeks, so we reunited for coffee and pastries in the café we used near the Frari. There we spoke about local affairs, work and exhibitions, mostly avoiding the former Palazzo Colonna-Ottoboni across the water, and the fate of Mia Haas.

As March approached and my new manuscript was passing the sixty-thousand-word mark, there came the customary dinner with Valentina in her husband Franco's Dorsoduro restaurant, Il Pagliaccio, a test of his new seasonal menu. Winter squash and Treviso radicchio giving way to *castraure* from Sant'Erasmo, early sprigs of green asparagus and a risotto with *bruscandoli*, those curly little shoots of hops.

Our only mention of the Teatro Maddalena was an agreement not to discuss the painful past. What was there to say? Mia had disappeared into the prolix labyrinth of the Italian legal system, moved from the women's jail on Giudecca to somewhere more secure. Valentina was adamant she'd no idea where. The case had been taken over by prosecutors from Rome.

All she principally wanted to know was much the same as the questions I'd got from Luca a few weeks before. How was I doing? What was I up to? Was everything okay? Did I have enough money coming in to pay the bills?

Of course I did. Mia's promises were kept. The balance of the advance on the book that would never appear had arrived in my bank account in the first week of January. She'd planned that beforehand, just as she'd planned convincing Hazard's people to lure me from the Teatro Maddalena so that I didn't get to see her shoot Vasyl Archaki dead.

After that I found a sudden need to write urgently. In two weeks, I'd finished the new manuscript, given it a title, sent it off to the only person I could think of.

With a title that came from nowhere, one that seemed to fit.

The third week of March I took a phone call from Andriy Kravchuck. He was back in London, on his own. Ellen Kim had returned to New York to build her career and broken off all contact with him. Kravchuck, it seemed to me, was not disappointed.

'And you, my knowledgeable friend?' he asked. 'How goes it?'

A question I never knew how to answer, so I went through the standard responses, about being fine, getting on with things, muddling through.

'Such a response!' he cried. 'They'll never take the Englishman out of you.'

'That would be difficult. I'm sorry if this offends but I need to ask. Did you know what Mia was planning? That she had a gun?'

He grunted and at that moment I could picture him precisely. The magisterial scowl, Samuel Beckett in the guise of a bald eagle. 'What kind of question is this?'

'The kind someone asks when they're struggling to understand what's just happened. How things came to such an awful pass. What led us there.'

He hesitated. 'You were closer to the lady of late. Had you any idea?'

'None whatsoever. If I had, I'd have dragged her out of that concert and snatched away the damned gun. Even if I'd known about her mother at that point. Which was why she'd made sure she got me out of the way.'

A long sigh. 'She told you about Elena?'

'No. She was offended I'd worked that out. I recalled what you said about Archaki and a woman from the Balkans. I remembered the odd way she spoke, or rather didn't, about her mother. When I saw Mia in prison, just once, I put two and two together. She didn't elaborate.'

Another grunt. 'They came to me about that son of a bitch. After they heard Mia had got me working with Marcus Haas. The British. That creature Hazard, a man I never understood. This crazy idea of using Vivaldi to lure him out of Russia. They said...' He paused, uttered a word in a language I couldn't understand, only enough to gather it was a curse. 'They promised Vasyl Archaki would go to jail for a long time and Marcus would be saved from prosecution. I believed them. More fool me.'

'A lot of trouble to go to for one man.'

'I can only assume they thought him worth it.'

'They did,' I said. 'They believed Archaki could bring down any number of corrupt politicians all over the place. Europe. America. The most important defector in years.'

'And in return walk free, to a comfortable, private life,' Kravchuck said in a low, hurt tone. 'Individuals mean nothing to these people. On both sides. I'd no idea she planned to shoot him. If I had, I'd have demanded the gun and killed the evil bastard myself.'

He was such a gentle, intellectual man at heart, even with that occasional temper. I was lost for words.

'Elena was the bravest woman I ever knew,' Andriy Kravchuck added. 'Until I met her daughter.'

'I can believe that.'

'Anyway,' he added, 'you know the project isn't dead?'

'Excuse me?'

There was a brief explanation of what had been going on behind the scenes. It seems Mia had held secret negotiations in early December with a Croatian hotel and casino chain. One she'd once worked for herself. What was originally planned to be a joint venture would now involve the company taking over the entire estate, running both hotel and auditorium.

'I'm to return in July to put together an opening season. It's still to be dedicated to Vivaldi. New musicians. Chosen more carefully this time. The Teatro Maddalena will rise again. Her work, her talent, her vision, will not be lost.'

But there'd be no sensational Vivaldi book to mark the occasion. At least, not the one everyone had expected.

'I look forward to seeing you again, Andriy.'

'In happier circumstances one hopes. You were duped, Arnold. How does it feel?'

I thought carefully before answering. 'I was. But willingly. By a woman who turned out to be more extraordinary than I appreciated.'

'Not just by her. I told you that fake score was real. I was part of it too. Don't forget that.'

'You were doing what you thought was best.'

'I was lying to you, damning the memory of Antonio Vivaldi, in the hope an evil man would receive justice. Typical musician. So naive. Mia admired you. She told me so. You were her rock when she needed one. I'm sure she felt truly guilty about that deception. Forgive her, Arnold.'

'Happily, if I ever get the chance.'

When I was off the phone I glanced at my new manuscript again. It had reached the stage where I was word-blind to the whole thing and could offer nothing more by way of revision. Someone with a more professional eye needed to take a look.

There was only one place to send it.

```
To: Reggie Davies
   Fond wishes wherever this finds you.
Please   find   enclosed   the   finished
manuscript   for   the   Vivaldi   book.   A
different   account   touching   on   more
recent  matters  as  you'll  see.  I  have
retitled  it  THE  FOUR  DEADLY  SEASONS
which I hope you think acceptable.
   If   you   could   find   your   way   to
suggesting  a  way  forward,  an  agent  or
publisher,  I  would  be  immensely  grate-
ful.  A  modest  advance  would  be  all  I'd
expect  in  the  circumstances,  though,
with  the  cost  of  living  being  what  it  is
right  now,  not  too  modest  one  would
hope.
```

It took just a week to get a reply.

```
To: Arnold Clover
   Season's   greetings   from   Melbourne
which   is   hot   and   sunny   and   quite
delightful  presently.  I  read  THE  FOUR
DEADLY  SEASONS  immediately  as  you  may
gather,  and  with  great  pleasure.  It  may
not  be  the  book  you  first  imagined,  but
```

it's quite a tale. You write like a professional, spin a good and colourful yarn, one that made me think again about the extraordinary events which surrounded us all in that strange and unpredictable year. I cannot thank you enough for the pleasure and insight your sterling work has given me!

If only I could be the bearer of more positive news when it comes to publication. In normal circumstances I would suggest you find an agent and pitch your tale at one of the commercial houses in England.

However, I feel there are several reasons why this will not be possible. First, compelling as your narrative is, you fail to nail the most important question every agent, editor and reader will want answered: why did Mia act as she did? Why kill this man? Perhaps you don't know. Perhaps you do and feel, for personal reasons you don't wish to say. Either way it leaves a Titanic-size rupture in the hull of your story, one that will sink it from the very start.

Then there's the legal side of things. As far as I understand it, a murder case has yet to be heard. I don't know the ins and outs of the Italian legal system, but it seems to me you would run the dire risk of being in contempt of it for treading on prosecutorial toes.

Italy being your home, I would regard
this as exceedingly unwise.

Lastly — and this is the clincher, old
chum — there's the plain fact that in
your earlier career with the National
Archives you signed the Official Secrets
Act. Rupert Hazard could, I'm sure,
explain the ramifications of making
claims about His Majesty's secret squir-
rels as you do. Come to that I could
offer the same since — time to admit it
— I signed the thing as well.

Just forget it, mate. You'd be doing
the lovely Mia no favours there, I
assure you. Matters are rarely as simple
or cut and dried as they might seem to
Joe Public which, in this case, is you.

Move on. As for money… well, I think
you know the answer there. There are
those who write for filthy lucre. And
those who write because they must. You
are among the latter. Shame about your
chosen subject.

PS. As for 'Rupert Hazard'. Forget the
man. We have.

Oh Reggie, I thought, *not you as well.*

By the end of the month, the revival of Mia's original plan was
now in the papers. The hotel would open after Easter, and
concerts resume under Kravchuck's leadership soon after. Not a

meaningful word about Mia anywhere. No court date. No inkling where she might be. A secure location for her own safety was all the papers said. Nor had anyone revealed Archaki's identity to the public.

On the second of April, a bright day marking the return of spring, the story broke.

I knew he'd call. Luca was frantic.

'Are you all right, Arnold? Seriously.'

'Kind of you to ask.'

'This is so awful. How do you think it happened?'

The details were brief and vague. A newsflash on the radio, now on the web. Doubtless in the local papers' first editions. Mia Haas, the woman charged with murder on the opening night of her auditorium in Giudecca, had been found dead in her cell in a secure location somewhere outside Orvieto. The cause was yet to be ascertained. The date of her death was a mystery, since it seemed to have occurred a week or two before, hidden by the authorities until now. Her remains were to be shipped home to relatives in Croatia. The investigation into the murder of a mysterious Bulgarian in the Teatro Maddalena was now closed for good.

'Would you like lunch?' I said.

'You sound remarkably calm.'

'The Pugni. Twenty minutes. I have a table reserved. It's time we resumed old habits.'

'Very well,' he said, sounding puzzled.

The dish of the day was *vitello tonnato*, cold veal in a tuna sauce. Something I'd never liked until I tasted it at a table at the back of our favourite bar next to the Bridge of Fists and Campo San Barnaba. I ordered it while Luca picked at a plate of *bigoli*

in salsa. Since he was of the opinion this was a wake, we were sharing a bottle of red. He was wearing the same mustard trousers and green hunting jacket I'd seen a year before. The feathered alpine cap was absent. No complaints there.

'I must admit,' he said, after some gentle words of commiseration, 'you're taking it very well.'

I concentrated on my meal.

'She was a fine woman,' he went on. 'A complex one, true enough. With her own agenda. But what she did with that place on Giudecca. It will live on.'

'Indeed. How's Silvia?'

He sighed and stuck a fork in his bigoli.

'Oh dear. Sorry, Luca. I didn't mean to be nosy. It's just that back in December...'

'That was winter. This is spring. She's been swept off her feet by some rich bastard from Rome. He's got a pad by the Tiber on the Via Giulia, a weekend apartment near Salute, and a yacht in Portofino or somewhere. I can't compete. Not with that.'

He seemed genuinely upset. Luca had a long history of brief romantic relationships, but they always ended on friendly terms from what I'd gathered. He was never a man keen on breaking hearts. And here he was, his own in pieces from what I could see.

'You know, if money makes a difference, it's probably best to bring matters to a close.'

'True. True... And who am I to complain? Next to your loss? Poor Mia gone. Do you know what happened? Did they even tell you where she was?'

'No. I saw her that one time in the women's prison back in January. After that nothing...'

'God... how awful.'

I'd never seen him so upset.

'Luca. I need you to promise to keep this between us. Always.'

He stared at me, surprised. 'I'm a man of the utmost discretion. Of course. I'm shocked you need to ask.'

'In normal circumstances I wouldn't. But...' I retrieved from my jacket pocket the postcard that had turned up three days earlier. A view of Dubrovnik, the port, the city walls and the Old Town.

Beneath, in a careful, flowing hand I recognised, there was a brief message.

> *Arnold. Do not believe everything you read. Remember: as I often told you, there's always an accommodation to be made. Farewell my too-brief Venetian lover and friend.*
> *xxxx*

Luca read it, astonished, mouth agape, after a long moment laughing so hard there were tears in his eyes.

'My God. What a woman. She's talked herself out of there. Out of a murder charge. Faked her own death. Really? How?'

I shushed him. 'Not so loud.'

'No, no.' The place was empty for once thank goodness. He whispered, 'How?'

Only Mia Haas, or whatever she was called now, could answer that. And she was somewhere in Croatia. Or so it seemed.

When I came to think about it after the postcard turned up, I realised the pointers were there all along, with some opportunities too. That coy message she gave me in the woman's prison. There were things she could reveal in court that might embarrass a good few people, not just in Britain, but in the Italian secret service too. Perhaps she'd waved the possibility of my manuscript becoming public in their faces. Reggie Davies seemed to hint at that when she wrote back to me saying I'd be doing Mia a favour by killing the book. That matters were 'rarely as simple or cut and dried as they might seem'.

Quite...

'I don't know,' I admitted. 'I doubt I ever will.'

He nodded and ordered two coffees. 'There's that catamaran from San Basilio to Pula. Only three hours or so. A very pleasant journey. Croatia's not so far away. You could always try and track her down and ask.'

'Dubrovnik's much further from Pula than Venice.'

'Ah.' He sounded triumphant. 'You've checked then?'

'What if she doesn't want to be found?'

Another nod. The coffees arrived.

'What a woman says she wants and what she really wants may sometimes be quite different things,' Luca said.

'Perhaps.'

'In the meantime, Dottore Volpetti prescribes intellectual activity. Work.'

I shuddered and said, 'I beg your pardon?'

'I've a rather exciting project on the cards. To do with cryptography and the like. We could use some help.'

'I'd rather not right now.'

'Let me send you a little something. See what you think.'

I thought back a year. To the fulsome lunch he'd treated me to at that very table before enticing me over the water to Giudecca.

'I'd prefer it if I enjoyed a little time without excitement if you don't mind.'

'Only a little. Let me pay for this. I insist. You remember the Doge they decapitated in the palazzo for treason? Marin Falier? Boy did Byron get it wrong with that one. This is right up your street, Arnold, trust me...'

There were times when I felt I ought to punch Luca

Volpetti. Or hug him. Or ask myself why on earth I allowed myself to become embroiled in his bizarre schemes even if, at first glance, they appeared rational and quite enticing.

But not then. I let him pay and we said goodbye outside as he headed off to see one of his old girlfriends, a married lecturer from Ca' Foscari he visited in the afternoon from time to time.

I wandered into Campo Santa Margherita, took a table outside Margaret Duchamp, ordered a post-meal spritz, sat and watched the familiar round of local life. The fishmongers were dismantling their stall as gulls swooped for titbits from the cobbles. Kids kicked around a football, students ambled across the square full of the bright spark of youth. A trickle of tourists, nothing more. It was too early in the year for the rush. A couple of youngsters were giggling at a terrier leaping at the trickle of water from the drinking fountain. A small dog dashed out from the inside the bar and began chasing pigeons around the square, yapping furiously.

It was almost a year to the day since I first walked across that wooden bridge into the Maddalena estate. The seasons had turned full circle once more, the way they always did.

My phone buzzed. An email from Luca with a stack of attachments that seemed to be about elaborate devices for codifying secret messages, Renaissance subterfuge, a photograph of the strappado rope in the Doge's Palace torture chamber, and links to an academic book about how the Venetian Republic's masters of the black arts invented the basis of modern spy craft. And a picture of a painting by Delacroix, the execution of Marin Falier, beheaded beneath a marble staircase in the grandeur of the Ducal Palace, watched by nobles unmoved by the sight of his corpse.

Somewhere in my mind I heard the call of the cuckoo, Rupert Hazard's clever bird. First in the minor third of the Devil's Tritone, then to the major. Finally, to the fourth. Dissonance to harmony. Chaos to concord. A movement, a chapter completed, followed by a new and empty page to shape, to enjoy, to fill with life.

Cuck-OO.

Mia was where she wanted. Gone from her dark and dismal past, starting somewhere fresh, anew, her mother avenged. I was glad, privileged, to be a part of that strange and necessary journey. Now I was back where I began, alone, idle, aimless. Perhaps a little wiser, who knew? Except when it came to the elusive Antonio Vivaldi. He was an enigma, a mystery still. As he deserved to be. His glorious music was legacy enough.

April was never the cruellest month, not in Venice anyway.

Acknowledgements

The poetic translations of Vivaldi's sonnets for *The Four Seasons* are the work of Armand D'Angour, Professor of Classics at Jesus College, Oxford (https://www.armand-dangour.com). I'm grateful to Armand for permission to quote them here. Karl Heller's *Antonio Vivaldi: The Red Priest of Venice* and Myriam Zerbi's *A Flow of Music: Antonio Vivaldi at the Origins Of a Rediscovery*, published by the Fondazione Giorgio Cini and available for free online, were invaluable sources of academic information about Vivaldi's time, work, travels and re-emergence.

Also by David Hewson

When the Germans Come

1940: Dover waits for the Nazi invasion… but what if Hitler's agents are already here, among them?

When the Germans Come is a thriller about the murky and frightening dark heart of wartime Britain we rarely see.

BUY NOW

A note from the publisher

Thank you for reading this book. If you enjoyed it please do consider leaving a review on Amazon to help others find it too.

We hate typos. All of our books have been rigorously edited and proofread, but sometimes mistakes do slip through. If you have spotted a typo, please do let us know and we can get it amended within hours.

info@bloodhoundbooks.com

www.ingramcontent.com/pod-product-compliance
Lightning Source LLC
Chambersburg PA
CBHW030525190726
48283CB00006B/1776